THE REFLEX - CONSOLIDATED VERSION

BOOK 1 IN THE REFLEX SERIES

MARIA DENISON

Maria
Denison
AUTHOR

PART ONE

PROLOGUE

APRIL 2014

THE LIGHTING IN THE ROOM is dim. Grime covers the floors and small kitchenette Cara has in her visual. The apartment looks like no one has lived in it for some time, much less updated it since its location in Berlin was called the German Democratic Republic. The décor is at least 25 years old.

So, this is how it ends for her. Her demise will be tragic and painful at the hands of the Albert Einstein look-alike who's holding a gun to her head. She will die alone, and only God knows when her body will be found. Not how she ever pictured her death.

Young Cara Bianco Andre never envisioned her mortality. She felt invincible. Taking chances with her life was the norm. The adrenaline rush was her drug. If ziplines and bungee jumping were around back then, she would have been all in.

At this point in her life however, those needs are in the distant past. They haven't made an appearance in years, closer to decades. She no longer enjoys the thrill game. If she's honest with herself, she's on the verge of a full-blown panic attack. Her only thought before she dies is to somehow leave a message for her husband and children. They are her world.

Looking down, she can see the puddle she left when she lost her bladder after the Taser hit. She could try to fingerpaint a message to them with her pee. What would she say, though? "I am sorry I was an ass and got myself killed?"

No, those can't be her last words. They are most definitely true, but something more emotional would be appropriate.

How about, "I love you three so much. I will watch over you forever, but please move on with your lives." No, Einstein with the gun will notice her writing all that. Einstein. That's it! She could leave a clue about him.

Something they can solve her murder with.

Wait, she doesn't know his name. "He looks like Einstein." No, that's not going to help them. Why has she never thought about her last words? Do most people? Maybe not. Especially if you have no regrets about the life you've lived. She wouldn't change a thing. Well, except for coming to Berlin.

Deciding it's now or never, she discreetly places one fingertip in the puddle and drags it out to spell, "sorry, love you."

Of course, Einstein notices, and says, "Eeewwww, gross. It's bad enough I'll have to drag your body out of here covered in piss. Now you've got your hands in it? I am going to shoot you twice for that."

She might have let a little more of her bladder go after that.

CHAPTER 1

FOUR DAYS EARLIER

CARA IS HAVING THE MOST sensual dream. She can feel full lips trailing softly down her exposed back. There is a sensation of warm fingertips following behind them. Her breathing speeds with her arousal and she smiles. It's been a while since she's had an erotic dream. She intends to enjoy this one, but a sudden slap on her ass jolts her awake. "Ouch!"

"Get that fine ass up now. This is the third time I had to come in here to wake you, Cara." Her husband has lost his patience. Every morning it's the same routine. Nic has fed their children, packed their lunches and finally, struggled to get her out of bed. "You have ten minutes before driving them to school."

Wide 8wake now, she whines, "No, I hate drop-off." She rolls to her side to get comfortable again, just to torment him.

"Gotta catch a flight, remember?" He leans in to brush his lips across hers. As soon as he hears her soft moan of appreciation, he yanks her up out of bed, sets her down in front of him and commands, "Get ready, now!" then walks out of the room.

Sighing audibly, Cara stalks around the king size bed with its disheveled bedding, evidence of a tantric evening. She picks up a thrown pillow and tosses it back on the bed, affectionately brushing her hand across the front of the hand painted armoire as she passes by. It's one of the first pieces of furniture she and her husband purchased together and a prized possession. Cara uses the toilet, brushes her teeth quickly, and pulls on the yoga pants, sports bra and T-shirt she'd left lying across her vanity stool the night before. She walks resignedly out of the bath, through the bedroom, and down the hall towards the smell of coffee. Even the length of the hallway is exhausting for her at this hour of the morning.

When she reaches the kitchen, Nic is just grabbing his leather messenger bag and heading to the garage. He stops abruptly, grabs Cara around the waist, and pulls her in for a long, sensuous kiss. Behind them, they hear, "Stop that. It's disgusting!" They end the kiss with an audible pop and glare at their daughter.

Nic instructs her, "Mia, be nice to your mother today, please," then turns back to Cara and says, "I'm in and out of Detroit." He points to a to-go coffee he left on the counter for her, waves and walks out the door.

Cara ignores her daughter in favor of her first sip of said coffee. After several gulps, she inquires, "Is your brother ready?"

Mia scowls, a consistent response for her. "Is he ever? He's still in his room messing with his hair. Total fem."

Cara looks around her perfectly designed kitchen. The granite counters shine beneath the detritus of breakfast plates and school lunch prep. She sighs audibly for the second time this morning. Nic is the most amazingly attentive husband and father, but cleaning up after himself is not his thing.

She leans into the back stairwell, which leads to the second floor of their home, and yells, "Max! Downstairs, now!" She grabs the two lunch sacks and her coffee and starts towards the garage exit, glancing back at her daughter. "I'll be waiting in the car."

As she walks into the garage, Cara suddenly realizes she's only wearing a T-shirt and the temperature can't be more than 50 degrees. Hopefully she can make it to the school and back without incident. She climbs into her Audi Q5 and positions Mia's lunch on the floor of the front seat, and Max's in the middle of the back seat.

And this is how it's been done, every morning, over the ten plus years since the twins started school. She raises the garage door and starts the car, immediately turning on the seat warmers for both front seats. Mia will pose a fit if her seat isn't sufficiently heated when she arrives.

And now, she waits. Mia emerges first, frown on her face, ready for the day. She climbs into the front seat, struggles with her backpack and settles in without a word. Cara does not look at her, because making eye contact with one's nearly sixteen-year-old daughter is, at any time, forbidden. Max comes out within seconds of his sister, looking like he fell out of an Abercrombie & Fitch ad. He is, by far, the most handsome boy at school.

The problem is, he knows it.

Again, no one speaks as Cara pulls out of the garage. As they turn onto the open road, Cara breaks the silence. "So, what's the afterschool schedule today?" she asks, tentatively.

Mia huffs out, "I don't know. I'll text you." Cara checks her rearview mirror when Max doesn't answer and sees he's wearing his earbuds. She waves a hand around between the two front seats until he notices.

He pulls one earbud out and grunts, "What?"

Cara inquires again, "What is the afterschool schedule today?"

"I have baseball practice after school."

"What time will you be done?"

"I don't know. I'll text you." So, ditto.

This is the sum total of conversation allowed during the drive to school. Cara sips her coffee to keep herself busy. Mia continues to frown and Max bobs his head to music. The stress of dealing with two teenagers is more than any one person should have to endure first thing in the morning.

Cara is about to take the right turn which will lead them to the drop-off oval for the high school, when she's forced to slam on her brakes. Another mom, with an obnoxiously large Lexus SUV, cuts her off by taking a left from the oncoming traffic. Cara takes a deep, cleansing yoga breath.

Mia hears it and immediately launches into the morning diatribe. "Don't even start Mom! I can't handle the way you and Dad freak out every morning in the oval. Can't you be like all the other parents and just deal with it?"

Holding her tongue, Cara is determined to get through this without a word. Suddenly, she sees a car headed straight for them, going the wrong way on the one-way access road. And she erupts, "What kind of assholes are these people? Since when is dropping your child off at school a frigging competitive sport? Why doesn't the school administration police this oval?" As if in answer to her screaming rhetoric, another car backs out of a parking spot, almost T-boning them. Cara lays on the horn to alert the moron that he has a rearview mirror; he should try looking at it occasionally.

A mortified Mia fumes, "You're actually worse than Dad! Did you have to honk?"

Regaining her composure, Cara calmly states, "No, I guess I didn't. I could have let him hit us." She feels bad, but honestly, Mia could use a taste of her own medicine. She never censors anything coming out of her mouth.

Cara's blood pressure has skyrocketed up 30 points and she's only halfway through. They're making their way around the top corner of the oval, where the activity is reminiscent of the final lap at Indy. Cars dart two, sometimes three wide, to get to the front doors. It's total chaos. Cara impatiently waits her turn and finally arrives at the entrance. She silently vows one of these days she is going for the checkered flag, and the win. Damn all these bitches to hell!

She pulls close to the curb, and her children climb out without a single word. She checks the backseat as Max exits. And, as usual, she yells, "Max, lunch!" He leans back in for his sack then slams the door. Cara still needs to negotiate her way out of the oval, but the worst should be over by now.

As she gets close to the exit, her cell phone rings. Cara answers with her usual, "Hello, bitch."

"Yo, not THE bitch today," her dearest friend corrects. "You should be hunting down the fake-boobed blonde in the Lexus who cut you off. I saw the whole thing."

"You know who she is?" Cara inquires eagerly.

"No, but I will make it a priority to find out...and then we will exact our revenge. You up for Starbucks?"

Looking down at herself, Cara answers, "Can't, not wearing a coat, underpants or shoes right now."

"You're my hero."

"Thanks Jinx. Coming from you that means a lot." Cara has early conference calls with clients but, "Can I meet you at 10:00? Also, need to hit Target. I promise to put on shoes, the panties are non-negotiable."

"OK, coffee, then wanna work out?"

She wants to decline the work out, but Jinx will just guilt her into it anyway. After a half-hearted 'OK', Cara hangs up.

Taking more deep breaths to decompress for the drive back home, Cara wonders how she would have survived living in Cleveland, of all places, without her good friend, Jinx. They were roommates for ten years when they both worked in Washington, DC. Then Jinx left to take a new job in Cleveland. Cara arrived at her doorstep several months later, broken and battered; with no clear direction where to go next after quitting her job. She was in a bad place, emotionally.

Her stay in Cleveland was supposed to be short-lived, just long enough to lick her wounds, but then life happened. And with no family in the area, Jinx became a critical element of her local support system, especially when the twins were young. Their friendship bloomed.

She swipes her card as she pulls through the entrance to her gated neighborhood and smiles as she passes all the lovely homes and manicured lawns. She knows how privileged she is to live in this golf course community. On her street, she slows to take in the side view of her home. It is truly magnificent. It's the dream house that, five years ago, Nic designed and built, and Cara decorated from top to bottom. The architecture blends classic English features with some Victorian touches, so it's not true to any one style, but it works.

Back in the house, Cara glances at the clock. She has one hour before her first client conference call. She'll use it to clean the kitchen, make the beds, and start a load of laundry. But, before she can attempt any of that, she makes herself another cup of coffee. As she leans against the counter enjoying the fresh taste of java, she sees her reflection on the glass of the built-in microwave. Apparently, she also forgot to run a brush through her hair this morning. She looks like a wild woman. "No wonder I don't have many friends here."

TWO

CARA GLANCES AT THE MIRROR after brushing her long, thick hair into a high ponytail. As she leans closer to examine her hairline, she spots more than a few gray hairs. Disgusted, she stomps out of the bathroom and into the massive walk-in closet. It is a thing of beauty. There are long rows of racks for clothes and shelves for shoes.

The right side of the closet is pristinely organized; clothes are color coordinated, as are shoes, by style and season. Every accessory is placed neatly in cubby holes or on hooks. Not a speck of dust can be seen. Then, there's the left side of the closet. Shoes are tossed haphazardly across the floor. Clothes are bulging from all the racks. Dust bunnies have collected around the tossed belts, scarves and discarded socks mixed in with the shoes. Cara turns left and kicks around for her sneakers. She snatches up two mismatched socks, smells them, and heads out of the room, grabbing a pullover sweatshirt on the way back to her car. As promised, sans underwear. By the time she pulls into the local Starbucks it's 10:05 and Jinx's car is already there.

When she steps out of her car, Cara hears, "Hey, slut, I'm sitting outside, and you're late."

Jinx has procured the premiere bistro table out front. "I'm only five minutes late, and you are the sluttier of the two of us."

Cocking her head, Jinx muses, "Is sluttier a word? Or is more slutty a better use of the term?"

Wordlessly approaches the table, she gives her friend a knowing smile to remind her she is well aware of all the men Jinx has slept with. When they lived together, Cara often joked that Jinx's bedroom needed a revolving door and a deli ticket dispenser outside said door.

Interpreting Cara's salacious smile, Jinx responds, "You get laid a hell of a lot more than I do now."

"Only because your husband is gone for weeks at a time. Good thing you have your electronic boyfriends," Cara quips as she takes a seat. Jinx's husband, Jake, travels all over the world, and is sometimes away for a month at a time. He never reveals his location or purpose for the trip, despite Cara's incessant probing. "Speaking of, when is Jack Reacher due back from his latest secret adventure?"

"JAKE," Jinx emphasizes his name, "is on his way home today. And, you know he hates that you guys call him Jack Reacher."

They know, but they do it anyway. Cara has the whole gang saying it. Jake is huge, mean and mysterious, a big bastard with a heart of gold. Although most people don't get to know that last part. "Jake gets pissed off because he thinks we're comparing him to Tom Cruise who played Reacher in the movie. Poor choice, by the way. The real fictional Reacher is totally your husband. Get him to read a book."

Jinx rolls her eyes. "Real fictional? Oxymoron, you moron."

"Whatever," Cara says smugly while she mentally calculates how long Jake has been MIA, "Hey, you want I take Elijah this weekend so you can get hot and heavy with your hot and heavy?"

"You calling my husband heavy?" Jinx asks with feigned indignation.

Cara laughs. Jake is six foot six and 270 pounds. He's a hot gorilla. He would make anyone piss their pants if they got caught alone in a dark alley with him. "He's seriously scary in a hot, BIG way. He's Jack Reacher."

Jinx knows she can't win this Reacher battle on behalf of her husband. She huffs loudly and retorts, "You're the last person who should talk about hot husbands. Nic is prettier than you."

"So true." Cara agrees, looking glum.

"Don't start that inferiority thing with me today. I didn't bring my Freud hat," Jinx cries as she pushes a grande skinny latte in front of Cara. "You're late, so it might be cold."

"Five minutes!" What is it with Jinx and time? "You're a horrific housekeeper and cook. You are so disorganized, and yet, completely anal about money and time."

Never without a comeback, Jinx points out, "Like the way you home cook every meal, and keep a spotlessly clean house, but compared to Nic's, your side of the closet looks like a cyclone hit?"

With a snort, Cara acknowledges, "Funny, I was just noticing that before I came over here." How can a man be so compulsive about his property and possessions? He can't seem to get a mug from the counter into the dishwasher or even the sink for God's sake. Cara is all about the appearance of organization. If the mess is hidden behind closed doors, then it doesn't count. Must be something she inherited from her mother. "Next time bring the Freud hat so we can explore that."

Before Jinx can comment, Cara adds, "Have any intel on the blonde with the Lexus yet? Because bitch is going down."

"No, but why were you there? Nic out of town? Man's a saint for dropping them off every morning." Jinx waits for Cara's confirmation of Nic's sainthood status.

Bowing her head, hands clasped in prayer, she answers, "Day trip for him."

"Are you here this week? Or are you off to the East Coast again? And why is it always East?"

She and Nic own a design and construction firm. As a native East coaster, Cara has more familiarity with the region so, given the option, she chooses to work in that area. They currently have job sites in Boston, Philly, Syracuse, NYC, and new projects just commencing in Greensboro and DC. Still, a lot of their work is client based, so it could land them anywhere and they each have their own set of regulars. "Some clients respond better to Nic, and some to me."

"You mean do they want to work with the hot guy or the hot girl?" Jinx asks, giving Cara a penetrating stare.

Cara shrinks into herself. It used to work that way, but Nic has aged better than she has. Her husband still thinks she's beautiful and tells her so. But with the passage of time, she believes it's becoming harder for her. "It might help if Nic had a dad bod and receding hair-line," she mutters under her breath.

Before she can spiral further down that hole, Jinx interrupts. "I would love you to take Eli this weekend."

"How is he getting along at school?"

Naturally shy and reserved, Eli keeps to himself and as such became the target of bullying in his freshman year. Cara admires Jinx for the subtle ways she helped him work through it. She is quite sure neither she nor Nic would show such restraint if either of their children were bullied.

Jinx sighs, "He's much taller than the other boys now and it appears they've backed off. But he still struggles with making friends."

Cara tries to formulate an appropriate response. "Well, he will always have my two." Eli loves the twins, and he's Mia's best friend, so he's always at Cara's house. She suspects he's fed better there, as well. And Mia is closer to Eli than she is to any of her girlfriends. Whether it's because they've been together since their births, or because they're both introverts, they are inseparable. "Mia and Eli are two peas in a pod."

Nodding Jinx adds, "Strange how your daughter and my son are closer than your daughter and her twin."

It would be strange, but Max is their complete opposite. Every student at the high school wants to BE him or DATE him. He's royalty and only a sophomore.

"Are the senior girls still calling him all the time?" Jinx asks.

"Yes, and it's stressing me out." Mia is the stereotypical teenager. Introverted and sullen, sporting braces and acne, and full of angst. Maximillian Andre is an anomaly. He's so excessively confident, she worries he's going to fall off the fifty-story pedestal he's on and really hurt himself. Elijah and Mia can look forward to things only getting better, but Max has it all. What happens if he falters? What happens if he fails at something? Despite Mia's constant state of distress, Cara and Nic worry more about Max. "Just be thankful you have an only child. This two kid thing sucks."

Jinx and Cara have seen and endured more than most people. They thought there was nothing life could throw at them they couldn't easily survive...until they had kids. In this alternate universe called motherhood, the constant state of anxiety over the safety and well-being of their children is all-consuming. Neither woman wanted to get pregnant again, ever. "Enough about the kids. Thinking of them is ruining my caffeine high," Jinx complains.

"Do you mind if I get a new latte? This one is cold."

"You were late!" Jinx shouts, loud enough for all to hear. She stands and holds a hand out to Cara. "You buy, I fly." Cara reaches into her pullover pocket and passes her a twenty-dollar bill. Jinx does her best catwalk strut from her chair to the building.

Cara uses the alone time to start stretching her legs and arms. Apparently, they are supposed to work out at some point this morning.

Jinx suddenly appears holding two cups and grinning ear to ear. "Cara, you need to get in there, NOW. They're playing your song!" She barely gets the last part out before dissolving into excited giggles.

Jumping up, Cara runs into the store where she is immediately assaulted by Duran Duran's, *The Reflex*, playing much too loudly through the store's speakers. She wants to laugh along with Jinx, but she's suddenly overcome with the strangest feeling, an ominous almost threatening sensation. "Don't you think that's weird? *The Reflex* playing in a Starbucks?" she asks when she comes back outside.

Jinx pulls herself together enough to respond, "It isn't normal Starbuck's Musak, but maybe it's 80's day. Speaking of which, the theme at 10:30 Zumba today is the 80's. Want to hit that?"

Cara releases the tension from her body. "Sure. Let's head out. I'll drive and then we can go to Target all sweaty after."

Their favorite thing is to run errands together. It makes life's annoying and boring to-do list so much more entertaining. Both women work from home and when they're not traveling, they spend a lot of time in each other's company.

They get to Zumba with seconds to spare and take up spots in the last row. That way they can watch everyone else from the back and make fun of them. It makes the time go fast and keeps them focused. Otherwise...they would both give up and walk out.

When class is over, Jinx wipes the sweat off her face with her arm and asks, "Target run?".

The TP supply at the Andre home is running perilously low, and Cara seeks to avoid an uprising at the house. "In and out quickly, though." She needs to get some work done before the incessant pick me up texts start from her lovely children.

Target, of course, is very busy and very red. Always. So. Painfully. Red. Cara grabs a cart and starts down the main aisle at warp speed. Jinx grabs her cart, and heads perpendicular, but with the same haste. Cara yells to

Jinx over her shoulder, "First one checked out and paid, wins."

She rushes to paper products first and then works her way back through the grocery aisles to Health and Beauty. She spots Jinx and slips past unseen. Feeling victorious, she rushes toward the check-out lanes to take the win. She no sooner gets in line than she catches Jinx in her peripheral vision. She stretches her neck to watch Jinx angling for the fastest lane. Is it the one with the mom and two small children and a half full cart, or the one with the older couple whose cart if overflowing?

Cara calls out to her, "Tough choice, Jinx. The kiddies or the ancients?" Everyone around her can certainly hear this, but no one seems to understand or pay her any attention.

When she turns back and sees the woman in front of her grabbing her receipt, Cara quickly moves forward to load her items on the belt. "The win is in the bag, full pun intended," she yells out to Jinx. The words are barely out of her mouth when she suddenly freezes at the sound assaulting her ears. The competition forgotten; she listens intently. It can't be? Again?

She calls out to her friend, "Um, Ellie?"

"You haven't won yet, don't gloat!"

"No, El?" The distress in Cara's voice plus the use of her real name stops Jinx in her tracks. She looks over at Cara, whose head slowly tilts up towards the ceiling. It takes Jinx a couple of seconds to catch on. And then, she hears it. Playing loudly through the store's speakers....Duran Duran's, *The Reflex.*

Jinx turns back to the cashier to swipe her credit card. Then in one fluid motion, she grabs the receipt, tosses her bags in the cart, and rushes to Cara's lane. "I win."

But Cara is still frozen in place. She doesn't move until the cashier's voice captures her attention. "Ma'am, form of payment, please." She swipes her card while Jinx transfers her bags into her cart. Neither one speaks as they exit the store.

They arrive at the car and Cara finally communicates, "You don't think that's weird? That we would hear *The Reflex*, twice, within hours, at two places that are unlikely venues for that type of music?" She pops the trunk and Jinx starts loading her purchases to the left side.

When she's done, she turns to Cara. "I don't know if I would call it weird...maybe coincidental." Cara, still in a daze, attempts to unload her bags into the right side of the trunk. But she's moving too slowly so Jinx takes over, emptying the cart and parking it in the corral. Back at the car, she reaches over and gently touches Cara's arm. "It's probably in the Musak loop today. You're overthinking this, Cara."

"You know there is no such thing as a coincidence," Cara whispers.

Jinx tightens her grip on Cara's arm to the point of pain. "Yes, Cara, there is. Get Connor Reed out of your head and calm the fuck down!"

Cara doesn't react to her friend's reprimand. She's in a fugue state, standing stock-still, a vague expression on her face. Cara has left the building. She does this, sometimes. She disappears into her mind like she's having an internal conversation. Everyone who knows her well has become accustomed to it. Jinx calls it her 'seizures.'

Jinx wraps her arm around Cara and soothes, "Listen, if it'll make you feel better, I'll do some investigating and find the source of the background music for both stores. Okay?"

Cara breathes out, "Thank you. I know I'm just being paranoid, but I really don't hear that song often... hardly ever."

"Is it in your iTunes library?"

This question finally gets a smile from Cara, "Of course," she responds flippantly. And just like that, Cara is back.

CHAPTER

THREE

T HANKFULLY, THE REST OF CARA'S afternoon proceeds as normal. Shower, hair, makeup, dress, emails, return calls. And then the texts begin. 'Pick me up', 'Drop me off', and then, 'Pick me up', again. Somewhere between all the chauffeuring, she manages to get a pot roast into the oven. It should be ready by 6:30, which is when, as the color-coded schedules on her smartphone's calendar indicate, everyone can eat dinner together.

That family meal is the one tradition Cara fights for. Food is the love language she learned from her parents, both Sicilian immigrants, and sharing that food with family, a demonstration of that love. It's not easy to execute in today's world but it's important to her. And on the rare occasion they all actually talk at that meal, Cara feels vindicated maintaining the custom. It remains to be seen whether tonight will be one of those occasions.

At five o'clock, Nic comes home, just as Cara is pulling in the garage with Max who's on the phone next to her, talking to a girl. Nic dashes into the house and heads directly to the lower level. No greeting, just straight for the stairs. He has that 'run to the office, I'm cutting it close' look in his eyes. He must owe some client an end of

19

day solution. Cara gives a brief wave and feels a nudge from Max. He's signaling for her to get out of the car and give him some privacy. She complies and heads into the house to set the kitchen table for dinner.

This mundane task is a daily reminder of probably their biggest source of marital conflict. Their children do very little to help around the house. She and Nic agree the twins should have chores; they just disagree on to how to make it happen. Some methods have worked better on Max, others on Mia, but ultimately everything failed.

Both kids are incredibly well behaved and every teacher has said, 'Pleasure to have in class.' Their grades are great and both are in Honors or AP level classes. They're both gifted musicians and singers. Mia plays in the school's Philharmonic and Max, opting out of band because of sports, practices music in his downtime. They're great kids, she muses, except when it comes to lending a hand at home.

Nic enters the kitchen and breaks her reverie. She looks down at the kitchen table and realizes she has been on autopilot, setting it and putting out the meal, complete with drinks during her mind hiatus. He pulls her into his arms. "Cara mia, I'm so sorry for dashing in the house earlier. I needed to adjust a quote before six o'clock. I think I made it."

Nic has called her, cara mia, since their first night together. He says it with an Italian accent, and it's a great play on words as it means 'my sweetheart' in Italian. Her birth name is Caralina, but she has gone by Cara, pronounced Car-uh, since infancy. Nic speaks fluent Italian along with several other languages.

Cara tilts her head back to kiss him on the neck. "I figured by the look on your face you were bee-lining it to your office for something. No worries. How was Detroit?"

Drawing her firmly against him, he quips, "It was Detroit. Still makes Cleveland look like grandeur." He releases her and walks over to the back staircase. He yells up, "Max! Mia! DINNER!" then gives her a contrite shrug and asks, "Why didn't we install an intercom system when we designed this house? Obviously, we never thought our offspring would be hiding in their rooms."

"And hide they do," she muses.

They sit in their usual spots, serve themselves dinner and discuss work. Halfway through their meal, Max and Mia come down in unison. Max is wearing board shorts and no shirt and looks like a bathing suit model. Mia has on a camisole and skintight yoga shorts. Their school attire comes off the moment they get home, usually tossed to the floor, and they are mostly naked for the rest of the night, even in winter.

There's no moaning about the menu tonight because they both like Cara's pot roast. They serve themselves and Mia keeps her head down while she eats. Nic and Cara keep their eyes averted, knowing better than to look directly at her. Max on the other hand, shovels food into his mouth, smiling in his untroubled way as if it's the best thing he's ever tasted.

When Nic and Cara are finished with their meal, Nic makes his usual attempt at conversation. "Anything interesting to report? How was school?" Mia grunts and Max stares at him, still smiling. No discernible words, just more silence.

Undeterred, Cara makes her own attempt, "How's the homework coming? Need any help? Or anything from us?" Again, a grunt from Mia, and Max continues to grin. It can be unnerving, but Cara continues, "Okay, you've been warned. No ten o'clock 'I needs' from either one of you, understand?" They both nod their affirmation.

Cara says this every evening at dinner, and she's getting better at really making good on it, but if she had a dollar for every time she hears, 'Mom, I need...' between 10 and 11 PM.

Mia stands from the table first, attempting to walk away empty-handed. Nic narrows his eyes at her and scolds, "Pick up your dish and cup, and place them in the sink, please." She reluctantly complies. Nic follows his daughter with his stare as she ascends the back steps. Despite Cara's constant advice to ignore the flippant attitude, she knows he'd really like to smack Mia sometimes. He turns back to the table in time to catch Max walking away. "Max!"

Max looks back at his father, clueless. "What?"

Nic repeats, "Dishes! Sink!" Max complies and promptly leaves.

Cara can't stifle the giggle. "They are oblivious."

Nic gets up from the table and puts his own dish in the sink. "If they weren't cute and smart, I would sell them on eBay."

Without another word, he heads down to the lower level where his office is located. It's one of several rooms in their finished basement. There's also a soundproof music room, a home theater, a billiards room with full kitchen and bar, a dedicated work-out space, and a bedroom and bath for their sometimes-live-in childcare provider, Sasha. Nic spends most evenings downstairs in his office or in the music room, where the twins and even Sasha often join him.

Cara finishes the dinner clean-up, then heads to her office, her sanctuary, if such a thing exists. Plopping down in the chair in front of her computer, she awakens the screen and decides Facebook needs a visit. She sees a post from her sister with a new picture of her young nephew and makes a funny comment. After getting caught up on social media, she pulls up mail and composes several work-related emails. She checks the time. 10:00 PM. She's suddenly feeling anxious. It's the witching hour. She gets up and heads downstairs to Nic's office. He's at his computer typing something between glances at the TV that's tuned to a basketball game.

NIC SENSES HER PRESENCE IN THE HALL OUTSIDE HIS OFFICE AND WITHOUT looking up for a visual confirmation, he calls out, "Are you spying on me, cara mia?"

"I'm not very good at it if I am."

"What's up? You hardly ever come down here."

"I don't know. Maybe I was thinking of hiding down here until the coast is clear."

Glancing at his clock, he immediately understands her appearance at his door. He waves her into his office and motions to the plush chair in front of his desk. His office is twice the size of Cara's. Long tables laden with blueprints and files line one wall. His TV, along with large whiteboards filled with project calendars, Post-its and schedules fill the other wall. It's his version of a war room. Cara sits down and stares at the TV.

Nic studies her for a moment. She seems unsettled so he asks, "Something bothering you?" Then more hesitantly, "Is there something you want to discuss?" He winces at his own question, knowing this could devolve into one of Cara's 'we need to talk' conversations.

Cara smiles at him, "No. No talking. Can I just sit here, quietly?"

Astonished, he mocks, "Can you? I mean, are you capable of sitting quietly?"

Scowling, she narrows her eyes at him. "Keep that up and we will be 'talking'. Really, I just want to sit here. Will that bother you?"

"Um, no, I guess not," he replies as he goes back to typing. After about a minute he stops and looks at her. She has stretched her legs out in front of her and is watching the game. She really is sitting quietly. It's unnerving. There must be something wrong. "Okay, that's enough. Tell me what's going on."

Snapping her head to look at him, Cara responds, "Nothing is going on. Am I disturbing you here?"

Nic needs to proceed with caution here. "You're not disturbing me, baby, it's just...I'm sensing something more. Like you NEED something."

"Maybe I just NEED to sit quietly in close proximity to you, and that's all."

"You miss me," he states with surety.

"It's possible," she retorts.

Nic smirks and gets up. He walks over and straddles her in the big chair, a knee on either side of her hips. Her head falls back against the chair, and she emits a contented sigh. "Love that beautiful face and those gorgeous ocean blue eyes of yours."

Undeterred by her flattery, he tries one more time, "Tell me what you need, please?" Cara licks her lips and places her hands seductively on his hips. "Like I said, I don't need anything but...I'm starting to want something." With that, she subtly shifts her hands towards the front of his jeans.

Nic grabs her wrists and holds them against his chest. He drops to his knees on the floor in front of her, slowly leaning in to brush his lips against hers. She murmurs her pleasure. He places gentle kisses on her chin, and follows her jawline, until he reaches her ear. "I'll make you a deal," he whispers. "You make sure the monsters are in bed, and I'll meet you in our room so we can finish what you started here."

She kisses his neck. "I AM bothering you sitting quietly down here."

He still has her wrists in his hands. Moving them down so she can feel his arousal stretching out his jeans, he retorts, "You are not bothering me, but you are a...distraction."

"Ha!" Cara chokes out as she pushes him off. She points a finger in his face and declares, "I will meet you in the bedroom in thirty minutes. Do not make me wait." She storms out of his office.

He watches her fine ass wiggle away and he chuckles. After all these years, he still loves the Tom and Jerry games they play with each other.

CHAPTER

FOUR

CARA IS EXHAUSTED AND DELICIOUSLY sated. It's well past one in the morning and Nic is snoring softly, his arms still wrapped around her. She eases away without waking him and shimmies to the other side of their king bed. She's as far from him as possible, hoping to diminish the sound of his snores so she can sleep. What seems like minutes later, she feels a tug at her hair. She murmurs, half asleep, "No, Nic, not again."

"No again, baby. It's morning. Time to get up." He yanks the covers off her.

"How are you so chipper?" she huffs.

"I got laid by a hot babe last night, how can I not be chipper?" he purrs over his shoulder as he walks out of the bedroom.

Cara glares at him. It's annoying to have a husband who's such a morning person.

She enters the kitchen sporting a clean pair of yoga pants and a clean T-shirt, still no shoes or underpants. Nic hands her a plated omelet and a cup of coffee as she passes him. Then, she stops dead in her tracks. Her two children are dressed and ready for school. She quickly glances at the kitchen clock, thinking they must be running

25

late, but they still have ten minutes to spare. She narrows her eyes at them. "What gives?"

"We forgot we need you to fill out some forms due today to go on the field trip to Chicago," Mia declares, before pointing at the counter and backing away from her.

Cara sees what appears to be a ten-page document waiting to be filled out. Trying to stay calm, she checks the clock again, and waving the paperwork that is now in her hand, says, "You want me to complete this in 10 minutes?" She looks to Nic for support but he only shrugs. Turning back to her children, no longer able to contain her frustration, she screams, "How long have you had these?!"

Mia doesn't answer her mother directly, just pleads, "But we need these today."

Cara shouts back at her, "But you can't get what you need right now!"

And then Cara hears it, the humming. She spins to glare at her husband. He's humming the Joe Jackson song *You Can't Get What You Want Till You Know What You Want.*

Max laughs out loud and starts singing to Nic's humming. After a couple verses, Nic joins him and the two of them are harmonizing.

Nic grabs Cara by the hips grinding to the harmony. He's trying to diffuse the situation because he knows his wife is on the verge of going postal. He takes her body and shimmies while Max air guitars and hums the instrumental portion. Soon, they're dirty dancing as Max reaches the final chorus, and Mia stares at the three of them in horror. She finally breaks into their revelry shouting, "Okay, I get it. NOW STOP!"

Nic laughs at his daughter, "I'm sorry, Mia, and I swear I wasn't humming aloud."

"God, Dad, you always say that, but we can totally hear you!

Everyone else must be deaf. And thanks, by the way, I now have a new song to add to the soundtrack of your life."

That's what his family call his humming thing. The Soundtrack of His Life. Cara believes it's a coping mechanism he developed as a child when life got too complicated or emotional. He played a song in his head that ultimately related to the current situation. When they began dating, she found it a bit peculiar, and he was embarrassed she could hear him humming. But it quickly turned into a game of 'Name that Tune' for her. He's tried to control it, but he can't, and he swears no one ever noticed it before her.

Not one to prolong their agony, Cara settles on a trade. She will complete the paperwork and deliver it to the school, if they apologize for screwing up, and make amends by cleaning their rooms for a 6:00 PM inspection. "Capice?" she adds.

Crisis over, Nic grabs the lunch sacks and heads out the door, calling back, "I'll be in the car."

When Nic returns from drop-off hell, he finds Cara slumped over the kitchen table, her head resting on the offending documents. "Baby, good job this morning. I know that was hard."

Without lifting her head, she groans, "It was draining. And my coffee is cold."

Nic taps the table. She glances over to see he has placed a large cup of hot, double D coffee in front of her. He leans in and places a kiss on her head. "You're welcome and no, I'm not helping you with the papers. They stressed me out this morning. I'm going for a run."

She takes a gulp of her favorite coffee from Dunkin Donuts, impressed and appreciative her husband battled the drive-thru after running the drop off gauntlet at the kids' school. "Mmmmm, thanks, and please keep your shirt on during your jog." Nic quirks his head at her, as if he doesn't understand. She narrows her eyes at him. This time slot isn't on his normal run schedule. "The neighborhood ladies will be sad if they hear Nic Andre passed by bare-chested and they missed it."

An hour later, Cara finally completes the five-page form in duplicate for each child, with the same information she has provided the school hundreds of times before, when her cell phone rings. "Hey Jinxie, what up?"

"Starbucks in ten minutes?"

"Stopping at the school office. Make it fifteen minutes and you have a deal."

"You know that means twenty minutes. Deal."

Twenty minutes to the second later, Cara pulls into Starbucks. Freaking Jinx and her timeline accuracy!

Jinx is sitting at the same table from the previous morning with two cups in front of her. As Cara approaches, she says, "Let me guess, they gave you the Chicago papers this morning?"

"Bingo."

"Did you go all thermonuclear?"

"Bingo, again."

"Well, welcome to Hump day, two more days and we can rest. Before you ask, no, I didn't get any details yet on the music from Starbucks or Target."

Cara is about to respond when she sees Jinx's eyes go wide at something beyond her visual. An audible sigh escapes Jinx's lips and she knows immediately what's coming up behind her. She leans into Jinx and commands, "Say nothing." She turns slowly to watch Nic running towards them, shirt off, of course, and tucked into the waistband of his shorts. Damn him.

He slows down and approaches their table. "Ladies," he greets them as he pulls his shirt out of his waistband and slowly wipes sweat from his chest, drawing attention to every sculpted muscle. Cara notices all the women outside are gawking. In her peripheral vision, she can see the women inside pressing their faces against the glass. It's a Magic Mike moment and Nic is clueless.

Now Nic has his arms over his head, reaching for the sweat on his back. This move amplifies the defined muscles of his broad shoulders and chest. There's a collective gasp from those around them. Cara wants to offer to wipe the sweat for him, just to stake claim on her man, but she knows that's not in her nature. Let the ladies enjoy. She asks sweetly, "Nic, you want me to run in and get you a drink."

"No, I can do it," Nic says, waving at her to stay seated.

Through gritted teeth, she mouths, "Put your shirt on before you go inside, please. You promised, earlier."

He leans down and, wrapping her ponytail around his hand, yanks her head back and gives her a wet kiss. He breaks away and whispers, "I never promised."

Hmm, so Nic isn't as clueless as she thought. Bastard.

Thoroughly entertained by the scene, Jinx blurts, "Nice show, Nic."

"I aim to please my fans," he retorts, brandishing a killer smile.

Cara grunts, "Shirt on, now!" He snickers and puts on his shirt while walking into Starbucks, making sure to stretch every muscle in the process. "And he wonders where Max gets it?"

Jinx giggles while nodding in agreement. "Sorry, but you must admit, it's pretty funny. They're all in there now, fawning over him." She continues to giggle, pointing inside the store. "They don't look at my Jake like that."

"I told you yesterday, Reacher is just as hot. But he's too scary," she continues with a laugh. "The women admire him. They just do it from a safe distance! Speaking of him, is he back tonight?"

Shaking her head sadly, Jinx responds, "No, he texted this morning to say he missed the last flight out and will be back tomorrow night."

"The last flight out from where?" Cara asks trying to trick Jinx into divulging.

Before Jinx can reply, Nic appears with a coffee cup in hand and interrupts with, "When's Reacher coming home?"

He takes the seat between the women and Jinx loses it. "You guys need to stop with that nickname! Wait, you got a coffee already?"

Nic shrugs. "They had my regular waiting for me. The barista said she saw me outside."

"Of course she did," Jinx mumbles under her breath. She informs them of Jake's arrival status but offers up no further details.

Nic stands and motions to Cara for the car keys. "I'm hitching a ride home. Ready?"

Cara looks at Jinx and then glares at her husband. "But I just got here."

Apparently, Jinx has also decided their little party is over. She stands up, mimes texting to Cara and grabs her coffee cup.

Shrugging, Cara tosses her car keys to Nic and asks, "Same time tomorrow, then?"

Jinx calls over her shoulder, "Sure."

FIVE

A COUPLE OF HOURS LATER, Cara is showered, dressed and settled in with her computer in her office.

She keeps two email accounts. The business emails go to a secure server. Her personal email, for on-line shopping, social media and other 'junk' mail go to a Gmail account she checks at best, once a day. She completes a call with a client, then downloads her unread Gmail. As she scrolls through, mostly hitting delete, she stops suddenly when something catches her eye. The subject of the email is Duran Duran Tickets.

Before she can stop herself, she clicks on the email. It opens and *The Reflex* begins playing through the computer speakers. Stunned, Cara immediately clicks off the sound.

She stares numbly at the screen, heart racing. Stay calm. Assess, calculate, formulate, and react. She focuses her eyes to read the screen. It's an email from a Duran Duran fan club announcing new tour dates and ticket sales. The email looks legit; graphics are clear; lots of details on upcoming shows, new tour dates, Ticketmaster schedules. But Cara does not believe in coincidences. Besides, is Duran Duran even touring?

Suddenly, Cara is startled right out of her chair by her phone's text message alert. Holy Shit! Get it together, girl. She picks up her phone to see it's from Mia looking for a pick-up at 2:30. Cara texts her back asking why she can't make the bus at 2:30? Her answer is, 'carrying too much stuff'. She gives up and tells her daughter, 'Fine.'

Although, the only thing worse than drop-off at the oval, is pick-up at the oval right at 2:30 when school lets out. She would sooner be water boarded. As if Mia has a moment of clarity, she texts, 'Sorry mom, but I can use the extra time to clean my room. Thx'. Did her daughter just show appreciation and manipulation skills? Impressive.

Still unnerved, Cara decides to investigate the email. She clips and pastes the sender's email address into the Google search bar. The fan club appears to be real. Next, she checks the Duran Duran site and, yes, they are touring, and yes, these are new tour dates. The Ticketmaster information is accurate as well.

She's feeling slightly better. But she's never signed up to be a fan of the band on any website. Preferences and contact info sold from iTunes or Apple, maybe?

As she's pondering these questions, she hears Nic coming up the stairs from the lower level. She quickly closes out of her Google searches then drags the original email into a folder. She manually turns off her speakers just as Nic walks into the room. "Hey, what's up?"

Without waiting for an answer, he launches into a request for help with a contract and hands her several sheets of paper. Lucky for her, Nic is oblivious to her worried state. Cara glances at her clock. Great. More paperwork today. When he's finished, she tells him, "I'll do what I can before I leave to get Mia for a 2:30 pick-up."

"You're going to do a 2:30 pick up? Have you lost your mind?"

"Quite possibly. In any case, I'll work on your shit until I leave, but after I come back with Mia, I need to do my own work, you understand?"

"Deal and thank you for reviewing that contract." He walks out and Cara realizes where Mia gets her manipulation skills.

She needs to compartmentalize this song obsession, or she'll never get any work done.

Making an effort to clear her desk, she takes some deep, cleansing breaths and lays out Nic's papers. She finishes her review, emails a request for updates on open items in the contract, as well as a short list of additions and deletions, grabs her phone and her handbag, and heads to the car for Defensive Driving 101.

After successfully negotiating the Oval, Cara and Mia head home, neither breaking the peaceful silence of the car ride. But no sooner does Cara pull into their driveway, when her phone pings with a text message from Max. 'I need to be picked up now.'

"No!" She practically pushes Mia out of the car and pulls back out of the driveway. This is ridiculous. How the hell does she ever get anything done? She's just reaching the main road when her phone rings. Not wanting her car's Bluetooth to pick up, Cara grabs her phone and answers, knowing it's Max waiting for a response to his text. Just as her hand slides across the bottom of the phone, she sees the caller ID reads, 'Unknown'. But it's too late. The call connects... and Duran Duran's *The Reflex* is blaring through her phone.

Cara throws her phone down on the passenger seat, yanks the wheel hard to the left, and pulls into the corner CVS. She isn't parked, she isn't moving; she's just sitting in the middle of the entrance lane staring wild-eyed at her phone while the music continues to play. The loud toot of a horn behind her snaps her out of her daze. She robotically pulls through CVS to the next plaza, circles around to the back of the building by the loading docks, out of sight from the main traffic flow. The music abruptly stops, and the line goes dead.

Putting her head down on the steering wheel, she lets it rest there. After a couple of minutes, she picks up her phone and texts Nic with shaky hands. 'Have serious work emergency. Caught between home and school, please pick up Max for me. On hold for building official, now. Thx'.

Once Nic confirms he'll run to get Max, she sits back and tries to calm down so she can think. On impulse, she picks up her phone, finds her favorites and hits 'call'.

She can picture somewhere in a Pentagon conference room a cell phone shrills to life. A very handsome man, in his late forties, casually gets up and walks away from the conference table. He steps outside into the hallway with his phone and answers. "C, what's up, sweetheart? You don't usually call during business hours. You just pester the shit out of me with texts."

"I need to clock in," Cara says firmly.

"Come again?"

"You heard me. I need to clock in. I'm booking a flight for tomorrow morning. I'll send you my itinerary when it's confirmed. Please provide standard protocol. I'll email my concerns to your secure address."

"I'll make sure I'm available for you," he promises.

"Please, do not reschedule any of your commitments for me. I can work with anyone there," Cara scolds.

"You let me worry about that, sweetheart. See you tomorrow morning." And with that, he ends the call.

When Cara finally returns home, she is composed. She heads down to Nic's office. "It's bad, Nic."

"What happened?"

Cara explains she's had a fiasco on her DC project. There was some obscure reference to the building as a historical landmark. The local architect never caught it. Of course, the building officials practically fell over themselves to deliver a cease and desist on the construction. "The whole project fell apart," she tells him.

"Did we hire the contractor and or architect?" Nic asks, truly concerned.

The Owner contracted directly with the GC and the design team. She's being paid to project manage this one, so they have no legal exposure, but she is still responsible for fixing the mess. "Client is having a meltdown. He wants me there tomorrow morning."

"Sorry, baby. Anything I can do to help?"

"Cover for me here tomorrow?" Cara lets out a huge grunt as she walks out of Nic's office looking defeated. That total lie went well.

CHAPTER
SIX

THE FOLLOWING MORNING CARA IS up by five o'clock to shower and dress. She replays the previous evening through her mind. She had kept her composure throughout the night's activities. Before dinner, she booked her flight to Dulles. At six, the twins' rooms both passed a hardcore inspection, although Cara did find some candy wrappers under Mia's bed. She got off with a warning. Dinner was served and kitchen clean-up was done by eight o'clock.

She texted Jinx about her construction emergency and bailed on their coffee date. She packed her carry-on bag, found her folders on the DC project, to maintain her cover story, and placed them, with her iPad in her Longchamp tote. She was in bed by 10.

She's blowing out her hair in front of the mirror, when Nic enters the bathroom, naked as usual, and begins to rub his morning wood playfully against her butt. Cara shuts the hair dryer off and turns to him. "Nothing is happening for you this morning, my love. I still must choose an amazing outfit and get out of here to make my flight."

"Wear the brown suede boots with the wedge heels. I love your legs when you wear those," he offers.

Surprised by his comment, Cara leans into him with a one-arm hug while still holding the hair dryer. "Thanks, babe, that helps me decide. Although, I'm shocked."

Her husband eyes her warily. "You're shocked I want you to look your best on the jobsite? I understand sex sells and you'll knock them dead. Or are you shocked that I don't mind you wearing the boots for Reed? You are seeing him while you're there, right?"

Cara lets him go from the hug and places a soft kiss on his lips. "And there it is...I was wondering when you were going to ask." Nic gives her a beseeching look. "Reed is in town. If I spend the night, we agreed I'd meet him for a late dinner and stay at his place."

"So, you may not see him?"

"He's in meetings all day and has an early professional dinner to attend. So, only if I must spend the night," she confirms, once again.

"Send him my love," Nic delivers with sarcasm.

"I will be sure to do that."

Cara is out the door by six, wearing the brown boots and a killer ensemble under her Burberry trench coat. At the airport, she gets TSA Precheck so the boots and coat can stay on, and, arriving at the gate, hears her name called for a complimentary first-class upgrade. So far, this is going well. On the plane, she's seated next to a man close to her age, who steals occasional glances but makes no attempt at conversation. Things are going even better.

At Dulles, Cara makes her way through to ground transportation. She recognizes her contact and walks towards him. The young man wearing a dark suit gives her the once over and says, "Ma'am, follow me," and takes her carry-on from her.

They walk outside to a waiting black town car. Her escort opens the door for her to enter, then stows her bag in the trunk before getting into the front passenger seat. The driver hurriedly pulls away. The privacy screen between the front and back seats is left open.

No one speaks during the thirty-minute ride. Cara texts her husband to say she has landed safely. She puts her phone away and stares out the window, caught up in the thoughts and memories swirling in her head.

Before she realizes, they've gone through two checkpoints and arrive at a building she doesn't recognize. She looks up and spots a lone figure standing with his hands in the pockets of his suit pants, his classic good looks evident even with the Ray Ban Aviators he's sporting. She can see his hard jawline, perfect nose and defined, full lips. The cut of his dark blue well-tailored suit molds to his muscular frame. His full head of mostly gray hair is cut short in a trendy style. His face is impassive as he watches their vehicle pull up in front of him.

Connor Mitchell Reed, Jr. is a man of tremendous power and position, the current Director of the CIA, and Cara's best friend. He opens the car door and drags her out into a bear hug. "C, I've missed you so much." He holds her at arm's length then pulls her back in for a kiss on her lips while he dips her.

She pushes at him. "Stop that!" He's causing a scene on purpose just to raise eyebrows; a nod to the scandalous rumors spread about him by former associates.

When he finally releases her, she points to his suit. "You're wearing Tom Ford? I'm pleased you took my fashion advice. You look extremely dashing."

"Thanks, you don't look bad yourself."

"Please, I'm so nervous. I changed my clothes six times this morning."

"Nervous?" Reed mocks.

"I haven't stepped foot on these hallowed grounds in seventeen years. And I've never been in this building." She points to the front doors. "Is this the new George Bush Center?"

"Yup. I figured I would walk you through here, first. It's the long way to my office, but I thought you might enjoy it."

Reed places her arm through his as they stroll into the building.

They bypass security and he hands her an ID badge with her picture and the name 'Chase Bennett' on it. Reed is rambling on about construction costs and delays with the new Center. He points out interesting items in the lobby and talks about additional square footage and facilities.

Normally, Cara would enjoy any conversation concerning the building of the new Center, but she hasn't heard a word Reed has said. She's only aware of the way everyone they pass is staring at them as Reed drags her through secure door after secure door, until she has no idea where she is within the framework of the site. They finally reach an elevator and take it up to the seventh floor.

They exit the elevator and walk through a bullpen of workstations, all grey, and all in need of refurbishment. Work stops and silence ensues as each person casts a glance their way. She's trying not to make eye contact, but her nerves get the better of her as she notices their stares are not for Reed. They're watching her. She whispers, "Why are they all staring?"

"Well, it's possible someone leaked the news that Chase Bennett is back for a visit," Reed tells her with a devilish grin.

"So?"

He chuckles softly, "Sweetheart, you're a legend around here."

"A legend? You make me sound like some old, medieval witch."

A broad smile appears on his face. "Witch wasn't the word I was thinking of, but let's go with that."

On an inhale Cara whispers, "You know the rules. If I'm a bitch, you're a prick." She pinches his side for good measure.

He yelps before adding, "Seriously, C, there are some people still here from your time, and others who have heard all the stories. Stories and legends built the walls here at Langley. You, of all people, should know about legends." Reed raises an eyebrow as he says this and chuckles, again.

"Nimrod."

REED LAUGHS A LITTLE LOUDER. SHE HAS MANAGED TO SLING HER THREE favorite insults at him already, and she's been in the building for less than ten minutes. Another involuntary chuckle escapes his throat. Cara is the only person in his life who would ever dare to put him in his place. Just seeing a smile on his face probably sent his staff into shock. Imagine if they could hear this conversation. Reed would never be respected again.

Waving his security fob as they pass through the next secure door, he heads down a quiet hallway past several conference rooms. Near the end of the hallway, through yet another secure door, they enter the Executive area and finally his office. He closes the door, after signaling to his Admin he's not to be disturbed.

Reed points Cara to a chair in front of his desk and he takes a seat behind it. For a moment he drifts into the past. He and the gorgeous woman sitting across from him were a team; young and idealistic looking to right the wrongs of the world together. Realizing he's been holding his breath, Reed shakes himself out of his reverie. "Memories," he sighs out.

Cara snorts, ruining his nostalgic mood. "Memories? This office is incredible. My memories are of you behind a World War II era metal desk, in a shithole office. God, Reed, I don't know what to say. The reality of THIS." She waves her arm around.

"To think I have another office just like this at the Pentagon" he responds, laughing.

"It blows me away. I'm so proud of you."

Reed shifts uncomfortably. "OK, enough of that nonsense. Let's get down to it. Let me see your phone." She pulls her phone from her handbag and slides it across the desk to him. He picks it up just as a new text arrives. He relays the message, "Mia needs to be picked up from school at three."

"Jesus, those kids never listen. Text her back and tell her to text her father, I'm in DC."

Shrugging at her typical demand of him, he texts back and

immediately there's a response. "She asked is DC a new grocery store? And where will you be parked at 3:00?"

"Ugh, damn kid! Give me the phone." She leans across the desk to grab the phone but not before flicking him in the head. He doesn't understand the attack. He hasn't done anything wrong...yet.

"C, remind me why we're best friends again?" She doesn't respond but continues typing on her phone. He leans in to see the text. It says, 'DC, District of Columbia, as in six hours away. Text your father for a ride. And NO, I won't text him for you! Stop bothering me, I'm WORKING!' She gently places the phone back in his hand and grins at him.

Maybe, it wasn't such a good idea allowing her back into the building. He glances up to make sure his office blinds are drawn and his Admin has not witnessed this exchange. "You do realize I run this entire facility now?"

"And you do that all by yourself?" she mocks.

She makes a valid point. He does have an amazing staff, and he has her to bounce all his issues around with.

Interrupting his internal dialog, she snaps, "And why are we making this about you? This is about ME, today."

He doesn't dignify the dig with a response. Instead, he pops the SIM card out of her phone. He opens his top desk drawer, pulls out a file and a new SIM card. He inserts the new SIM into her phone, then takes the original out to his Admin.

When he comes back in, he opens the file and places three sheets of paper in front of Cara. "You are correct. This is about you." He details their investigation so far. Both the Starbucks and Target music systems were tampered with. The email is from an unknown IP address. Not a legitimate Fan Club email. "None of this type of hacking is difficult, but it proves the music you heard was not a coincidence, and the email is a plant."

Cara takes this in trying not to show any sign of the panic growing inside her. Something is wrong, possibly very wrong. She's felt it for days. She's repeating to herself the mantra Reed taught her so many years ago. Capture and contain, capture and contain. She doesn't want Reed to see her unbalanced if she's going to solve this mystery her way.

She focuses on her breathing and continues, "So, we know that someone knows who I am... or who I was...whatever, someone knows I am the Reflex."

"It would appear that way, sweetheart."

He details his investigation into all her known adversaries. Most of them are either dead or have gone legit, and in any case, he doesn't see how they could've made the connection between Chase Bennett, the Reflex, and Cara Andre. More importantly, he can't come up with a motive for any of them.

He pulls a fourth sheet of paper from the file and lays it out in front of her. "Here's the list of anyone you tangled with who's still alive."

Cara reads through it quickly. It's short. "Six people left, that's it?"

"Sweetheart, you removed the other threats."

Examining the list more closely, she addresses each name. "Well, I'm sure you know I'm Facebook friends with Javier and Lucien... well...I'm friends with their alter egos. They're not a threat."

"Yeah, about that, do you think that's wise? Facebook, Instagram, and Twitter? Posting pictures?" Reed asks, his disproval on full display.

"Connor, first, I use the tightest security settings on the sites and I'm careful about what pictures of me are posted. Secondly, it would be far too suspicious if a middle-aged mom didn't participate in social media. Talk about red flags." She waves her hand at him dismissively, but she's not fooling him with the cavalier attitude. Her eyes must reflect her concern.

Giving up, Reed exhales, "We'll continue that argument another time. As for the other four names on the list...they're all doing well financially, and I can find no motive, so I can't see any reason to investigate them further."

Besides, if they wanted to hurt her, they could have found Cara in Ohio and killed her there. That's more their style. "I agree. So where does this leave us? With one of the supposedly 'dead' threats?" she asks.

"It's possible one of the dead is still living; maybe faked their death. But even that list is short. And again, they would've had to make the connection between Chase and Cara." He assures her there's no record of Cara Bianco or Cara Andre anywhere within the government's systems.

"Maybe not here at Langley. But Cara Bianco worked for World Bank from 1989 until 1999," she reminds.

"All of the precautions I took for you are still in place. Solid," Reed assures her again. When she left the Agency, and forfeited her pension, he swept her record and removed any reference to Cara Bianco. Only her decade of service at the Agency as 'Chase Bennett' remains. And no known whereabouts since 2000. A search for Cara Bianco will take anyone only to her years at the World Bank from 1989 until 1999.

Before Cara can ask her next question, Reed receives a call. He picks up, listens for a couple of minutes and with a frown hangs up and says, "That was Agent Carter. We were able to triangulate the call you received yesterday to cell towers in Berlin, Germany."

Cara's brows shoot up as she looks back down at the short list of remaining suspects. "Olaf Stein. He and his company's headquarters are based there." Cara jumps to her feet and turns towards the door.

Reed is quick to intercept her. "Where are you going?" he demands.

"To Berlin to visit Olaf."

"It's not that simple."

"Of course it is."

What's left of Reed's patience is gone. He grabs both of her arms and plants her firmly back in her chair. "You. Are. Not. Going. Anywhere."

Cara sets her jaw and stares defiantly back at Reed. Quickly sensing she won't win this battle of wills, she softens her gaze and runs her hands up his arms into his hair, pulling him in until their noses are touching.

Licking her lips slowly, she purrs, "Please?"

Reed lets out a long sigh. He brushes the corner of her mouth in a light kiss before resting his forehead against hers. He looks into her eyes again. "Can I at least do some recon first?" She shakes her head and Reed growls through clenched teeth, "Damn it, C! I've got a bad feeling about this."

Holding her ground, willing Reed to concede, they are interrupted by a knock on the door. Reed releases her, and quickly steps back to lean on his desk, before commanding, "Come in, Carter."

A tall, very muscular, young man with amazing light brown skin enters the office. He strides over to Reed and hands him a file folder. Reed takes the folder then thrusts his right hand out to shake. The Agent is obviously caught off guard by this gesture and hesitantly puts his own right hand into Reed's. Clasping the young man's shoulder in a fatherly way, Reed turns him towards Cara who has risen from her seat.

There's a moment of uncomfortable silence while Reed wars with himself about how best to make this introduction. He finally inhales softly, then blurts out, "Agent William Carter, I would like to introduce you to Agent Chase Bennett. You will be accompanying her to Berlin within the hour."

CHAPTER

SEVEN

CARA, CARTER AND REED WALK quickly out of the building and back to the waiting town car. Reed opens the door and settles himself with his two agents inside while instructing the driver to head to the air base. He closes the privacy window between the front and back seats and turns his focus to Carter and Cara to reiterate their mission objectives.

They are to visit Olaf Stein tomorrow morning, first thing. They've hacked into his schedule, and Olaf will be in his office by 7:00 AM to prepare for a meeting. After initial contact, they are to go directly to the designated meeting place and do nothing else. Reed will attend his afternoon meeting with the Joint Chiefs, the White House dinner tonight, and then take his Gulfstream to meet them.

Cara interrupts him to the noticeable shock of Carter. "Reed, you don't need to meet us in Berlin. You have Carter babysitting me... that's enough!"

Reed continues, ignoring Cara as if she hasn't spoken. "Carter, you brought your service weapon and a Glock 43 9mm for Agent Bennett like I requested?"

"Yes, sir."

"And you are NOT to give her the gun, unless there's no other choice, correct?"

"Life or death only, sir."

Cara is outraged and interrupts Reed, again. "That's ridiculous, why can't I have a gun?"

This time Reed acknowledges her interruption and calmly responds, "Because you can't be trusted to follow orders when you're armed." Then he turns to Carter and warns, "She is very cunning, Carter. Don't underestimate her."

For the first time since they were introduced, Carter shows some personality. He slowly turns to look at her, a wry smile on his face. He flexes his muscles and drawls, "Sir, there will be no trouble from Ms. Bennett."

Cara's head snaps in Carter's direction and with steel in her eyes, declares, "First, that's Agent Bennett to you," then, "and second, how can you be so sure I won't be trouble?"

"Ma'am, I have never met a woman I couldn't handle."

"Really? Out of what...the maybe two you've had so far? What are you like, 19?" Cara snorts.

"I'm 27, Special Forces trained. I've seen action in Afghanistan and I've been with the Agency for three years. AND...a gentleman never talks about how many women he has 'had'," Carter responds unfazed by her.

"Huh," is all she can come up with in response.

Reed interjects, "I see you two will get along fine." He glances out the window as the car slows to a stop. "We are here. I have you both on a military transport. Sorry for the sub-par accommodations, but this was the quickest way. Carter, do you mind giving Agent Bennett and me a moment, please?" Carter grabs his bag and Cara's and exits the car, shutting the door behind him.

Reed immediately pulls Cara into a bear hug. He doesn't speak. He just buries his face into her hair inhaling her scent. There's an anxiety creeping through his blood.

She was his best agent, and he's always had complete faith in her, but he hasn't sent her on a mission without him in a very long time. At this moment, he feels that faith wavering. He gazes over at the transport plane. Every bone in his body wants to get on that plane with her. But a last minute cancellation of his schedule today, would be too suspicious. He can cover up their trip on the cargo transport but flying his plane to Berlin after cancelling his commitments at the eleventh hour, would raise a red flag. He has a hunch he needs to keep all of this under the radar, for now.

His lips to her ear, he whispers, "Please be careful. I'm worried to death right now. Please do as I say and only talk to Olaf...and don't hurt Carter. He's a great agent...but I know you," he continues, pulling away from their hug to look her in the eyes. "You were and are a very dangerous woman, C, impulsive and arrogant...please wait for me before you pursue any leads. Please, promise."

Cara gives him her duh face. "Stop whining. It doesn't become you. Besides, it's like riding a bike, right? I'll be fine. And you know I've never listened to you. If I feel time is ticking, I won't be detained."

Reed leans down and places a gentle kiss on her forehead, "Carter will stop you."

As she starts for the door, Cara turns back towards him and quips, "I'd like to see him try." Then she smiles, blows him a kiss, shuts the door and heads for the transport.

CARTER SLEEPS THE ENTIRE TIME ON THE PLANE. CARA CAN'T IMAGINE HOW. It's noisy, bumpy and entirely uncivilized. How did she ever travel this way? Of course, she was a younger woman the last time she was strapped into a stripped-down cargo plane. This is an Airbus, but it doesn't ride like or remotely resemble any Airbus commercial flights. Is it the plane, or are the pilots flying crazy? Must be the pilots.

She inspects the seat. It doesn't recline; there's no padding and it's hard as a rock. It resembles the plastic seat on a city bus. She mumbles, "Hemorrhoid Makers." To make matters worse, she is harnessed in, so everything she's wearing will be a wrinkled mess. She's feeling out of sorts and needs to get a grip.

She understands she should try to sleep, but she can't comprehend how. It takes her half a Xanax at home to get to sleep on a $3000 mattress. When did she become so soft? Oh yes, when the kids came! That's when she started worrying about everything...and a good night's sleep became a thing of the past. She was trained to grab sleep anywhere, when she could get some, like all members of the military. Guess that training disappears once you have children. She just hopes she hasn't lost her edge.

Her thoughts turn to her family. She needs to call Nic when she lands. She'll tell him she's staying in DC an extra night and hope he doesn't ask many questions. To begin with, he's never happy when he thinks she's with Reed. The two men have a grudging respect for each other, grudge being the operative word. Mildly antagonistic is another phrase to describe their relationship. Cara won't give either man up, though. After 16 years of marriage, she hoped Nic would finally accept that Reed is in her life to stay.

He's gotten marginally more accepting but he's obviously not ready to give his stamp of approval. Reed is her best friend and Nic is the best husband, ever. There's bound to be jealousies.

She and Reed don't get together near as often as she'd like. When she left the agency, her life went in a different direction and Reed's career took off. He's a powerful player in D.C. now and his job keeps him very busy. There are times she misses him like crazy.

For the decade Cara was at the Agency, Reed was her handler, her protector, trainer, confidante, and partner. He was Cara's White Knight. Their friendship has endured 25 years. No one knows her better than Reed. Not even Nic.

Their friendship began while Cara was in college. When she graduated with no job prospects, Reed brought her to the Agency to work for him. Her colleagues picked up on their close relationship and were less than friendly. They believed she received preferential treatment, when the truth was, Reed worked her harder, cutting her no slack, expecting the best. And she did her best to exceed his expectations.

The pilot's voice announcing their descent into Berlin drags Cara back to the present. Carter wakes up and gives her a devilish grin. Ugh, she should have played a prank on him while he slept instead of losing herself in the past.

Reed has somehow arranged for a town car to meet Carter and Cara on the runway at Tegel near Berlin. It's a commercial airfield but they appear to be bypassing customs. The man's reach never ceases to amaze. As expected, the driver has already received his orders and as soon as they're settled, he speeds out of the airport and heads straight for the hotel.

Inside the car, Cara spots a box on the seat with a card addressed to 'C'. She opens the card, and reads, 'Sweetheart, because I knew you would break into the local Olaf store tonight, I decided to save you the trouble. Enjoy. Love, Reed.' Cara laughs out loud. He knows her well.

Carter peeks over her shoulder at the card and gives her a puzzled look. "Director Reed knew I wouldn't go see Olaf Stein without wearing one of his designs," Cara explains while she opens the package.

"You mean the Olaf Stein we're going to see is Olaf, the fashion designer?"

She snaps, "Did you get no intel at all? Of course it's the same Olaf! And 'WE' aren't seeing him. I am. You're waiting outside."

She takes the lid off the box and squeaks as she pulls out a gorgeous cashmere coat, off-white and collarless with wide lapels. Classic Olaf! Underneath is a pair of amazing black suede over the knee boots with stiletto heels.

She's blissfully caressing the garment when Carter wrecks the mood with, "You're stroking that coat like it's a cock. You're kinda turning me on, Agent Bennett."

"Nice mouth. Agent Carter. You implied you were a gentleman.

Could have fooled me with that comment," Cara scolds. "And I'm a married woman, so keep your trashy thoughts to yourself."

Carter snickers, "You're married? Poor sap."

"What? Why would you say that?"

"Darlin', you...with Director Reed? Not cool."

Cara is about to set him straight but stops short. Why should she explain herself to this infantile moron? He's as bad as her former colleagues at the Agency. They all assumed she was fucking Reed for special treatment. It became tiresome defending herself, so she finally gave up. It was easier to just ignore the gossip and speculation.

Cara turns her head to watch out the window and let her thoughts drift back to her first time in Berlin.

It was just after the wall came down. Things were crazy and chaotic, but even then, the town vibrated with an energy she'd never felt before outside of New York City. It was raw, and edgy, full of purpose and determination after so many years of disrepute. It was a breakout period for the city that, to no one's surprise, would become the thriving business and cultural scene it is today, in just twenty-five years.

Olaf Stein must have felt it, too. It was in Berlin he launched his immensely successful company. Today, Olaf Designs is to Berlin what Burberry is to London. He started with women's clothing and before long, added a men's line, shoes, handbags, and most recently domestics for the home. His unique clothing concept marries outrageous design with subtle sophistication; Gaultier meets Prada. Olaf's biggest draw, though, is the extra sensory feel of his creations. The fabrics feel as good as they look and some limited-edition garments are even infused with a signature fragrance. The wearer enjoys a sensuous experience in one of his creations. And that's what sets him apart.

The fashion community spurned him initially, but women loved him. Very soon supply struggled to meet demand and customers were paying a premium to get their hands on an original Olaf.

Today his house of fashion is considered one of the best in the world.

For almost 20 years, Olaf Stein has been known as 'Olaf', having dropped his last name and expended considerable effort to conceal his identity. He's regarded as a recluse. He refuses to be photographed, only appears in public at the end of his runway shows, hides behind his latest sunglass design, and always sports a bald head and full beard. Of course, the mystery of Olaf has only added to his appeal.

Cara smiles to herself. She has enjoyed following Olaf's career. Partly because she loves fashion, which is by no means evident in her daily life of yoga pants and T-shirts. But it was secretly her favorite part of the job at the Agency. Cara loved when she was allowed to prep for a covert mission with an expense account that included designer wear.

She could never have afforded that wardrobe on her salary. The best part was Reed letting her keep all of it after the mission, writing each article of clothing off as 'collateral damage', although, sometimes, they really were destroyed. She had to promise Reed she would never jeopardize a mission to save her Louboutins from the mud. She did try to, though, always.

When she left the CIA and Virginia, Cara left everything behind except her treasured designer swag. Pity, within two years, most of it would never fit her again. Having twins does that to a woman. Her foot size grew along with the rest of her body as she ultimately gained 60 pounds by the end of her pregnancy.

Fortunately, her children were close to 6 pounds each, and very healthy at birth, but Cara's body never completely recovered. She lost most of the weight, but she'd never got back to a size four. Even Cara's feet refused to go back to her original size eight, so she ended up consigning most of the items.

Since then, Cara hasn't purchased many designer pieces. She and Nic generally reinvest their earnings into the business they started 17 years ago. They were fortunate at the time to have had enough capital between the two of them for the venture. Cara opted for a buyout rather than a pension when she left the government, and she isn't entirely sure where Nic's money came from, but she was thrilled to discover he had plenty to contribute.

Done reminiscing, Cara's mind focuses on her imminent mission. It's been over twenty years since she last saw Olaf Stein.

CHAPTER
EIGHT

CARA FIRST MET OLAF when they were both staring down the barrel of a Heckler and Koch P7 semi-automatic pistol in a back alley during 1994 Paris Fashion Week. Olaf Stein was an East German born KGB agent who fell off their grid and was considered having gone rogue. He had a penchant for Paris, especially during Fashion Week, and Cara was tasked to find him and determine his loyalties. Of course they weren't referred to as the KGB by then, but the SVR. Reed used to joke it was like the Russians put lipstick and make-up on an ugly girl. Same management style and methods, just a new name; and the poor girl was still butt ugly.

The Russians were not exactly forthcoming regarding their concern for Olaf's allegiance, but it was clear to the CIA there were a lot of unanswered questions. Reed was of the opinion Olaf could honestly be waiting to make contact with the US, but he could just as likely be a set up in another attempt to bring down the CIA.

1994 was a particularly painful time for the CIA. The Aldrich Ames scandal was in full bloom, and all hell had broken loose at Langley. Reed, and every Team Leader or Section Head, was nose deep in shit and bureaucracy, spending all their time digging up answers for the brass and the Deputy Director. Because Cara was Reed's best agent, she was chosen to determine Olaf's intentions.

Cara had this weirdly uncanny ability to quickly decipher people and situations. She still does but back then she's sure it's what made her effective at her job. She has spoken at great length with Navy Seals and Special Ops guys who, like her, say they can feel a prickle on the backs of their necks when danger is near. Also like her, they'd come to rely on that sensation as much as all their training.

Reed found her talent to read people fascinating and initially called it her special intuition. After he met Cara's family, though, he began to call it something else.

Growing up in the Bianco household was not easy. Noone escaped criticism and the jump from 'first glance' to 'the verdict is in' was almost instantaneous. To say her parents are a tad judgmental is an understatement. Once judgment was passed, there was no second chances. It was hell making new friends and forget dating. She and her sister were so traumatized by 'told you so' bad dates; they eventually stopped dating all together.

Sure, there were one-night hookups as she gained independence from her parents, but that's generally as far as Cara would take it. You can't escape your upbringing, so as Cara got older, she became her own judge and jury. She knew a guy wasn't for her the moment she met him. Her body might be screaming 'sleep with him' but her head was screaming 'loser'.

It wasn't until she met Nic that her mind and body were finally in agreement, intense, total agreement. And at that moment, nothing could have scared her more.

Cara is shaken out of her thoughts when the town car pulls up to the Hotel De Rome. "Wow," she says in almost a whisper.

"What's up?" Carter asks.

"Reed didn't spare any expense; this place is 5-star and THE place to be seen at in Berlin. I'm surprised he chose somewhere so public."

They approach the desk where Carter checks them into their

rooms. Cara wouldn't normally defer, but since Reed hadn't shared any details about the arrangements, she would let Agent Carter wear the pants...for now. She turns her phone back on, noting the time; 5:00 AM Berlin time, which means 11:00 PM in Ohio.

As it powers up, her phone registers several texts from Max requesting pick-up, typical, and a call from Nic while she was in flight. Clutching her tote and the gift box, she follows Carter who's carrying the rest of their bags to their adjoining rooms on the 5th floor.

After thoroughly checking Cara's rooms for God knows what, Carter turns to her and hands her the key, "I will pick you up at 6:30 AM to head over to Olaf's building."

"K, bye."

Carter leaves and she immediately dials Nic's cell phone. It goes right to voicemail. She leaves a quick message saying she hopes to be home by late tomorrow night and she misses him. She tries texting him, next. No response. Suddenly concerned, she decides to call Sasha, Nic's brother and their sometimes live-in Manny. Sasha answers immediately.

"Sash, I'm sorry to call so late, but I was trying to get ahold of Nic, and my phone went dead earlier at dinner. What's up?"

"Yeah, he was trying to call you. Something came up with his Cincy job, and he had to get down there. I'm here with the kids," Sasha replies in his typical unruffled manner. No inflection, business as usual.

"How are my precious little ones?"

"Predictably, driving me nuts." Still no inflection.

"You love it. Do they miss me?"

"Cara, they don't even know you're gone. Mia just called out for you to sign some form she needs for school tomorrow. I didn't bother to remind her, again, that her parents have left the building."

"So, you forged my signature and hopefully yelled at her to go to bed?"

"Obviously." Total deadpan.

Cara hears a soft knock on the connecting door. She walks over and opens it to find Carter standing there. He's wearing sweatpants but is otherwise, barefoot and bare-chested. She motions to him with one finger to wait. "Sasha, hang on one minute, I have another call coming in." She mutes her call, and pointing to his lack of clothing, says to Carter, "What the hell, Agent?"

Carter smirks, flexes his biceps and responds, "I decided I shouldn't trust you. I need you to keep your connecting door open a crack. I don't want you slipping out before our 6:30 meet up."

"Fine. Now can I get back to my call?" She turns away and unmutes her phone. Carter doesn't move. "Sasha? Sorry about that. Apparently, a few people were looking for me while my phone was dead. Do you know when Nic is coming back?"

"If all goes well, he should be back by tomorrow night, but it could be a couple of days. How about you, still scheduled for tomorrow?"

"No, that's why I'm calling." Cara gives him some bullshit about her DC project.

"Sorry, Princess, sometimes we need to work a little harder for our money, right? Are you with Reed and staying at his place while you're there?"

An involuntary sigh escapes Cara's throat. Sasha can be as hostile towards Reed as Nic. It's bad enough she's constantly dealing with Nic's jealousy of her relationship with Reed. She doesn't need Sasha's judgment, too.

"Yes, Sasha, I had a late dinner with Reed tonight. He just left, though, on a trip abroad, so I'm by myself at his place." Cara makes a face at Carter after the 'by myself' comment and tries to close her door. Carter places his foot against the jamb to prevent her from shutting it.

Cara continues her conversation, turning her back on Carter again. "Do you have the twins' schedule for the next two days?"

"Good with tomorrow, can you forward Friday's? Are all kids this busy all the time? It gives me a headache," Sasha adds with only minimal inflection.

"Don't know. Don't wanna know. I believe ignorance is bliss when it comes to parenting. Saves me a lot of second-guessing."

"Wise words to live by, Vizzini."

Sasha has his share of pet names for Cara, most of them references to the movie *Princess Bride*. His favorite is Vizzini; the overly confident but ultimately flawed Sicilian thief. She was annoyed at first, to be compared to a short, balding, ridiculous character, but then realized any attention from Sasha is a gift. He's a man of few words and fewer emotions. Speaking of which... this is the longest phone conversation she's had with him, ever. Strange.

"Very funny, Sasha. Please make sure my children are in bed. And please tell Nic I'll try him midday tomorrow, but to text me if he needs me. Thanks, and love ya."

"Will do, um...and...take care, Cara." Odd. Sasha never fumbles his words.

Cara ends the call and Carter steps into her room. She puts her palm out to stop him from coming in any further. "What do you want Carter? I need to get into the shower and get dressed."

"Is Sasha your nanny? Is she hot?"

Cara pauses before she answers, not wanting to correct him. "Yes, nanny, and yes, hot...in an untraditional way."

Carter slowly heads back to his room, shaking his head and mumbling, "It must be really interesting at your house; that's all I can say."

CHAPTER

NINE

CARTER ARRIVES AT THE connecting door promptly at 6:30 AM. He knocks, even though the door is technically not closed, but Cara gives him credit for being considerate. He is wearing black slacks and a cream-colored silk collared shirt, tucked in with a black belt. Cara is wearing a grey silk shell and matching push-up bra over a black pencil skirt and the suede Olaf boots.

Several buttons are left undone to display just enough of her breasts and her lacy bra to call attention to her D cups and still maintain decorum. She has spent extra time on her hair, straightening it and parting it to the side so it sweeps over one eye.

Carter is trying hard not to look at her breasts and is failing miserably. She ignores his lecherous stare and begins her own assessment of him. She slowly moves her eyes down from Carter's face to take in the way his silk shirt clings against his biceps and pecs. She can see the outline of his nipples in the fabric. The shirt is not fitted so it's tucked loosely into his waistband. She trails her gaze down to his groin. His pants are also loose. She looks back up at Carter's face and finds him staring at her, nervously.

With one finger, she signals him closer to her. He hesitates a moment, then obeys. She continues to motion him forward until he's only a foot from her. She raises her arms to unbutton his shirt.

She gets one button undone and Carter grabs her wrist. "Agent Bennett...umm...I'm not comfortable with this."

Cara pulls her wrist from his hand and replies in a mocking tone, "Ummm...Agent Carter...what is it you think 'this' is?"

Carter stutters, "I-I think you have enough men in your life already, ma'am."

Cara drops her arms to her sides and with a grave look asks, "Agent Carter, is this your first covert op?"

He quickly and vehemently responds, "No."

"Are you sure of that?"

"Yes!"

"OK, I'm going to dumb this down for you. We do not have an appointment to see Olaf this morning. You know that, right?" He nods. "All we know is Olaf will be in his office at 7:00 AM and we need to just walk in like we belong there. Do you understand the consequence of that, my young Padawan?"

"Is this a test?" Carter chokes out.

"Not sure what you kids call this nowadays...scam, cheat, sweet talk? But we're going to con our way into his office this morning." Carter nods like he's following. Earlier, she told him he wouldn't be a part of her plan, but now that Cara sees him in silk, she has a better idea. "Now let me fix you up – and NO, this isn't a play for your body, so calm yourself."

She undoes three more buttons and rolls up his sleeves until the material tightens around his biceps. Then she looks down at his crotch. "Where's your dick?"

"What!?" Carter sputters.

"Your dick, your cock, where are you hiding it?" she inquires, calmly.

"Oh my God, I have it positioned appropriately!"

"Well, un-position it and give me a bulge, please."

With great reluctance, Carter reaches into his pants and yanks his dick front and center. He pulls his hand out of his pants. "Like that?"

Cara studies the bulge with a critical eye. "Take your pants off and give them to me."

"What?! No!" his indignation ramping up.

"Oh, for God's sake, just do it. We're running out of time here!" Carter quickly unbuckles his belt, unzips his pants and pulls them off. He throws them to Cara, who catches them with one hand and heads towards her luggage. She pulls out a small stapler type device and uses it to take in the butt seam of his pants.

Carter's face finally registers clarity and he sighs, "You're making my pants tighter, so my bulge will show more. This is part of my disguise. Why didn't you just say so to begin with?"

"I don't know? I guess I never met a man who..." She doesn't finish her thought as she hands him back his pants.

Once he has the pants back on, she stands in front of him, palms out near his crotch, trying to magically place his dick into the right position without touching it. Giving up, she finally requests, "Move him two inches to the left, please."

Carter rummages around in his briefs again until Cara nods her satisfaction with the cock placement. Then she tugs all the loose material of his shirt to the back, reaches into his pants and staples the shirt to his waistband. She steps away, looks up and smiles. "Now, we're ready to go."

"No, we are not. Where am I supposed to conceal a weapon in this outfit?" Carter fumes.

"You won't need one."

Hands on hips, feet firmly planted, he responds, "I'm not going anywhere without a weapon."

"My handbag, then. Put them in my handbag, Carter."

"Doesn't that break Director Reed's number one cardinal rule?" he asks, believing he's found a loophole.

"No, because YOU will carry my handbag."

"Argh!!"

Cara hands him her purse and motions for him to hurry up. He reluctantly takes her bag back to his room and places both weapons inside of it. Cara grabs the Olaf coat and heads for the elevator, Carter just a few steps behind.

Outside the hotel, the same town car and driver are waiting for them by the curb. Before climbing in, Cara puts her hand up to stop Carter. "You're going to have some difficulty sitting with the staples I used on your pants," she informs him. "Bending at the waist may cause injury."

"You're not serious!" Carter growls through gritted teeth.

"Oh, but I am," Cara responds, straight-faced. "You wouldn't want to, you know, pop one of your nuts," she adds, climbing in first.

She watches as Carter struggles to get into the car without bending. She's trying not to give in to the giggle that's bubbling up. Finally inside, he sets his ass on the edge of the back seat, legs stretched out in front of him. The bulge in his pants is front and center now, on full display. She reaches into her coat pocket removes her phone and lines up for a photo, trying to get his whole body in the picture. Carter lunges to grab the phone, but Cara has the leverage, because her ass is firmly planted on her seat. She finally giggles.

"You did all of this on purpose!" Carter spits out.

"No, no, I didn't, I swear, but I couldn't resist getting the money shot."

Carter clenches his teeth and snarls, "I am going to kill you!"

She only laughs at him, reminding him the Director did warn him about her. "Did you underestimate me because I'm a middle-aged woman? Tell me, my young Padawan, because we are only getting started."

Carter chooses not to speak. He faces forward breathing slowly to calm himself. When he's finally under control, he turns to her and asks politely, "Are you going to tell me what the plan is now?"

"I don't have a plan," she shrugs.

All control gone again, Carter spits out, "What?!" as he loses his balance and topples onto her.

"You say 'what' a lot," she states, pushing him back onto his seat. Then, deciding she has tortured him long enough; Cara takes pity and attempts to explain.

In a covert con such as this one, there is no real gameplan. They can make assumptions about what they might encounter, but they must be ready to improvise. And in any good improv, tools are critical. Cara points to her breasts, and explains how showing them and wearing the Olaf coat will help her blend in. Carter is masquerading as a male model, but his look can alter, quickly. He can become a businessman or bodyguard, should the gameplan need to change.

"So, see? We have a plan. It's just fluid. You don't need to worry, just let me lead and react appropriately. Try to go with the flow and things will work out fine."

Starting to look a little less angry, Carter asks her, "Have you ever done this before?"

"For over 25 years, darling, 25 years." Cara drones.

CHAPTER

TEN

T HEY ARRIVE AT THEIR DESTINATION at 6:53 AM. Cara notes the time and knows she has seven minutes to get upstairs. She does a quick assessment of the street, building, and block, and then marches into the building. There are guards positioned behind a circular reception desk, mid lobby, and there's a clear path to the elevators. The high security must be on the Olaf floors.

She grabs Carter by the arm and says loudly, as they waltz past the reception area, Beeil dich! Wir müssen in drei Minuten beim Meeting sein." She sees one of the guards glances up at them, but he doesn't intercede. The elevator arrives and she pushes the button for the 17th floor, her best intel for the location of Olaf's office. When the elevator door closes, Cara glances at Carter. He's still as a statue. "Carter, breathe."

"What did you say in German?"

"I said we needed to hurry to my office for the meeting. They need to think we belong in the building. Show confidence and no one questions you. That part was easy. It may get trickier up here. Remember, follow my lead."

The doors open and they are immediately confronted with another receptionist and two guards wearing hip holsters, their weapons tucked safely inside. In her peripheral, Cara can see two secure doors leading from the lobby, one on the right and one on the left. She does some quick mental calculations of the building layout she studied on Google Earth and she decides. She pulls Carter from the elevator and drags him towards the door on the left. The guards watch, but don't make a move to stop them. She attempts to pull the door open, but it doesn't budge. Sighing in frustration, she tries again.

At this point, one of the guards walks over and says, "Haben Sie eine Sicherheitskarte?"

Cara answers quickly, in a rough New York City accent, "What? Do you speak English? My German is horrendous. I don't have my Karte on me. Open this door, this instant! Don't you know who I am? I need to show Olaf this boy for the Vanity Fair shoot. He must approve him. We have a 9:30 flight to New York we must be on. You know Olaf personally approves substitutions! Schnell, Schnell!"

Peeking at the clock above the receptionist, she screeches, "OH MY GAWD! It's 6:58! We have two minutes to get to Olaf! Machen Sie die Tür auf!"

The guard sends a questioning glance to his partner who simply shrugs back, as does the receptionist. With his own shrug, he swipes his fob over the reader and the lock releases with a click. Cara pulls the guard into a hug, pressing her breasts against his chest before shoving Carter through the door. "Danke," she adds before sliding through herself, as it closes.

Carter is shaking his head. "Fucking unbelievable. You got more of that?"

Cara places her hand in his and quickens their pace through the offices. Her assumption based on the architecture of the building; is that Olaf's office is situated at the very end of this section. It would afford him the largest number of windows, and the best views of the city. She can only hope she's correct.

They near the corner of the building, and she's sure they've found their objective. Cara leans in to whisper some direction to Carter and they approach the Admin. "We're here for Olaf to approve this model for substitution. I'm sorry we're late; I hope he's still available."

The administrative assistant, a man in his early forties with a full head of dark hair and a wiry thin body, gives Carter the once over. He doesn't even glance in Cara's direction. He asks Carter, "What's this about, sugar?"

Carter folds his arms across his chest, causing all kinds of muscles to ripple and stretch. He looks directly into the man's eyes and sighs, "I'm supposed to be approved by Olaf for the shoot in New York. Does he want to see me with my clothes on or off?"

The admin's mouth forms a perfect 'O'. Carter slips his hands into his pockets to draw attention to his nicely cached junk and purrs, "I need to catch the 9:30 this morning to New York if he approves. We just need two minutes, pretty pleeeeeaaaase?"

The admin immediately gets up, grabs Carter by the hand and leads him through Olaf's door where he announces, "Olaf, I need a quick substitution approval," while discreetly slipping his business card in Carter's pants pocket.

Carter is now standing in the center of an enormous space, at least 30 feet deep and 40 wide with large windows on three walls and a sweeping view. The floors are black lacquered wood and the walls are white. At one end sits a glass desk in front of a series of glass built-ins. The furniture, a sofa and four plush chairs, is upholstered in buttery black leather. The only splash of color is the reds and purples of the crazy geometric rug centered in the room. Seated at the desk, is a handsome man with a shiny bald head and a full salt and pepper beard trimmed short but with enough coverage to conceal his jawline. His eyes are a piercing teal color.

Olaf lets a smile form on his lips as he addresses Carter. "What's your name, beautiful?"

But before Carter can answer, Cara walks into the office and states, "His name is Carter, Agent William Carter." She has the Glock in her hands, and it's aimed directly at Olaf.

Carter immediately places the admin in a headlock, securing him. Olaf just stares at Cara. He doesn't react to the fact there's a gun trained on him. He slowly stands and continues to gaze at her. Olaf isn't a small man. He must be at least six-foot covered in 220 pounds of what looks like pure muscle.

Olaf finally speaks, and it comes out a whisper. "Chase?" Cara lowers the gun as she nods in confirmation.

Olaf, still whispering, asks, "What are you doing here?"

Cara has the Glock pointed down to the ground now. She walks towards Carter, keeping her eyes trained on Olaf, and she responds in a whisper back, "I was hoping you could tell me." She hands her gun to Carter requesting he take his new friend outside and make sure she and Olaf get some privacy.

Carter leans into Cara while they're both still watching Olaf. "I don't think that's a good idea."

"I didn't ask you."

Carter looks at the gun in his hand, obviously shocked to see it out of her handbag.

"Leave us, Carter...please," she pleads. Carter releases the admin from his hold but guides him by the shoulders out the door and closes it behind them.

"I think Tomas was enjoying the choke hold Agent Carter had on him," Olaf muses.

Cara gives Olaf a big smile, raising her hands and taking off the coat, slowly, so he can see she is unarmed.

"Do you think that I believe you would hurt me?" he questions.

She stares at him open-faced, vulnerable. "I would never hurt you, but I'm possibly thinking you want to hurt me."

"Hurt you? Darling, I spent two years paying people to find you! I thought you were dead and my heart broke" As he speaks, he cautiously approaches her.

Cara is frozen to her spot. "Find me? When? Why?"

"Why? Because look around you, Chase. All of this?" he continues, his arms sweeping the room, "This is all because of you."

"I don't understand."

Olaf take her face in his hands for a moment, then quickly scoops her up around the waist and spins in a circle whooping with delight. He stops suddenly and leads a laughing Cara to the sofa, motioning for her to sit down. He takes a seat next to her. "Do you remember Paris?"

Nodding, Cara affirms, "Of course I remember Paris. First, we almost killed each other, and then we almost got our asses shot off, together."

"Yes, fun times. Do you remember your orders?"

"Sure. Locate the target, you, determine your loyalties, and take you out, if necessary."

"No, not that part. I mean the additional order Reed gave you for the first time ever." Olaf is getting more animated now.

Cara's mission was to seduce Olaf, even if it meant bedding him. She had never actually fucked anyone during the course of her work. Seduced and teased, yes, but Reed had never asked one of his agents to sleep with a target. The request was a last-minute mission change, and it hurt, but knowing Olaf's reputation as a Lothario, Reed believed it might be the only way Cara could get close enough to determine his allegiances. With a bemused smile, Cara admits, "I forgot I told you about that."

Olaf laughs, "You approached me at the Hermes after-party."

CHASE CAME ONTO TO HIM WEARING A DARK BLUE YSL DRESS AND CARRYING a Hermes evening bag. She threw herself at him, openly flirting. Olaf surmised she was the American agent they called, Reflex. He knew she was sent find out where his loyalties lay. He was enjoying her obvious attempts to seduce him and decided he would let the evening play out. When Chase asked him back to her hotel room, Olaf went willingly, figuring it was as good a place as any to kill her. Thus far, he had purposefully resisted all her advances and was amused by her evident frustration.

Olaf was on the bed, Chase on top of him wearing only her undergarments, when she reached into her handbag and produced her Glock. She pointed it right at her own head and implored, "Just admit you're gay, and confess you want to be free to live your truth, and I won't kill myself."

He stared at her for the longest time before pulling the gun away from her head and placing it on the nightstand. Then, he started to cry. No other woman had ever suspected his true sexual preference. He was so taken aback; he ended up confessing everything to her. How he didn't want to live that lie anymore. How he wanted more than anything to leave this life behind him and have the freedom to pursue his real passions.

"It was as simple as that," he says softly, reminiscing about that long ago encounter. "Just one statement from you and my world jerked, tumbled and righted itself."

Chase places her hand on his cheek. "I felt heartbroken for you. I never meant to upset you. I'm so sorry for that."

"I was so empty...Do you remember what we did after that?"

"If I recall, we got very drunk and talked for hours about clothes, and designers, and your love of that world," They also spoke about the brutality of their jobs, and how they both wanted out, but how difficult it is to walk away, particularly for Olaf because the SVR would want to ensure his silence.

"You suggested I let my superiors know I'm gay. Do you remember that?"

"Um, I was pretty drunk..."

Chase believed it could be his insurance card. They would be embarrassed if it got out, and he would be embarrassed if it got out. 'Tit for Tat', she had said. It was too simple, but it did get Olaf thinking she might be on to something. Maybe, he did have some leverage.

"Is that what you ended up doing?" Chase asks amazed her drunken advice had any merit at all.

"A more complicated version of it, and I got some inside assistance, but, yes, it is."

"I don't want the details," she says, giving him a look of understanding. Some SVR agents were able to get out without a bullseye on their backs, but it usually involved money, bribes, blackmail, and more money. "As far as I'm concerned, it's none of my business. Every agent deserves a life after what we have all done for our countries. No judgments from me on that topic."

Wondering, Olaf must ask, "Did you get your life, Chase? Did you get to fall madly in love, have babies, and live happily ever after?"

Chase sucks in a breath when he says this. "Is that what I told you I wanted that night?"

"Yes, you were, how do you say it in English...emphatic." Olaf can see she appears distressed. "Have I upset you?"

"No, it gives me chills to think I don't remember telling you and yet, that's exactly what I got." She looks into his eyes and continues, "I did get my happily ever after and that's why I'm here; on a mission to rule out threats against my blissful existence."

"Darling, I don't think you understand. I owe you my life." If it wasn't for Chase that night in Paris, he's sure he would not have survived long enough to come to terms with all of it. He was a hunted man. He may have figured it all out eventually, but he saw the timing of her intervention as a sign because he knew there was no 'eventually' for him without it. Olaf turns to her on the couch and takes both of her hands in his. "Tell me why you've come to see me."

Chase spills everything to him. She summarizes her life since leaving the Agency. Shows him pictures of her family and talks about her company. She tells him about the song at Starbucks and Target, the email, and ultimately the anonymous cellphone call from somewhere within Berlin.

While she's speaking, he calls for Tomas to bring Carter back in with coffee and breakfast. After they eat, Olaf studies Carter and the obvious hack job done to his outfit. He rolls his eyes at Chase and tells Carter to go with Tomas. "Have him get you dressed appropriately, please."

Carter looks imploringly at Chase to intercede on his behalf. She waves him out of the office. He leaves with Tomas, but not before turning back to her with a steely glare.

Olaf waits until Carter is gone and asks, "So, you came to me because of the lead on the call?"

"Reed and I never actually thought it was you. But Berlin being your home base, there was a chance you might have knowledge of nefarious activity in the area," she answers honestly. Then in a more contemplative tone, "We've all tried to leave our past in the past, but it has a way of staying only a few steps behind."

"Why didn't you just phone me?" he questions. Sneaking into his building and barging into his office seems a bit extreme.

"You know we left each other in Paris years ago under…how can I put this…duress? I had to see you to be sure there weren't any hard feelings." Chase makes a concerned face.

Clarity dawns on him. "Oh, you mean because you shot me?"

"Um, yeah."

Again, he laughs. "Chase, my darling, I understand why you did it, and it was brilliant."

"Please, call me Cara. We're going to be friends, yes?" she asks, looking more relieved.

After the gun incident and Olaf's unburdening in his Paris hotel room, the two former adversaries headed to a small, local bar where they drank, talked, and laughed, for hours. They emerged from the bar, categorically plastered, and stumbled into an alley where they came face to face with the Ukrainian Agent, Lucien Romanov.

Olaf knew Romanov wasn't there to chat. His gun was pointed directly at Olaf's heart. He was there to kill him. Olaf's own gun was in a holster at his back. There was no way he was going to get to it in time to save himself. But, before he could react, he felt another weapon, this one pressed to his temple. It was Cara's Glock. In his drunken stupor, he could barely stand much less figure out how Cara was able to pull out her weapon. He could hear her screaming at Romanov, while he was still processing his options.

"He's mine! I found him, first! Back off!" she screeched. Romanov wasn't listening. He drew closer, and the next thing Olaf knew, Cara had lowered her weapon and shot him in the foot. Nice clean shot. Olaf dropped to the ground in agony. This unexpected development distracted Romanov and Cara's next shot knocked the gun out of the Ukrainian's hand.

"I heard Romanov screaming, and I did what any trained agent would've done...I got up and ran away as quickly as my shot foot would take me!" Olaf laughs uncontrollably as he finishes the story. When he can finally speak, he asks what he's always wanted to know. "What happened to you after that?"

Trying to speak through her own laughter, Cara cries, "I was so drunk! I was aiming for Romanov's arm but made a direct hit to his gun instead! YOU ran away and I was left watching poor Lucien writhing on the ground holding his wrist. When my eyes finally focused, I realized I shot a good portion of his middle finger off. I felt terrible. I started frantically looking all over the ground for his finger – and I found it!"

Olaf exhales a convulsive laugh, "Why on earth did you want his finger?"

"I just reacted! I grabbed what was left of his weapon, ran back into the bar to get ice for his finger, then hailed a cab. I sent him to the hospital with a bar napkin wrapped tightly around the stump of his middle finger, and a bag of ice with said middle finger in it. I apologized, profusely."

Such compassion for a foe? Olaf doesn't understand why she would bother. Before he can inquire, she rattles on, "I helped him to the cab and before it could whisk him away, I assured him you weren't a threat to us or the Russians. He was to leave you alone or I would tell everyone a girl shot his finger off."

Olaf is staring blankly at her, so Cara quips, "What can I say? I was drunk."

He must ask, "You didn't kill him?"

"No! Why would I do that? He wasn't a threat to me anymore. And I felt badly I might have destroyed his career. I mean how was he going to handle a weapon with a missing finger?"

Olaf's only encounter with the Agent known as the Reflex had led to his freedom to build a successful business and a life worth living. So, he knew she could be fair and just, but still. "Do you know what happened to Romanov?"

"About six months after the incident, I received a letter at Langley from Lucien. It would've been cryptic to anyone intercepting it, but I understood its meaning. He was thanking me for my mercy that night. He left his job, changed his name and found more rewarding employment."

She pulls out her phone to show him a picture of the man who almost ended his life. He's standing with his arms around a woman and two beautiful little girls. She explains, "Lucien and I have kept in touch. He has a wife, family and a lucrative career."

Olaf is holding the phone with shaking hands. That night led to him and Lucien both getting out...and all because they crossed paths with Agent Bennett. He looks up from the phone and whispers, "You're our angel."

She scoffs, "More like devil with the blue dress on."

"Wait! That's a great idea for a collection! 'Devil with the Blue Dress'. Again, you inspire me!" His mind is already picturing wicked manipulations of blue silks, chiffons and lace.

Snapping her fingers in his face, she brings him back to the present. "Earth to Olaf, back to my concerns, please. Do you know who may be hunting me after all these years, or have you ever heard rumblings of revenge?"

"I haven't heard anything, ever. I told you, after I made a deal with my superiors, I got out and started the Olaf line." After some initial success, Olaf had the money to pay a couple former colleagues to look for Agent Bennett. He felt he owed her in some way.

She was no longer employed with the Agency, and penetrating the US government files produced nothing at all. His people worked on some leads, but they all led to dead ends. However Cara got out, she did it perfectly. Chase Bennett was dead; and there were no clues to a new alias. Olaf gave up looking. He hasn't heard anything about the Reflex in the years since.

She digests this information before asking, "And these folks you paid to find me? Could they have betrayed you? Found me and didn't share with you?"

"Absolutely not." Those men are part of his security team now and have been with him since the late 90's. He trusts them completely.

Olaf pauses to study her quietly while he connects the dots. "About three months ago, my laptop was breached and someone got into my personal contacts list. At the time, we presumed it was benign, but what's interesting is...we traced the hacker's IP to here in Berlin."

Her eyes light up. "It might be related!"

"It's possible they were looking to see if I had contact info for you." The IP address led them to the Prenzlauer Berg section of the city. It's a very bohemian area, so they didn't bother to do much investigating. "We figured it was a fledging young designer, or someone looking to get info on a celebrity I outfitted."

Olaf moves to his desk to search for the address as Carter makes his way back into the office. He is dressed to kill in a beautifully cut dark gray suit, black shirt and no tie. He opens his jacket to reveal a black snakeskin shoulder holster with his weapon tucked inside. He stops in front of Olaf and pointing at the holster, exclaiming, "I LOVE this. It's my favorite design of yours. Thank you."

Olaf snickers, "You must have made quite an impression on

Tomas for him to give you one of my exclusive designs. Those are reserved for me and my security team."

Carter smiles and waggles his eyebrows. "Maybe I did."

Olaf grins back while he slowly checks out Carter's body fitted inside one of his designer suits, "Well, Agent Carter, if you ever want to do any modeling on the side, give me a call."

Cara huffs, "Please don't compliment him. His head is big enough as it is."

Addressing Cara but still staring at Carter, Olaf comments, "From here, seems to me Agent Carter's head is just right." Of course, his gaze is not directed at the head sitting on Carter's shoulders. Carter flushes crimson and looks down at his pants. When he does, Olaf slips the paper with the address into Cara's skirt pocket.

"On that note," Cara giggles, "we should be going." She leans in to give Olaf a big hug and whispers a 'thank-you' in his ear.

But before she can pull away, he stops her. "Wait, I need to send you with some of my designs! You can't leave here empty-handed, I forbid it. Tomas, when's my next meeting?"

"9:30. I cancelled your earlier ones," Tomas answers absently, admiring eyes still trained on Carter.

Olaf looks at his watch and announces with glee, "That gives me 15 minutes to raid the closets for her."

He grabs Cara's hand, pulling her out of his office while she protests, "Olaf, look at me, none of your samples are going to fit my frumpy, middle-aged ass."

"Stop being so modest! You're still a total knock-out...for a girl that is." And with that, Carter picks up Cara's handbag and the bag of additional clothes that he received and follows them out.

Olaf returns to his office with only seconds to spare before his 9:30 conference call with his London team. He's feeling elated Chase, or Cara, was back in his life and he had managed to find her a few great articles of clothing and some wonderful bags and shoes.

He can't contain his happiness. He shuts the door of his office and quickly strides to his desk. With his mind still distracted by the unexpected events of the morning, he doesn't notice the tall man hidden in the shadows at the far corner of his office. The intruder slowly emerges pointing a Beretta M9 with a laser sight aimed at Olaf's forehead.

Olaf freezes when he recognizes the man. He speaks cautiously, while slowly raising his hands. "I guess it's finally my turn to meet my maker. Welcome to my office, Dark Angel of Death."

CHAPTER

ELEVEN

THE TOWN CAR PICKS UP Carter and Cara for the ride back to the hotel with their care packages from Olaf. She starts to calculate the math in her head. It's 9:30 in Berlin. The best Reed's going to do for time is a noon arrival. She needs to decide if she's going to bring Carter in on the new intel about the address in the Prenzlauer Berg, wait for Reed to go and check it out, or get rid of Carter, forget Reed, and go by herself.

She'll lose two and half hours if she waits for Reed. She could be there and back, having investigated the lead, in much less time. And she has no aversion to Carter coming with her, except the prickling hairs on her neck are screaming, 'GO. NOW'!

"Carter, I must tell you, I was pretty impressed with your quick pick up when we first got to Tomas' desk this morning. Score one for Team Carter."

"Thanks," he deadpans. "Maybe you won't treat me like a useless tool from now on."

"Let's not get ahead of ourselves there, big guy. It's a long game, Carter. What's the plan now?"

The town car is pulling in front of the hotel. Carter grabs all their bags and opens the door to head out. "We wait for Director Reed. And get some rest before he arrives." Not the answer she was looking for.

The lobby is empty as they wait for the elevator together. The doors open, and Cara, seeing the elevator is also empty, steps inside and turns to face Carter. His head is down, and he has the Olaf bags in both hands. She gives him a swift kick to the groin, and as his body involuntarily bends forward, his head connects with her upraised knee. He is down for the count. Cara quickly ensures the Olaf bags are fine, she has her priorities, then pushes all the buttons on the elevator before running back out into the lobby. She hails the first cab outside and heads to the Prenzlauer Berg.

Agent William Carter comes to some moments later on the floor of the elevator with the Olaf bags neatly stacked next to him. There are several sets of eyes staring at him. He slowly pushes himself to a sitting position. A short, round older woman asks, "Brauchen Sie einen Arzt?"

Carter's very bad German skills assume she's asking if he needs a doctor. He shakes his head and leans towards the elevator panel to hit the five button. No one wants to get on the elevator with him. By the time the doors open on the fifth floor, Carter's head is pounding and he's feeling nauseous.

Worst of all, his nuts are on fire. What the hell is he supposed to do now? How could a woman in her 40's take him down? Reed is going to fire his ass. Oh no, Reed. He has to call Reed and tell him. He drags himself and their Olaf bags out of the elevator and makes it to his room. He takes some deep cleansing breaths and dials Director Reed.

"Reed."

"Director, sir."

"You lost her, didn't you, Carter?"

"Yes, sir. Sorry, sir."

"She kick you in the nuts?"

"Yes, sir."

"My bad, I should've warned you. It's her go to maneuver."

"Sir, I understand if you want to re-assign me off the case or out of the department. Hell, sir, I would understand if you terminated me right now."

Reed lets out a soft chuckle, "Carter, don't be so hard on yourself, she is very crafty. She has taken down threats bigger and badder than you. Besides, I assumed she would lose you. Those Olaf boots I gave her, is she still wearing them?"

"Yes, sir."

"There was no way I was going to let Agent Bennett wander around Berlin unchaperoned. The trick is to always be a step ahead of her. I had a tracer and audio device installed in one heel so I could track her movements. Give me a second for the satellite to uplink from my plane and I'll send you the GPS coordinates of her location. Are you in any condition to go after her?"

"Yes, sir," Carter lies.

"I'm arriving in less than an hour. I will proceed directly to whatever coordinates I get from the trace unless I hear from you otherwise. And Carter?"

"Yes, sir?"

"No more slip ups."

CARA ARRIVES AT THE ADDRESS AND IS SURPRISED TO FIND HERSELF IN A FUN, diverse neighborhood full of coffee shops, restaurants, funky boutiques and music stores. There are lots of young people loitering around. Probably unemployed. A door located between a coffee shop and a record store, with actual vinyl albums in it, looks to be the entrance she wants.

Earlier, in Olaf's sample room, she managed to swipe the Glock back out of her purse without Carter seeing. He really is sort of slow on the uptake. But the gun, her phone and some Euros are the only thing Cara has in her coat pockets.

She tries the door and it's open. According to the address Olaf has written, they were able to pinpoint to an actual apartment number on the second floor. She wonders if they can really be that accurate. It seems unlikely in a multi-tenanted space, but how would she know? Her grasp of the latest technologies is sufficiently lacking.

She makes her way to the second floor, looking for Apartment 24. She places her hand in her coat, and around the handle of her weapon. Walking slowly, her back against the wall, she stealthily moves down the hall checking apartment numbers as she goes.

When she gets to 23, she looks across the hall to a door marked 24. She pulls out her Glock and faces the door to Apartment 24, when suddenly, she hears the door to Apartment 23 open behind her.

Before she can spin around, her world tilts. She feels her body lift off the ground, and her brain scrambles. She loses control of her bladder, and everything goes dark.

When Cara starts to see light beyond her closed eyelids, the overwhelming stench of urine is the first thing to invade her senses. Soon after, comes the memory of that last moment before she passed out. She'd been Taser'd! And, holy shit, she'd peed herself.

Quickly setting aside the humiliation of that, she again, wishes she knew more about the latest technologies. She has no clue how many volts of electricity she just received, or if it's normal to lose your bladder. And will she have any permanent damage? She's feeling extremely inadequate. She can describe the entrance and exit wounds of every possible cartridge or bullet and yet, she knows nothing about a Taser.

Even her arms feel dead. But they aren't dead; they're tied behind her back. Cara tries to remain calm as she attempts to work out the situation. She's on the ground in a pool of her own urine with her arms bound. She listens for sounds. She can hear breathing and movement to her left.

Very cautiously, she lifts her eyelids. Her vision is blurry, but she is certain she's looking down the barrel of a semi-automatic pistol. Not good. She might be able to reach her puddle of urine with her bound hands. Maybe she should leave a message? She discreetly puts one fingertip in the puddle and begins to drag it.

It only incites the Einstein look-alike who's holding the gun. Feeling chastised but suddenly more focused, she glares at him.

Einstein speaks, "Welcome, Agent Chase Bennett. Or should I call you Cara Bianco, or is it Cara Andre now? My, you do have many names. Maybe I will just call you Reflex."

The man is quite unattractive. He's mid-fifties, short, big bellied with a large nose. Wisps of hair protrude out from the sides of his head. His accent sounds Russian, could be Slavic. He knows Cara, but she's never seen him before. Time to work out more details before mounting a full panic attack. "You know my name or names, what's yours?"

"My name is Vlad, Vlad Chekov," the short man offers freely.

"Chekov, like the Star Trek character?"

"Yes, yes, you may have heard of me?" he asks looking for validation.

"No, should I?" Cara is attempting to get to a sitting position with her back to the wall she is lying next to.

"Well, maybe you know me as Vlad the Impaler?"

Vlad the Impaler? Seriously? She has never heard of this guy. What the fuck? "That's not ringing a bell either. Sorry, have we met?"

"No, we have never met, but I thought you may have heard of my reputation." His shoulders go back and his spine stiffens with pride.

"Your reputation? Are you former KGB? I know a lot of those guys. Some of them, I even consider friends."

He deflates. "I was KGB trained, but I haven't been part of that organization for a long time."

Always keep them talking. Time for chatty Cara. "So, forgive me for being forward but, if we've never met, and I don't know who you are, why am I tied up at gunpoint like I'm your hostage?"

"Oh, yes, this...you're my shining star," He blurts with great pride, again.

"Care to elaborate, please?"

He shrugs, "I'm a contract killer, now. Three months ago, I was asked to find the Reflex and kill her. Largest offer I ever had for a disposal. I've heard of you, of course, but I also heard you were untraceable. I started to think, maybe everyone was going about finding you the wrong way."

"How did you go about finding me, then?"

He taps his temple. "I have a friend who's a wiz with computers and conveniently owed me a favor. I wanted to see if it was possible to take a picture of the Reflex from the 90's, age-progress it, and then search the Internet for any matches. I knew we were going to end up with lots of people, but I wasn't concerned.

So far, he's making sense. She asks, "So, how did you weed out all the mismatched folks?"

"I narrowed it down to about 50 people, 38 in the US. I focused only on the ones in the US. I eliminated age differences, background discrepancies, or any obvious inconsistencies. That narrowed the list down to eight women."

"How did you get backgrounds and pictures?"

"Social media, of course. I used professional sites like Linked In, as well." He's looking at her like she's a dumb ass.

Which, apparently, she is, and Reed is going to kill her if Chekov doesn't. "I still don't understand how you found me," Cara inquires casually, trying to keep him talking.

"I didn't try for you, specifically. I used the music, the emails and the phone calls to get to all eight of you. I figured the only one that would react would be the real Reflex, right?"

"That was really smart!" She decides she should compliment him. "But, how did you find me here in Berlin?"

He straightens to his full height, looking very smug. And it hits her. Olaf. Vlad must have known the story of Olaf and Lucien.

With a tremulous voice, she answers her own question. "Paris. You know what happened in Paris with Olaf."

Vlad confirms, a wicked grin stretching his thin lips. "I overheard an agent talking about it in a bar in Budapest one night. Confirmed it was true you shot Olaf in the foot, then shot Lucien's finger off."

It's all coming together in her mind. "You knew I would trace the call to here in Berlin." She wants to be devastated, but the only emotion she feels now is genuine praise for his plan. "It was you who hacked into Olaf's personal contacts three months ago from this address, but across the hall, knowing when I found out the blocked call came from Berlin, Olaf would be the first person I sought. Right?"

Her back against the wall, Cara is slowly rising from her seat on the floor to a standing position. "So, essentially, eight women get the same messages; only one reacts and makes her way to Berlin. You wait patiently and abracadabra, she, well, me, delivers herself right to your doorstep! It's genius!" she exclaims, having seriously underestimated this short, overweight man.

Using her peripheral vision, Cara takes in the apartment. She's looking for anything she can use as a weapon. The apartment is completely empty save for the contents of her coat pockets lying on the counter in the grimy kitchenette area. Her Glock, her phone and the Euros are there. Otherwise, the place is bare. Could he have been sitting on the floor waiting for her for days? Maybe he has a camera or some kind of surveillance on Olaf's building.

Cara stops her 'good for you's' to ask, "Wait, how did you know when I would get to Berlin? You couldn't have been waiting in this apartment for days?"

"Easy. I paid someone to watch Olaf's building when he was in town or in the office. They had pictures of the eight women and called me early this morning to say you had arrived with a male escort. So, I came to the apartment to wait."

"But what if I brought an army of people with me to this apartment?" She needs to buy more time.

"You underestimate me! My eyes at Olaf's followed you back to your hotel. I was prepared to stake out there, but I didn't have to. You were back out, by yourself, within minutes of arriving. I knew you must be headed here."

Reed is really going to kill her if she doesn't die now. "Let's go back to my original question. Why are you trying to kill me?"

Cara notices her breathing is quick and shallow. Her heart rate is elevated. She's beginning to perspire. She's losing it. Focus! She can't. Pictures of her family are flashing in front of her eyes. Max, first, with all his beautiful out of control blonde hair and his constant smirking smile. The one that says he's up to no good. The cocky walk and bold strides of her beautiful baby boy. And Mia, her Mia, all five foot ten of her always mouthing some complaint...when she speaks, that is. The raving beauty and confidence she doesn't even know she possesses. They act like they don't need their Mommy, but that's no consolation right now. Deep down, Cara knows they need her.

"I told you I will be paid very handsomely for your body. I'm getting on in years. I need this to retire. You understand," Vlad adds, almost apologetically. He's closer to Cara now. Gun still trained at her head.

He's getting ready to shoot. She can go for the head butt, but she needs him closer. He's angled away from her, prohibiting the old faithful kick in the nuts. It's like this guy knows all her tricks. Her arms are bound, so she has little leverage to work with. "But who hired you?"

Vlad shrugs his shoulders. "I don't know. I did learn they were very impressed with how I found you, though. But, as long as the second half of my cash is paid when I deliver your body, I'm good. It doesn't matter to me who they are."

Her anxiety peaks, preventing all subtlety and she shouts, "It matters to me! I want you to tell me who hired you!"

"I told you. I don't know. You are a dead woman in less than thirty seconds. Don't worry yourself about it." He takes his shooting stance.

THE GPS COORDINATES FROM REED TOOK CARTER TO THE DOORWAY between a coffee shop and music store. Based on the three-dimensional grid display on his phone, Bennett should be in one of the right-hand side apartments on the second floor. Carter enters the building through the unlocked door. Once inside, he pulls his gun into a two-handed grip, holding it out in front of him. He stays to the shadow side of the stairwell and climbs as quietly as he can to the second floor.

He waits on the top step to listen for movement. He hears water running, but no voices. He proceeds slowly down the hall, passing the first two apartments, one on each side of the hallway. He releases one hand from his gun and searches in his pocket for his phone. He glances at the screen. His target is further down the corridor.

Again, he moves cautiously towards the next set of apartment doors. He stops and listens, no abnormal sounds, no voices. Another quick glance at his phone tells him to keep moving. He approaches the doorways for Apartments 23 and 24. All is quiet, but the image on his phone indicates she is in Apartment 23 on his right.

Before Carter lifts his eyes from the screen, his right wrist is jerked backwards by a hand from behind him, the fingers wrapped around the barrel of his handgun. To prevent his wrist from breaking, he releases his grip on the gun but throws his head back in an attempt to head-butt his assailant. It's a classic, surprise street-fight maneuver, except his head is met with nothing but air. Carter loses his balance and stumbles.

He regains his footing and finds himself locking eyes with a tall, muscular man who is now standing motionless holding both his gun and Carter's, one in each hand. No expression on his face. Just cold, dead eyes staring menacingly back at him. Carter lunges, except the tall man is quicker. He steps forward and kicks Carter in the nuts – again. Carter lurches forward, and the last thing he remembers is being dealt a left upper cut to his jaw. Lights out.

CARA IS TREMBLING. NO, MAKE THAT, SHAKING UNCONTROLLABLY. AND FOR only the second time in her life during a mission, she's crying. It's over. Her only clear thought is how unfair to meet death at this age rather than when she was young and rash and irresponsible. She would've faced death with more dignity back then because she felt invincible and the job was everything. Now, like this, convulsing, crying, and coated in her own urine, she will die an undignified death and leave behind a husband, two children and a beautiful life.

She turns her head away from the handgun. Cara is so hopeless; she can't look death in the eye. Then her despairing thoughts are suddenly interrupted. Kabul. 1998. It was the last field mission before she quit, the only other incident that left Cara in tears, and an emotional basket case. All her emotions from Kabul come flooding back into her. She prayed for death in Kabul, and her prayers were answered in an unexpected way.

Suddenly she finds the courage to pick up her head and look at Vlad with silent tears streaming down her face. She swore to Reed she would be careful. She has broken her insincere promise to her handler for the last time. Cara is crying so hard; her vision is blurring. She's seeing spots.

No, it's just one spot. She tries to focus. And there it is again. A mark on Vlad's forehead. A red mark. At just about the exact millisecond it takes for Cara to register what the spot is, Vlad makes the same connection. Both sets of eyes travel the length of the laser causing the red spot, in slow motion. When they finally find the source, Cara's jaw drops in astonishment.

Standing completely still, two hands wrapped around the handle of a Beretta M9, is the most frightening man with the coldest dark gray eyes ever seen...and looks just like her husband.

CHAPTER

TWELVE

NIC? NO, NOT HER NIC. SOMEONE who looks like Nic. This Nic is wearing leather pants, a matching fitted leather jacket with a hood and biker boots. This Nic has the cruelest, coldest eyes Cara has ever seen. And they're not blue. They're a dark gunmetal grey. This Nic is a thug, a badass. His hair is slicked back like a mobster's. Nic's doppelgänger? He hasn't blinked even once. His eyes haven't left Vlad's face, not even to glance in her direction.

Peeling her gaze away from Nic's evil twin, she focuses on her captor. Vlad's eyes are shifting at top speed between her and the Nic twin. There's a fine sheen of sweat on his face; the gun hand trained on her trembles.

Vlad hisses, "Nicolae? Nicolae Andrychenko?" Evil Nic twin continues to glare in stony silence. The Beretta's laser sight doesn't flinch. Vlad takes a second to better compose himself. "They said you were dead. Died at the hands of Golov." He slowly inclines his head and whispers reverently, "Agent Bennett, have you met the Dark Angel of Death?"

Cara is staring wild-eyed at Vlad. Uncontrolled tears are still spilling from her eyes. She is terrified.

"Agent Bennett, you are a very popular woman." Vlad tries to lighten the mood. "Seems you have incited the wrath of the Dark Angel, as well." Vlad raises his weapon and presses it against Cara's temple. He turns his head ever so slightly towards evil Nic. "Nicolae, do you remember, friend? It is me, Vlad Chekov."

For the first time, evil Nic speaks. His voice is low, and in a heavy Russian accent, he says, "I have no friends." Her Nic does not have an accent.

Vlad tries again, "Yes, we worked some missions together, remember?"

There's a moment of uncomfortable silence, then evil Nic declares, "She's mine."

"Does it really matter which one of us shoots her? Allow me the pleasure for old times' sake," Vlad asks, wanting to hold on to his prize.

Evil Nic couldn't be clearer when he growls his next statement. "She's MINE."

Vlad is growing petulant. "I found her first."

And just like that, all of Cara's training kicks in. She refocuses and directs her gaze on the Nic look-alike. When she feels she has his attention, she shifts her eyes to Vlad's leg, and then slowly back to evil Nic. She blinks three times through her tears. To her astonishment, evil Nic blinks three times back at her.

She starts the count in her head. One...Cara shifts her weight to her right leg. Two...she bends her right knee. Three...she throws her head forward, raises her left leg and lands a chop kick into the side of Vlad's knee.

She hears a gun go off and suddenly feels her body being propelled to the right. Her hands are bound so she can't control the fall. She hits the ground hard, landing on her right side. She's not sure she's breathing.

The next sensation is of a cold blade against her wrists, then being jerked up from the floor. Her hands are free, but she can't feel them. Evil Nic has his hands on her body, and his lips are moving but Cara can't make out what he's saying.

Stripping the Olaf coat from her, he tosses it to the side and runs his hands over her. Checking her body for damage? He places his hands on each side of her face, capturing it. "Cara, look at me, baby, I need you to look at me. You're going into shock. I need you to try to focus. I can't find any wounds. Are you hurt?" he asks, panic in his voice.

Cara squints up at him and slurs, "I-I don't think so."

"Good girl. Was Vlad alone? Was there someone else here, Cara?"

She shakes her head then looks past him to the left, to the spot she last saw Vlad. He lays crumpled on the ground. There's a small red dot in the middle of his forehead and the back of his head is completely gone. She follows the trail of blood, skull fragments and brain tissue leading back to where she was laying. Raising her arm, she touches her hair, then brings her hand in front of her face and looks at it. In a flat voice, she croaks, "I have brains in my hair."

"Yes, you do, baby. It was unavoidable. I'm sorry."

For the first time, Cara really looks at the person hovering over her. Her hand touches his chest. He places his hand over hers. She whispers, "Nic?"

"Cara mia."

"Who are...how did...," she stutters.

"No time to explain now. We need to get you out of here and cleaned up, then we'll talk. Please, Cara," Nic pleads, softly.

Cara scrutinizes his face, befuddled, but then he's leading her by the hand towards the door. She glances over at the kitchenette where her Glock, phone and Euros are still sitting on the counter. Nic reaches to grab all three and stuffs them in his jacket pocket.

They step out into the hallway where Carter is sitting with his back to the wall adjacent to the apartment door. He's conscious but not moving. He looks like hell.

CARTER breathes out a huge sigh. She's not dead and she looks unharmed. He heard the single gunshot but had no idea who would be walking out of that apartment. His attacker is clutching her to his side, but she's not resisting. Carter finds his voice. "Are you okay?"

Agent Bennett doesn't answer, but stares blankly at him before shifting a concerned gaze to the man who has her in his arms. She whispers, "Did you do that?" pointing at Carter.

"Yes." The mean man speaks, and he's unapologetic.

Looking back at Carter, she whispers, "Sorry."

Carter tries to move, but the large man makes a stop motion with his hand and warns, "It would not be prudent for you to try to stop me."

The man gets down on his knees and, keeping his eyes on Carter, unzips her boots and gently pulls them off. When she's standing barefoot, he tosses the boots at Carter. "Give your boss a message from me. Let him know I have her." Then, gesturing towards the interior of the apartment, he growls, "He has clean-up duty." The hostile man opens his jacket and pulls Agent Bennett into it, concealing most of her upper body and head. He turns her towards the stairwell, and they walk away with his arm around her waist.

Carter barely managed to catch the boots. He can't believe he couldn't save her. He attempts to get up, but nausea overtakes him, and he falls back down to his butt. He's unsure how much time goes by, before he hears footsteps on the stairs. Director Reed appears. He has a Glock in his hand, and several men following behind.

His eyes are wild with panic as they dart frantically around the space. He yells at Carter, "Where is she? Where is she!? I followed the tracker here when I didn't hear from you!"

Carter tries to articulate his answer to the Director. "Sir, she was here, in Apartment 23. She was being held at gunpoint by the man in there. I was on my way to her when, out of nowhere, I was attacked from behind, Sir."

Director Reed opens the door to the apartment and surveys the scene quickly. He turns to Carter and demands, "What did they do to her?"

"It was only one guy. Mean son of a bitch, Sir. He put me down, like I was nothing, then took my weapons and my phone after I passed out. I am so sorry, Sir. He went in there and he shot the man holding Agent Bennett. He came back out with her, threw her boots at me, and left with her about 15 minutes ago."

"Was she hurt or struggling?" It's apparent Director Reed, who is pacing now, is trying desperately to keep his alarm under control but is losing the battle.

"I think she was in shock, but she didn't appear hurt, Sir. She just let him lead her. He spoke to me. He said to tell my boss that he had her, and that you had clean-up duty." Carter points to the apartment.

The Director stops his pacing and slowly turns on Carter. "What did this guy look like?"

"Like I said, mean son of a bitch. Cold, dead eyes. Maybe around your age, but blonde, Sir."

Leaning in close, the Director asks, "A little taller than me, and a little bigger? Very good looking?"

Carter can't stifle a snort. "Handsome like the Devil himself."

Falling back against the wall, Director Reed exhales very loudly and let's all the built-up tension leave his body. He brings one trembling hand up to his face and stares at it. His legs give out and his body sags down the wall until he's squatting next to Carter. His head droops, and he replies quietly, "You did meet the Devil, Carter." He drops his hands and numbly continues, "Consider yourself initiated. You're only my second agent, in almost 30 years, to survive a close encounter with the Dark Angel of Death."

Alarmed even more, Carter asks, "Sir, who was the first?"

A slight frown crosses his features when he answers, "Agent Bennett, 17 years ago."

"The man is a monster. How did she survive, Sir?"

The Director mumbles dispassionately, looking Carter directly in the eyes, "She married him."

CHAPTER

THIRTEEN

N IC KEEPS MOST OF CARA'S head and upper body covered with his coat as he makes his way to the motorbike he left in an alley. She has no shoes on, and he lifts her onto the back of the bike. He doesn't have a helmet with him, but they don't have far to go. He mounts the bike in front of her but needs to reach back for her arms to make sure she wraps them around him. Her body quivers against him. The tears are gone, but she hasn't said a word. He tells her, "I'm taking you to my apartment. We can get cleaned up there. It's just a few blocks away."

It was late 1989 when Nicolae Andrychenko first heard of the Reflex. Talk among the agents was the Americans had a new operative who was beautiful, cunning, lethal, and she could creep up on you undetected. His superiors at the KGB shared her description with every agent, but there were no pictures. Nic didn't pay much attention. By the time she was on the scene, he was already considered one of their best. He was assigned the highest profile and most dangerous missions. He didn't expect to cross paths with an American woman anywhere he would be.

Nic continued to hear stories from other agents who had seen the

Reflex in action and lived to talk about it. They all spoke of her talent and beauty. Some of the agents truly admired her. They said she was a woman of honor, no cheap shots, and always open to negotiate. But Agent Chase Bennett was not in Nic's league. He had bigger bears to hunt.

In the early 90's, Nic's handler, Alexander Golov, managed to acquire a picture of the Reflex. It was taken from a distance, but it gave the office a general idea of what she looked like. Nic studied the photo for posterity purposes only. She was attractive, but not beautiful. He didn't share the sentiment of the others, nor was he interested in wasting any energy on her.

It wasn't until Kabul in late 1998 that would all change. By then, Russia had been out of Afghanistan for nine years. The Taliban had seized the Afghan capital and declared Afghanistan an Islamic emirate, recognized by Saudi Arabia and Pakistan. Osama bin Laden and his Al-Qaeda had issued their first fatwah, declaring war against the United States. The previously anti-Soviet Massoud was now allied with Russia in its decades long battle with the Taliban.

The former Soviet Union, provided old tanks, built bridges and printed money in solidarity with Massoud's efforts to sink the already crippled Afghan economy to break the Taliban's stranglehold on the country. Nic's mission was to arrange for assistance to the remaining Massoud forces.

There was some chatter the Reflex was in the region. Nic heard it but couldn't believe her handler would allow it. Women do not perform effectively in covert missions within that misogynistic culture. He assumed the intel was incorrect.

His meeting was with six contacts at a specified location in Kabul. He was on his way, expecting to arrive early, when he heard some commotion. Nic stopped and took protective cover in the shadows. Peering around the corner, he saw some men dragging a woman in full burka into an alley just ahead. He knew what their intentions were. These were his contacts, but they were animals, filled with hate and rage, depravity at its worst. He watched as the woman continued to struggle but to no avail. They groped her, unarmed her, and finally pulled her hijab off.

He recognized her immediately, except she wasn't just beautiful like his colleagues had described, and she wasn't just attractive as he had thought previously. She was breathtaking. He felt his heart tighten and his body stiffen when he laid eyes on her. She was the most beautiful woman he had ever seen. Never in his life, did he have such a visceral reaction to a woman.

Worst of all, he could feel her terror. He knew those men would gang rape her and kill her. He didn't stop to think. He pulled out his weapon and shot all six of them without remorse or a thought to the consequences.

His heart was pounding so hard in his chest; he swore there was movement from behind. So, he turned to ensure he was alone. When he turned back, she was gone. He assumed she ran off. He wanted to run after her, but he finally had a clear thought. Nic was certain the Reflex hadn't seen him. He was still using the corner of the building as cover, but he would only scare her more if he gave chase. He rushed towards the bodies and quickly removed any identification, bringing his hat down low over his forehead to hide from the figures he spied in the windows and balconies of the apartments facing the dusty alley.

His mission blown; he made a hasty departure from Kabul. His first failure. His handler was very disappointed, but Golov understood the mentality of the region, and how tenuous any associations were there. Nic never told him the truth about what happened. He never told anyone.

Pushing memories aside, Nic steers the bike to an alley that opens into a courtyard. This is the former East German side of Berlin. It's known now as the courtyard district or Mitte. Clutching Cara to him as he lifts her off the bike, he scans the area, searching for eyes. He looks up at the buildings, finding it ironic they are standing in an alley, once again. Although, the Mitte's cobblestone back streets bear no resemblance to Kabul's dirt paths.

Using a key, he opens the back door and pulls her in. They walk silently up two flights of stairs. The hallway is well decorated. The building is clean and modernized, but at least a century old. Nic places his arm around her again and approaches an apartment door. He pulls another key and lets them in.

They enter the small but very quaint apartment. The colors are muted, and there are lovely furnishings. The compact kitchen is entirely updated with granite counters and stainless-steel appliances. There is one bedroom with a European double bed and a couple of dressers.

Nic releases Cara and turns to lock the front door. At the kitchen table he removes all the weapons from his jacket pockets. He pulls knives from his pants. Removing his jacket, he hangs it on the back of one of the two kitchen chairs. Next, he peels off his leather pants and places them over the jacket.

Cara only watches. Her eyes are picking through the large number of weapons on the table.

Clad only in his briefs and a T-shirt, Nic is still wearing his holster which is outfitted with two more guns, one under his arm and one on his back. He sits down on the only other kitchen chair and pulls off his boots, but not before removing a smaller .22 automatic from the inside of one boot and a knife from the other.

He approaches Cara, and taking her hand, pulls her gently into the bathroom located between the kitchen and only bedroom. He closes the door to the bathroom and locks it. He hangs the shoulder holster over the hook on the door before leading her into the large walk-in shower.

The shower has been obviously renovated. New porcelain tiles cover the walls and there's marble on the floor. A shower seat is built-in to one side. He turns on the water and adjusts the temperature before pulling off his T-shirt and throwing it in the corner. Turning to face her, he carefully unbuttons Cara's silk shell. He extricates her arms, then reaches around her to unzip her skirt, letting it fall to the shower floor. He tosses both items to the corner with his shirt. She is now standing naked except for her matching grey lace bra and thong.

Satisfied the water is warm enough, he pulls Cara under the showerhead. She shudders when the water hits her. He wraps one arm around her waist, pressing his body close to provide warmth. Removing the head from its mount on the wall, he uses it as a hand-held. He runs it over her hair until it's sufficiently wet. He pours out shampoo and begins slowly massaging it through her hair.

When it's thoroughly lathered, Nic turns her to face him and uses the handheld to rinse out the shampoo. When he's done, he replaces the nozzle and twists a dial to activate the large rectangular rain head centered above them. Gentle, warm droplets leisurely fall into the shower stall.

Bending his knees to be eye level with Cara, he rests both his hands on the nape of her neck. He hesitantly brings his lips to hers, brushing across them ever so slightly. Gazing into her still dazed eyes, Nic knows all his apprehension has led to this moment.

When he and Cara finally met face-to-face sometime after Kabul, she introduced herself as Cara, and not as Chase Bennett. He would find out later it was her real name. Cara said she was a recently unemployed banker. She never let on what he knew was her true profession. That initial lack of disclosure compelled him to be discreet as well. He gave her his cover story and nothing else. But as that first evening progressed, it became clear she truly didn't know who Nic was.

She was never frightened or concerned for her safety that first night with him. Had she known he was the Dark Angel, she would never have willfully gone back to his hotel suite with him. Even Reed seemed unaware. The man was her handler, a CIA Team Leader, and eventually the Director, yet he let his best friend marry the Dark Angel of Death. In the 17 years to follow, Nic could only assume neither Cara nor Reed ever became aware of his true identity.

He breaks their visual connection to whisper, "Please, just remember, I love you more than you can ever know." Nic sits on the shower seat, placing her between his legs with her back to his chest. He wraps both arms tightly around her and confesses what he did and how he felt in Kabul.

After the incident in Kabul, Nic returned to Moscow a mental wreck. He spent the next few weeks trying to get the Reflex out of his mind. She became a compulsion, though. He was feeling all kinds of things he had never felt before. Strong emotions are dangerous in his line of work. Emotions will get you killed.

His next assignment was still pending when he learned about the upcoming European and American mini-Summit to be held at the UN in Geneva. He heard through the grapevine the CIA would have agents there so Nic convinced his superiors to choose him to represent the SVR. He just hoped she would be there.

And Agent Chase Bennett was there, with Agent Connor Reed wrapped around her like a glove. The famed and feared duo of the Reflex and the White Knight were schmoozing it up at the dinner. He knew Reed was her handler. And he had heard the speculation they were not only an effective team, but they were a couple.

Nic couldn't imagine she could look even more breathtaking than in Kabul, but she did. The Reflex was a knockout in an amazing red gown. She had the attention of every man in the room, but it was Reed whose arms were around her. He was acting like a man in love, gazing at and leaving kisses on her lips, face, bare shoulders and hands. Nic found himself trembling with rage and jealousy as he watched the two of them together.

It was only when he stopped looking at Reed and just concentrated on her that he could see...she was smiling, but the smile never made it to her eyes. She appeared distracted. Her mind was elsewhere. Occasionally, her eyes would dart around the room as if she was looking for something or someone.

Nic stayed in the shadows during most of the dinner but decided to finally get closer to them once the dancing commenced. He grabbed a fellow female agent when he saw the Duo headed towards the dance floor. He tried to steer his dance partner in their direction to get a better feel and possibly overhear any conversation. But that damn Agent Oksana was talking his ear off. She was running her hands through his hair and disrupting his hearing. He kept trying to tell her, as discreetly as possible, to shut the hell up and stop touching him, but she was incorrigible. And that's when he noticed Reed yanking Cara abruptly off the dance floor. Nic turned to watch as Reed practically dragged her out of the ballroom.

He ditched Oksana so he could follow them, but it was too late. They were both gone. He took a chance and went to the hotel he heard the CIA had taken a floor on. He worked his charm on the girl at the front desk and got their block of rooms. Nic rode up and as he came out of the elevator, he had to immediately take cover because Reed came storming out of one of the rooms. He had his luggage with him and headed straight into the open elevator car.

Nic came around the corner and headed in the direction Reed had come from. That's when he heard the sobbing. It was coming from the room Reed had exited, and he knew for sure it was her. Nic wanted to break down the door to get to her. What had Reed done? Did he hit her? Hurt her in any way? He had to get a grip on himself before he did anything rash. He listened more intently and that's when he realized she didn't seem to be in physical pain. Her cries were more emotional.

Nic leans into Cara's ear as the droplets of water roll down his face. "I decided to just stand outside your door and listen. My heart was breaking for your pain. I must have stayed there an hour until you finally stopped crying. I presumed you and Reed had some sort of blowout, and he left. He left you alone and in distress."

With that final statement, Cara bends forward against his restraining arms as if in pain. Wincing, she tries to speak for the first time since the shooting. Her voice is more of a croak. "I can't believe you were there, outside my hotel room that whole time. So close...if you wanted to check on me, why didn't you just knock?"

"Cara, when one is known as the Dark Angel...." Nic pauses before continuing, "Honestly, I thought you'd recognize me and shoot me." If he was Cara, he would have shot first and asked questions later. It was one thing to try to see her in public, but knock on her door in the middle of the night?

He shifts their positions until she is directly on the shower seat. He kneels in front of her to force her to look into his eyes.

He waited outside her hotel room in Geneva all night, dodging other agents and any activity in the hallway. She finally emerged around 7:00 am with her bag. He followed her out of the hotel and to the airport. Nic watched her board a flight to DC. He assumed she was headed back to Langley.

Running back to his hotel, he grabbed his bags and his American cover documents and boarded the next direct flight to Washington. He had to know what this thing was between her and Reed. But what he really needed was to understand this compulsive feeling he had toward her.

He arrived in DC and used his contacts there to find out where she was living. It was easier than he thought. By the time he made it to her apartment, she was packing her car. She looked lost. Not much different than she appears now.

Nic runs his hands down Cara's hair and around to her shoulders. "I knew you were leaving town. I didn't know at the time that you had quit. I would learn that later. But I followed you for the next six hours until you arrived outside of Cleveland at Jinx's apartment. During the next two days, I staked out the apartment and tailed you, not that you left much."

The problem was Nic couldn't stay in the States. His superiors would think he'd gone rogue if he didn't check back in. He only hoped Cara was at Jinx's for a while. He flew out of Cleveland and back to Moscow that afternoon. As soon as Nic arrived, he found Golov and told him he needed some mental health time off. Nic always had a very close relationship with Alexander, and he wanted to be honest. Nic explained he met a woman and needed to explore the relationship because she was causing him all kinds of turmoil. He wouldn't be able to perform his job until his head was on straight. It was the truth. He was surprised when Golov was sympathetic about it. He told him to take three weeks, and then report in.

"Of course, I didn't tell Alexander who the girl was. He would've had you shot." Reaching for the shower gel, he starts soaping up Cara's feet and legs.

After his conversation with his handler, Nic spent the remaining day making arrangements for himself. He needed to put some insurances in place before he left Moscow to avoid a target on his back. He packed everything he thought vital to his mission. For him, it became the most important mission of his life. He flew back to Cleveland and was relieved Cara was still at the apartment. He waited for his opportunity, finally deciding he had spent too much time being the creepy stalker.

He followed Cara to the Ritz Carlton downtown, where she was meeting three men for a late lunch. Her outfit, body language and what Nic could hear of the conversation led him to conclude it was a job interview.

Nic pauses in his confession here to massage the soap onto Cara's hands while very gently making his way up her arms. His eyes on what he's doing and not on hers, he continues, "I watched you wrap up your lunch and extend your thanks. And I headed into the bar."

Earlier, Nic had decided the restaurant and bar at the Ritz provided the perfect opportunity to make first contact. He booked a suite to ensure their privacy to talk, if he could get Cara that far. As luck would have it, he never had to intercept her. She finished her meeting and walked right towards where he was sitting at the bar.

Cara places her hands on his shoulders causing Nic to still for a moment. When he looks up into her face, she sees the steel has left his eyes and they're back to that most beautiful ocean blue she has always loved. She whispers, "I didn't see you at the bar. I only saw the five women around you. I needed a stiff drink after that interview."

Nic finally flashes her one of his signature smiles. The one that makes his eyes twinkle. He pulls her right hand down from his shoulder and places it over his heart. "Those women were fodder compared to you."

Cara smiles for the first time since she's seen him in Berlin. "That's exactly what you said to me at the bar."

She was about to pay for her drink, when suddenly, there was a hand on her wrist. She thought one of the women grabbed her, but it was a man's hand. When she looked over, Cara could see Nic literally pushing a couple of girls aside to reach her. He told the bartender to put the drink on his tab, pulled the twenty out of her hand, and placed it on the counter in front of her.

Nic has more shower gel in his right hand and rubs it across her rib cage brushing the bottoms of her breasts. When she doesn't protest, he releases the front clasp on her bra as he asks, "Do you remember what you said to me?" Now both hands are rubbing soap on her shoulders as he removes the bra straps from her arms.

Cara brings her hand back up and into Nic's hair and smiles at the memory.

She politely thanked him for the drink but told him he had more than enough women at the moment. That's when Nic gave her the first of many, 'killer' smiles and replied with the fodder comment, loud enough to send the other women off in a huff.

Nic winces slightly at the 'killer' adjective. "I knew the instant my hand touched your wrist that if I didn't get you out of my system, I was a dead man. I felt all my blood rush to my groin. I had to turn my body towards the bar to hide the raging hard on that simple touch produced." With his hands, he begins to skim over Cara's breasts, lightly brushing her nipples. She shudders from the arousal and moves her hands onto his nape. "What did you say next?" he pushes her.

"I asked you why I was different from the other women. You said because I was the most beautiful girl in the room."

Cara laughed at him in the bar after he gave her that line. She accused him of using the most unoriginal pick-up line, ever. Nic's expression turned serious after that. He looked her straight in the eyes and confessed he had never said that to any woman, EVER.

He pulls Cara closer to him and she wraps her legs around his waist. Nic moves one hand through Cara's hair, pulling gently to bring her head back. He places tender kisses along her jawline. "It was the truth. But I didn't think you believed me." He continues his kissing along her neck, occasionally letting his teeth lightly scrape her skin.

Cara closes her eyes as her husband's lips sensuously incite her passion and the memories of that long ago first connect with him.

When her drink was delivered, Nic picked up his glass and clinked it to hers. He toasted to good girls and bad girls. She didn't understand the toast and asked him to expound.

With his lips against her jaw, Nic whispers into her flesh, "What did I tell you, cara mia?"

Cara smiles to herself as the memories are now pouring into her brain. "You said something about good girls are sweet and kind and can be rather boring. Bad girls are hot and sexy, but too high maintenance. Then you asked me which one I was, good or bad?"

Nic makes his way back to Cara's chin and up to her lips to softly brush them with his. His breath is hot against her when he whispers, "You didn't answer me at first. You paused. Then you did something I didn't expect. You leaned forward very slowly, eventually bringing your mouth to my ear. You said..." Nic moves his head in the same manner she had 17 years ago, bringing his lips to her ear, whispering the words she spoke on that unforgettable day. "I am neither good nor bad...I am dangerous." Nic gently bites Cara's ear as she had done to him at the bar.

Pulling back to look at his face, Cara brings her mouth down on his. Their kisses go immediately from gentle and tentative to hard and passionate. Nic runs his hands down her back getting to her bottom and pulling at her thong. He rips the delicate fabric off her, then stands, her legs still wrapped around his waist. "Baby, take off my briefs."

Cara leans to one side and tugs at his waistband, jerking his erection free, and getting his briefs halfway down his leg. He wiggles them the rest of the way off while still carrying her. He turns and places her back gently against the side wall of the shower. The water has turned colder but neither of them notices. Nic gazes into her eyes and admits, "I knew then, with those words, I was a goner. I had to have you. No getting to know each other. No courting you, no romance. I just needed to be inside you. That was the only clear thought in my head."

And with that declaration, Nic lowers Cara onto his waiting erection. He slides slowly inside her watching her eyes again. "This is where I belong, cara mia. It was then, and it will always be my place and mine only, in your body, in your heart and in your soul."

He begins with a slow thrust into her. His eyes never leave hers until her head rolls back and a moan escapes her lips. He thrusts harder and Cara groans appreciatively. He takes one of her nipples into his mouth, and her breath hitches, "Nic, more." He moves his mouth to her other breast before quickening his pace.

Cara arches her back, her head resting against the hard tile. Her mouth is open, and her breathing has quickened. Nic coaxes, "I can feel you, baby, you're ready, come with me." And with that command, Cara cries out and Nic plunges into her one more time, pressing her back against the shower wall as he releases everything he has for her.

FOURTEEN

CARA IS CLINGING TO HER husband as she drops her legs and he leans in for a passionate post coital kiss. She wants to smile, but is holding back. He just took her exactly like he did for the first time in his hotel suite at the Ritz. He shut the door, pushed her into it, and fucked her with such need; they still had some clothes on when they were done. But he was only getting started. Nic had her on every surface in the suite at one point or another. She couldn't believe any man could have the stamina and the ability to recoup with such speed. He was a machine, physically, but there was a sensuality to his love making that she had never experienced before. He had a deep emotional desire to please her and care for her from the very beginning.

Nic releases her and grabs the shampoo for his hair. Cara adds conditioner to her hair, before reaching for the shower gel and stating, "You know the water is freezing."

He smirks, "I don't feel a thing."

Cara rubs the gel across his chest while he rinses his hair. She takes her time, working it all over the front of his body, making sure to spend a little longer around his already firming manhood. His head drops back, and all he can do is groan. Moving to his back, she rubs gel everywhere, again spending more time on his gorgeous ass. He abruptly shuts the water off, opens the shower door and grabs a huge towel. He spins it around the both of them, and with an arm around her waist, lifts her up, and out of the shower.

He towels the both of them off, spending some time removing the excess moisture from her hair. He then grabs her hand with his left and leads her out of the bathroom, snatching up his holster with his right hand and taking it with him.

Nic brings Cara into the bedroom. He places the holster with the two guns on the floor by the bed then picks Cara up to toss her onto it. He growls as he crawls onto the bed on top of her. "First time I needed fast and hard. The second time, you are going to get slow and torturous."

Cara's eyes widen, "That's what you said 17 years ago!"

Nic smiles and brushes his lips gently across hers before pulling her lower lip and biting it. "I may not be able to go 12 for 12 like I did years ago, but I have a couple more in me today." With that he takes her mouth.

Cara awakens with a smile on her face, feeling very satisfied. Then the memory of the last 24 hours comes hurtling back. Frowning, she checks the clock, then reaches over in the bed for Nic, but finds she's alone. She falls back on the mattress and stares at the ceiling.

She has never really understood why she was sent to Kabul. She had always disliked the region and had only ever gone there on assignment with Reed and a detailed mission plan. Besides the obvious reasons, her hair never cooperated in that climate, her shoes were always ruined, and it smelled bad. For some reason though, the Deputy Director at the time insisted she go. He made it an order. Despite her aversion to Afghanistan, the lack of proper intel, and the fact they were sending her in without back up, she felt compelled to comply.

Cara ended up in Kabul at the right place but the wrong time. She was informed of the Dark Angel's meeting, and planned to position herself in the window of one of the apartment buildings adjacent to the alley selected for the meeting. She staked it out the previous day, and was prepared to arrive early, excited to finally see the Dark Angel in action. Her so-called contacts, however, gave her bad information. She ended up walking into the alley just minutes before the event was to take place and ran right into the six men who were there for the meet-up.

Suddenly, they're all yelling, 'hey green eyes', and 'where do you think you're going, girl' in their native dialect. They grabbed her and she tried to fight them off, self-preservation instinct and training kicking in. Except there were too many of them. The more she fought, the angrier they got. Two of them secured her, while the others groped her breasts and placed their hands between her legs. When they pulled off her burka, Cara knew she was about to die a slow, brutal death.

She's not a religious person but at that moment she prayed. She begged the heavens for a miracle, or at least a quick and merciful death before these men could do what they intended. And then, her prayers were answered. A bullet whizzed by her ear and she thought, 'oh good, someone will shoot me and this will all be over'. But unbelievably, within seconds, the arms restraining her were gone. The hands all over her body withdrew. She looked down, and the men were laying in lifeless piles on the dusty alley ground. She didn't think. Cara didn't even breathe. She just ran.

Cara shudders at the memory and sits up. She notices a robe at the foot of the bed. She gets up and puts it on, tightening the sash as she approaches the bedroom door.

When she opens the door, she finds Nic just finishing up in the bathroom. He's wearing rubber gloves, jeans, his shoulder holster and nothing else. He has bagged all of their clothes and there's a heavy scent of bleach coming from the walk-in shower. Cara checks out her bare chested, gun-wearing husband. He looks smoking hot. She decides the next round she'll have him wear just the holster. No, she needs to focus. Stop thinking about sex and talk to him.

Nic glances up and grins when he sees her. "Hey, baby, you passed out on me after round three. Figured I would start cleanup. Bathroom is done, and I've cleaned the Beretta and my leather. All stored away where they won't be found. Unfortunately, I have nothing for you to wear. But I imagine it's only a matter of time before Reed shows up."

Reed? "Oh my God! I totally forgot about Reed!" Cara exclaims. He's surely coming to kill her.

"I'm actually glad to hear you say that," Nic teases.

As if on cue, there's a knock on the door. Nic quickly removes the rubber gloves and tosses them into the trash bag with all their clothes. He pulls the gun from his holster, and gently pushes Cara back into the bedroom, mumbling, "Just in case it's not your boyfriend." He walks towards the front door and listens.

They hear Reed say, "It's me, Nic. I'm unarmed. Well, not really, but come on, just let me in, please."

Cara snickers when Nic rolls his eyes at her. He unlocks the door and opens it wide. He's standing there looking a little less menacing in only jeans and his holster. Gun, of course, still in hand.

Rushing forward, she decides she may need to place herself between these two. Reed is standing just outside the doorway with Cara's carry-on in one hand and four large shopping bags with the Olaf logo on full display in the other.

When he walks in, Cara squeals, "You brought my stuff!" She jumps up into Reed's arms.

Reed drops the bags and catches her, squeezing her tight. Almost too tight, and he's not sure if it's from relief or rage. He decides it doesn't matter.

She's rubbing his back sensing the mixture of emotions he's

feeling at the moment. He's still running on the rush of adrenalin from the fear something had happened to her. He whispers softly in her ear, "Sweetheart, are you okay?" Cara lets him put her down. She smiles at him and nods while she holds his hands.

She refocuses on the overstuffed shopping bags. "What's all this? Olaf only gave me two bags of stuff."

"I was hoping your husband could answer that question," Reed inquires while peering over at Nic.

Nic shoulders his weapon and just shrugs. He has retrieved Carter's gun and phone and hands them to Reed stating, "Agent Carter misplaced these."

Reed pockets them with no comment and explains a courier delivered two bags of merchandise to Cara's hotel room with a note for the 'Dark Angel'. "And they weren't Carter's size, so..."

Nic breaks into one of his killer smiles and nods in recollection. "Olaf... this morning. I was waiting in his office for him when he returned from the sample rooms with you." He points at Cara and admits he had Olaf in his sights, and was prepared to torture him for intel. Olaf, however, was unfazed by the weapon trained on him. Instead, he barreled into Nic, open armed, and pulled him into a bear hug. He then started yapping on and on about how he couldn't believe Nic married the Reflex. "Apparently, my wife showed Olaf pictures of her family. Olaf told me Cara never mentioned my name. She only said, 'This is my very hot and wonderful husband'."

Nic shudders at the memory, slightly repulsed by the designer's over-the-top reaction. He was able to rush through a quick recap with his old comrade, but Olaf wouldn't let him leave. "He insisted he had to 'measure my inseam.' No one ever told me that was code for 'I want to violate you'."

Reed and Cara burst out laughing. Reed asks through his snickers, "Nic, can you show me on the doll where Olaf touched you?"

Cara is howling but soon raises her hand to Reed in a stop motion informing him he shouldn't laugh too hard. "Olaf has been following your career. He clips your photos and watches all your TV coverage. I'm pretty sure he's developed a crush. He asked me to relay a message to you, Connor. Olaf does not appreciate you wearing Tom Ford. He wants to 'measure your inseam' so the only thing on your body is Olaf! He expects a visit before you leave Berlin," Cara giggles out.

Now Nic and Cara are laughing at him. Before he can respond, Cara continues, "And he said seeing you never married, and have no known serious dating record, Olaf is fairly certain you're the man for him!"

Reed is horrified. Nic's still belly laughing but begins poking through the bags. He pulls out a beautiful chocolate leather jacket and puts it on.

"Reed!" Nic exclaims, "This coat is amazing. You've got to feel this." He strokes the leather and pleads, "Please sleep with Olaf so we can get more swag." Cara and Nic both dissolve into more laughter.

Reed does not see the humor. "I am not amused, guys, and I AM NOT GAY!"

"Oh, the lady doth protest...," Nic spits out.

Before he can rip back into Nic, Reed considers that he might get laid more often if he was gay. But before he can continue on that bizarre train of thought, he pulls up short as Nic raises both hands and stops laughing. His face tightens and his eyes go back to that odd steel color Carter was talking about.

"What did you say when you came in, Reed? Did you say Olaf sent the clothes to the 'Dark Angel'?" No one answers. Nic stares at his wife as realization slowly spreads across his face. "You both knew who I was, didn't you?"

Reed looks imploringly to Cara, but she's just standing there biting her lower lip. She only bites her lip when she's emotionally stressed. He glances back at Nic and can sense he's about to erupt. Reed's at a momentary loss. Should he stay and assist, or leave this to Cara?

He finally speaks. "I purposely gave you guys a couple of hours to sort this out. I immediately knew where you went because I replaced the SIM card in Cara's phone and tracked her here. I...I...am leaving." He makes a hasty retreat out the front door, calling over his shoulder, "I'll be at the café across the street, when you're done."

THE DOOR SHUTS BEHIND REED, AND CARA IS LEFT WITH NIC AND HIS awful, menacing stare.

Shit. Evil Nic twin is back. Reed and his impeccable timing. Tentatively, Cara begins, "Nic, my love, I swear I was just about to tell you when I came out of the bedroom." Sometime during Nic's confession this morning, Cara realized he thought she was still unaware of his true identity. She probably should have told him right there and then. Too late for woulda, shoulda's now.

"When?!" Nic barks out, making her jump.

"When what?"

"When did you know who I was?!" he yells.

She blurts out quickly, "Kabul, I knew in Kabul!" Nic is now roiling with genuine rage.

Wait, why is he so angry? Confusion overtakes her. "Nic, how could you think I didn't know? I mean on the surface that's rather insulting. Do you think so little of the CIA, and of me and Reed, to believe we wouldn't have intel on what you looked like...or heard all the stories?"

Nic doesn't answer her. He only glares with those cruel eyes.

Still sensing hostility, Cara starts to ramble, "Reed was one of your biggest fans. We had pictures of you, one a clear close up." They all feared Nic, but respected him for his skills. Reed promised he would never send one of his agents up against Andrychenko or his handler, Golov. It wasn't that Reed didn't have faith in his team, but faith wouldn't save their asses against either Russian.

"Reed thought of you two as the deadliest weapons the Soviet bloc ever produced. He told us you were labelled the Dark Angel of

Death because you looked like an angel but had the heart of the devil, and no soul to speak of."

Cara pauses to tamp down the hysteria she feels rising, then continues, "It was actually a mistake that I was in Kabul. Jinx was my regular analyst, you know that, right?" Nic gives a small nod.

Jinx had just quit to take the job in Cleveland, which Cara has always suspected was a front for the NSA, but Jinx will never admit it. Back then, Cara was assigned a new researcher, and he wasn't very good. They were having some difficulties getting along. Reed was out on assignment when she got the order to go to Kabul, leaving immediately.

She was not to engage. Only witness and report. She should have called Reed, and informed him of the assignment, but she didn't. Cara felt foolish tracking him down while he was possibly under-cover, and whining to him about it. If Jinx was there, she would've had better intel, or she would've stopped Cara if she didn't.

As usual, Cara ignored Reed's orders to never go there alone, much less possibly run into the Dark Angel, and took the next trans-port to Kabul. Suddenly, she stifles a sob at the memory. She stops rambling and hesitantly continues the story.

After she ran away from the blood bath in the alley, full of ques-tions like 'What the hell just happened?' and 'Who in the hell could have taken those shots?', she had a moment of clarity. The only possible scenario included him, the Dark Angel, Andrychenko, but why?

Because she had to know, she circled back, this time skipping the alley and entering the apartment building she had staked out earlier through a different door. She dashed up the stairs to the second floor window and carefully looked out. The Dark Angel was there. He was bent over the bodies removing their weapons and ID's. His move-ments kept her spellbound and more baffled than ever. What was his motive? Wouldn't the cruel and vicious Dark Angel have a motive for everything? But oddly, she wasn't feeling it. From her vantage, he looked more resigned than calculating. Then it happened. A gust of wind blew through the alley and his hat came off. He turned his face and she had a clear view.

Her legs went weak as she stared at that face. Her knees buckled, and she dropped to the floor, her breath leaving her lungs with a whoosh. He was the most spectacular creature she had ever seen. The pictures they had did not do him justice. She was totally captivated by his face. He had the looks of an angel and a body built for sin. He was her angel, her guardian angel. She was hanging onto the windowsill for support, looking like a Peeping Tom, when he glanced up, almost like he knew she was there. Cara backed away quickly, escaped down the hallway and out of the building, and kept running until she was safely on the next transport.

When she got back to Langley, she had to report what happened. Essentially the transaction she was sent to witness didn't go down, but Cara was hesitant to document everything that happened that night. Reed hadn't returned from his assignment, so she bought herself some time and didn't report anything. She made excuses, took some time off, and within a week, Reed was back.

It felt like the longest week of her life. She couldn't get Nic's beautiful, angelic face out of her mind. It was making her crazy. She told Reed everything. Listened to him yell at her for even going to Kabul in the first place, and then listened to him lecture her for turning back to see the Dark Angel after the shootings.

Reed tried to convince her Nicolae Andrychenko did have motive, and if he had caught her, her fate would've been sealed. She never would have made it back from Kabul. But, for the first time since she'd known Reed, Cara wasn't buying his assessment. And that made him even more irritated, except he didn't yell again. Instead, Reed decided she was experiencing some sort of PTSD over the attempted gang rape. He furloughed her, and sent her to five sessions with a shrink before she could come back to work.

Interrupting her story, Nic demands, "Geneva. Tell me what happened in Geneva."

Cara is exhausted. She hasn't slept in 36 hours, she almost died, and now this. She walks over to a plush chair and sits down tucking her legs beneath her. Nic is still standing in the same spot, not having moved a muscle since she started confessing. Throwing her head back, she concentrates on the ceiling and whispers, "I needed to see you again. Counseling didn't help. It only reinforced the strong connection I felt to you, like we were linked somehow. Like some thread had been sewn between us."

She found out Reed had been invited to Geneva. She knew several of the higher profile Russian agents would be there with their diplomats so there was a chance one of them would be the Dark Angel. For some reason, she believed, if he's there, it will be because of the thread. It will mean something.

She begged Reed to let her come as his plus one. He finally agreed on the grounds she had to act like his date. The Americans were to only have a certain number of agents present. When they arrived at the kickoff Gala, she immediately spotted Nic in the shadows.

Unfortunately, so did Reed. She would swear he took the whole 'date' thing to a new level that night. Nevertheless, she felt excited Nic was there. It proved to her the thread existed. Kismet, karma, long shot, chaos theory, mathematical improbability of coincidence, whatever it was called, she was feeling all of it.

Cara kept track of Nic all night, but he was always a distance away. She finally saw her chance when he showed himself near the dance floor. She grabbed Reed and started in the same direction. She just wanted to catch his eye. She can't explain why she felt that way. She thought if they could just make eye contact...but the leggy blonde Russian agent he was dancing with kept getting in the way. She was all over Nic, practically fondling him. And every time he was about to turn his face to look in Cara's direction, the blonde would turn it back toward her.

She was so focused on trying to get Nic to look at her; Cara didn't notice Reed watching her. He pointedly asked her what the hell she thought she was doing? And what the hell was she trying to prove? She was so determined to get near Nic, she just ignored Reed's cross-examination until it happened. Nic's face broke into a genuinely amazing smile... his killer smile. It wasn't directed at Cara. It was meant for his dance partner, but Cara went down hard.

"For me, the thread pulled tight, right there and then, Nic. I was devastated you weren't experiencing the same sensation." Cara shuts her eyes recalling the intense emotion she felt on that dance floor so many years ago. "But after your confession this morning, I know now, you did feel the connection between us."

"But what happened with you and Reed?" Nic asks.

Cara takes a deep breath, letting the painful memories flood back. Slowly, she articulates her side of what happened the night after Reed dragged her from the party.

As the story continues and the memories become more and more painful, she begins to sob. Nic just stares, listening intently to every word she utters about the horrible night that ended with her walking away from Reed, her career and her home. When she finishes, she looks up at him, hoping to see her loving husband's gentle face, but instead she gets the mask of the Dark Angel of Death.

Making no comment about her Geneva admission, Nic jumps forward to their first night together at the Ritz, and asks with piercing eyes, "Why weren't you afraid when you saw me in the bar? I always assumed it was because you didn't know who I was, but you did recognize me, and yet..."

Cara rises from her chair and approaches her husband. She chooses to stand directly in front of him despite his height and his still steely glare. She looks into those cruel eyes and answers, "And yet I let you drag me back to your hotel suite within an hour of meeting you, unarmed, and without letting anyone know where I was. I would NEVER do that with a complete stranger, yet, I let a known killer have me. Is that what you're asking, Nic?"

Before he can answer, she continues, "Because of the thread, Nic, the thread. You found me. You found me because you pulled the thread, and all of it was wrapped around me! If you were there at the hotel to kill me, then so be it. I would rather have died than continued the insanity. That's what I was thinking that late afternoon at the Ritz."

She raises her hand to place it on his heart, but he catches her wrist and snaps at her, "Don't touch me."

Cara tries to yank her hand away, but his grip is too strong. Nic has her hand and arm immobilized. Instead of fighting him, she steps in closer so they're mere inches apart and she stares into his eyes.

She can feel the fury he's barely holding back, but she doesn't understand it. Calmly she inquires, "Why are you so angry? I'm sorry I didn't interrupt your heartfelt confession to add mine. I was traumatized by the events with Vlad. I've always wondered what led you to me. And I waited 17 years for that story, Nic."

"You really don't get it, do you?" he snaps at her, again.

"You're starting to aggravate me, Nic. I'm warning you." She has no idea where this is coming from. They are both to blame for the lack of disclosure all these years. It's nonsensical to lay this lie of omission only at her feet. Nic isn't budging, though. He's still holding her wrist and glaring down at her.

Cara narrows her eyes, her mouth tightens, and she loses it. With her free hand, she grabs the back of Nic's neck to yank him down nose to nose with her, and through clenched teeth she commands, "You can stop this right now. Stop being a smug, sanctimonious, ice-cold BASTARD!"

And with that, Nic releases her wrist, grabs her by the shoulders and pins her between himself and the kitchen counter. All of his weight presses against her, causing Cara to wince. He further imprisons her with his hands on the counter, one on each side of her, and leaning into her face, he spits out, "That's it, Cara! That's just it. I AM an ice-cold bastard."

He's watching her face to see a reaction, but she continues to stare wild-eyed back at him. "More importantly, I am YOUR bastard!" Nic is yelling in her face now, "Your own personal lethal weapon!" Again, he searches Cara's face for something, but she still has the same clueless expression. Nic, disgusted by now that she can't figure this out, knows he'll have to spell it out for her. "What's the first thing you do when you determine there's a viable threat to you and possibly your family?"

Watching her expression finally change to one of comprehension and remorse, he drives it home. "You don't come to the man who sleeps with you every night. The man you have children with. The man who would lay down his life for you. The man who, you know, can protect you better than ANYONE! NO! YOU. CALL. REED!" He pushes off her after this pronouncement.

She is dumbfounded. She shakes her head trying to formulate a response but her mouth just keeps mumbling, "I'm so sorry, I'm so sorry," over and over. Her head is down because she can't look at him. "You more than deserve an answer." Her knees give out and she drops to the floor, her back against the cabinets.

He feels justified being this angry and disappointed with her. How could she lie to him? How could she exclude him from all of this? Federal secrets and loyalties aside, he is her husband.

She's still on the ground mumbling something about Pavlovian reactions to threats and not thinking straight. The tears are streaming down her face, again. He has rarely seen her cry. Between finding her in tears with Vlad, having her finally divulge what happened in Geneva, and now this, he's starting to wonder what's going on with her. She's been an emotional wreck for the last six hours.

Nic walks away from her to the pile of luggage and Olaf bags. He opens her carry-on and pulls out a matching set of bra and panties and a pair of jeans. Next, he rifles through the designer pieces from Olaf and separates the men's clothes from the ladies. He wants to give Cara some time to sort this out, but he needs answers. He spies a cashmere sweater with a cropped front and a pair of camel colored soft leather mid-calf height boots with a modest heel.

He takes all of it and walks back to Cara, dropping the outfit in front of her. "Get dressed," he commands her. "We need to go."

His rage and jealousy have subsided, only disappointment remains. Her running to Reed when she felt threatened, he can rationalize away as being habit, but not telling him? When she knew who he was? And how delusional was he to believe his wife, a prominent ex-CIA agent, would not know about the Dark Angel?

She's correct, of course, about him being guilty of omission, as well. He didn't believe she could love a man like him. He never imagined his life would take such a left turn, landing him blissfully happy and content with the woman of his dreams. He knew he didn't deserve her or this perfect life after the sins of his past. A past he never wanted to contaminate the life they shared.

Nic makes another pass back to Cara with her cosmetic bag and she grabs his arm, "Nic, I love YOU. Please, never question that. You are a wonderful husband and father and you've earned your happiness. I should be questioning whether I deserve someone as amazing as you. Not the other way around."

Walking away from her, Nic is always astounded she can so clearly read him. Then again, except for this recent miscommunication, he can always read her. He knew she was lying about the DC job in his office. He could tell she was upset and distressed the night before. Yesterday morning when she flew to DC, every alarm bell in his mind went off. He and his wife have been strangely connected and entwined like threads to each other from the first moment he laid eyes on her.

Cara sheds her robe and starts getting dressed. She's mumbling again. "When we first met, aside from the obvious spy versus spy omission, I felt we were being honest with each other. I wanted to get to know the true Nic, the man who wasn't a monster. The man whose heart didn't belong to Satan but was full of love and passion. The man who had a soul, the sensitive soul of a poet."

She heads into the bathroom to do something with her hair while still spewing indiscriminate memories of their early relationship. Recalling the first few weeks and months of their relationship, she admits "Even though the passion between us was off the charts, we also spent time talking about dreams and desires; planning what the perfect business venture would be for us. And somewhere along the way, for me, the Reflex and the Dark Angel ceased to exist. The memories faded. The legends became vague. Of course having twins can fully dominate anyone's mind. But that aside, I stopped seeing us as anything but Nic and Cara, couple, parents, and business owners."

He's getting dressed while she's still in the bathroom, making an attempt at make-up and a loose ponytail for her hair. She hasn't stopped talking. "When I started to hear the music everywhere and sensed something was wrong, my first thought wasn't to see what the Dark Angel of Death thought about my predicament. My first thought was to run to my handler. The man who trained me and protected me for a decade. The man I still consider to be my best friend. I am truly sorry, my love." She peeks out the door looking devastated.

Again, he can overlook Cara's habitual nature of running to her best friend. Reed has the means, as the current Director, to make things happen. But it doesn't excuse her most recent lie. He cannot forgive her for the fear and anxiety she caused him when Nic sensed she was heading into danger yesterday. She may have been a formidable agent in her day, but she went off half-cocked and sloppy this morning. She walked into a perilous situation with no strategic plan.

Good God, had he been only seconds later, the life he has treasured would have been destroyed. The woman who gave him a reason to love, two amazing children and 17 years of bliss would be dead. He shudders at how close they came to that.

Cara is walking out of the bathroom with her cosmetic bag when she adds, "But, on the other hand, this morning with Vlad, I didn't think you were my Nic."

She has his full attention now. "What about this morning?"

"You looked different, like a mean, violent version of yourself. My Nic's cruel evil twin."

He was wearing clothes she has never seen him in. And he's aware his eye color alters when he is enraged. Years of training kicked in and he became his alter ego, devoid of all emotion.

"It's like you were wearing a mask." She points to his face, "I don't know that face. I have never seen it before."

She zips her bag closed while Nic places his shoulder holster back on. She notices his collar is caught on the leather straps of the holster, and leans into him to adjust it. The gesture feels natural. Fondling the holster, Cara whispers, "I have never seen you in action. I didn't actually witness you shooting the Afghani men in Kabul. Until this morning, I had no real firsthand knowledge of your reputation."

Forcing his chin down so he has to look at her, she gently rubs her fingertips across his lips. "Most importantly, Nic, you will always be the Zen Master of our family. You are the patient and impartial parent, and the devoted and loving husband. A brilliant entrepreneur, a hardworking business owner, a passionate, avid and talented musician, and to me, you are the antitheses of a killer. This morning was shock and awe, a total surprise." She is gazing at him with such devotion in her eyes, Nic has to release the rest of his disappointment. He is a sucker for that look of love.

Her eyes turn reflective before she admits, "I think I may have been more afraid of you than Vlad. You really scared the crap out of me this morning."

He relinquishes and pulls her into a firm hug. She grips him back harder, both of them needing the contact. They stand clinging to each other until he whispers, "I scared the piss out of you, not the crap."

Cara stiffens at the humiliation of that, and whines, "It happened when I was Taser'd."

"I know. I'm just teasing. Trust me, nothing can be worse than watching them slice you in half to rip out our two children."

"You didn't have to watch them give me a C-Section."

"I wasn't taking my eyes off you or our children during any of that," Nic says sternly.

She spends a moment rubbing her lips along his neck before pulling away. "I've always felt safe with you. I know you will protect us. I ... didn't give you the respect you were due and I'm sorry for that. You are amazing!" she says with genuine admiration. "The way you took down Carter. The way you got into the apartment so silently. The head game you had going with Vlad, and that shot from the other side of the apartment. I am your newest, biggest fan, Dark Angel."

Before he can speak, she continues, "And I promise the following. A. full disclosure on everything. B. I will respect the skill," she bows before him with that, "And C. we start the next phase of our marriage by including our past, and learning to incorporate it into our future."

Nic pulls her into a hard kiss. The kiss turns passionate, but he breaks it off, and holding on to her jaw he concedes, "I'm good with those promises, cara mia. Now, let's go meet your boyfriend. He's across the street, probably apoplectic by now."

Cara winces at the thought, but then asks as they're walking out with their bags, "By the way, how did you find me, and how did you rent this adorable apartment?"

Nic says as he's locking up, "The first part is a story for later, and the apartment...I'm glad you like it...because we own it."

CHAPTER

FIFTEEN

A S THEY ENTER THE CAFÉ, Nic takes a more protective stance with Cara, grabbing her hand and pulling her closer behind him. The café is mostly full, and they spot Reed at a table in the back. They place their luggage against the wall and sit down, Cara next to Reed and Nic across from him.

Reed breaks the awkward silence after visually inspecting both of them. "Are we good?"

Nic retorts, "We are not good. My wife and I need coffee, immediately. And we're starving. Otherwise...yeah, we're good."

Reed motions to the waitress to come over. She's very young and approaches hesitantly. Nic smiles at her then launches into flawless German as he orders a carafe of coffee, cream, and breakfast food for the table.

When he's finished ordering, he turns his attention back to Reed, "I count seven plain clothes agents in the café with us. Tell them to stand down. They're nervous and jumpy." Reed rolls his eyes.

Cara leans past Reed and taps the shoulder of the customer sitting head down with his back to them. "Carter, darling, how are you feeling?" she asks solicitously.

Carter slowly turns his head, and replies, "Between the two of you, I may never father any children, but otherwise I'm fine. Thank you for asking."

Cara turns to Nic. "You kick him in the nuts, too?"

He grins, "I couldn't help myself. I saw the way Carter took the stairs when I was following him. I presumed you got his boys earlier." He apologizes to Carter, but there's not an ounce of sincerity in it.

Reed whispers something to Carter who gestures with his hands. The other agents in the café noticeably relax. Then, Reed fills them in on his progress.

They swept Apartment 23 for prints. As expected, most of them belonged to Vlad with only a few that would have implicated Cara. Nothing else of interest was uncovered. They took Chekov's ID and his phone, which they're still running diagnostics on. Vlad was in Berlin less than a week before the encounter. And after listening to the recording transmitted from the audio device in Cara's boot, they're pretty comfortable that aside from the hacker he used, Vlad was working alone. They hope to identify the hacker via Vlad's phone records but have little confidence they will lead them to the person or persons who funded the hit. They found a homeless man who Vlad had paid to watch Olaf's building. Reed has some of his local contacts following up on a few other leads.

The coffee arrives and Nic pours a cup for Cara and then himself. Cara guzzles hers down and refills her small cup a second time. Nic considers Reed's narrative and says, "The hacker will be of no assistance, and knowing Vlad and his training, I'm not surprised your search of the apartment yielded nothing."

Confused, Cara declares, "You told Vlad you didn't recognize him."

"Really, Cara?" Nic mocks, "You think I forget anyone?"

Nic worked a couple of missions, with Vlad as his researcher, but they were never in the field together. Vlad was a substandard agent at best, and just an average analyst. Golov would only send the most accomplished agents in the field with Nic. He held his comrades in arms to some pretty high standards, and cocky as that makes him sound, he had the skills and success rate to back it up. He makes no apology for it. "Anyway, Chekov's usefulness had expired and he was out of the game by the late 80's. I'd heard he became a contract killer and I vowed to put him down if we ever crossed paths again."

"Well, you're a man of your word, then. Time to get out here," Reed announces. He doesn't believe there is anything left for them to do in Berlin. They need to get back to Langley and do some research. He has the Gulfstream ready at the airport. No need to stay in Berlin any longer and draw suspicion.

"I agree. This lead has gone cold," Nic concurs.

Seemingly out of nowhere Cara asks, "Hey, what time is it?"

Reed answers, "3:30 here, why?"

Cara turns to Nic with an insightful glance and replies, "Can you check in with Sasha and see how the kids are doing? Let her know we're together. Tell her we will text her before we get in the air."

Nic stares blankly at his wife, at a complete loss. Her eyes are boring into his. Sasha...her? Oh God. Cara knows. He smiles as blandly as he can and agrees, "That's a good idea. I'll call her outside."

Nic gets up to leave, turning his back on Reed and Cara, but inclining his head just enough to see them in his peripheral vision. He observes Reed grabbing Cara by the arm and dragging her to him with some force. Good boy, Reed. Nic had been wondering when Reed was going to reprimand her for the disgraceful way she conducted her mission this morning. About time he acted like her handler instead of making her husband be the bad guy.

Happy with this turn of events, Nic exits the café to make what should prove to be an interesting phone call. He keeps an eye on his wife and Reed and their heated discussion through the front window, and makes the call to Sasha.

CARA HAS A BITE OF FOOD ON HER FORK WHEN SHE'S JERKED HARD TOWARDS Reed. She watches as the food falls from her fork onto the table.

Reed tries to keep his voice low as he snarls, "What the hell did you think you were doing this morning? You're fired."

"I can't be fired. I don't work for you."

Reed grips her arm and leans into her face. "Disobeying direct orders, assaulting an agent, contaminating a crime scene, breaking and entering, cavorting with the enemy AND THAT WAS IN THE FIRST 3 HOURS YOU WERE HERE!"

"My personal favorite was the cavorting," she winks.

"Not talking about Nic, you pain in my ass. Olaf! Olaf is not cleared."

Cara counters, "Olaf gave me swag. You know I'm easily bought. We're Facebook friends now." She waits for the FB lecture but it doesn't come.

Instead, Reed hugs her tight. "You're being glib, C. You were scared this morning. Admit it."

Acquiescing and exhaling a breath, she confesses, "I totally lost control, Connor. I failed to see the threat, and then I failed to neutralize it."

Cara pulls away from their embrace and sets her eyes on Reed. If it weren't for Nic, she may have been collateral damage, even if Carter got there in time to take out Vlad. Nic determined that in his weird mental assessment thing he does. He knocked Carter out so he could control the confrontation with Vlad. It was brilliant, really. She owes Nic her life for a second time now, and she's feeling very inadequate. "I think it was wise I quit 17 years ago. I suck at this now. I'm so sorry I kicked Carter in the balls and disobeyed your orders. Mostly, I'm sorry I made you worry."

Wrapping his fist around her ponytail, he yanks her head closer to him. "Argh, how do you do that? Turn it around so I stop being angry?"

Cara gives him another quick hug before pulling away, "I PROMISE to be careful and follow your orders from now on."

Nic's voice startles both Cara and Reed out of their chairs. "YOU WILL NOT MAKE THAT PROMISE!" He's standing directly behind them with his arms folded across his chest.

"Jesus Nic, how do you do that? Appear out of nowhere!" Cara exclaims.

"Baby, no promises to Reed. I will handle your protection and this investigation from now on. I'll work with Reed and you will report to me. Capice?" Nic asserts.

Cara is about to argue, but then remembers the deal she made earlier with Nic, her confession to Reed just now, and most importantly, the fiasco with Vlad this morning that almost cost her life. Surprising them both, she quietly agrees, "Nic is the lead on this."

Reed's eyebrows spike up. "Wow, C, appears you have a new handler."

Contemplating her response while she eyes both men, Cara finally states, "Not a new handler. I'm not releasing you of that honor, Reed. Instead, I have a new partner."

CHAPTER

SIXTEEN

O N THE LIMO DRIVE BACK to the airport, Reed shares more details on the information they have accumulated so far. He passes Nic a ballistics report from the crime scene, records from Vlad's cell phone and rental information on the apartment, amongst other intel. Nic reads through all of it, occasionally asking Reed a question. Then, the two men work on possible motives and suspects, discussing strategies, protocols and outstanding items.

Cara sat away from them lost in her own thoughts for most of the ride. Now, she's looking at the two of them. They're both in their element and more in sync than she's ever seen them, deferential and respectful of the other's talent and intelligence. To think it only took an attempt on her life to bring them together. It's their shared concern for her that's binding them. Maybe this is a turning point for all of them.

What's odder than these two working together is she has no interest in what they're talking about. They keep glancing over to her, looking for input, but she has none. Instead, she's letting something weave its way through her mind. It's there, but just below the

126

surface. Something about Vlad that's a clue of some sort. It came up in that final conversation with him.

She's replaying the dialogue in her head when it occurs to her that she's fallen into another fugue state. One of her so-called seizures. She isn't zoned out. She's actually hyper-focused, shutting out the outside world and deliberating in her mind. After all these years, it's intriguing she just made the association. Perhaps the stress of her recent ordeal brought with it some clarity? She snaps out of her reverie as the car stops at the hangar.

Reed and Nic exit the limo first, and Reed heads into the building. Nic hangs back for a moment and watches as one of Reed's agents grabs their bags from the trunk and follows him in. When they're both out of earshot, Nic takes Cara's hand and helps her out of the car. He brings her close and whispers, "How long have you known?"

Cara doesn't bother to whisper back. She is well aware of his new concern. "From the first time we met, I knew. It didn't take a brain trust to figure it out, Nic."

"I am so sorry it didn't come up earlier during our confessions. I forgot. I owe you a considerable apology for that omission. It's possibly... unforgivable." Nic lowers his head, feeling shame.

Grabbing his jaw, she gently forces him to look up at her. "Don't ever think you need to defend your actions on this one," she scolds. "More importantly, you must know I am not upset by it. Let's keep it in the past. We're good. It was a long time ago."

The beautiful frown lines between his eyes are still furrowed. "And Reed?"

Raising her hands in prayer and her eyes to the heavens, Cara tells him, "Obviously, Reed doesn't know yet, and God help us when he finds out. He's going to have a complete meltdown, but he has to be made aware of it now with all that's going on."

"You were having a seizure in the car. I was worried you were having a meltdown over all of this," a worried Nic responds as they head towards the hangar.

Cara stops abruptly. "No, I was in my mind palace." She smiles at her nod to one of their favorite shows, the BBC's *Sherlock* series. "They're not seizures. I just figured it out. I go to the palace for insight." She stands proudly in front of him like she won the spelling bee.

"Find anything of interest swirling in there, Sherlock?" he jokes.

"Something Vlad said is bothering me. I can't put my finger on what it was. I'm letting it float around in the palace for a bit." She motions to her head.

"How about you let me be your Watson?" Nic inquires as they walk into the hangar, hand in hand, where Reed is on the phone. Carter is there, as well as the agent with the bags, and two more men who are wearing casual street clothes.

Motioning them to follow him into an office within the hangar, Reed hangs up his call and asks, "Who's Watson?"

Nic and Cara smile at each other while Reed takes a seat behind the desk, gesturing to the two chairs in front.

Cara shakes her head, "Watson as in Sherlock Holmes. And I don't feel like sitting." She begins pacing the long length of the office as Nic drags a chair halfway down until he is centered on her pacing path.

"Okay," Nic directs her, "start throwing me those thoughts from your 'mind palace'."

Cara begins this game they play often, which evidently now has a name. As business partners and marriage partners, she and Nic have developed this as a way to cope with conflict. Sometimes they weigh out tough business decisions. Sometimes they hash out marital issues. They've even begun using it to work through issues with the twins. She always leads with the pacing. For some reason her thoughts are clearer if she's in motion. Nic always sits within close proximity of her. No one takes any notes. The sessions are more productive if they are unrestricted and fluid.

Reed opens the small refrigerator in the office and removes three bottles of water. He delivers one to each of them, then goes back to sit on the edge of the desk, curious to see what will play out next. Cara's never introduced him to this game. And oddly, now that she thinks about it, she hardly ever has one of her seizures when she's alone with Reed.

Speaking out as thoughts begin to form, she says, "Reed and I have already agreed we're missing motive. We went through lists of possibilities back at Langley and could identify no known adversaries for me, so keep that in mind. It's my conversation with Vlad that's bothering me...there's a clue there...something he said..." She looks to Nic, "Was he always so self-important?"

Nic considers the question before speaking. "Yes. But more so, the approval of others was important to him. I wouldn't say he was delusional, just insecure."

"That was my feeling as well...he was very proud of how he found me...as if finding me was a bigger prize than killing me." She is still pacing back and forth in a rhythmic pattern. "Vlad said whoever hired him was impressed with how he found me. So he/she or they knew how he did it."

Nic interrupts her, "Why do you say he/she or they? Are you getting any thoughts on which it is?"

"They. Definitely leaning on 'they'...a collective group, small... I'm not sure he even knew but the inflection in Vlad's voice leads me to a 'they'. Could be it was an attempt by the originator to throw him or me off, but I don't think so."

Nic affirms, "I agree. Let's work with a 'they.' What is their objective?"

Cara continues her march, except the rhythm has slowed and she shakes her head at Nic's question. "Before we go there," she asks, "is it possible others were hired to find me, multiple contracts?" She directs the question to no one in particular.

Reed and Nic had discussed just that in the car, while she was zoning out. "It's possible," Reed says. In a preemptive move, he's already placed tracers on all of her social media accounts. Going forward, they will be able to see anyone trying to access those accounts who are not 'friends only'. He says this using air quotes, "I did it as soon as I heard how Vlad found you."

Cara turns to Nic, "What made Vlad leave your group in the late 80's? Specific event?"

Vlad had a sharp mind and was pretty focused in his analyst role most of the time. He wanted to be Nic's analyst, but because he did not perform consistently well, and was not always at the top of his game, Golov told him he needed to work harder to earn that right. Vlad would whine and insist he needed to work with Nic because it felt right. Golov found that a bit creepy, so he kept them mostly apart. Vlad finally left because he wasn't happy with his assignments, and they had no use for him as anything but an analyst. The odd thing is Vlad wasn't a good field agent. Nic thought it strange Vlad would go on to find work as a contract killer. "He really didn't seem the type to..."

"That's it!" Cara interrupts. "He's not the type, and I would venture to guess his forte was finding people, not killing them." No one speaks, so she continues to toss more ideas. "So let us go with this coincidence; the one person in this world to locate the Reflex in almost two decades happens to also have some strange obsession with you, Nic."

Nic tilts his head. "I did have quite a few fans. As feared as I was, I could draw people to me like a moth to the flame. Hence, the moniker's real origin, like the Dark Angel of Death, attractive, tempting, and alluring but ultimately deadly. I was apparently, judge and jury damning someone to hell for an eternity," Nic utters with disgust in his voice. "Nice, huh?"

Her eyes roam up and down over Nic's body. If getting to fondle that is hell, she means to live there indefinitely. Refocusing her thoughts back to the issue at hand, she makes a request. "Do the math thing in your head, Nic. You know where you calculate probability? What are the odds of the actual connection? Me, you, and Vlad. Furthermore, what are the odds that we would end up together in the apartment here in Berlin?"

Nic's face changes slightly as he thinks, and then his face grows blank. "Less than 1 percent on the first, fractional from that for the second scenario."

"Now calculate the odds that it wasn't a coincidence that Vlad was chosen to find me, but chosen because of my known connection to you."

Nic is ready with an answer, having already predicted Cara's direction. "46.54%."

Reed lets out a slow whistle. "I will take those odds in Vegas any day."

"So, this isn't necessarily about you, but more likely about me or us. That was actually my initial reaction and my reason for coming here, to be honest," Nic states matter-of-factly.

This admission gives both Cara and Reed pause. She eyes her husband carefully before speaking, "Your gut told you I was being led away from you, wasn't it?"

"Yes, and then I discounted it. I thought I was being super paranoid and possessive. Making it all about me instead of the threat to you," Nic confirms.

"That's very sweet of you, babe, but I'm thinking your instinct was on the money," Cara smiles at her husband. She wants to continue with this train of thought, however likely or unlikely. She was led to Berlin as a diversion, whether she was killed here wasn't important. What was important was Nic following her or losing her in the process.

"Well, Vlad was definitely surprised to see me. Shocked would be a better word, so he was unaware of our relationship, despite being privy to your fairly active social media posts," Nic adds.

Nodding, Cara agrees. "Yes, but if Vlad wasn't aware of your existence in my life...and he was just an average analyst...did he have the smarts to pick up on any possible connection?"

As usual, Nic is quick on the uptake. "Conceivably no, but the more intriguing question is would he have shared what he found in detail with the folks that hired him?" If they profiled Vlad based on his history, they knew he would want to share any and all details of his findings in order to garner more accolades and improve his self-worth.

Cara chimes in, "But you don't believe he would show all his cards initially. You think he waited until he had me in Berlin this morning so the timing would be to his advantage."

"Yes," agrees, Nic, "garner the praise when the risk for failure was minimized."

"Would you say you are a habitual hunter? One who uses patterns that can be mimicked or followed?" Cara inquires.

"No," Nic states vehemently.

"That's what I thought. Whether you follow me here or not, the odds of you ending up here with Vlad and me don't change. Is it still less than 1%?"

"Yes, but if you include any pre-knowledge he may have had of our association with each other, the odds go to 5%." They both nod to one another, easily following each other's train of thought.

Cara has her back to both men as she paces North away from them. "Stick with the diversion scenario, first. I am led away from you..." She turns 180 degrees to pace South when she notices Reed shaking his head, his lips quirking up in a mystified grin. She stops pacing, takes a sip from the water bottle and points inquiringly at Reed. "What is so humorous?"

Reed smiles more broadly and raises both his hands in a protective gesture. "I don't know how you're doing this, but I am enthralled by the both of you." He points, waving his finger between them. This process they have mastered with each other. "It's fucking remarkable." Nic and Cara have debunked more theories and explored more scenarios in the last five minutes than Reed's whole team has in the last six hours. He let his mind wander, and he couldn't think of a time when Cara was this good at strategizing. Partnering with Nic suits her, intellectually. "I was smiling because I'm seeing right here in front of me, my dream team of operatives. Together, you make a perfect pair. I was shaking my head thinking how I wish I had you both together 25 years ago."

Cara's stops abruptly, a look of horror forming across her features. She walks stiffly towards Nic and grabs his shirt, bunching it in her hand as she stares at Reed, asking him to elaborate.

He rises from the desk, knowing she's upset, and apologizes for the 25 years ago comment. He didn't mean to make a jab about their ages.

"No!" Cara barks out, "before that!"

Reed tries to think, and then it dawns on him, "You mean the dream team thing?" he offers. "I couldn't help myself. Just pointing out the astounding combination of talent and genetics between the two of you."

Cara's water bottle slips from her hand, and crashes to the floor. Nic rises so quickly from his chair, he knocks it over. Cara still has his shirt bunched in her hand, but she tightens it while Nic grabs her shoulders and roars, "It's 78%. It's fucking 78%!" He releases Cara's shoulders, brushes her hand off his shirt, rifles through his pocket for his phone, and runs out of the office.

Reed is left feeling more horrified than Cara looks. "What the hell did I just miss?" he shouts. Cara turns to him, and tears spring from her eyes as she slowly approaches.

"Sweetheart, tell me!" he demands, stalking towards her.

Cara is shivering and stuttering, "Missing motive...always about finding...diversion...Dream team...genetics."

Then it hits him, the impact taking his breath away. This is most likely the rationale for hiring Vlad. Reed grabs Cara as her knees buckle and she drops. He's immediately seized by the overwhelming need to protect. He lifts her up and cradles her against his chest. He guides her to his chair and sits down, placing Cara on his lap. He's wiping her tears, gently, murmuring, "It's going to be okay. They're going to be fine."

Cara stares at him with a look of loss he has never seen on her face, "My babies, Connor, someone wants my babies."

Bursting back into the room, Nic, uncontrolled and frantic, has panic written across his face. Reed has never seen Nic look like this before either. He informs them, "Sasha and Jake are on their way to the school to get all three kids out of class and bring them home. Jinx will meet them there. Sasha will phone when they're safely home. Carter is having the crew refile their flight plan to go directly to Cleveland Hopkins airport. We should be on board in 15 minutes."

Then he adds, "Carter may need your influence with the tower in Cleveland, and he would like permission to send some local boys to the house to await our arrival."

Reed stands up without a word, deposits Cara into her husband's arms and darts out of the room.

CHAPTER

SEVENTEEN

CARA CAN HEAR REED'S VOICE barking commands into his phone just outside the office. She's wrapped in her husband's arms and he is clinging to her so fiercely; she's having difficulty breathing. Nic is murmuring words, but Cara can't make them out. Maybe he's humming. Either way, she isn't sure who is comforting whom. They stay like this for what feels like hours but must only be minutes when Nic's phone rings.

He breaks the embrace and grabs his phone. He opens the connection but doesn't say a word. He nods his head, then in a low voice tells her, "They have the kids in the car. Jinx has secured the house. Their ETA is two minutes to the neighborhood gate." Cara exhales loudly, and dries her tears.

Having heard Nic's phone, Reed walks back into the office, his own cell phone still attached to his ear. Reed touches Nic's arm. "Tell them local FBI will be there within 20 minutes. Five men in two cars. Let your gate guard know. Code for the men is 'Sold the Renoir'." Reed walks away again to continue his conversation.

Nic relays the info to Sasha and tells him to text when they arrive and are completely secure in the house, and text again when the FBI

135

team arrives. He'll call Sasha back once they've boarded the plane and have their own ETA for Hopkins Field.

After he ends the call, he meets Cara's eyes. "Sold the Renoir? That's funny, actually." He presses his lips to hers with only the slightest pressure and she lets go of some of her tension.

Reed reenters the office. He apologizes that he can't get the FBI to the house sooner. "I don't have any agents in the area and the FBI has jurisdiction anyway and should be involved. But I had to go across agency lines to get them. Thus the delay."

Nic raises his hand at Reed, stopping him. Without thinking, he says, "Sasha and Jake are armed to the hilt. I have full faith in them until the FBI arrives."

Slightly alarmed, Reed peers questioningly at both Cara and Nic and inquires, "Why is your babysitter 'armed to the hilt' and this Jake? Isn't he Jinx's husband?"

"Uhhh, how much time do we have before the plane is ready?"

"They're fueling the plane now, but the flight plan is in, and the tower in Cleveland has been alerted. About 15 minutes to board. Enough time for you to answer the question," Reed barks with more authority.

Cara nods her approval to Nic and takes a seat. Nic closes the door and advises Reed he may want to be sitting when he hears their explanation.

"Why am I suddenly feeling like things are going to go from bad to worse?" Reed inquires as he heads back to the chair behind the desk. "Hit it, Nic."

With some apprehension, Nic takes a deep breath and begins. Seventeen years ago, after locating Cara in Cleveland, he returned to Moscow and made arrangements with Golov to take a three-week leave because he met a woman. "I never went back. I was a deserter, and as our relationship developed, I realized I needed to deal with Golov and my deliberate absence from my obligations."

Reed interrupts him, "Word on the street was Alexander Golov killed you, and was executed sometime later in the UK."

Nic ignores Reed and continues his story. He kept buying more time with Golov, using the truth as his excuse, but never divulging the girl's identity. He got about four months out of it by doing a few minor jobs for Golov in the States; but only out of necessity to keep his superiors at bay.

Golov allowed Nic the freedom because they had always been like family. So when Nic asked Cara to marry him, he knew it was time to come clean with his friend and handler. He wanted out but he needed to tell Golov in person. He owed him that much.

So Alexander made his way to the US under cover of his forged American papers and Nic met up with him in New York City. The meeting did not go the way Nic had hoped. "He basically went bat shit crazy on me," Nic recalls. "I suspect Cara got the same reaction from you; except I'm hoping you didn't take multiple swings at her like Golov did with me." Reed gazes over at Cara as if recollecting, but otherwise remains silent.

Nic and Alexander trashed a hotel room going nine rounds with each other. But when they were done, Golov just stared at him. They were both bruised and bleeding and he said, "Do you love her enough to risk everything?"

Nic told him, "1000 times over."

Golov nodded and said, "So be it," and quietly left. Nic and Cara married, and she was immediately pregnant with the twins. Nic sent another message to Golov informing him of the upcoming birth, but he didn't hear from him for months. Just a few weeks before the twins due date, Golov made an appearance.

Before Nic can go on, Cara stops him and looks pointedly at Reed. "Sweetheart, you're not going to like this next part but please try to stay calm. This all happened over 15 years ago. Just keep that in mind." She motions for Nic to continue, but as tough as he is, he's lost his nerve. She proceeds for him. "Connor, you know the Russians have nicknames like we do, right? Dick for Richard, Bob for Robert? Do you know the Russian nickname for Alexander?"

The silence in the room is epic. Nic can actually hear Reed's brain working it out.

The light bulb goes only a split second before Reed jumps to his feet and shouts, "GOLOV IS YOUR NANNY!" Reed sweeps everything off the desktop causing a huge crash.

The door swings open and Carter with a second agent barrel through with their guns drawn. Reed ignores them and continues his rampage trashing everything within arm's reach. Carter motions to the other agent to stand down, but he keeps his gun out. Cara is sitting calmly, legs crossed in the middle of the war zone, somehow avoiding the flying debris.

Reed is gesticulating wildly, and trying to form words with his mouth when, Carter whispers to Cara, "You seem to have this effect on men." He signals to the other agent, and they both leave, shutting the door behind them.

When Reed is finally able to speak, all that comes out is, "Someone better start talking, NOW!"

Nic decides he needs to man up here, so he picks up where he left off. Golov, or Sasha, showed up at their door two weeks before the kids were born. He offered a solution for Nic's desertion that would release him from any repercussions from their organization. Nic introduced him to Cara that day as his brother. And until today, he believed that's who Cara thought he was.

CARA TAKES OVER THE STORY FROM HERE. SHE DOESN'T KNOW, NOR DOES SHE care, what Nic and Sasha worked out, but by the time it was finished, Sasha was at the hospital with them while she gave birth to the twins. To say the man fell in love that day would be an understatement. Alexander Golov cradled her babies like they were his own, and swore to guard and protect them at all costs. It was at that moment, Cara knew he would be with them always, a welcome member of their family unit.

Ignoring Reed's scathing sneer at her, she calmly says to him, "You remember our conversation when you found out about Nic and me. That went completely sideways. So having just undergone an emergency C-section to deliver not one, but two babies, the last thing I wanted to deal with was telling you about Sasha."

Reed finally interjects, his volume intensifying with each syllable, "So, you're telling me you allowed the original Widow Maker of Russia, the notorious Alexander Golov, to reside under your roof and watch over your children since their birth! Have you completely lost your mind?!"

Cara takes a deep, cleansing breath, grasping at control. When she feels she's ready, she simply stands, leans into Reed's face over the desktop, and with measured calm, recites, "Yes, the great Widow Maker, the handler for the Dark Angel of Death, and unarguably one of the most lethal men in the world, helped raise our children. He has been the grandfather who dotes on them; the uncle who plays with them. He's been my right hand along with Nic in their mentoring and education, and most importantly, our children ADORE him. He has taught them everything that is good and kind and wonderful in this world, and I would not change a minute of it." And with that, she sits back down.

Reed is rendered momentarily speechless. So Nic continues his account. "Sasha turned to his contacts in the UK with a tale of the Dark Angels' demise for desertion at his hands. He then paid off an MI6 agent to claim knowledge of Golov's death. The stories took hold, and we have both been left alone by Mother Russia ever since."

Capable of speaking again, Reed glares at Cara and says, "I did a full background check on Sasha as soon as you told me about your new nanny. I didn't find any of this."

"Of course not," Cara acknowledges, "That part was all Jinx." Cara knew Reed would run a check, was actually counting on it. So she had Jinx hack into Sasha's original cover story, remove references to Sasha Andre, create a new surname for him, then fabricate a new online presence for her fictional nanny, changing him to a her in the process. Sasha has been transgender ever since.

"I don't think Sasha knows this," Cara admits, smiling at Nic because well, Sasha as a girl is just plain funny. She's never discussed it with Nic either. It's been that way for 15 years. The final requirement to keep the secret buried was to warn the twins not to speak about their Uncle Sasha to Uncle Reed because, she explained to them, it would make him jealous. "I feel awful including the kids in the ruse, but it couldn't be helped."

Now Nic is staring at her in disbelief right along with Reed. But before either man can speak, Carter steps in to announce the plane is ready to board.

Nic jumps to his feet and heads to the door, calling back over his shoulder, "Sasha just texted. They're all in the house, and the FBI agents are outside awaiting further instructions from Reed." He's still shaking his head at the details Cara just divulged as he grabs their stuff and makes his way onto the plane.

A petulant Cara watches her husband go. Nic is not happy with her, but it's not her fault she knows him so well. Just like Cara knew Reed would run a background check on her new babysitter, she knew Nic would never guess at her scheme to physically shield Sasha from Reed. He couldn't see past his bitter jealousy of Reed to imagine she was running her own game, so there was no reason to clue him in.

Cara never invited Reed to visit the house when Sasha was around, and there are no pictures of Sasha on display in her home. If she visited Reed with the kids, she generally left Nic home reasoning he and Sasha should spend some boy time together.

Of course, Nic wouldn't want Reed to meet Sasha, so without knowing it, he was helping her perpetuate the subterfuge. That's the beauty of manipulation. If done well, the minds you're controlling truly believe they are acting of their own accord.

CHAPTER

EIGHTEEN

REED IS STILL IMMOBILIZED WITH SHOCK, ANGER and disappointment. He glares at Cara from across the desk. In the last 24 hours he's gone from concern for her safety, to irritation at her disregard for the rules of engagement, to terrified at the possibility she might be dead. And now this revelation! For the first time in decades, he really wants to choke her.

Ignoring his outrage, she gets up and walks over to him, leaning in to wrap him in a hug. "Today was a day for big revelations. And as with any secret, these all started out with the best of intentions. Please know I never meant to hurt you, or jeopardize your position. I simply did what I needed to do to keep my family together. And Sasha is family to me-just like you are." Cara presses a quick kiss to his lips and pulls back from her embrace.

Reed grabs a fistful of her sweater with each hand and pulls her back in until they are nose-to-nose. There's more to her deception than Cara has owned up to. He can feel it. He's sure she has another motive for keeping Sasha a secret from him. He wants to shake it out of her, but she's had enough excitement for one day. He can wait for the truth.

He traces her lips with one finger before slowly shaking his head at her. He's partly to blame for this. He created this woman. He trained her, coached her, and taught her everything he knew. But there are aspects of Cara no one will ever comprehend. Some truly gifted, wicked impulses only she can navigate with such ease.

She must know she just dealt him a serious sucker punch; the kind of blow that could damage any relationship, even theirs. Her face turns resolute when she admits, "You know this morning, at the apartment, when I told Nic we've always known his real identity? He wasn't just mad because we never let on, he was infuriated because I knew, and yet...the moment I felt threatened I didn't turn to my husband who could obviously protect me ...I went running to you." Cara raises her eyebrows at him, tilts her head, leaves a small kiss over his heart, then walks out of the office to board the plane.

Well played, Cara, well played. Way to get in the last word while giving him a sense of priority. Soften the blow. Maybe she's become more dangerous than he ever gave her credit for.

THE PLANE IS A GULFSTREAM GV, A SMALL TWIN ENGINE JET COMMONLY used by US corporate types and Military VIPs. It's parked out in front of the hangar, engines running, readying for take-off. Although the aircraft has been assigned to Reed, he's very careful about using it strictly for business travel. At the same time, he's quite adept at maneuvering around the rules and avoiding red flags. She wonders what story Reed has spun to cover his unscheduled trip to Berlin, and now, a flight to Cleveland.

The plane is equipped with two rows of twin seats that slide and lock on a track so they can be relocated next to each other for private conversations. A conference table and series of chairs that swivel are located at the back of the plane as well as two plush first-class chairs, one on each side of the plane. The only bathroom is in the front of the plane behind the cockpit across from a small galley. The interior is unpretentious, but a vast improvement over the military transport, and certainly more luxurious than any commercial flight.

Cara spots Nic in one of the private rows when she boards the plane. He's typing on his iPad, his leather duffle on the seat next to him. She notices her carry-on bag is in the overhead compartment above.

Nic looks up and points at her bag, inquiring whether there's anything she needs in there for the flight. Cara shakes her head and he moves his duffle to the floor so she can sit.

"I'm sending an email to Sasha asking him to investigate a few leads while we're in the air." He sends the email request, closes the iPad and turns his full attention to Cara. "So...that went well," he says sardonically. "I'm a little afraid for round two in this game of Secrets and Lies we're playing."

Cara is worried what Round Two might bring as well.

Sensing her agitation Nic says, "You're compartmentalizing right now. You're worried about the kids, and that mind palace of yours is searching for answers."

"I am terrified for the kids right now." It's true she's doing a mental Google search for answers to this threat. She does feel better knowing Sasha, Jake and Jinx are protecting her children, but she's concerned with how long they can keep them safe. "You know we have to tell them the truth."

"Sasha asked me if we were going to come clean with the kids. The twins are asking questions. Not many, mind you. They're still teenagers with short attention spans, but they are curious." Nic gives Cara a light lip to lip caress and murmurs. "I love you. I...no WE...will make this right."

Just then Reed walks by them and snorts, "Are you two always making out?"

Cara retorts, "Not always!" and makes a face at him before locking lips with her husband again.

Reed drops his bag in a bin at the back of the plane and takes a seat in the row behind them. He lowers the seat back tray table and piles his laptop and phone on top. Apparently, he's immune to FAA regulations governing the use of seatback tray tables during take-off and landing. Cara turns to watch him get comfortable and soon hears the tap of keys as he begins to type.

She leans out into the aisle and spots Carter sitting in the first seat on the left. The agent who's been with him all day is seated across from him. He hasn't been introduced to her yet, but she's thinking he must be Reed's far guard. At least that's what she thinks he's called. Political VIPs are assigned a near guard and a far guard. The near guard acts as a personal bodyguard, and the far guard watches his subject's back from a short distance, checking for any incoming threats. Reed would have opted out of a near guard, considering it unnecessary with his training, but he may still respect the need for a far guard.

The flight attendant performs the usual safety demonstration, then the pilot announces they are getting into the queue for take-off.

CARA FALLS ASLEEP BEFORE THE PLANE IS OFF THE GROUND. LIKEWISE CARTER and Far Guard. Nic watches his wife sleep, hoping she'll nap the entire flight.

She's exhausted, and will need her strength for the kids once they land. He needs to figure out how he's going to break Part Two to Reed. He can hear Reed still typing furiously on his laptop behind him and figures this is as good a time as any. The pilot turns off the seatbelt sign and the flight attendant begins to make her way through the cabin towards him.

He flashes the attendant one of his killer smiles and requests a couple of pillows and blankets. When she returns, he asks for two glasses of bourbon, straight up, to be delivered to Reed's seat. Nic releases his seat belt and gently lays Cara down across his seat, placing the two pillows under her head. He maneuvers out into the aisle and covers her with the blankets.

He steps up to Reed and, pointing to the empty seat next to him, asks, "May I?"

Reed nods hesitantly then motions for Nic to sit. The attendant immediately arrives with the two glasses. She hands them to Nic, who keeps one and passes the other to Reed.

Reed narrows his eyes and takes a sip. "What's this for?"

"In Russia, it's customary to start an important exchange with a drink."

"Do you know what the percentage of alcoholism in men over age 45 is in Russia, Nic?"

"I'm well aware, Reed." Then he toasts, "To new beginnings, I hope."

Reed is still eyeing him warily, but he takes another sip of the bourbon. He swishes it around his mouth and grins devilishly at Nic. "Angel's Envy bourbon. How serendipitous."

Nic matches him sip for sip, saying nothing. They both sit looking forward, waiting each other out. When their glasses are empty, Nic catches the eye of the attendant, waving his tumbler in the universal gesture for a refill.

While they're waiting for their second round of drinks, Nic decides to break the silence and offer an olive branch. "I want to sincerely thank you for keeping my presence in the States all these years a secret." Nic understands now what a risky venture it has been for Reed and by extension, Cara. Aware of Nic's true identity, and never letting on, was akin to harboring a criminal.

If he had wanted to, Reed could have made one phone call to the SVR and severed Nic and Cara's relationship. But he didn't. Reed never got in their way. He could have made Nic's life hell, but instead he looked the other way. "When Cara told you about me, I know you two must have come to blows over it, figuratively, I hope. I need you to know how thankful I am."

Reed continues to stare straight ahead. "I would do anything for her. She loved you and I knew it. What could I do?" Reed shrugs as he continues, "You're a parent now. If Mia comes home with a boy you dislike, but she claims to love him, what would you do?"

Without hesitation Nic declares, "I would kill him."

This elicits a small chuckle from Reed. "Very funny, but you would break your daughter's heart? I think even the Dark Angel would try to avoid that."

"That's true."

"Don't get me wrong. I never gave C my blessing. I simply let her go."

THERE HAS NEVER BEEN ANYTHING SIMPLE ABOUT HIS RELATIONSHIP WITH Cara. They share a closeness that is unparalleled, odd from its origin, progressing into the abnormal as the years rolled by. She has been his companion, his partner, his confidante and his closest friend. For reasons neither of them can interpret, they understand each other on a molecular level. He realized that the instant they met.

Cara's a total pain in his ass, but she's also easy to be with. She can anticipate Reed's thoughts and feelings, and through her wisdom and support, she's made him a better man. He'd never had such a devoted friend, and normal or not, appropriate or not, he's run every move he's made by her first, almost since the beginning.

"I know my wife pesters you on a day-to-day basis, much more often than she does me." Nic admits he's peeked at some of the texts they send each other all day long. "You two act like the old married couple, devoted to each other but bickering and nitpicking at every opportunity." Reed laughs at the apt description. "By the way, why do you call her C?" Nic asks.

"That's an easy one." When Reed first met her, she was Cara Bianco, a coed attending the University of Connecticut. When he recruited her to the Agency, they agreed to keep her employment there a secret. Her parents would have freaked out; her mother, particularly, would have gone ape shit with worry if she knew what her daughter was really doing.

Consequently, he created paper and digital trails for Cara Bianco that maintained she was employed by World Bank as an assistant in the International Banking department. He set up an office for her in their building in DC with a phone and voicemail where her friends and family could leave messages. Cara received a check from the bank every other week deposited directly into a checking account in her name. She even received a couple of promotions during her tenure at the World Bank.

Reed created another alias for Cara to work under at the Agency. There she was Chase Bennett with a manufactured past, education and a new social security number. No one at the Agency, other than Reed, knew her as anyone else. In the beginning, though, he had some issues remembering to call her Chase. He kept catching himself calling out 'Car', so, he nicknamed her 'C', instead. Over time, Chase became easier to remember, but he continued to call her C. "Which thankfully became a habit, because when it was time for Chase to go back to being Cara, I would've been fucked."

Nic smiles at this. "I was thinking it was far more sentimental. May I ask another question?"

"Shoot. Hopefully, they're all this easy."

"Your published bio says you went to Harvard undergrad, and then did a year at their Law school. You eventually completed your J.D. at Georgetown. If that's all true, how did you and Cara meet at UConn?"

Reed takes a deep breath, stalling while he thinks about how to respond. Those first few months after meeting Cara changed his life, in every imaginable way. How does someone explain to the husband what a profound impact his wife had on another man's life? If ever there was a time for diplomacy... "After I left Harvard I joined the FBI, in the Hartford office. My first field assignment, when I was only an analyst, was to assist in the investigation of a series of rapes at UConn."

Nic's eyebrows shoot up but Reed cuts his concern off quickly. "My job was to interview anyone associated with the victims; witnesses and such." Cara was his third interviewee on his first day. To say he was shaken up after that interview would be a serious understatement. "She marched in, yanked the file out of my hands, and read through it before I could stop her." Of course, the fact she was disarmingly beautiful may have contributed to his loss of control over the meeting. "Before I could protest, she had processed the info and was spewing out conjecture and possible leads, all of them viable."

Cara was already familiar with the rapist's MO since she had found his fourth victim. The girl was a housemate of hers so she was particularly invested in nailing the perp. "She blackmailed me. She promised not to tell anyone I allowed her to look at the file if I let her assist in the investigation. My first chance to prove my worth in the office and I get Cara Bianco stuck up my ass!"

Nic is stifling a laugh. Reed wants to gloss over as many details as possible so he decides on a comedic approach over full disclosure. "A fifth rape occurred while I was investigating some of C's ideas so the Special Agent in charge decided I needed to go undercover as a college student."

From the moment he entered the campus as a coed, every move he made on the investigation was orchestrated by Cara. "We had decided the perp was mostly likely a frat boy so I masqueraded as her boyfriend from Harvard so I could get into the frat parties. I was only 24 at the time so it wasn't a stretch.

"She kept a calendar of each weekend's frat parties, decided which ones we would attend, and chose the appropriate attire for me. So, not only did she dictate my schedule, she's going to tell me what to wear! And what did I do? Exactly what she told me to do!"

They both dissolve into quiet laughter at this, the two bourbons and 35,000-foot altitude surely contributing. They shush each other, trying not to wake the others, until Reed motions for Nic to relocate to the conference table at the back of the plane. He waves to the flight attendant for another round as he follows Nic to a new seat. "So we spent the next 6 weeks as a couple with me on campus every weekend to attend the frat parties."

Nic stutters, "Wwwait, you spent the night with her?"

Reed turns serious now, knowing where Nic's mind has gone. "She was a senior, so she had a single, a tiny room with a double bed in it. The first night we were to spend together I panicked because, well what is she expecting from me? Before I could overthink it, she said..."

From directly behind them Cara yells, "Don't panic, Connor, keep your clothes on. Nothing is going to happen!" He and Nic are so startled, Nic spills the remaining bourbon across the table and Reed bangs his knee on the table leg.

CHAPTER

NINETEEN

N IC SHOUTS AT HER, "HOW the hell did you..." pointing ahead of him, and then behind him.

"I guess sleeping with you has its benefits. Ghost by injection," Cara teases, raising her eyebrows at Nic.

"Seriously, what the fuck, C, you were sleeping two rows up. You made me bang my knee and Nic wasted a perfectly good drink," Reed whines.

"The bourbon might explain how I got behind you both and you never noticed. How dare you drink without me." She catches the flight attendant eye and raises three fingers. Might as well join the boys.

The shock of her sudden appearance, having worn off, Nic makes a rolling motion with his hand. "Keep talking, buddy. There has to be more. What did Cara do?"

Cara heard most of the conversation and was thankful Reed was less than forthcoming on some of the details. Although they became friends ten years before she ever met Nic, she's been reluctant to explain the fiercely powerful connection she still shares with Reed. Or is it just too hard to articulate? It's time however Nic understood why Reed is so important to her. In fact it's long overdue.

So, after a nod from Reed, Cara takes up the story. "To start with, I called him Connor." Reed covers his face with his hands and growls. She giggles, "Reed doesn't like to be called Connor."

Reed confirms through gritted teeth, "Connor is my father's name! I go by Reed."

Cara waves off his whiny response. "Our first evening was spent alone together in bed talking for hours; Reed confessing to his Daddy issues and me venting over my crazy family." Reed flicks her head at the dig before grasping her hand.

That evening and all the ones that followed were filled with revelations about themselves, their family relationships, their passions, their hopes and dreams. They laid the foundation of their enduring relationship during this time, and although they became intimately familiar with each other both physically and emotionally, their relationship was never sexual.

Reed admits, "I told her that night, and every one after, shit I had never confessed to anyone. I still struggle to understand why, but I admit it was oddly cathartic." He releases the death grip he has on her hand and subconsciously strokes his thumb over her palm.

Narrowing his eyes at their clasped hands, Nic inquires calmly, "You mean to tell me you had my wife in bed with you for a dozen nights and you didn't try to fuck her?"

Cara winces at his choice of words, and then glares at her husband. "Not every hetero relationship is based on sex. What is wrong with you?" But she knows nothing is wrong. It's a valid question for Nic because sex is at the core of their relationship. If they're fighting with each other, they have sex. If they're happy, they have sex. If they are feeling vulnerable, they have sex. It's their cure all. It works for them. And honestly, it's pretty fucking awesome.

Alarmed, Reed, responds without thinking. "I was a 24-year-old with a strong sex drive. Of course I wanted to fuck her. But that would've been inappropriate on so many levels. I went to bed stiff, and woke up the same way, but between feeling guilty for involving her in the investigation, and knowing I wasn't hanging around after the assignment, it was just not possible."

Nic murmurs, "How gallant of you."

"Precisely!" Cara shouts, but then points to Reed. "White. Knight." She cocks her head at her husband. "Get it?" It was the name Cara jokingly bestowed on Reed during her time at the Agency and it stuck. Pretty soon everyone was referring to them as the Reflex and her White Knight.

"Anyway, for the next six weeks, we went to all the frat parties but nothing happened." On the seventh weekend, though, they decided to change things up. They arrived at the party together as usual, but quickly separated once inside.

Cara partied and danced with her sorority sisters while Reed flirted with another group of girls. Pretty soon a boy she didn't know asked her to dance. "He was reserved and unassuming but there was something about him," she muses.

Reed scowls at her, remembering the night. "C decided that it was safe to go with this kid into the backyard alone. He told her she could help him retrieve more beer from a cooler back there. Before I knew what was happening, I lost sight of her."

Sighing, Cara recounts the life altering events that followed. The boy, Ed Grotto, took her to the darkest corner of the yard and pulled a knife on her. He was suddenly crazed, telling her she had been the one he was looking for and all those other girls were mistakes.

Cara was fairly confident Reed followed her outside, but she couldn't see him in the dark. She didn't call out to him because she didn't want Ed to know he was there.

"When I got to the yard, I heard Ed telling her she was his and they would be together now, forever. And I knew C had found our serial rapist." Reed is shaking his head at her. "I pulled my gun from my boot and cautiously approached them. I could see the knife in Ed's hand, but he was too close to C for me to take a shot."

Reed studies her for a moment before turning his gaze back to Nic. Poor Connor. He looks as grim as he did that night so long ago.

"I knew Ed intended to make a move so I bolted towards them. Before I reached him though, C had stepped forward, forcing his knife hand away from her with her forearm, while simultaneously jabbing an elbow into his throat. She spun back, landed a kick to his nuts, and as he was going down, she grabbed his head and forced him face first into her knee. By the time I reached them, Ed writhing on the ground, blood pouring from his nose, and C had the knife in her hand. She was screaming, 'I'll cut your nuts off for what you did!'" Reed concludes.

"I still haven't forgiven you for stopping me. Slicing off his balls was the least he deserved," Cara intones.

"SPD moment?" Nic questions his wife.

Reed responds, "Her Sicilian Personality Disorder aside, there is a process in this country, and I certainly wasn't going to have her jeopardize that process, and get him off on a technicality. I wanted Ed Grotto put away for a long time. I cuffed him, read him his Miranda rights, and called it in."

Nic blinks several times in reaction to their tale. And Cara continues, "While Reed and I were waiting for the police, the adrenalin wore off and I began to freak out."

Nic is about to offer her some comfort but Reed cuts him off. "She wasn't losing it over Ed. She was a mess because she didn't want her mother to find out."

Comprehension dawns on Nic's face. He's had 17 years of dealing with her nutty family, from her father's boisterous personality to her mother's strict, often overprotective approach when it came to her children. Nina, her mother, would have shit a brick if she found out her daughter put herself in harm's way. Cara learned early on the less her parents knew about her life, the better. She instructed her younger sister on the benefits of selective disclosure, as well. It was never about disrespect. It was always about survival.

"Reed agreed to connect me to the story only as Ed's last victim.

No one, friends, family or otherwise would ever know of my part in the investigation or my assistance with the case."

Nic is now glaring at Reed. "Just to be clear then, you took all the credit for the capture? Your career catapulted off the back of Cara's ordeal."

Cara jumps in then to defuse the tension. "Nic, he only did what I asked. Neither of us would have survived the repercussions were the real story to get out. If a side effect of our deception was the launching of Reed's career, then so be it. It made no difference to me."

"Where is this Ed now?" Nic demands.

"He's doing life in a state penitentiary with no possibility of parole. I keep tabs on him and will be notified if that ever changes. Unlike C, I'm convinced she was his intended target all along," Reed asserts as he glances over at her.

They've often argued this point over the years. She believes Ed was simply nuts, but Reed is not so sure. Ed changed his MO with her, but Cara thinks he just didn't get the chance to complete his objective.

She can almost hear her husband's scrambled thoughts as he processes what he's just learned. Before he can make any further judgment, she calmly adds, "Nic, my love, you are the first person to know this story. Reed and I have never shared it...with anyone."

Nic takes in a deep breath and exhales, "What happened to you, Reed, after the ordeal?"

Reed slumps forward over the table and hisses out, "Give me a moment before I divulge federal secrets to a former high-level KGB operative, whose live-in nanny was once considered the most notoriously cunning handler and spy in Russia's Foreign Intelligence history."

TWENTY

BEFORE THE TRIAL WAS EVEN over, Reed received a call from the CIA. The man had heard of the UConn case and wanted Reed to come to Langley to discuss an opportunity that had just arisen. They were starting a new program to train a younger, more 'hip' group of operatives to address newer concerns they believed would arise from the predicted fall of the Soviet Union. This modern team would be autonomous within the Agency with only a few guidelines to follow. It was a trial operation that would be re-evaluated after two years.

While responding to interview questions for this opportunity, Reed couldn't help but think about Cara and the manipulative approach she used to insert herself into the rape investigation. His answers were influenced less by his Quantico training, and more by the lessons he learned and the rules he broke working with Cara to find a serial rapist.

When he was asked how he would choose a team, if he were to head up the operation, he was floored by the question. He just assumed the opening was for a team member, not the team lead. Again, he thought of Cara before he answered. She would expect nimble, out of the box thinkers, not afraid of change and ready to ditch the old school ways. They'd be open to new technology as it becomes available, and not fear innovative approaches to training.

His answers were apparently spot-on because he was offered the assignment and signed a non-disclosure before heading back to Connecticut.

On the ride home the irony hit him like a freight train. He just secured the job of a lifetime because of what he experienced over the last four months with Cara. Did he interview as Cara, or as the man he had become because of her?

"It was then I realized what a profound affect she had on my life. I was a different person; changed because of her. I no longer felt guilty for what happened at UConn, or how I handled it, because in the end, we got the job done. I understood then some rules are meant to be broken, and others can be bent if your gut and intuition lead you there."

Reed can feel the hostility rolling off Nic but he doesn't care. After all, he is not the one referred to as the Dark Angel of Death.

"You got the team leader job, then dragged Cara in," Nic states bitterly. But before he can correct Nic, Reed feels Cara's foot pressing against his under the table. He glances over to see her scratch her hand and then her nose.

During the course of their training, Reed and Cara developed a series of hand signals to silently communicate with each other. She had just signaled him to omit from the script and quickly summarize. Then he catches her putting two fingers into her mouth, the signal to spoon feed. He's not entirely sure why Cara doesn't want him to share the events of the pivotal evening he decided to hire her. But, he understands from her signal she needs time to break this story down into smaller pieces for Nic. Reed touches his ear in confirmation.

CARA LETS OUT A SIGH, LOUDER THAN SHE INTENDED, RELIEVED REED understood. After all of the confessions today, she's happy to slow walk this one. Cara cringes at the thought of Nic's response to the full story. The atmosphere is already too highly charged so the sensible solution is to wait. For now, they'll just give him the highlights.

Reed did not hire her immediately after accepting the CIA position. It was in fact six weeks later, during the summer after graduation. Reed put her up when she came to DC to interview for a job at World Bank. The interview was a bust, but the events that followed spurred Reed to add her to his team, commencing her employment with the CIA.

That's as much as she wants to reveal for now so she turns the subject to Jinx and how they met. "I assume you know Jinx worked for Reed, too?"

"Eleanor Evans, aka The Jinx? Yes, I know she was your analyst. Did you hire her?" Nic inquires.

Reed answers for her. "No, Jinx was already employed by the Agency when I was hired. She was a brilliant analyst and white hat with burgeoning cyber technology. Still is. But no one would work with her. Apparently, her intel was always on the money, but one thing or another would go wrong in the field. Hence the nickname. There was nothing the woman couldn't hack into though, so the whole bad mojo thing aside, I knew I wanted her for my team."

Cara breaks in, "Reed sent Jinx to collect me from the lobby the first time I ventured into Langley." Cara finds herself grinning at the memory. Jinx was wearing a dowdy navy-blue suit with a white shirt. She was a blonde bombshell trapped in plain Jane clothes. Cara, of course, was wearing ripped jeans and a halter-top. She thought she was having lunch with Reed not heading to an interview.

By the time she and Jinx arrived at Reed's office, Cara was in love. Jinx chatted her up the entire way. She asked Cara if Reed was available because in her mind, he was by far, the hottest guy at the

Agency. She even went so far as to warn Cara she was determined to get into his pants. Of course that never happened, but Jinx did become Cara's right hand, her roommate and her dearest friend.

"Jinx left me at Reed's office, which by the way, was the shittiest office I have ever seen." He had a gun metal gray desk and one metal folding chair. The walls were painted a dull gray like the rest of the facility. The whole place was joyless and depressing. "It was *Fifty Shades of Grey* without the fun sex and bondage."

Reed laughs and declares, "And from that day forward, you became my best employee, my best friend, and the biggest pain in my ass."

"Wait!" Nic stops them. "That's it? You just said, yes, I will be an agent?"

Cara looks at her husband in disbelief. "Nic, besides sex, how many times have I just said yes to you in almost 17 years of marriage?"

Nic ponders the question before answering, "I can count on one hand."

"Exactly. I said yes to Reed, with a short list of conditions."

"Short list!" Reed snorts. "Try like twenty conditions. Besides the whole Cara Bianco needs an alias and separate employment in case her family asks questions, she said she would not wear the uniform."

Those hideous suits in blue or black and the white, gray or light blue tailored shirts? A travesty. "Who could feel inspired in those. You wanted to instill your team with inventiveness and creativity, you needed to let them wear what they wanted," Cara argues.

Reed concedes, "This, I agreed, was a good point." She also wanted artistic freedom for her teammates, which meant letting them choose to paint their area any color they wanted. All of her conditions were of course, calculated to secure maximum results from Reed's team. "C had changed the look and feel of an entire project within twenty fucking minutes of stepping into the building."

"Jinx was also looking for a roommate to share rent, so I had a job, a place to sleep, and a new name all before lunch. How awesome was that?" Cara takes a gulp of the bourbon.

Nic is looking at her like she has three heads. "Just like that. No formal background. No training. No military exercises. Nothing."

"Jesus, Nic, don't start with your Russian angst." She explains to Reed, "I call Nic, Moody and Sasha, Broody. I attribute it to all the dark, torturous Russian training they went through. The KGB produces unmitigated killing machines, but at the slightest provocation of emotion, they fall apart. Total angst."

Turning to her husband with a look of disdain, "And to answer your question, Nic, yes, I took the job without over thinking it. I was unemployed, and living with my parents! I was between purgatory and hell. I would have worked for you Russians to get the hell out of there!"

Nic lowers his head and says very quietly, "I'm not Russian."

Both Reed and Cara have the same visceral reaction. "What?!" they shout in unison.

CHAPTER

TWENTY-ONE

NIC LOOKS UP AT THEM, AN UNREADABLE expression on his face. "Did I tell you I was Russian when we met?"

He told Cara he was a freelance interpreter who traveled all over the world working for various clients. He inferred he was educated in Europe, and that's where he began his career. Of course, she never pressed him for details, just as he never dug into her banking job. Both of their jobs required international travel, and their discussions only went as deep as destinations they'd been to and plans for future travel together.

"Um, no. You only said you were born in Germany, but I assumed that was a cover." Cara finally responds.

"Not a cover. I'm German."

They continue to stare at him in shocked puzzlement. He watches his wife, carefully. Nic was always honest with her about his lack of family and his lonely childhood, although she never probed for more details. His only omission was the real reason for his travels. Had she requested more details on either subject, he was prepared to share them, but again, she never did.

Shifting his eyes from Cara's face to Reed's and back again, he decides it's time to share those specifics.

Nic was born in Berlin, coincidentally, but on the wrong side. His parents were teachers at the University. He's pretty sure they both taught sciences, but they were also gifted musicians. He was an only child and he remembers feeling loved and protected.

His parents adored entertaining guests in their home. Sometimes, they would play music and dance and sing with their guests and sometimes, the group would engage in vigorous debates over books and propaganda. But the atmosphere was always cheerful.

One night, when Nic was eight years old, he was asleep in his parents' bedroom when he woke to the sound of a loud argument. He thought his parents were having one of their lively debates with their friends, but the arguing turned to pleading, and he can't recall why, but he crawled under the bed, afraid. And that's when he heard the two gunshots. Nic froze, too scared to do or say anything.

Cara gets up from her chair and makes her way around the table to sit on Nic's lap. She puts her arms around him resting her hand on his heart. Reed remains motionless, completely engrossed.

Thinking back, Nic was so frightened. He stayed under the bed until he heard the neighbors calling his name. He crawled out and, although they ran to him to try to cover his eyes, he still saw them, his parents. Someone had shot them in the head, execution style. The police came and they questioned him, but he was so traumatized, he couldn't speak.

He was placed in an orphanage after that. The boys there were cruel, telling him he would die in that place because he was too old to be adopted, and no one would want him. But still, he didn't speak.

Only two weeks went by before a Russian couple arrived at the orphanage to claim him. They told him he would be coming home with them, and that everything was going to be fine. They spoke very quietly to him and he knew enough Russian to make out what they were telling him. At the time, however, Nic wasn't sure what was scarier, going with two complete strangers, or staying at that wretched place. But still, he did not speak.

They brought him home to a nice apartment in St. Petersburg; Leningrad back then. They told him he would be called Nicolae, and his new last name would be Andrychenko. He had his own room. They bought him books and treated him well, but he couldn't say thank you.

"I was sent to a school for children who are...special," Nic admits. The teachers tried diligently to get him to converse. His new adoptive parents would come in every afternoon to check on his progress. One day about six months in, the school fire alarm went off. Nic could smell smoke and knew enough to use one of the fire exits to vacate the building. As he ran towards the door, he noticed the teachers running from the building, leaving the more helpless children behind.

He turned back to retrieve the kids who remained and made sure they exited safely. His parents heard about the fire and arrived to find him escorting the children out, and talking to them in perfect Russian, trying to keep them calm. They couldn't believe what they were hearing. They cried, "You can talk. And you speak fluent Russian. How?"

Nic just told them, "I listen."

That's when they moved him to an elite private school for children who are the other kind of special. He thrived in the new classrooms, studying math, languages and the sciences. He even had access to books normally banned in the Soviet Union. He loved it there.

Nic didn't interact much with the other children. He had difficulty making friends and was happy enough by himself, just learning. Life was good with the Andrychenko's. But his happiness was short-lived. They died in a car crash seven years after adopting him. He was only fifteen.

Stopping his story, he looks up at Cara. A lone tear runs down her cheek. He wipes it away and says, "Same age as Max and Mia."

Cara wraps her arms around his neck, burying her head in his chest.

After a moment's silence Reed gently asks, "Nic, what happened after they died?"

"I didn't even have time to grieve." He lost everything when they died, his home, his school, and the life he had come to enjoy. The private education was no longer affordable. Because Nic's grades and attitude were so exemplary, the headmaster recommended him for a private military school. He was told to pack one bag, with anything he valued, and was shipped off to an all-boys military academy located outside of Moscow.

He discovered quickly it was no academy of learning. It was a training facility. Nic was highly intelligent for his age. He was already fluent in seven languages, was doing math at a graduate level, and studying chemistry, physics and biology at the college level. His IQ tested over 180, but he had never been in a fistfight. He was a pacifist, a scholar.

Nic looks at his wife and again digresses to the present, "It would be like throwing Max in prison now, and telling him his survival is in his own hands." Cara shudders and even Reed reacts with a frown on his otherwise impassive face.

Nic was placed in a large open dorm room shared by 13 other boys his age. The boys tormented Nic, taking shots at him whenever possible. He was pretty beat up by the end of his first week there.

He was able to hold his own, one on one, because he was bigger than most of the boys in his residence. So by the end of his first week, they started to come at him in groups of two, three or four. Nic was at a breaking point. He would rather die than continue to endure the beatings.

He was ready for death when four boys cornered him in a quiet hallway. They taunted him, calling him pretty boy, mama's pet, and geek. They held him down and gave him his worst beating yet. Just when he believed it was finally his day to die, the boys suddenly stopped.

They had all turned to stare at a lone older boy who had entered the hallway. He was bigger than all of them, his face a cold, hard mask. One of the younger ruffians who was holding Nic down watched the boy approach wordlessly and asked him what he wanted. The older boy responded, "I want you to leave and give me the pretty boy."

One of the boys who had been hitting Nic challenged the older boy saying, "You will need to fight us if you want him." Before he completed his sentence, the older boy punched him in the throat, then kicked his legs out from under him and the second boy went down. The third boy came at him from behind, but the older boy anticipated the move and spun, connecting with an upper cut to the boy's jaw. The boy holding Nic down ran away.

Bleeding from multiple cuts, and now alone in the hallway with the frightening older boy, Nic got to his knees trying to determine his next move. The older boy yanked him up by his shirt and pulled him outside the building to a dark corner. Nic was hurt and scared and couldn't muster the energy to fight him.

Then the most unexpected thing happened. The boy declared, "I've heard stories about you; that you're extremely intelligent. Is that true?" Nic wasn't sure how to respond, so he just shrugged.

"You've never been taught how to fight?"

Nic admitted his only education had been academic. He doesn't know what made him tell this menacing young man the truth. As soon as he said it, he wondered if he had made a huge error in judgment.

The older boy began to examine Nic's injuries. Nic flinched at his touch, but the boy didn't take notice. He was rough, but somehow gentle at the same time. Then he backed up and simply stated, "I will teach you to fight, Nicolae. Those other boys won't bother you for a while as you are under my protection now. But that will only last so long. It will be hard work, but you must train with me every chance you get. Do you understand?"

Nic was stunned by the offer, but somehow wanted to put his

trust in this unexpected ally. Then again, what choice did he have? He nodded yes, and then said thank-you.

The boy offered his hand and introduced himself. "My name is Alexander. My friends call me Sasha. You will need to earn that right."

Silent tears roll down Cara's cheeks as she listens to Nic's tale. She's clutching his shirt with both hands.

Alexander found time to work with Nic every day the next week. They started with the basics of hand-to-hand combat. Nic caught on quickly, emulating Alexander's moves with ease. But more importantly he began to understand the psychology behind the fighting. His brain processed the mechanics and came up with strategies to keep him one step ahead of his opponent. Alexander was impressed with his progress and, recognizing Nic's brains over brawn mentality, recommended some books on the art and science of combat.

Nic read every one of them over the weekend between other schoolwork and training. The following Monday, he was feeling more self-assured. He was in the commissary, eating alone at a table, when Alexander approached him with another boy his age. Alexander pointed at Nic and told the other boy who was much larger than Nic, "This pretty face has angered me. Please, teach him a lesson."

Bewildered by this turn in Alexander, Nic questioned why would he ask another boy to fight Nic? Before he could make sense of it, or get up from the table, the other boy was throwing a punch at his head. Then, the most amazing thing happened inside Nic's mind. He began mapping his immediate surroundings in search of possible weapons, computing distance to his adversary and calculating mass, speed, and volume, all at a lightning pace.

He grabbed his food tray and blocked the punch to his head. Then he flung the tray hard into the boy's nose, giving himself time to get up from the bench. He was pummeling the boy's torso when he heard Alexander say, "Stop! This is the wrong pretty boy. Sorry.

My mistake." Then he leaned to whisper in Nic's ear, "Now, you may call me Sasha."

"Then, with this smug smile on his face, he just turned and walked away, leaving me standing there," Nic concludes with a grin in memory.

"HOLY SHIT!" Reed responds.

"I know, right? The commissary was full that day, so lots of witnesses to the fight. Needless to say, I was left alone for a few more weeks."

He continued his one-on-one training with Sasha and for the first time Nic had a true friend. Sasha was easy to be around. He understood Nic in a way the others didn't. Sasha was also a good match intellectually and they found they had much in common.

"Interesting," Reed muses. "So what happened after that first year?"

"I learned everything I could from him. I trained hard. He taught me everything he knew about hand to hand, guns, knives, all aspects of weaponry. Then we moved on to the more psychological aspects needed for covert operations, concealment, blending in, and role playing."

Sasha threw everything he could at teenaged Nic, explaining that he'd need these skills if he wanted one of the prized undercover assignments in the KGB. Otherwise he'd end up in a much less glamorous military position like most of the other boys. KGB covert ops offered plenty of freedom and latitude that was not available in the military. "He explained the whole 'game' to me, making sure I understood what my limited options were, and which would ultimately suit me best."

When Sasha turned 18, he was sent away for special training. Nic didn't understand at the time what made this training so special, but he did notice only the better-looking boys were chosen. The Sasha who returned four months later was a colder and harder version of the boy who left.

Nic often pressed Sasha for details of his time away, and when he finally opened up, he admitted the training was sexual in nature. Sasha described it as the worst experience of his life. Nic didn't understand at the time but would later find out about the cruel and degrading assaults on the men in the program meant to teach them sexual stamina, control and the 'art' of seduction. They had come to call it Whore School.

About a year later, Sasha was assigned a position with the KGB. By then, Nic was 17 years old and was targeted for Whore School in six months. Just before Nic was to leave for that training, he received an order to report to KGB headquarters in Moscow. When he arrived, it was Sasha who greeted him, explaining that Nic's expertise, high intellect and willingness to advance made him an excellent choice for a fast-track to the KGB.

He would later find out Sasha had pulled a multitude of strings to get him out of Whore School and placed on Sasha's team. They shared an apartment together, and have been together since.

Sasha was an expert at hiding in plain sight. He could alter his appearance completely and become almost anyone. Nic was as talented, but his size, his blonde hair and blue eyes, made successful covert missions in some countries near impossible. He was, also, too noticeable. He stops to ask Cara, "You and Jinx tease that I'm too beautiful? Well, in reality, I'm just too easy to recall. Not exactly an attribute in a deep cover situation, as you know."

Sasha's assignments were generally long term; he would sometimes be gone for months. It was after one assignment in England Sasha came back damaged, not physically or mentally, but emotionally. "He's never talked about it, but after that, he was reassigned as a handler, and I was assigned to him. The rest you know."

Wiping away her tears with her sweater sleeve, Cara suddenly narrows her eyes and jolts her head toward Reed. "Nic introduced Sasha to me as his brother and Sasha IS his brother."

"Sasha protected me from the time I was a scared 15-year-old boy. He is the big brother I never had. As my handler, he made sure I was given the best missions and assigned the most highly trained back up. You understand now, when I had the opportunity to give him something in return, a family, a life and love, I didn't hesitate to repay him." This earns him a big hug from his wife.

She pulls away to question him from her position on his lap, "The apartment you purchased in Berlin; the one we were in this morning? It's the one you shared with your parents, isn't it? Where they were murdered?"

An overwhelming sadness seizes him. "Yes. I've been in search of a motive for my parents' murder for years."

At every opportunity, he worked on their cold case but his investigations turned up nothing. He never gave up, but the more time went by, the harder it became. When the apartment went up for rent, he took it thinking he might find a clue. He stumbled on a number of secret hiding places, but found nothing of interest inside of them. Eventually, the apartment building was converted to condos and he bought it.

Reed's turn, "And do you suspect the Andrychenkos' death might not have been an accident?"

"How do you put it, there's no such thing as a coincidence? The question becomes, are the two incidents related, and was I being manipulated? The math leans hard to a yes."

"Last question from me," Cara states. "If Nicolae Andrychenko was your adopted name, what is your given name?"

The choking emotions he felt telling them his story come back. He slowly exhales and answers, "Herrmann. Maximillian Herrmann. My father was also Maximillian. My mother was Maria Herrmann."

CHAPTER

TWENTY-TWO

CARA IS RENDERED ALMOST SPEECHLESS. SHE whispers, "Max and Mia."

"Yes," is all Nic can get out before breaking down.

Reed rises immediately, excusing himself, but not before giving each of them a shoulder squeeze as he passes behind them. Cara tangles her fingers into Nic's hair, pulling his head down and cradling him to her chest. She is still sitting on his lap and neither of them speak.

It's all so dreadful. Cara always knew Nic's angst came from somewhere. She just didn't know the details. Does the knowing make it better? It makes it real. She feels his pain right now, and his shame. Why shame? He didn't ask for that life. Maybe the shame of an eight-year-old boy who believes he could have saved his parents. Or the shame of a grown man who thinks he should have been able to solve their murder?

She gently cups Nic's face with her hands and brings her lips to his. She gives him their soft lip-to-lip caress before placing her cheek against his. "I love you. Thank-you for sharing all of that with us. I didn't think it possible, but I may love you more for it."

Nic shifts her body so she is straddling him. He pulls her in until they are chest to chest. He looks into her eyes and gives her quick, soft kisses that promptly grow longer and deeper. They pull apart before they lose all control, and Nic gazes into her eyes. "Cara mia, I have no regrets knowing my life has led me to you and our children. For that, I am eternally grateful."

It's surreal when she thinks about the upbringing she and Reed had compared to Nic's tragic history.

Nic cups her cheeks, and the sadness is back in his eyes. "After hearing you and Reed talk about your past, I realized how much you two are alike. He's your synonym and I'm your antonym."

"It is like we're from different ends of the color spectrum," she agrees, then shakes her head at him. "Yet, despite, or maybe due to the disparity, we complement each other. I won't deny Reed and I are like alter egos of each other. But you and me? We fill in all the empty spaces we each have. I mean what's an alter ego anyway? It's just an imitation."

Nic breaks into one of his killer smiles. "I like your analogy better."

Reed is approaching with a pot of coffee and some snacks. Nic lifts Cara to standing, and directs her back to her chair on the other side of the table. Reed places the tray on the table and retakes his seat in the corner. He informs them dinner will be served shortly. The flight attendant is serving the pilots first.

Everyone is haggard at this point. Cara's messy ponytail is hanging in strands around her face. Nic's hair is mussed and standing on end and he looks wiped out. Reed's shirt is wrinkled and the sleeves rolled up. Serious shadows have developed under all of their eyes.

The sky outside is growing darker as they approach the East Coast. Lights in the cabin are dimmed, casting a supernatural radiance across the table. They are preoccupied with their own thoughts as Cara pours some coffee for each of them. She makes eye contact with her husband, willing him to make the final confession to Reed and get it over with.

Giving her a subtle nod of understanding, Nic intones, "So... there's one more thing..."

"Wait, wait!" Cara exclaims. "It's...*Something's Always Wrong*, by Toad the Wet Sprocket." In her off-key voice, she sings the first verse of the song he's humming.

Nic leans over the table and covers her mouth. "You know you're not allowed to sing." He continues the song's next verse with perfect pitch.

It's after the chorus that Nic and Cara notice the look of utter confusion on Reed's face. Nic stops singing and Cara starts laughing. "Sorry Reed, Nic was doing that 'Soundtracks of His Life' thing, again. You heard him humming, right?"

"You told Reed about my tic?" Nic asks, affronted.

"Yes, long time ago, though. You remember, don't you Reed?" Reed still looks bewildered and Cara realizes he has no clue what she's talking about. She enlightens him, "You know, the weird coping mechanism Nic has where he sings songs in his head, and then starts humming the tune when he gets really emotional." Reed still looks befuddled.

"It's humiliating enough that you and the kids constantly point it out, Cara. Must you tell everyone?" Nic snaps.

"Reed isn't EVERYONE, he's, you know, just Reed," Cara counters.

REED FEELS HIS STOMACH DROP, HIS BLOOD PRESSURE SPIKE, AND HIS HEART race. He's trying desperately to keep his emotions in check. Something is wrong. No! Everything is wrong. His eyes dart back and forth between Cara and Nic as they continue to argue. He's starting to perspire. A cold sweat breaks out across his forehead, and he covers his face with his hands, swallowing hard in an attempt to keep down the bile rising in his throat.

Reed closes his eyes and tunes out their bickering. His mind is racing through the last 25 years. From the moment he met Cara in that campus police interview room to now. His brain is systematically picking through events and processing. It was all there. He's trembling now. He's falling apart. Cara is still trying to get him to recall the coping mechanism. He drops his hands and stares blankly at her.

She grabs his wrist and says soothingly, "Sweetheart, it's fine if you don't remember. Please, don't get so upset."

He can't articulate. His stunned face is evidence he is distraught, but Cara doesn't understand why. It's a moment of illumination for him filled with knowledge, insight, reconciliation, regret and guilt. His heart is hammering in his chest. He can't take his eyes off Cara... because Nic was not humming just now.

Trying desperately to regain composure, he gives a faint smile and addresses Nic. "By the way, I've forgotten what an amazing singer you are. Is there anything you can't do?"

Nic quips, "Control my wife."

Before he can respond, or make sense of his monumental epiphany, the plane plummets forward tossing them out of their seats. The flight attendant screams. Instinctually, Reed grasps the stationary table as he reaches for Cara, just before she flies out of her seat. Nic also clutches the edge of the table and somersaults over it. Still holding on with one hand, Reed sets Cara back down in her chair with the other arm. "Buckle up, sweetheart." Once she has the belt around her waist, he raises his eyes to Nic. "Turbulence?"

Nic is easing himself off the table with care as the plane tilts downwards. "I don't think so, Reed. We're descending rapidly." He jerks his head, signaling they should make their way to the front of the plane. They move cautiously towards the cockpit and see Carter and the other agent still strapped in, the flight attendant and the contents of a dinner tray in Carter's lap.

Reed can't remember the name of the flight attendant. This screaming one isn't his regular. Bonnie? Connie? Lonnie? "Are you hurt?" he finally asks without a name. She stops screaming long enough to shake her head. He grips her around the waist and shifts her off Carter and into the seat next to him. "Buckle up, and please try to stay calm."

"Reed!"

Reed's head whips forward to see Nic standing in the now open cockpit doorway. Beyond him, both pilots are passed out over the controls. Holy shit. He turns back to look down the cabin. Cara is leaning into the aisle, her eyes locked on the sight. That's his girl. She's not a screamer. He trained that shit right out of her, but she most definitely isn't breathing, either. Her eyes are wide and her lips are turning blue. He turns back to see Nic pulling the pilots away from the controls.

"Reed, stop gawking and help me!" Nic demands.

The sound of Nic's shout startles him into action. He reaches the doorframe as Nic is yanking a comatose pilot out of his seat. He quickly motions to the empty dinner trays on the jump seat as he crawls into the now vacant pilot's chair.

It takes a moment for Reed to interpret Nic's meaning. And then it clicks. Calmly, he turns back to Carter and crew and inquires, "Have any of you eaten dinner yet?" Carter motions to the food all over him and shakes his head in response. "Good. I don't recommend the selection this evening." Turning to Nic, who is flipping switches on the control panel, he asks, "Poison?"

"Probably, but they're still breathing. Get this other pilot out of here and see if Carter can rouse them and make them vomit. Do you have any medical supplies on board?"

Reed is staring blankly at Nic because he has no clue. Thank God the flight attendant finally decides to do her job. She tells them there is a defibrillator as well as IV for fluids on board.

Nic looks back at Carter as the plane starts leveling off. "Carter, we're stable. Get to work on these two." He gives Carter detailed instructions on the medical care for the pilots while Reed just stands there, one hand on the captains' chair. "Reed! Look alive, please, and get into the other chair."

Again Nic's command spurs him forward. He climbs over and buckles himself in.

"Cara! Get over here!" Nic continues barking.

Her eyes still wide, she steps over the two pilots in the aisle to get to the cockpit.

In a calmer voice, Nic tells her, "Baby, clean the trays from the jump seat, dump the contents, wash your hands, come back, sit and buckle up."

Following her husband's instructions, Cara makes it back inside the cockpit and into the small seat. Reed reaches one hand back to her and she entwines her fingers with his.

The warmth of the touch revives him and Reed finally focuses. He takes a big breath and asks, "So, Nic, you have a plan?"

Nic turns his most dazzling smile on him and responds, "I'm going to fly us to Cleveland."

Reed stops himself just as the words, you can fly a jet, are about to rip from his mouth. Of course Nic can fly a jet. He kills, he sings, he can leap tall buildings in a single bound. Fucking Superman in a golden god facade. He decides to take an alternate approach. "Now we know there isn't anything you can't do besides control your wife. But, can you get us on the ground?"

Nic glares at him before asking, "Do you have Wi-Fi on here?"

"Of course."

He tips his head back towards Cara whose lips are finally returning to their natural color and commands, "Get Sasha on the phone for me." She digs her phone from the pocket of her jeans and dials. Satisfied, Nic turns his attention back to Reed. "Do you think you and my wife can do something productive, like start an investigation into who had access to the food service?"

Cara starts giggling as she hands her phone to Nic. Jerking a thumb towards her husband, she asks Reed, "Did you think it's been easy for me living with Mr. Cocky Pants and the Brilliant Bastard he's on the phone with?"

Fairly sure that Nic might have this disaster under control, Reed finally smiles and responds, "I'm sure you held your own, sweetheart. You should be very proud." He squeezes her hand with affection before letting go and getting to work.

NIC HAS PLACED THE PLANE BACK ON COURSE AND TURNED ON THE autopilot while he waits for Sasha to research the schematics for this model jet. Cara and Reed Facetime Reed's office for an update on who handled the food. Apparently, the dinners were delivered onto the jet before it took off from the government hangar at Dulles. It was never restocked in Berlin. His staff is scrambling to identify how the meals were tampered with, when and by whom.

In the midst of this crisis, Sasha asks him, "Have you told Cara and Reed about Jake yet?"

"No, I was just about to when the pilots keeled over. You, have come out of the closet, though." He tells Sasha how Reed trashed an office after being given the news.

"How pleasant," Sasha deadpans.

Snickering, Nic asks, "Has Jake offered anything?"

"No, but he and Jinx are sequestered in your bedroom. I can hear yelling from here."

Averting his head from Cara and Reed, and speaking more softly, Nic asks, "So our bet that Jake was unaware of who Jinx and Cara were and who they worked for still stands?"

"Based on the argument coming from your room, that's my supposition. And we can still assume Jinx never knew what Jake was up to." After a moment of silence, Sasha finally adds, "Nic, land the plane safely before you tell Reed. Sounds like he might put a bullet in you when he finds out."

"I will take that under serious advisement. Now, feed me the details on the jet."

Cara gets up from the jump seat and peers into the cabin. Both pilots are still out cold. Their vitals are stable but they appear to be heavily sedated. A popular theory is the dinners were laced with Rohypnol, the date rape drug. Carter assures her he has everything under control. She steps back and closes the cockpit door. Nic is still on the phone with Sasha and it sounds like Reed is just finishing a call with the FAA.

In the military this is called a Charlie Foxtrot. A clusterfuck. For the second time today, she has almost lost her life. This time they were willing to take down a whole plane to do it. But was she the only target? If the food trays were the culprits, how could they know Reed and crew wouldn't have consumed them on the way to Berlin? It was an overnight flight taken late in the evening, so they ate the breakfast aboard on the way over, but the dinner could have been eaten as well. And how could they know she would be on board on the way back? And Nic?

Carter is trying to unravel the pilots' movements and what they may have consumed while they were waiting in Berlin. It's quite possible it wasn't the dinner trays at all. They will be tested once they land. In the meantime, retracing the pilots' steps is proving difficult without their participation.

Cara's eyes lock on her husband. The man of the hour. She isn't surprised he can fly a jet. In fact, there's not much that would surprise her when it comes to Sasha and Nic and their abilities, both innate and learned. She's had to work hard to keep up with them. She isn't joking when she says living with Moody and Broody hasn't always been easy. They are demanding and controlling.

Then her eyes shift to Reed. He is just as demanding and controlling. Why does she surround herself with all these alpha males? Nic and Sasha tease her relentlessly. Only Reed openly admits she can give as good as she gets. But somehow it all works because as much as they push her around, they certainly have not been able to suppress her.

Speaking of macho men, Nic was just about to spill the beans to Reed on their Jake connection when the plane took a nosedive. Jake Bishop, a man of mystery, is Jinx's husband. He came on the scene a few months after Cara met Nic. Jinx suddenly had a boyfriend, or at least a guy she was fucking on a regular basis. Which for Jinx, constituted a boyfriend.

She shared many a story with Nic about living with Jinx and her revolving door. She escaped to Reed's whenever possible and was honest with Nic about their interpersonal relationships. She only lied about where they all worked. She told him Reed was a government employee while Jinx worked for the Defense Department. Then years ago, when Reed's position as Deputy Director of the CIA became public, she said he was promoted to the position from outside the agency.

She feels a tug on her ponytail and snaps out of her daydream. "C, come back from wherever you are. You're zoning out again." Reed is in her face. Her hair is wrapped around his hand and he's looking at her with concern.

Nic pipes up from his position in the chief pilot chair, "Baby, how come you let your boyfriend snap you out of your seizures but not me?"

"They are not seizures! In my mind palace! And...I was thinking about Jake." She waits to see if Nic cringes before continuing, "Specifically, about how I used to live with Reed to get away from Jinx and her sexual escapades before Jake came along." This gets a chuckle from Reed before Cara adds, "Well, unless Reed was getting laid, too. Then, I was homeless."

"Hey, I went elsewhere to get laid whenever I could and left you in peace at my apartment. Don't I get credit for that?" Reed challenges.

Cara pats his hand "Yes, you get points for that, but you also had to make sure I was well rested. I was your best agent, so the sentiment is diluted."

"Wait, Reed had dates and got laid?" Nic taunts.

Reed's body jerks in the co-pilot chair. "What the hell...you think I'm some sort of eunuch? C. WAS. NOT. MY. GIRLFRIEND! I'm not sure when you will finally get that straight inside your thick, GERMAN, skull.... She makes a hell of a wingman, though."

"You helped him get laid?!" Nic rails, a little loud for the tight quarters they're in.

"I'm an awesome wingman. Pity, you will never find that out," Cara replies, indignantly.

DAMN, JUST WHEN HE THOUGHT THEY WERE FINALLY GOING TO BREAK THEIR silence about Jake, they are digressing again. Reed takes a big breath and gets back on the crazy train. In a much lower voice, he explains Cara's method. She would lay it on thick in front of the woman he chose. It could be a breakup scene, leaving Reed broken hearted and looking for a sympathetic ear, or a jealous ex-lover pining for the great lay he had been. She had a million tricks up her sleeve. Cara always knew exactly what was going to get the woman practically undressing for him. When he thinks back, he has another moment of illumination.

Before Nic can make some snide comment about needing assistance to get laid, Reed explains. He refused to date anyone at work. No one, in any way, shape, or form related to the government. "Shit like that comes back and can bite you in the ass, especially as I climbed up through the Agency." So, he and Cara would get out of Dodge and go trolling where no one knew them. He was only looking for a simple one-nighter, quick, safe and fulfilling.

"Cara," Nic butts in, "was Reed your wingman? Did you go trolling too?"

Reed can't contain his mocking laughter. Cara sneers at him before responding to her husband. "First of all, I never needed a wingman to get laid. Second…I'm not comfortable with the direction of this conversation. Let's get back to the Jake story, please."

"Answer the question, baby," Nic commands.

Cara sneaks a peek at Reed before answering, wondering if he's going to sell her out. "No, mostly no."

Reed decides to out her. "C doesn't need a sex life. She could've been a nun."

"Really?! YOU don't need sex?! That's news to me," Nic says way too loudly again.

"This is why I don't like the direction of this conversation. Jake. Please, tell us about Jake," Cara tries again.

Surprised by Nic's response, Reed can't let this go. He's desperate to hear about Jake but this is also breaking news. "Wait, are you saying you two have an active sex life?"

"ACTIVE?! My wife is insatiable!" Nic's voice reverberates around the cockpit.

Cara is banging her head on the fuselage. "Nic, please, TMI, TMI!" She gives her husband the hairy eyeball and snaps Reed's hanging jaw closed. "Nic, if you want to talk to someone about our sex life, talk to Jinx. She's the one I confide in on that subject. Not Reed. And none of this is relevant. We need to hear about Jake."

Nic seems to ponder this, then says, "But au contraire, mon frère. Our sex life is what started this whole Jake story."

Reed's not giving up. He's going to ride this coaster even if it kills him, because he's gaining insight to a Cara he doesn't recognize. He stares at her as he asks, "What did you mean when you said, 'mostly no,' about getting laid?"

Cara stares back at him, blankly. "Um, I wasn't as encumbered by your ban on government employees. When Jinx and I went out without you, I may have taken a boy, here or there, home with me."

Cara raises her brows at him. He's speechless, so she narrows her eyes and adds, "I'm no nun, Connor."

Nic shouts, "Amen to that!"

"Wait, what do you mean our sex life started this?" Cara pokes at her husband.

CHAPTER
TWENTY-THREE

NIC WAS SERIOUSLY HOPING to have this Jake discussion either after he's landed the plane, or if one of the pilots has retaken the controls. They have left him in a precarious position. If he admits what's really going on, there is a very good chance Reed will kill him in a fit of rage, and they will all die when the plane crashes. Giving Reed a sidelong glance, Nic inquires cautiously, "If I tell you two this story, you must promise not to hurt me until we land. Then you can kick my ass. Deal?"

The scowl on Reed's face doesn't give Nic much confidence, but then Reed says, "I promise. I happen to value my life and the lives of everyone on this plane. But, once on the ground, all bets are off."

Only slightly mollified, Nic considers his words carefully. It's a long, sordid story when it comes to Jake. The details will either exonerate him or indict him depending on how they are interpreted. But instead of trying to soften the blow, he decides to look straight ahead and blurt, "Jake blackmailed Sasha and me to run missions for him."

His wife's mouth drops open but it's Reed's face that seals the deal. It's gone red up to his ears. Nic turns to his wife and adds, "It happened right after the twins were born. Jake figured out who

Sasha and I were. He told us if we didn't run missions for him, he'd turn us over to Interpol and we'd be deported." Then before either of them can respond, Nic adds, "We thought about killing him. But...I couldn't do that to Jinx. They weren't married yet, but I also couldn't leave Elijah without a father."

Reed is glaring at him, but Cara's mind is whirling. He can almost hear her connecting all the dots in her head. She leans into him, with her voice barely above a whisper, and states, "All those boys weekends the three of you took. All missions."

Nic nods and confesses it started when Jake questioned him about his relationship with Cara on a couple's weekend away. "He and Jinx heard us having loud sex from their adjacent room. Jake already knew who I was, and he interrogated me about my intentions. He wanted to know why the Dark Angel of Death was carrying on with Cara Bianco." Jake made it sound like Nic was taking advantage of a poor, unsuspecting civilian. "I don't think he knew your alias, and I definitely didn't say anything to him about Reed."

To this day, neither Sasha nor Nic know who Jake really is. They have run over 30 missions for him in the last 15 years. Most were kidnap and rescue, but some were more political in nature.

"And Jinx?" Cara whispers, again.

"Based on the dissension between them right now, my guess is Jake had no clue until today that you and Jinx worked for the CIA." Nic can see Reed is ready to burst, but he must get this last part out. "After an initial six missions, Jake decided to stop blackmailing us." He inhales deeply and comes clean with the rest. "He began to offer missions to us, instead."

"And you took them," Cara says as a statement of fact.

Exhaling for the first time since his confession, Nic admits, "Not all. We only chose the ones we were confident would be successful, and where we thought we could make a difference."

Eventually, the three became close. Jake wanted to be the husband and father Jinx and Elijah deserved, but he knew he was leading a dangerous life. So, without revealing too much about himself, Jake asked Nic and Sasha to watch over Jinx and Elijah when he wasn't around. He wanted to propose to Jinx, and make them a family, but he would only do it if Nic and Sasha would agree to ensure their safety.

"He married Jinx when he trusted you and Sasha to keep them protected," Cara says, confirming what she just heard. She pulls out her hair tie and massages her scalp. Her hair cascades down to her shoulders in beautiful waves he would give anything to run his own fingers through.

SHAKING HER CRAZY HAIR OUT TO BRING MORE CIRCULATION TO HER BRAIN, Cara asks, "Is it time for the Q&A yet?"

"WAIT, both of you. Before you go at each other, I need some questions answered, NOW!" Reed barks, actually causing her to jump. She can feel his rage as he points a finger in Nic's face.

Nic shifts slightly away and says, "Shoot, but not literally, please."

Reed's fists are clenched. "You really don't know who Jake works for?"

Raising his hands as if at gunpoint, Nic answers honestly, "No. And trust me, Sasha and I have really tried. I can tell you we've been backed up by various military units as well as black ops types, but we haven't seen a regular pattern." Reed doesn't react, so Nic tries to lighten the mood with, "You know, Jake is so secretive about his trips away from home, Cara started referring to him as Jack Reacher."

Reed turns his head to look at her so quickly, his neck makes a clicking sound. "Why do you call him that?" he snaps.

"Um, I don't know. Sasha has nicknames for everyone, and Jake didn't have one. We're always commenting about his 'walkabouts' away from home, and he's really big and mean looking. He just reminded me of the Jack Reacher character. You know, roaming around the country as a vigilante looking all disheveled and scary," she explains quickly.

Reed shakes his head at her and scowls. "Yes, I know the fictional character, but doesn't he resemble Nic more? Isn't he big and blonde?"

"Well, yeah, but he's supposedly Jake's size, even bigger than Nic, and well, the wandering thing is what jumped out at me. He hates it."

"Who hates it?" Reed demands.

She and Nic respond simultaneously, "Jake!"

Nic goes on, "He hates that we all call him Jack instead of Jake or just 'Reacher' now. He gets all riled up about it. So, we do it more, of course."

Reed starts snapping his fingers. "Pictures, do you have a picture of him?"

Nic still has Cara's phone, and he begins flipping through her photos. He finds the folder from the twins' last birthday party and hands the device to Reed. "Scroll through these." Reed starts swiping and stops at a couple shots to look more closely. Cara is watching his face and at one point she swears an almost imperceptible smirk forms on his lips.

Suddenly, the air around them crackles with tension. Cara senses Nic feels it too because he quietly asks, "Any more questions?"

When Reed looks up, his expression is hard. This is the Reed most people see, the intense, unsmiling Director of the CIA with the piercing, ice blue eyes. "No more questions."

Nic asks hesitantly, "Do you want to hit me?"

Reed gives Nic his iciest glare and articulates a response, enunciating each word. "No. But I'm going to give you a direct order and you will accept it without question. You and Sasha will no longer work for Jake, under any circumstances, EVER again. You want to run missions? You'll do it for me. Got it?"

"Yes," Nic responds immediately.

At this point, Cara grabs Reed's arm and suggests they check on

Carter and the pilots. She needs to separate these two. Their lives all depend on it.

Reed continues to glower at Nic, but he unfastens the harness and follows her. The pilots are propped up and belted into two passenger seats, still unconscious. Reed and Cara confer with Carter who reports two town cars and an ambulance will be waiting for them when they arrive.

Gently pulling Reed toward the conference area, Cara directs him to the back of the plane. He heaves himself into a seat and pulls her onto his lap. He wraps the seatbelt around them and sits in silence.

She leans back and puts her hand on the nape of his neck. She slowly pulls his face down to hers and they let their foreheads touch. This is their thing. They do this when one of them is upset or emotional. It's weirdly intimate, yet perfectly innocent, and it centers them.

Reed breaks their connection but only to scrutinize her face. He looks battered and beaten and he studies her as if all of life's answers are written in her eyes. She feels horribly guilty for the day he's had. The resignation on his face is foreign to her. Has she finally managed to fry his last nerve? Lifting her fingers to his temples, she rubs slow circles. While he still watches her closely, she whispers, "Are you gonna be OK?"

His eyes close and a sigh escapes his lips. She moves her fingers into his hairline and works his scalp. His head tilts back but otherwise he remains still and silent. After what seems like a lifetime, he finally responds, "Can you play copilot for a little while? I need to get some things done before we land."

She only nods and gets up from his lap. Quiet Reed is a bit scary. "I understand you need some alone time to process all of this. For what it's worth, I am sorry. Now, I'll go deal with my Angel."

TWENTY-FOUR

NIC IS ON THE PHONE WITH SASHA again when Cara reenters the cockpit. She takes the copilot's seat and fastens the harness. "Look, I'm flying the plane," she tells him and makes a goofy face.

He interrupts his conversation and bellows, "You're doing nothing of the sort. Only touch what I tell you to touch."

She grabs the phone from him to say hello and he hears Sasha on the other end ask her if she knows anything about aviation. She cocks her head in thought and then nods before telling him, "Well, I know the appropriate size carry-on luggage that will fit in the overhead compartment of almost every plane model. Does that count?"

Nic rips the phone away from her and bids farewell to Sasha. "We have about 30 minutes before I need to turn off autopilot, contact the tower, and punch in our descent and landing pattern. I suppose you want to 'talk' now?" He uses air quotes to demonstrate how little he wants to re-hash his recent admission.

She shakes her head, unfastens the harness, locks the cockpit door, and straddles him.

"Baby, I don't think this…" She covers his mouth with hers in an impassioned kiss.

She breaks free to catch her breath and nips at his jaw, then down his throat. Unbuttoning his shirt, she climbs off his lap, kissing her way down to his abs, and the happy trail leading into his jeans.

"You don't seem as angry or disappointed as I expected. This is the third time today you've surprised me with your calm," he declares in an effort to remain cool as his wife devours him.

"Third time's a charm," she murmurs and unbuttons his jeans.

"What are you doing?"

Her perfect pout disables him. "I need some skin. It's been a very draining day, and it's only going to get worse."

She wins. He unzips his jeans, then bunches his fists in her hair. A small moan escapes Cara's mouth.

She wedges herself in front of him in the tight compartment, and releases just the head of his cock from his boxers. Placing her tongue along the waistband and pulling gently at his pants, she tugs them down just enough to expose a little more skin. His erection is straining against the fabric. She takes pity, and pulls his jeans down further, just enough to free his hard on. When she runs her tongue from the base to the tip, he inhales sharply.

She delivers those long licks paying special attention to the underside of the head, wrapping her tongue and mouth slowly around and sucking only there. She teases him, licking and sucking in small sections making him squirm with desire. His wife is so very talented at edging. Cruelly so.

He tries to push her away, but she resists. "Are you going to lie to me anymore, Nic?" she whispers as she continues her deliberate assault on his manhood.

"Is that what this is? My punishment?" he softly moans. He needs to misbehave more often. Cara's teeth nip at his sensitive nerve endings. He shudders from the pain. Damn, she always knows what he's thinking.

"This is your penance, my love. Beg me for more." Cara's eyes shift up to his face with a wicked gleam.

"Cara mia, please, give me more," he pleads in a whisper.

Cara gives him just a bit more, grasping the base with her hand and slowly bringing it up and down with firm then light touches, still teasing the head with her mouth.

The sexual charge is excruciating. "Oh God, please more."

"God has nothing to do with this, Nic." But she complies and lowers her mouth leisurely down the shaft, keeping her tongue flat against the ridge. She sucks a little harder until she hears his familiar soft moan. She snakes her fingers up his inner thighs, gradually reaching his balls, massaging underneath as she takes him deeper into her mouth. Her movements are painfully slow. His legs are beginning to tremble from the pleasure and pain she's inducing.

She knows his breaking point, and he's so close. Her mouth moves more quickly up and down, increasing his pleasure while making sure she still teases his head with every pass.

This is torture for him. His muscles become taut as he loses himself, but he still has the wherewithal to imprison her with his legs, keeping her from hitting the controls. She just needs to speed up, suck slightly harder, to send him over the edge. But she waits, this she-devil, a little longer. Just when he can't take it anymore, she draws him in deeper, sucking hard and hitting the back of her throat.

It only takes seconds and...he can't breathe. He's sucking at air, and it takes every ounce of energy to refrain from screaming. And then his body goes limp. "You're such a fucking bitch," he gasps breathlessly as she licks her lips. "And I LOVE it."

"I know."

Cara straddles him again, taking his mouth passionately, robbing him of the oxygen he so desperately needs. He finally uses one hand to pull her hair to break the kiss and catch his breath. His hand still in her hair, he deposits small kisses along her jawline, nipping her lightly with his teeth as he moves. His other hand reaches under her sweater, his fingers brushing beneath her breasts. He releases her hair and moves his other hand under her sweater. He covers her nipples, letting the lacy bra rub against them, and watches as Cara drops her head back in pleasure.

"I know how turned on you get when you tease me. Torture is a two way street, baby," he breathes out while unclasping her bra and letting her breasts drop into his hands.

His fingertips continue to rub lightly, teasing her nipples until they are hard pebbles. He knows she loves this. The anticipation of a firmer pinch, and then a lighter brush will send her anywhere he needs her to go.

Cara's breathing catches and he raises her sweater to place his lips on her breast. He gets the desired effect when he sees Cara cover her mouth to prevent any sounds from coming out. He lets one hand drop between her legs, rubbing lightly at first, but then harder. Her hand goes for the button to undo them, but Nic bats her hand away. "No, baby, I'm not ready for that. Beg for it."

She doesn't hesitate, "Please, Nic."

He unbuttons her jeans, pulling down the zipper and letting his fingertips brush across her sensitive spot. Cara shudders just from the light touch. He pulls her jeans down further before dipping one finger into her tight sheath. She bucks from the penetration, but he holds her hips firmly, preventing any movement.

He continues to taunt her with his fingers, bringing her so close, then backing away. Eyes closed and head thrown back, she tries to move her hips closer, but he stops her. "Say that you trust me, baby."

"Always, my love."

He slips two fingers inside her while his thumb strokes her clit. She gasps with eagerness. "Look at me, baby." She opens her eyes to meet his and he gives her that killer smile. "I need you to watch me enjoy this as much as you are," he whispers just before she lets loose.

She sees Nic's pleasure at watching her and she can contain hers any longer. She grabs his head to hold him tight against her. Her hands are shaking, and her mouth is open. The sounds of life around her cease to exist. Nic takes one final, long, slow swipe and sends a post-climatic shudder through her.

Still experiencing the pleasurable aftershocks, Cara is barely aware of Nic yanking one pant leg from her. He moves her hands to grip the chair arms. He's not finished with her just yet. With both hands he lifts her ass and positions her over his fresh arousal, driving into her as she moans.

He pushes her hair to one side, and whispers into her ear, "Perfect…so perfect…it will never be anything but perfect." Cara can't think; he feels wonderful. She cradles his head with one hand and Nic thrusts up harder in feverish pleasure, moving one hand back under her sweater to lightly stroke her nipples. He knows just when she's about to shatter and lets himself go.

She giggles in his ear. "We have done this while you drove a car, but never while you flew a plane. It's a first for us."

"You are a very wicked woman, cara mia. Proving to me once again your love for danger." It's at this moment they both hear the buzz indicating it's time to release the autopilot.

"Timing is everything." She smiles at him and does a little wiggle. "Do you need me now, because I have to pee."

"You always have to pee afterwards."

"It's a universal rule." Snaking around him, she winks at Nic before unlocking the door and swinging it open.

She runs right into Reed standing arms akimbo, glaring at her. She pats her hair down. She must look a mess. Talk about walk of shame, the look of outrage on Reed's face is mortifying.

She pushes past him towards the bathroom, but he grabs her arm. Trying, she stutters out, "We…we needed some privacy to work things out."

"I'm sure you did." He leans in and sniffs her. Yikes. Does she smell like sex?

She lowers her head, not bothering with a retort. He clips past her into the cockpit, closing the door behind him. As she passes Carter, he puts his hand out, palm up and mouths, 'mile high'.

Cara giggles. Guess they were obvious. But hey, it's getting harder and harder for them to achieve firsts concerning their sex life. Pun intended. But when opportunity knocks...

CHAPTER
TWENTY-FIVE

CARA AWAKENS WITH A JOLT when the plane hits the ground. It takes her a second to recall where she is and what is happening. And then she sees Nic and Reed wearing headsets and high fiving each other.

"We're on the ground," she says, stating the obvious amid sounds of whooping and clapping from the cabin.

"You couldn't have been too concerned, C, you fell asleep," Reed notes. He's directing Nic to the NASA Glenn Terminal although it's hard to miss with all the fire trucks and ambulances out front.

"I was tired." She hasn't slept in days. "Sorry, I wasn't much assistance."

"It's fine, baby," Nic smirks, "we never ended up needing your expertise on overhead luggage sizes." He leans back and winks at her.

She takes the opportunity to squeeze his shoulder in appreciation. She never doubted he would get them safely home. Nic is a superhero.

Still so exhausted, she can barely get herself off the plane, much less assist in getting the two pilots off and into the medics' hands.

Reed and Carter handle it while Nic confers with some other agents. This is where hanging with alpha males pays off. She just grabs her luggage and makes her way to the exit. Reed, the miracle worker, has insured once again, they pass through the airport undetected, avoiding both customs and the concourse.

There are two empty town cars parked by the emergency vehicles. Far guard jumps into the driver's seat of the first car. Seeing this, Cara climbs into the back seat of the second car.

Once all the macho men are done collaborating, Carter and Reed get into the car with Far Guard and Nic gets behind the wheel of Cara's car. Without acknowledging him, Cara opens her door and walks to Reed's car.

"Get out, Carter. I need to talk with Reed. You ride with Nic." She tugs his arm and pulls him out of the front seat.

Carter is horrified. "You want me to ride alone with Mean Man?"

"Yes, and I promise he won't bite," she assures him as she drags him away.

She pushes Carter toward the passenger side, prompting him, "Hop in, big boy." After he's seated next to Nic she adds, "Oh...I promised Mean Man wouldn't bite, but I didn't say anything about kicking and punching." She slams the door with the sound of Carter's protests and Nic's laughter escaping through the windows.

Cara slides into the back seat with Reed. She closes the window separating them from their driver and commences speaking. "Um, there are some things you need to know before we get to my house."

"About?" Reed asks without looking at her.

"Mostly about Sasha."

Reed nods slowly and turns to look at her. "Oh, I thought you were going to tell me what the hell you were doing in the cockpit earlier." Cara immediately turns a bright shade of red. "Judging by your new skin tone, I was correct in my assumption."

"I thought we were quiet," Cara whispers, sheepishly.

"You were quiet, way too quiet for a couple looking to fight in private, C. Nic wasn't exaggerating about your sex life. Why wouldn't you talk about that with me? I don't mean the details, but you never even gave the impression there was any level of intimacy between you two."

Cara, feeling a little less embarrassed and a little more defiant, almost shrieks, "After what happened in Geneva, you expected me to freely discuss my raging sex life? You and I went almost four months without speaking to each other after that incident."

The topic of sex never comes up in their conversations; not who's getting some, and with whom. Forget how often. She's certain he's getting laid, but he doesn't share that with her, so why should she divulge? Besides, she's pretty sure the topic of sex became taboo after their last night in Geneva. They still haven't made peace with it. "If you want the sordid sensual and erotic details of my sex life, you need to man up and discuss Geneva," she says shakily but manages to compose herself before adding, "Is that what you want to do?"

This shuts Reed down completely. He stares out his window, ignoring her. There, she initiated the discussion. He may not be ready yet, but when he is, she WILL go there with him.

Reed sits in his thoughts after her threat. Geneva. Fucking Geneva was the biggest disaster of his life, and another fucking illumination. He makes yet another attempt to get his emotions in check as the roller coaster they are on careens and banks hard to the left.

He lets a few moments pass, then turns back to Cara and calmly requests, "Tell me about Sasha."

Cara releases the tension in her shoulders and starts, "Sasha is... an enigma. Have you ever seen pictures of him?"

"Yes and no." They had photos, but in each one he had a different look. Golov was a chameleon, easily transforming himself, and for that reason the Agency always feared him the most. They knew they wouldn't see him coming.

"Well, he still maintains his mystique," Cara confirms.

Shaking her head, Cara struggles to describe her brother-in-law. "He is many things and none. He's layered like an onion. Every time you peel one back, and you think you've gotten to the heart of him, there's another layer cloaking his secrets."

Her gleam softens, "There's Uncle Sasha, who on the daily spends countless hours teaching and nurturing my children. He has this innate sense to intuit what the kids want to do. He was their personal clown and playmate when they were toddlers. Then, he was their mentor, patient and persistent, introducing art projects and the alphabet. He's taught them kindness and tolerance. He even developed a separate and distinct bond with each of them.

"Whereas Nic and I would group our children as the 'twins', Uncle Sasha would entertain each child, individually, based on their preferences. With Mia, he cultivated her love of hands-on projects. Finger-painting. Tie-dyes. Macaroni necklaces. And Sasha, of course, would wear whatever she made him. When she advanced to more complicated art forms, she would draw on all his clothes with fabric paint, even bejeweling some of his jackets. The work they did together on her crafts, deepened their bond.

"With Max, Uncle Sasha, was the rough houser. He had him shooting baskets by three. Sasha was the one who explored all of the sports options in town and signed Max up for all of them. I would sometimes catch him studying rules and strategies for each sport. He took Max to all of his games and even coached or volunteered if a team was in need. As Max grew older, the two of them became more like partners in crime with Sasha allowing Max more freedom to act out and just be a boy. In that respect, Nic and I are the disciplinarians, and Sasha, the favorite uncle, literally."

Reed always prided himself on having a great relationship with her children. He wasn't local, but he did see them at least 5 times a year and for two weeks in the summer when they would vacation together. He loves those kids, but envy for Sasha's role in their lives is adding to the multitude of emotions he's feeling. The Widow Maker, of all people, was privileged to see all their firsts.

Rationally, he understands it's due to the close relationship Sasha shares with Nic, but still, it chafes his ass he was left out. Particularly the last couple of years, when he's been busier, and the kids have more activities. Come to think of it, it's been at least 6 months since he's seen them.

He sets aside his jealousy and regret and listens as Cara continues, "Although Nic helped influence the twin's love of music, it was their Uncle Sasha's endless hours of tutelage that made them the skilled musicians they are today. He always made learning fun, and they excelled with him as their teacher.

"Max and Mia's connection with Sasha is in a lot of ways, separate and distinct from their relationship with Nic and me, their actual parents," she says dryly. "They have TV shows they only watch together, interests they only explore together, favorite places to dine together, the list is endless."

He knows she is not intimating Uncle Reed could have done more, and yet, that's how he's feeling. He won't let her know that, but he can't help but comment, "Sounds to me like Uncle Sasha has spoiled your children."

"Spoiled them incredibly!" Not the reaction he was expecting. "To make matters worse, they view Nic and me as the bad guys because we're the hard asses who have to take a stand with them."

She reaches over to intertwine her fingers with his and whispers, "Then... there's my Sasha."

Cara's Sasha? He inhales sharply, his thoughts in disarray. Wasn't it painful enough to share her with her husband all these years? Did he lose her to yet another man? It's too devastating to consider.

Sensing his distress, she squeezes his hand, "For me...Sasha's been the man who always knew when I was at my wit's end. When I was overwhelmed with work, it was Sasha who saved the day by going grocery shopping or cooking dinner. He would help around the house with anything I needed done. He would even take the kids to run errands, something I avoided like the plague! And he never complained. His tender regard and the small smile that accompanied every task he undertook got me through the hardest of my days."

Reed is very uncomfortable with the direction this is going in. "Just how close are you and Sasha?"

"I love and adore him. Honestly, I don't know what I would have done all these years without him," Cara admits.

"So, your relationship with him is like ours?" he inquires with hesitation, not convinced he wants her to answer. He turns to stare back out the car window because he can't look at her.

Her fingertips make contact with his chin and gently turn him back to face her. She shakes her head slowly and looks directly into his eyes. "Sasha is like a brother to me. You and me...not the same."

Why is he so relieved by that? Not an emotion he's ready to explore with everything else that's going on. Instead, he lowers his voice and asks, "What does he look like?"

Reaching into her tote bag, Cara pulls out her phone and finds her favorite photo of Sasha with her children. "They were five years old on the morning of their first day of kindergarten." She turns the photo towards him. He sees Sasha, sporting a broad smile, a child under each arm. "It's his eyes that have endeared me to this picture. They tell the real story. They are filled with fear, trepidation and loss."

She expands the photo, so the picture is a close-up of Sasha's face. "We went together and dropped the kids off at school for their first day. When we got home, we sat on the couch and I cried while Sasha held my hand. We didn't have to say anything to each other; he just understood." She takes a sharp breath before adding with a chuckle, "Meanwhile, Nic did a happy dance, thrilled the kids wouldn't be underfoot for at least 6 hours, five days a week."

Reed studies the photo while Cara relives the mixed emotions of that day. He can see what she means by Sasha's eyes. They are sad, but also filled with love. It isn't the only thing he notices, though. He's handsome. Very. "Like Nic, he doesn't look Russian," Reed observes.

Cara takes the photo back and studies it. "All these years and I've never really considered that. Sasha is more Mediterranean in his coloring, except for his eyes. He has the most captivating indigo blue eyes." She thinks about this for a moment. "I don't know his history, but you can see how he can pass himself off as Spanish, Italian, Lebanese, even Iraqi. He can be anyone from anywhere."

Reed has so many questions; he doesn't know where to start. "Does he live with you?"

"Most of the time, but he also keeps an apartment just outside our neighborhood. I think he needs alone time, occasionally. When the kids were young, Sasha would entertain them at our house so Nic and I could sneak off to his apartment to fool around," she giggles. "Sometimes, we still do. We tell the kids we need to go out of town for work, and then spend the night alone at Sasha's. The privacy is VERY rewarding."

Shaking the image of them from his mind, he redirects with, "Does Sasha date?"

She releases his hand and shrugs, "You and he have more in common there. I believe he trolls outside our general area. Nic and I have run into him on dates, but he never gets serious with anyone. I think he just gets laid. He's a fuck boy like you."

"Does he have a job or does he just raise your children for you?" Reed jabs after the last comment.

Cara gives him the hairy eyeball, then softens and clarifies, "Sasha has been both mother and father to my children on many occasions. After they started school though, Nic recruited him into the business. Sasha is Nic's right hand man now. He runs the crews and does a lot of the daily fieldwork. The crews love him. They see Nic as the 'boss man' and Sasha, one of their own. We don't generally have him interact with the clients. Nic and I maintain those relationships. All in all, it works out well."

Reed is staring at Cara. His mind is racing with questions, some of which he doesn't want to ask.

Sensing his hesitation, Cara offers, "Sasha is many, many things to me, but the one thing he is not, is the Notorious Alexander Golov. When I first met Sasha, I assumed he was Golov. I answered our front door looking like a whale at nine months pregnant. He didn't even look at my face. He just stared at my belly and his whole demeanor softened. Nic wasn't home so I invited him in. This Golov was no monster."

"I can't believe you didn't grab a sidearm!" Reed blurts out.

Cara waves him off, "The Golov standing at my door gave off no evil vibe. If anything, his body language read gracious and considerate."

"Still! It's not like you to be so susceptible." Reed has to stop himself and remember this was years ago. And he's grappling with Cara's so called "intuition" at the moment, as well.

"Connor! Sasha ought to be canonized for the patience and fortitude he has shown ME and my children over the years. He has given all of his love to us, unconditionally."

In other words, Sasha sees her, and loves her anyway. Cara is not your average homemaker and soccer mom. Reed, of all people, knows this. The woman is a demon.

His thoughts turn quickly, though, as a slow realization creeps into his mind. It was easy for them to put their past and all of their secrets behind them because their collective past was the anomaly. Their lives, all these years together as a family, is their truth.

Cara holds his face gently in her hands, and whispers, "Can you ever forgive me, Connor, for keeping Sasha from you?"

Reed studies her and decides it's time to call her out. "C, I know you better than you know yourself. You hid Sasha from me all these years because you were keeping him for yourself."

She bows her head in supplication. "You always figure out my motives." If Cara told him, he would have taken Sasha from her. And eventually, Nic would have followed. She knew they missed being in the field. And she knew how much Reed respected their skills. With Sasha concealed, the past could stay in the past, and in her mind at least, they could continue to live their ideal, happy, mission-free lives.

Cara inhales deeply, trying to control a sob. "Today has changed everything, Connor. My life will never be the same and I'm afraid my happily ever after will end."

Reed pulls her into his arms and hugs her to him. "You purposely looked the other way with Jake, too. If you admitted the truth to yourself and to them, your men would have run even more missions for Jake. You never wanted them back in that line of work, risking their lives...for Jake or for me. So you hid them and convinced yourself it wasn't happening."

Reed can feel her nod against his chest. He strokes her hair wanting desperately to give her courage. She is going to need it, because he's about to send her reeling. The fairy tale existence in her Land of Denial is about to come crashing to a halt. There's one more monumental bombshell about to drop.

Still holding her, Reed picks up her phone and studies the photo of Sasha. He can't help but ask, "I can't tell from this picture, but is Sasha big and buff like Nic?"

"He's slightly shorter than Nic but they work out together all the time." Cara gives Reed the once over before finishing, "He's more your height and weight. About six foot two and built like you."

She runs her hands across his shoulders and biceps. She knows he's wondering if he could take Sasha in a fight. She's assessing him. She lets her hand skim back down his chest while she considers this, then pinches his nipple and adds quietly, "My money is on you."

"Ouch, but thanks. Glad to know you still have some faith in me."

She grabs him by the nape and brings his face close to hers. "Always, sweetheart, my faith in you never waivers. Feel free to question my motives, but never question my confidence in you. I take full responsibility for being a selfish bitch and keeping Sasha hidden", she admits, "but the decision had nothing to do with a lack of trust in you."

"That's why you called me, first." Reed watches her shrug.

Honestly, he hadn't even thought to ask Cara if she had discussed it with Nic when she came to Langley. He just naturally went into protection mode. He's done it so often; it is second nature. So he understands why Cara's knee-jerk reaction to a threat was to reach out to him. But somehow Nic knew enough to go after her, despite her silence. Another illumination.

For the second time, after Cara directly disobeyed one of Reed's orders, it was Nic who saved her. Reed still can't believe he never put two and two together until now. She's always been teased about her seizures, but damn, the fucking truth is going to break her.

Cara pulls Reed from his deep reflection. "We're almost home. We need to talk about one more thing before we arrive. And that's Jake. You know who he is." His lips twitch and it's all she needs for a confirmation. She holds both hands up, palms out. "Don't tell me. I don't want to know right now. What I do want is to explain Jake's connection to my family."

He cocks his head, waiting for her to continue. "Jake has become part of our little Cleveland clique. His son, Elijah, is always at my home. He's Mia's best friend, and very close to both Max and Sasha, who has taken Eli under his wing the same way he's done for my kids.

"Jake is married to Jinx, and you know we are each other's support system here. We are closer now than when we worked for you. And although Jake is gone a lot, when he is home, he's very present in our lives. He's also developed a real friendship with Nic and Sasha. I suspect that might have to do with the missions they've been running together that I didn't know about." She rolls her eyes in irritation. "But nothing is going to break their bond, Reed. Nic promised you he wouldn't work for Jake anymore, but he will be Jake's friend."

Ah, Jake. Antagonizing Jake is going to be more fun than Reed has had in a long while. It's the only confrontation he's looking forward to. "I understand that, C. I could tell from Nic's words he has a great deal of respect for Jake."

She smiles broadly, and gives him a wink. "In conclusion...you're about to walk into enemy territory. I think you know that already. But like always, and I mean ALWAYS, I have your back, sweetheart." Cara waits for him to respond, but instead he pulls her in for a tighter hug. Just then the vehicle enters the driveway.

Reed releases her and looks towards the garage. One door is wide open and he sees a man holding an umbrella and wearing a V-neck T-shirt inscribed with, 'Fuck, Fuck, Fuckity, Fuck' and jeans decorated with painted skulls, demons, and pentagrams. His long salt and pepper hair hangs to his shoulders, and partially covers an unshaven face. His arms are covered in dark hair. The same hair is pushing its way out of his collar. He looks like a vagrant. He doesn't resemble the photo, at all.

"Ahh...Sasha's sporting a halfway decent look this evening," Cara muses.

"This is decent?" Reed is horrified.

"For Sasha, absolutely."

TWENTY-SIX

NIC BOLTS OUT OF HIS town car with their luggage in tow. He gives Sasha a quick greeting and grabs his shoulder in a display of affection before he walks into the house. Sasha walks to Cara's side of the car with the umbrella and opens the door for her.

"Vizzini, so nice to have you home," is his greeting. She gets out, staying under cover of the umbrella, but manages to punch him in the chest for the jibe. Sasha grabs her with his free hand and pulls her into a hug. "You gave me a scare there, Ms. Reflex. You will not do that again, capice?"

"Sash, please, I don't need another overprotective man coddling me. I'm fine, and we have a lot of work ahead of us."

Sasha whispers in her ear before releasing her from the hug, "I heard you knew, all along. I can never thank you enough."

Cara leans back into him and places her cheek against his. "I'm the one who should be doing the thanking for everything you've done for me and the kids. Please, never forget that, and let's not speak of it again."

She pushes his hair out of his face and behind his ears. They share a momentary look of understanding, then break apart. Less is more when it comes to Sasha and emotional displays. Cara has learned to refrain from any overt displays of affection with him. He carries an underlying anguish. She can feel his love for them, always, but there is a deep pain beneath it. She suspects it has something to do with the younger Sasha's long-ago assignment in England that Nic spoke of on the plane. She'll need to tread carefully if she ever expects to draw the answer to that mystery out of Broodyland.

She leans her head back into the car where Reed is picking up his belongings, and eavesdropping on their conversation. "You need any help there, sweetheart?"

Reed gives her a dirty look before opening his door and stepping out of the car. Cara places her arm in Sasha's, and strolls with him towards the cover of the garage. There's a steady gentle rain tonight, a welcome constant of Ohio's spring. When Reed reaches them, she decides introductions are in order.

While Sasha is folding the umbrella, Cara announces, "Director Connor Reed, I would like to introduce you to Sasha Andre." There's no sound and no movement as the two men size each other up. Cara lets it go on for about ten seconds, then, "For God's sake just shake hands and stop being alphaholes. You can swing your dicks later."

"Nice mouth, Vizzini!" Sasha calls out.

"Says the man wearing that T–shirt!" Cara calls back, pointing at his chest.

Reed can't control himself and starts chuckling. "Did he just call you Vizzini? Like from the *Princess Bride*, the little Sicilian guy who kidnaps Buttercup?"

She nods unhappily while Sasha breaks out into laughter, a rare display.

"Now, that's funny," Reed continues, still smiling, "And something else you haven't shared with me."

"Shut up, Reed. I guarantee Broody will have a biting nickname for you by the end of the night. Now shake or I'm kicking some ass," she warns.

Reed reaches out with his hand and Sasha doesn't hesitate. They shake, but it's quick, just borderline cordial.

The door leading to the house opens and Nic leans his head out. "Have they started fighting yet? We're laying odds on when it will start and who will win."

Reed answers him, "Is there a line on 'Vizzini' kicking both of our asses? Because she just threatened to do it."

Nic's face falls. "I hadn't considered that scenario. Shit, this is going to mess up the wagers. He pulls his head back in and closes the door.

All three smile, then Cara's mood becomes serious. She addresses Sasha directly. "I didn't ride with Nic so I have not been updated. Tell me what the kids know so far."

Sasha grows solemn as well and explains, "It was difficult to keep everything from them. They're smart kids. They know they were pulled from school and the FBI has the house surrounded. Max is fantasizing that you and Nic made your money running drugs and now you've been caught. He thinks it's 'awesome'. Mia, on the other hand, is convinced your Sicilian ties finally caught up to us, and the FBI is about to take you down for your mob connections."

"Sasha, I'm seeing a pattern here," Cara says, appalled.

"They're your children, what can I say? They think the worst of you." He smirks at her before admitting he was just teasing. "Remember, they are teenagers, and the idea of their parents going all gangster is far more exciting to them than the truth will be. The only thing I told them was their parents were not being arrested for any crimes. They were both sorely disappointed."

Reed snickers at this portrayal, and Cara feigns a glare at him for laughing about her children. "Okay, let's get in there and get this over with." She starts for the door.

Reed stops her and asks, "Are you expecting Sasha or me to be a part of this discussion?"

"No. Why?"

He addresses Sasha. "This would be a good time for you and me to have a conversation. Get to know each other, agree?"

Sasha replies in his usual deadpan, "I've been expecting it. We can use the Music room downstairs. It's soundproof."

At this, Cara rushes to the kitchen with Reed and Sasha following more slowly behind her. Nic, Max and Mia are at the table running numbers on a sheet of paper. "Are you guys odds making?" They all look up and nod. "Well then, you should know Reed and Sasha are about to have a 'chat' in the Music room."

"That changes everything," Nic states as he rips the paper they were working on to shreds.

Max and Mia get up to greet Reed who envelops Mia in a big hug, "It's been too long, sweetheart. You're growing more beautiful all the time," he says sincerely.

"Thank-you, Uncle Reed," Mia responds graciously.

"Does that get me your bet in the fight?" Reed pokes her playfully.

Mia embraces Sasha with one arm and confesses, "I have to put my money on Uncle Sasha, you understand, don't you, Uncle Reed," while winking at Reed and signaling her money is really on him.

Sasha leans into Reed and whispers, "Master manipulator like her mother."

"Yes, I see that," Reed confirms.

Mia pulls on her Uncle Sasha's unruly locks and reminds him, "You promised to let me braid your hair later." Then she winks again at Reed and whispers, "That should help emasculate him enough so I get the assist."

"Did I mention cruel as well?" is Sasha's comeback

Max approaches Reed while Mia is still in Sasha's embrace. He places his hand out to shake, but Reed grabs it and yanks Max in for a firm hug. Cara's heart swells. It's such a thrill for her to have him here spending time with her children.

Reed steps back and looks closely at her son. "Max, has anyone told you...you're looking more and more like your mother." Glancing over at Cara, he adds, "He has his father's coloring but I see much more of you in him now that he's maturing."

"Uncle Reed, are you saying I look like a girl? Dad, my money is definitely on Uncle Sasha," Max calls out.

Reed pulls him back for another hug, whispering loudly in his ear so everyone can hear, "No, I'm saying your mother looks like a boy."

This gets a laugh out of everyone except Cara who scowls at her boyfriend, which makes them laugh even harder.

Pulling both of her children away from the two men, she points them in the direction of the kitchen table. Once they're seated, she turns to Sasha and Reed and motions them to the kitchen island. "Kids, pay attention, this is tonight's first revelation." She turns back to the two men and demands they surrender every weapon they are carrying and place them on the counter. She wants a clean and fair fight. "Do it!"

The two men look at each other and shrug. Reed removes his suit jacket and reveals a black snakeskin holster.

Cara jumps at him. "OH MY GOD, you did go see Olaf, you dog, and he gave you this!" she exclaims touching the snakeskin leather on the holster. Even Sasha reaches out to stroke it.

Now Nic is laughing hysterically. "Reed has a new boyfriend! And we're going to get a lot of swag!"

Reed growls at him, "Of course I went to see Olaf. You didn't think I was going to miss the opportunity to make that connection, PROFESSIONALLY, Nic?"

Sasha is still admiring the holster, so Nic teases some more, "Don't sweat it, Sash, Olaf gave me two. Um, he wanted you to have one. Something about how he owes you? Care to elaborate?"

Sasha stops fondling the holster and flips Nic the bird behind Cara's back so the kids don't see.

"Don't you boys fight over Olaf, too." Nic continues with his tormenting. Now they both flip Nic off so the kids do see.

"That's enough," Cara cuts in. "Get back to it, guys. Let's go."

Reed takes the holster off and Sasha reaches behind to pull a semiautomatic from the back of his T-shirt. They both start to leave. As far as their concerned, the task is complete.

"Really, have you both forgotten who you're dealing with? Reed, pants, left leg, now. Sasha, right leg and your waist band." Sheepishly, they locate and surrender the additional arsenal. The countertop is littered with weaponry, but she's not done. "Boots off. Sasha, you have a knife in one and a small revolver in the other. Reed, the .22 and a poison dart." Cara glances at the widening eyes of her children then watches as the men remove their boots. Reed and Sasha are now shoeless and looking defeated. "Nic, did I miss anything?"

Nic, narrows his eyes at them and adds, "Sasha, switchblade left pocket. Reed, the garrote inside your waistband. Now they're clean."

"Gentlemen?" Cara cautions them.

While they remove the final appliances, Nic adds, "If either of you damage anything in the Music room or anywhere in the house during your 'discussion', I will personally kick both your asses. You know I'm capable, and I've already calculated the odds in my favor. Now, go have fun, gentlemen."

"Oh, and Sasha, can you please give Reed a tour of the lower level before you hurt each other? I'll show him the rest of the house later," Cara adds and walks to the table to take a seat.

THEY BOTH EYE EACH OTHER AS IF SIZING UP THE COMPETITION, THEN SASHA motions for Reed to follow him. They start down the long hallway and Sasha, speaking with a posh accent, says loudly, "On your right, Director Reed, is the Great room, commonly known as a living room. To your left is the butler's pantry and entrance to the formal dining room. We will be utilizing the front stairwell system to gain access to the lower level." He and Reed hear the four in the kitchen burst into chuckles.

Sasha stops talking when they hit the stairs. He walks down

them in silence, and heads towards the large recreation room which is equipped with a kitchen, a bar, and a billiards table. He goes behind the bar and pulls a chilled bottle of Chopin Vodka and two shot glasses from the cooler. He leads Reed to the next door and opens it to reveal a small theater room. He gives Reed a moment to view the set up, then closes the door and keeps walking.

The tour continues like this until Reed has seen the large bedroom with en-suite, Nic's office, and finally the music room. Here, Sasha stops and motions for Reed to enter. The space is beautifully appointed and houses an impressive array of musical instruments, including a drum set, electric guitars, acoustic guitars, and an electric bass. There's also a cello, a violin, an electric keyboard and a small upright piano. Several brass instruments rest on a shelf, and one whole wall is dedicated to mixing equipment.

Reed stares in amazement as he walks the perimeter, examining each piece of equipment. Sasha pulls two chairs to the center of the room, positions a small table next to them, and places the vodka and glasses on top. Then he walks over and shuts the door.

Reed is the first to speak. "You guys can play all of these?"

"What can I say? It's a hobby." Sasha answers flatly.

"This is impressive. Cara told me Nic and the kids are musicians. But I had no idea," he says, waving his arms around the room.

Again with no inflection, Sasha responds, "Music was very important to Nic. I found myself getting caught up in it with him and...well, I guess I had some natural talent." He becomes slightly more animated as he brings up the children. "The twins are extremely gifted. They each play several instruments and have great singing voices."

"Well, they didn't get that from their mother," Reed cracks.

"No, Vizzini isn't allowed in here, and she can never sing. Her voice hurts us."

This elicits a chuckle from Reed who heads to the chairs and sits down. He rolls up his shirtsleeves while Sasha opens the bottle and pours two shots. Then Reed does something unexpected. He sits back and crosses one leg over the other, an entirely non-confrontational pose.

Sasha picks up the two shots glasses and, handing one to Reed, asks, "We are not going to fight, are we?"

Reed raises his glass to Sasha and downs the shot, wincing at the bitter taste. Sasha does the same, then places his glass back on the table, smiling at Reed's discomfort. "It's not smooth like the vodka you're used to. Most vodka now is distilled wheat. This is potato vodka. I won't drink the other shit."

He's still standing in front of Reed when he admits, "If we are not fighting, please, let me introduce myself more appropriately." He puts his hand out. "Alexander Golov, it's such an honor to finally meet you, Director Reed."

Reed grins and shakes his hand. "The honor is all mine, and please, just 'Reed'. There's no need to fight, but you and I have much to discuss."

Sasha sits down and pours two more shots. "Nic's told me you know of Jake and what we've been doing for him."

"Yes, and we'll talk more about him later. I'm not prepared to play my hand with him...yet. All I will say on the subject is you're done working for him."

"You know who he is?" His interest is piqued.

Reed admits he does, but doesn't offer any other info. He holds no grudge against Sasha or Nic, but his business with Jake is incomplete. Reed asks Sasha if he would consider working for him in the future. "Full disclosure, I'm beside myself with envy knowing you and Nic were providing your services to Jake rather than for me. I have been a big admirer of you both for a very long time. If I wasn't, Nic would not be here. I would've found a way to separate him from Cara. But instead, I respect him, and of course, I trust her."

That's interesting. "And when you learned of my presence here?" Sasha inquires.

Reed reassures him, "Water under the bridge, as they say. I'm reconciled to it so it's a non-issue at this point."

"So, what is it you want to talk about, then?" Sasha asks while reaching for the second shot and swallowing it in one gulp. Reed grabs his and knocks it back. It seems to go down much easier this time for him.

"It's something you'd never expect, but I think you're the only one who can help me with it. I need you to be both open-minded and honest with me, and to hear me out before you pass judgment."

Sasha is intrigued but he takes a moment to study Reed before he responds. This first encounter with Cara's best friend and former handler is not at all what he expected. Cara only shared with him bits and pieces of her escapades with Reed, so he got most of his information from Nic. A decidedly slanted view of the man. Nic was either complaining about their relationship, or making fun of the goofball behavior he witnessed when he was forced to spend time with them. He found it hard to believe they were ever operatives, let alone the reputedly feared Duo.

Sasha would always take the higher ground, reminding Nic that Cara was close to Reed long before she met Nic and married him. His jealousy was counter-productive and certainly wasn't going to change anything. There's no question Cara is loyal to Nic, and it's obvious she adores him. Nic knows all this and yet, he would just feel better if Reed wasn't so handsome, successful, witty, single and unquestionably, heterosexual.

During the last few years, as Reed's career transported him into the public eye, Sasha was able to form his own opinion. He watched his appearances on CSPAN and saw an eloquent, intelligent, composed, and powerfully confident figure. There was absolutely nothing silly about this man, and Sasha finally understood how he earned his reputation.

Refocusing, Sasha again takes that higher ground. "Because Cara is very important to both of us, it would mean much to me if we could be friends. Please appreciate I want to work towards that."

Reed gives him a serious nod then drops his head for a moment. Potentially in thought? When his eyes meet Sasha's again, he drawls,

"That's a very mature, and touching sentiment, Sasha. Cara give you a vagina, too?" Then the son of a bitch actually winks at him. "Don't sweat it, bro. I've had mine for 25 years."

He can't prevent the snort of laughter that comes out of him at Reed's self-deprecating humor. The defeated look on Reed's face makes him laugh even harder. He pours two more shots of vodka and toasts this man who Nic refuses to appreciate. This powerfully formidable figure took control of the conversation but managed to level the playing field using compliments and humor. Sasha can add gifted diplomat to Reed's list of admirable traits.

Handing Reed the next shot, they each toss back the alcohol before Reed sets his jaw in grim determination.

He leans further back in his chair, takes a deep breath and begins. "People say that couples who have been together often finish each other's sentences." He inhales once again. "Have you ever noticed how C and Nic don't just finish each other's sentences; they actually speak an entire thought at the exact same time?"

Sasha is utterly confused by this sudden topic shift but his first instinct is always to protect Cara and Nic. He answers, "They are a very intimate couple, Reed. Always in sync with one another."

Reed shakes his head. "It's more than that. And that's my whole point, here. Did it ever occur to you they are too in sync and it happened too fast? They've been this way since the beginning."

Sasha doesn't want to take this inquiry seriously, but he can see it's important to Reed. He thinks back to when Nic asked him for time off after Geneva. He was shocked by the request. Here was a man who never dated, and rarely went out and got laid, despite women falling at his feet. Then, suddenly, he's an emotional basket case over some woman he literally saw from a distance in Kabul, and spent three weeks with her in the U.S. By then, completely smitten, he was ready to abandon ship, risking his career and possibly his life. So out of character for Nic. Sasha thought him immature and naïve, but he's spent the last 17 years with them watching their bond grow stronger every day.

It's truly astonishing, but even more so is his ass ending up in Cleveland with them. Who in the hell would have predicted he would walk away from his post to live with Nic, his wife and their two children? "Okay, I'll bite," Sasha finally concedes.

"The humming. Nic's humming. Do you hear it?" Reed asks, clearly spooked by something.

Sasha shrugs. "The Soundtrack of His Life? No, but do you know how many times I have fired a weapon?" He waves his hand by his ears.

Reed leans forward and points to his own ears. "I can hear just fine. He's not humming."

Sasha tilts his head trying to work out Reed's meaning. Reed raises his eyebrows questioningly and a light bulb comes on. Sasha's eyes go wide, his mouth drops open, and his hands fly to his face. Holy shit! He doesn't know how he already gleaned Reed's meaning or concern, but he has. And he has a million questions.

TWENTY-SEVEN

"SO YOU'RE SAYING THAT LIKE A HUNDRED years ago, Dad was a KGB agent for Russia and you were a CIA agent working for Uncle Reed?" Mia asks with a touch of cynicism.

"Mia, it wasn't a hundred years ago. It was 17, more or less, when we walked away from all that," Nic responds trying to keep his cool.

Max chimes in, "And Uncle Sasha is not your blood, but another agent for the KGB that was like a brother to you? And you're not gangsta, at all?"

Nic is growing more frustrated. "If it makes you feel any better, Uncle Sasha and I are considered very OG in Russia, original shoot to kill."

"Cool," Max says, more impressed.

Cara tries to explain. "In order to live here with me in the States, your dad and Sasha had to pretend they were dead so they could change their identities, and avoid potential criminal charges, or worse, an extermination order from Russia."

Mia, starting to actually believe them, asks, "Why would the people you worked for want you dead?"

"Because our positions gave us access to a great deal of classified information. And it wasn't all about Russia. Our mission scope often included secrets about other countries; things they would do anything to keep under wraps. So if an agent went rogue, or tried to cut ties, the top brass would order them to be exterminated. They believed, better off dead than a threat to their national security." Nic explains with as much patience as he has.

"Were all agents exterminated?" Max questions.

"No, it depended on their level of expertise and the security clearances they had. The more they knew, or the higher up they were, the bigger the threat." Nic continues, his patience wearing thinner.

"You and Sasha were pretty good agents, then?" Max asks again.

Cara answers for Nic, sensing he is clearly exasperated by these questions, "Guys, your father and Sasha weren't just good agents; they were the best." Then after a moment's indecision, she brags, "And they weren't just Russia's best agents, they were considered two of the most dangerous operatives in the world."

Max and Mia do that twin thing, like they know what the other is thinking. When they look away from each other, Mia proclaims, "We think you guys might be exaggerating. I mean, you have to see this from our point of view. Like you, Dad. A dangerous agent? And Sasha?! He lets me paint and bedazzle his clothes. And don't even get us started on Mom as a CIA agent. Well, that's just not happening." Mia waves her hand near her mother in a dismissive gesture.

Now rubbing his forehead, the worry lines on Nic's face must be deepening. "Cara, I could, in a split second, jump over this table and grab Max in a choke hold while sending an upper cut to Mia's jaw. Do you think they'd believe it then, cause I'm this close..."

Cara places a reassuring hand over the two fingers he's holding up an inch apart, and pleads, "Kids, can we pleeeease, for the moment, agree to disagree about your father's danger factor and your mother's potential lack of skills so we can move on to why the FBI is currently surrounding our house?" her voice rising a decibel or two by the end.

Mia crosses her arms and huffs, "Fine!" but that doesn't stop Max.

"Can you really cross the table that quickly, Dad?"

The words are barely out of his mouth before Nic is behind them, a hand on each of their necks, tilting their heads back and their chairs with them. Cara reacts with lighting speed and is across the table and standing in front of the kids before Mia has a chance to scream. The shriek leaves her throat just as Nic plants a kiss on the top of her head.

A wild-eyed Max yells, "Holy Shit!" once he catches his breath.

Nic releases both of them and scolds, "Language, young man!"

Undaunted, Max argues, "Come on Dad, what the hell? You scared the crap out of us! And Jesus, Mom, how fast did you vault the table? That was impressive."

Nic drops a hand on each child's head, "What do you think, Cara? Is this our new form of discipline?"

"I like it," Cara confirms as she walks back around the table instead of over it.

"Can we get back to the issue at hand, now?" Nic asks as he takes his seat at the table again. The twins nod quickly, not wanting to test him again. "So," he begins more calmly this time, "we think someone discovered that we married and had two children. And we're guessing they may have their sights on you two. They believe you inherited whatever genetics gave us our abilities but with double the effect."

Max bursts out laughing. "Someone thinks Mia has skills?"

Mia ignores her brother and asks earnestly, "So...we're like the *Spy Kids*?"

Cara squints, trying like Nic must be, to call to mind the storyline of this particular movie from the library of mindless kids' films they've had to endure over the years. They're both drawing a blank. "Remind me again about this movie?" Cara requests.

"Mom, they made like three of them," Mia gasps. Then in a run-on sentence she explains about these parents who were spies, and they have a fake uncle that watches over their children, and then the kids get kidnapped, but they have all these skills and they free themselves, and then they help their parents take down the bad guys.

Cara gawks at their daughter in horror, then wails, "Dear God! We're a fucking cliché!" She's out of her chair, bouncing up and down on her toes, pulling at her hair. "When did our life become an unremarkable kid's flick? Oh yeah. It must have been after I fell in love with the handsome Russian agent on a Lifetime channel!" Now she's yelling, "We're a live action B grade movie! The kind that goes straight to DVD! No wonder the kids think we're full of shit! I think we're full of shit!!" Meltdown in progress. He was wondering when she would finally snap.

The twins are horrified, frozen in their seats, watching their mother unravel. Nic is at her side trying to calm her but she pushes him away. "Cara, you're scaring the kids, and frankly, you're scaring me."

"SCARED? WHY WOULD YOU BE SCARED?" she shrieks, "This is B grade, remember? THERE'S ALWAYS A HAPPY ENDING!"

"OK, baby I need you to take some slow, deep breaths. Please?" Cara is trembling. "I think you're going into shock," he says and sends Mia for some water and Max to Cara's bedside nightstand for a Xanax.

She snaps, "It's not shock, it's TOTAL INSANITY!"

"You haven't slept in over 48 hours and your brain wants to shut down, that's all."

The twins are back and Nic gets Cara to swallow the pill. She's about to throw the glass at the wall, but he stops her just in time and wraps her in a bear hug, pinning her arms to her sides. He understands what's happening.

"Cara mia, I know what you're doing. You're blaming yourself for the position we're in. You're thinking if you and I hadn't met, none of this would be happening, right?" He clutches her firmly to his chest.

If things had been different, she could've had a normal life. And if maybe she hadn't met Reed, she'd be an innocent housewife, with a nice banking career, living in a modest home complete with a white picket fence, a mild-mannered husband and 1.8 children. Why did she choose the path she did? Her friends all have normal lives. Maybe not the Hallmark movie variety, what with their unhappy marriages, soul-crushing careers, and disagreeable children, but they're at least living a normal life.

Nic can see all of this in her wild eyes. The second guessing and the comparisons. He needs to make her see that the other choice; a life with no missions, no guns, no danger, no drama, also means a life with no thrill. And he just can't see her missing out on that.

"Of all the people you know, whose life would you rather have? Name one person. Look at me, Cara. Can you do that?" Nic demands.

She finally stops her flailing.

"I believe you were fated to meet Reed that day at UConn," Nic continues, "and I believe, cheap TV movie or not, that my path was always meant to cross yours. You believe it, too. You told me yourself, remember? You felt the pull of a thread."

Cara had told Nic she followed the thread that led her to him. He believes she's been following that thread her whole life. And maybe the thread knew she was meant for bigger things. "The thread took you where you needed to be."

He spins her so she can see the twins. "These are our children, Cara. I would argue they are also on the life path the thread has chosen for you. Consider if you had taken another path that didn't produce these two people you love more than anything else in this world."

Her body relaxes and she begins to cry. "I'm so sorry," she mumbles to the kids.

Mia shrugs, "No big deal. We all have meltdowns."

Max adds, "Maybe you're getting your period soon." Mia hammers him hard in the chest.

Cara's shoulders sag, "You still sure the thread wanted them?", she teases, a small smile playing at her lips. Nic lightens his grip on her but keeps her nestled in his arms. kissing the top of her head.

"Oh, please," Mia cries, clearly unaffected by her mother's tantrum. "Stop with the lovey-dovey stuff. I am out of here. Call me when the food is ready, I'm starving."

Nic assures her the Bishops are bringing Chinese food and will be there soon.

"I'll be in my room," Mia yells over her shoulder as she exits the kitchen.

"Ditto on that," Max mumbles, trailing behind her.

Nic holds onto his wife as he watches his children climb the stairs to their bedrooms. The conversation didn't go as well as he hoped, but it was more dialogue than they've had with their kids in a month.

He carries Cara to their bedroom, lights their gas fireplace and sits with her on the floor in front of it. Shifting, she snuggles up to him, leaning back against his chest. They sit in comfortable silence, with Nic stroking her hair, one hand wrapped around her waist.

Soon, he hears two sets of footsteps treading up the front stairwell from the basement. They stride to the kitchen and he listens as weapons are lifted from the counter, probably being returned to their assigned hiding places.

"Um, is there anyone home?"

Nic calls out to Sasha, "We're in the bedroom."

Sasha and Reed make their way to the open doorway of the bedroom and peer in. Sasha continues the tongue-in-cheek tour with, "And this, Director Reed, is the Primary Suite."

Nic motions for them to enter, but then stops them to scrutinize their appearance.

He doesn't realize Cara is doing the same thing until she drops her head back against his chest, and slurs, "I win."

"Damn, Reed, I thought you'd at least take a swing at Sasha," Nic proclaims.

"I knew they wouldn't fight," Cara says slowly, but more coherently. "It's like I said...Reed's going to have a girlfriend AND a boyfriend now."

TWENTY-EIGHT

REED IS WATCHING SASHA CRINGE, which is frankly insulting, because, "If I were inclined that way, I would be an amazing boyfriend for Sasha."

Cara busts into giggles and waves her arm at them.

Reed stares at Cara for a moment, then declares, "I imagine the talk with the kids didn't go so well. Is that Xanax Cara with us now?"

"I love Xanax Cara. She's funny," Sasha says taking a seat on the floor to Nic's left. Reed decides he'll make it a love fest and sits to their right. He's pleased to see Cara laughing even if it is drug induced. He wonders if they should put her to bed or wait for the food. She should probably eat something. "Who wants to decide?"

"I was just thinking the same thing," Nic answers, and decides she should have dinner, then go right to bed. He inquires causally, "Reed, are you going to behave yourself around Jake? Cara can't take any more stress right now."

Cara is still waving her arm around, and now she's snapping her fingers at nothing.

Reed grabs her hand and promises, "I'll behave." Honestly, even he doesn't have the energy for more confrontations. "I'm exhausted.

you must be, too. You saved your wife from an assassin, and then all of our asses on the jet."

Nic waves at him like 'twas nothing', but says, "Between the kids and Cara's total meltdown, I'm zapped now, too."

"You know I'm right here," Cara calls out. "And I'm suddenly feeling much better and more focused." She squeezes Reed's leg then leans back against Nic and takes in the scene. "This is nice, though. Can we just sit here until the food arrives?"

It really does feel comfortable, all of them together like this, Reed observes. An intimate moment shared by friends old and new. Cara gives Reed a discreet wink and smiles at him. The wink, he's sure, is because she knew he would like Sasha and he does. He's forgiven her for being selfish and keeping Sasha a secret.

Reed lays on his side, stretched out on the carpet. Sasha leans against the chaise lounge. "This IS nice," Nic agrees. "I feel more energized. Physically, I'm toast, but mentally, my mind is alert."

Cara turns to her husband. "You don't think we could have done this 15 years ago? We found our way, the four of us, to this place because of the thread, right?"

Nic leans forward to kiss the top of her head, "Yes, cara mia, the thread brought us here. I don't think this would have worked 15 years ago."

Reed can feel the lasers and shifts his eyes to catch Sasha staring intently at him. He gives the man a subtle nod. When he turns his gaze back to Nic and Cara, he realizes Nic caught the tail end of their silent communique. He's looking slightly wary. Brace yourself, Reed thinks. Soon enough, they will understand.

A FLASH OF LIGHT IGNITES THE BEDROOM, STARTLING SASHA WHO OPENS HIS eyes and reaches for a weapon. He turns to sees Jinx standing in the doorway, her camera phone aimed at them.

"What's going on in here?" Jinx asks. "Did you guys drink the Kool Aid? What am I witnessing?"

Sasha mumbles something about falling asleep waiting for the food. The others appear to still be sleeping until Reed reaches up and grabs Jinx's leg, bringing her down hard on top of him. She feigns a struggle, but is laughing by the time Reed flips her so she's wedged underneath him.

"I've missed you, Jinx." He plants a huge kiss on her lips. "You're looking pretty hot. You still wanna have sex with me?"

Jinx pushes at Reed, "I wanna have sex with every hot guy."

Cara's eyes flutter open at this and she adds, "It's true. Hot guys are Jinx's kryptonite."

"Wait, so you also want to have sex with me, then?" Sasha asks, affecting a hopeful countenance.

"A dream of mine," Jinx admits wistfully.

"Will you do me before Reed? I guarantee you won't want him after I'm done with you," Sasha says with a wink.

Jinx thinks about this. She looks back and forth between him and Reed, then answers in earnest, "No. Reed is first. I've wanted to get into his pants far longer."

Before Sasha can plead his case, Cara interjects, "No, Nic, I know what you're thinking and I didn't forbid it. It was Reed's rule, remember? No cavorting with the staff."

"Not that Jinx ever adhered to the rule," Reed maintains, standing up and pulling Jinx up with him.

"How was I supposed to get any work done?" Jinx protests, loudly. "There were so many distractions in the office. I had to get them out of my system."

"I'm feeling left out, will you have sex with me?" Nic asks trying to sound hurt.

With a broad smile, Jinx admits, "Now Cara did forbid that."

Cara laughs at her friend and starts to rise slowly. She looks completely spent. Nic also struggles to get to his feet as Sasha watches, motionless, from his position on the floor. He's too tired to move.

It's then they hear a new voice join the conversation. "Nobody is having sex with my wife without getting past me, first. Although I admit, the conversation is turning me on."

They all snap their heads towards the doorway where a menacing looking Jake is standing, hands on his hips. He's dressed in black cargo pants and a very tight white T-shirt making his tanned skin appear shades darker in contrast. His tattoos stand out, sharp and vibrant against the bleached cotton. Jake is tall and broad-shouldered and takes up the entire doorway. The man has a way of sucking all of the oxygen out of a room.

"Dude, we're just theorizing, but we're happy to enhance your sex life in any way we can." Sasha gives him a broad grin and two thumbs up. Now he's glad Jinx chose Reed to go first. He'd rather Jake kick Reed's ass.

Jinx takes this opportunity to make introductions. She grabs her husband's hand and pulls him forward until he's standing in front of Reed. Jake is a good four inches taller than Reed, and has about 50 pounds on him. "Director Connor Reed, I would like you to meet my husband, Jake Bishop."

Reed's smile disappears and his features harden. He narrows his eyes and puts a firm hand out. Jake hesitates a moment, then shakes Reed's hand.

Reed raises an eyebrow and asks, "Is it 'Jake'? Or do you prefer the nickname 'Jack'?" Ah, Formidable Reed is back.

Jake responds, obviously not intimidated, "It's Jake, and I could use some help putting the food out if you're up to it?"

"Lead the way," Reed offers, motioning to the doorway.

Jinx has already set the table and sent Eli to find Max and Mia. "They're all in Mia's room and said to call them when the food's been dished out," she explains, then murmurs under her breath, "the spoiled brats."

Staying behind, Jinx quietly shuts the door once Reed and Jake are gone. She turns to Cara with a look of concern on her face and Cara motions for her to sit. "Start talking," she commands.

This, Sasha wants to hear. He only caught portions of the shouted conversation between Jake and Jinx. He needs to know the rest.

JINX WAS HOPING TO PUT OFF THIS DISCUSSION. SHE TRIES TO DELAY THE inevitable, saying instead, "Nic, thank-you so much for saving my little buddy's life...twice. I can't believe you can fly a jet. Jake and Sasha admitted they can, too." Three sets of eyes are laser focused on her. She takes a deep breath and sighing resignedly, finally concedes, "Jake admitted a lot of things to me. Most of which I already suspected." Their stares sharpen. "None of which I'll admit to you guys." Disappointed faces. "His story is not mine to tell. I'm sure when he's ready, he'll disclose all." If he has a confrontation with Reed, it may be sooner than later.

"Did he know you and I were agents and we worked for Reed?" Cara whispers as if it's still a secret.

Jinx snorts, "Jake had no clue! Can you believe he was ripping mad at me earlier? Said I betrayed him! The nerve! He lives a lie, and I'm the traitor? Asshole."

Sasha snickers. "Is that what all the screaming was about?"

"Yes!" Jinx hangs her head. So what if she had her suspicions about her husband's line of work. That didn't mean she had to fess up to hers. Like Cara, it was just simpler to live the lie. She signed an NDA when she left the CIA and Reed set up her interview in Cleveland. He also altered her employment records to ensure her privacy but maintain her pension. Her job as an analyst with the Agency had been interesting and exciting, but she was starting to burn out. Reed understood this, and helped her get out and start a new life. Anyone checking up on her now would find she worked for the Defense Department in a minimal capacity.

"Reed gave me a glowing recommendation and described my background to the hiring manager. I scored an awesome job at triple my pay scale." As much as she hated to leave Cara behind, Jinx was confident Reed would protect her. She certainly didn't expect Cara to show up on her doorstep only months later, an emotional wreck after a weekend in Geneva.

"Ellie, you were suspicious of Jake's career, but...what about his motives?" Cara inquires with as much finesse as she ever displays.

"I'm not dumb," Jinx says giving Cara an eye roll. "Jake was HOT, but I was no honeypot. He wasn't going to get any confidential info out of me. I told myself I would fuck him and steer clear of the pillow talk. And that's what I did, and did I mention he was HOT? Hot enough to keep wanting him."

She knew Jake was fishing and probably dangerous, but it added to the eroticism. She wasn't sure what he was looking for, or if he was even a real threat, but she couldn't deny the thrill of not knowing.

But then she got knocked up. That was not part of her fuck the hot, mysterious guy plan, but Jinx was 32 and her biological clock was ticking away. She wanted the baby, and soon after breaking the news to Jake, felt a shift in their relationship. She realized he was really into her, not just using her for cover or a good lay. He wanted to be a part of it all. At the time, she was uncomfortable telling Cara about their growing attachment to each other, particularly because Cara made it all too clear she didn't approve of Jake.

"I'm sorry, but I didn't think you would understand, so I kept our true feelings to myself. That is, until he dropped out of sight at the end of my pregnancy. I was a wreck. I was pretty sure I knew what kind of job he had and I thought he was dead." Jake finally did show up in the middle of her labor. He was haggard and contrite and incredibly apologetic as he threw Cara and Nic out of her delivery room.

But what finally clinched it for Jinx was when Nic and Sasha started getting really close to Jake. She knew they didn't go to Vegas on their first guys' weekend getaway. "No way. You came back too clear eyed and your clothes too clean. There was no scent of the smoke and depravity that boys will get up to when let loose in Sin City."

"That's what I thought, too!" Cara exclaims. "I knew they were lying."

"Smoke and depravity?" Nic muses. "That was our big mistake?"

"Absolutely", Cara confirms. "Think about when Jinx and I go, or I meet Reed or my college girlfriends in Vegas?"

Nic considers this. "You come home exhausted, hung over and broke. Smelling of sweat, booze and ashtrays. Come to think of it, what the hell do you do there?"

"Our secret, we aren't sharing. But you guys came back almost exhilarated. All wrong." Cara gives them a disapproving look. "Not smart, boys."

Every weekend away supplied more clues to their true purpose. But Jinx wanted to believe it would all be fine. Nic obviously trusted Jake, and she respected Nic, so what could go wrong? "I stuck my head in the sand, went to Cara's Land of Denial, and pretended everything was normal. I love Jake, whoever he is." Then she peers at the closed door and admits, "Jake knows Reed. That's why he was so mad at me. He thinks Reed is going to do something...bad."

Jinx had stayed back to give Reed and Jake time to, hopefully, just chat. She figured there would be a confrontation, so she's somewhat confused by Reed's restraint. Why didn't he unmask Jake? He's either being charitable or is up to something. Withholding Jake's secret from Cara and Nic can go either way. Her money is on Reed spinning it to his advantage. Maybe for a favor...or five in the future.

Changing the subject, Jinx declares, "I'm beat. And by the scene in here when I arrived, I assume none of you slept recently, either. Let's eat and all get some sleep."

They all get up to leave but as they approach the door, Nic asks, "What can we expect from Reed and Jake when we get out there?"

Jinx shrugs her shoulders, "Hope for the best and prepare for the worst." With that pronouncement, Sasha checks for his weapon. She punches him.

"Hands off the gun, Broody."

CHAPTER

TWENTY-NINE

AS SOON AS THEY OPEN the door, they hear voices and laughter from the kitchen at the other end of the house. They approach cautiously, and find the kids all seated and already eating. Jake and Reed are seated next to each other at one end of the table with the kids on either side of them.

Jake addresses the foursome entering the kitchen. "We were just about to send a search party for you guys. The food is getting cold."

Without word, they take the remaining seats and start passing around cartons of Chinese food. Cara notices wine glasses and bottles of Shiraz and Pinot Grigio on the table. Good old Jinx. She won't cook, but she sets a mean table and thinks of all the little things.

Cara opts out of the wine and goes for ice water instead. She peers at Reed as she contemplates what might have happened between him and Jake. She's getting nothing from his face, but neither man appears injured. "What was so funny?" she decides to ask.

Before either man can speak, Mia pipes up, "We were talking about your code names. So lame, by the way." She rolls her eyes.

228

They get the meaning behind Nic and Sasha's, but the kids are having difficulty understanding Cara's. "Uncle Reed said we have to ask you if we want to know," Mia adds.

Cara freezes, water glass halfway to her lips. Nic reaches for her leg under the table and says in a stage whisper, "Don't go there if you can't handle it this evening."

There's a loud, derisive snort from Jinx. "The kids are going to LOVE this story!" Then she yells down the table to Reed, "Shall I start and you finish, or vice versa?"

Reed furrows his brows and eyes Cara with concern. She shrugs her shoulders in defeat and points to the bottle of red wine, "Go for it, but I need to be drinking."

Nic kindly pours as Reed begins.

He turns to the three kids and admonishes, "Everything you heard today and everything you hear from now on is strictly confidential. I trust you three with this information. You're not little kids anymore, and you have the right to know, but with that right comes responsibility. I expect the highest degree of discretion from you as I would any of my agents. Swear to it."

All three kids nod seriously, raising their right hands as if they're in a court of law. Nic and Jake smile at their reaction.

Having made his point, Reed continues with the story. "When I started at the Agency, both of your moms were on my team. We trained in marksmanship, weaponry and hardware. We practiced sleep deprivation and hand to hand combat, lots of stuff you might do in military basic training.

"One of the facilities at Langley housed simulation rooms. Back in the 80's they were equipped with a mechanically driven series of diversions and obstacles. Agents had to hit targets with a certain degree of speed and accuracy in order to pass the course."

Mia interrupts, as she's prone to do. "Like in the old movies? When the metal plated ugly mobster comes flying around a corner, and you have to put a bullet in him before he gets a shot off at you?"

"Yes, exactly like that!" Reed exclaims. "Your Mom excelled at most of the other training, but in the simulator, she was awful." Reed slides his gaze in Sasha's direction.

NIC NOTICES CARA IS GUZZLING HER WINE. STRESS DRINKING? SHE'S looking away from the captivated audience so he places his hand on her leg under the table in solidarity. She gives him a smile, thankful for his support. When Nic turns to smile back at her, he catches Sasha and Reed glancing at each other. Just like earlier. What's up with those two? They can't honestly be dating already?

Reed continues his story admitting Cara is anything but a quitter, "She kept going back to the simulator, sometimes late in the evening, to try to better her scores. And just when she was showing improvement, I would completely rework the program because I suspected she was memorizing the movements. Sure enough her scores dropped again."

Cara glares at Reed. He winks at her and keeps talking.

"C decided the sounds were a distraction, so she started running through the simulator wearing headphones and listening to music. This was years before the iPod. All we had back then were Sony Walkmans and cassette tapes.

"She did show improvement with this method. I changed the program again, and she continued to score in a decent range. She was definitely on to something. So, I suggested she plug her cassette player into the simulator speakers and ditch the bulky headphones. I thought shedding that equipment might help increase her scores."

The kids are on the edge of their seats fully engaged in Reed's story, as are Jake and Sasha. Nic can hear Cara regulate her breathing in an effort to stay calm.

"The modification worked and her scores did improve. She was still below average but she kept working at it. Then one day, late in the afternoon, we were all gathered in the team room when something activated the pager system." Reed motions, handing the baton off to Jinx.

Jinx works hard to maintain a straight face. "The next thing we heard was *The Reflex*, by Duran Duran blaring over the speakers throughout the Langley facility. I knew right away where it was coming from so I yelled to Reed, 'Bennett's in the simulator!'" Jinx is struggling to breathe and continue the story, between bursts of laughter. "You see, Cara had a huge crush on Simon LeBon, the lead singer, and she loved all of Duran Duran's music. But she especially loved *The Reflex*.

"Apparently, Cara screwed up the connection and plugged her music into the wrong speaker system. Reed went running to the simulator, but by the time he got there and disconnected the player, the song had played all the way through." Jinx is wiping tears from her eyes. "As luck would have it, the facility was packed full of people that day, in high level meetings or mass training exercises. There was going to be hell to pay!" Jinx screams through her laughter.

Reed jumps back in, "The Deputy Director summoned us to his office. He wanted answers. I didn't have a choice. I had to tell him the truth."

Cara is covering her face with hands that appear to be trembling. Nic can't tell if she's laughing or crying but before he can find out, Reed goes on. "The man was shouting at us when we walked in. Before we had a chance to even begin apologizing, he ordered Cara to get down on one knee. He pulled a huge sword out of a sheath he had hanging on one wall, and pointed it at her.

"Now I'm freaking out, thinking he's going to hurt her. But then he taps each shoulder, then her head with the sword." Mimicking an English accent, Reed quotes, "'I dub thee Sir Reflex from here on in', and then he bursts out laughing at her!"

Everyone erupts into laughter when they hear this, except Nic and Cara. She is mortified, her face burning with embarrassment. Nic however, is too disappointed to laugh. "That's it? That's why everyone called you the Reflex? Because of a pop song by an 80's band?" he exclaims.

His disdain only sends everyone into more fits of laughter.

Sasha tries to speak between gasps. "We all thought it meant you were quick and agile, like you actually had good reflexes. Instead you got the name because you put your plug into the wrong hole!"

More laughter ensues. Adding insult to injury Reed advises them, "Word got around and there was no way she could shake the name after that."

"Okay, stop already, will you?" Cara pleads. The three teenagers decide they've had enough of the adults and leave the room, but not before Mia runs over to whisper in Sasha's ear.

With the kids gone, Cara takes the opportunity to bring up the topic that brought them all together tonight. "Do you see now why I was so freaked out when the song kept popping up in the most random places? It's not like that story was public knowledge outside of Langley. How did Vlad know my code name came from the song?"

"It was the reason I took the threat so seriously when you emailed me," Reed confesses. "I'm still looking for possible connections." He turns to Sasha and asks, "You guys really didn't know any of this? Vlad was in your employ. He didn't get this information from you?"

Sobering, Sasha shakes his head. "Not us. But somehow, he knew the song would goad Cara into action. We should be exploring other known associates of Vlad. It is very likely he heard the story from someone who was connected to the Agency during that time period."

Reed already has his analysts working that angle. He agrees to loop Sasha in on the investigation and asks him to add anyone they haven't already considered. The two agree to meet at 10:00 AM tomorrow, deciding everyone is too tired tonight to be worthwhile.

Nic watches this exchange. It's as if he isn't there. This morning Reed knew nothing about Sasha and now they're suddenly BFF's? What the hell? He's the husband and father whose family is being threatened. What do they think his role is here?

He doesn't have a chance to process these feelings because there's a sudden commotion in the great room. The three kids have returned. They've obviously come from the music room. Mia walks into the kitchen and hands Sasha a guitar and him a wireless microphone. She whispers in his ear. Nic grabs his daughter by the chin and kisses her nose. Mia gives her mother a wicked grin as she strides back into the great room to the baby grand piano.

CARA IS DISCONCERTED. HER CHILDREN THINK SHE'S A JOKE AND HER husband, the music snob, is disillusioned with her. Why, oh why did this story have to come up tonight, her ridiculous moniker? Nic and Sasha's code names define them, or at least the roles they played. And Reed? Well, he embodies the term 'White Knight'. She gave him the name and it stuck. He is the heroic warrior righting wrongs, an honorable creature, respectful to men and women alike. Her stupid code name is another example how women need to work harder to get any respect.

Before she has a chance to wallow any further, Carter enters the house carrying two empty plates and some silverware. Cara assumes Jake and Reed must have served them food, but told them to eat outside. Poor bastards.

So, switching the topic away from her distress, she demands of Reed, "Why are Carter and Far Guard eating outside. It's too rude and improper for my Sicilian blood. This is MY house and people Eat INSIDE! Capice? And while we're on the subject of good manners, have you been shown to your rooms yet?"

Jake answers, "I did it when you guys were in the bedroom, and I took Reed on a tour of the house when we fetched the kids for dinner." Cara nods and smiles satisfied something has gone right.

"By the way, sweetheart, beautiful house," Reed says as a compliment. He senses Cara is still reeling from her recent humiliation and wants to lift her spirits. Plus it's the first time he's been to this house.

"Nic designed it and you did the interior, right? It's all very impressive."

She and Nic have traveled extensively. They both used the places and things they've encountered in their designs, a principle they have in common but have never actually discussed. It's a way for each of them to extract the positive from their pasts and leave the unpleasantness behind. "Despite being there for more nefarious purposes, we have seen some of the most beautiful architecture and artfully decorated rooms in the world. We each took that into consideration with the design of our home."

Jake asks, playfully, "Are you saying as you were being chased through the Hermitage you stopped to admire the frescoes?"

Reed looks at Cara and gives her the nod to respond. "Something like that, yes." She gets up and meets Carter at the sink. "Carter, please help yourself to anything in the house. You are my guest here. Do not eat outside anymore. Understand? And tell your nameless friend, too."

Carter nods graciously, and then asks, "What are they doing in the living room?"

"THEY are setting up to mock me, my children and Mean Man. Please, stay for the entertainment portion of this evening."

Carter peers into the living room then wanders in. Cara continues to clear the dishes, choosing to ignore everyone. With Reed's help she has the leftovers put away and dishwasher loaded by the time she hears an all too familiar sound coming from the living room.

The three kids are singing background...

"Ta, nah, nah, nah, Ta, nah, nah, nah"

Then comes the first verse, Nic's voice, sounding better than Simon LeBon could ever dream of.

Reed attempts to drag Cara into the living room, but she's resisting. He finally picks her up and throws her over his shoulder. Jake, not wanting to be outdone, throws Jinx over his shoulder and the two men move to the doorway. The girls clasp hands in an effort to prevent the boys from making any forward progress, but they fail and they all end up sitting on the floor in front of the performers.

Mia is at the piano and Sasha on acoustic guitar. Elijah is playing an electric bass guitar and Max has dragged up a small drum kit and cymbals. And look who has joined them on the saxophone. Great, even Carter has other talents.

They've given the song a more contemporary arrangement. There's a Lady Gaga/Usher feel to it. Nic winks at Cara as he belts out the chorus.

Reed leans into her ear, the music surrounding them from the plug and play

Bose sound system. "Holy shit, I had no idea they were this good!"

Cara replies with delight, "They are. They make me proud." Music is their outlet, but they could honestly tour, they're that good." And Cara is all for encouraging them, even when it's at her own expense.

All Reed can say is, "Amazing."

Nic launches into the second verse adding a little hip movement for the full rock star effect. Then Sasha starts a guitar solo his fingers flying over the strings. As soon as he finishes, Carter commences his own sax solo, then waves Mia into action on the baby grand piano. She earns a round of applause for her performance as she nods to Elijah to bring it home with some complicated riffs on the bass. Jake and Jinx hoot and holler along with the rest of the crew. Finally, Nic switches places with Max, taking a seat at the drums and handing over the microphone for Max to rap the next verse.

Cara is watching Reed and his expression of awe is priceless. Max is ever the showman, mixing a few of his own digs at his mother with the lyrics. She is beaming.

Suddenly, through the clouds in her head, she's outside of herself staring with wonder at her amazing family. How lucky she's been to have grown up in one incredibly loving family and then acquire a second, equally wonderful family...in one lifetime. Why did she not see this before? Why had she questioned the road she has taken. This...the people in this room... are everything to her.

"Don't do that."

What? Cara looks at Reed. *Was I just biting my lip? Reed hates it when I do that. Reed isn't paying me any attention, though. That's weird; I swear I just heard him speak. I'm losing it. Bedtime for Bonzo as soon as they're done mocking me.*

The song is finally finished and the performers all bow to a standing ovation. "Bravo, Bravo to all of you," Cara says with pride. "Can I go to bed now?"

"Just one more," Nic replies and sets the microphone stand in front of Sasha. He turns to Cara and bows. "May I have this dance, my lady? Or should I say, Sir Reflex?"

The kids rearrange themselves on the instruments. Elijah moves to the piano, Carter, the electric bass. Sasha picks up the electric guitar and with Mia on her cello they begin with a haunting extended intro to *Secrets* by OneRepublic. Nic takes Cara in his arms and they slow dance to the serenade. Jinx and Jake follow suit. Reed switches to one of the overstuffed chairs to watch the impromptu performance.

Sasha starts the song, his beautiful soulful voice filling the room. The lyrics are poignant and evocative, the melody cathartic. His face is etched with pain as he sings the words, the instruments growing louder with each refrain.

Cara notices Reed watching closely. *I wonder if he senses Sasha's anguish.*

"Sasha loves this song, and it's appropriate for this evening," Nic whispers, pulling her attention back to him. "The kids like playing this one with him, but it's his voice that tells the story. Full of pain."

"I was just thinking that, too."

"How are you, baby?"

"Ready for bed and a new start tomorrow."

CHAPTER

THIRTY

CARA PROMISED SHE WOULD MEET JINX at 8:00 AM to run the front nine of the golf course. The exercise sounded like a perfectly good idea the night before, but when the alarm goes off, she's not so sure. She was asleep last night as soon as she fell into bed and before Nic came out of the bathroom. She looks over and sees that his side of the bed is empty. She gets up and readies herself for what better be a slow jog through the neighborhood.

When Cara enters the kitchen, Nic is at the stove. He's already served up sausage, bacon and hash browns and is working on another serving of scrambled eggs. Carter is eating at the table and a dirty plate sits in front of Reed, who is drinking coffee and working on his tablet. Jinx is next to Reed with her own cup of coffee.

"Order up," Nic says as he serves Far Guard three eggs over easy.

Cara grabs a large mug and prepares a cup of coffee, then sits next to Carter. He stops eating from his full plate long enough to remark, "Mean Man makes a mean breakfast." Reed and Jinx both inhale sharply and start laughing at their simultaneous response. Carter gazes at them confused, "What?"

"Agent Carter, no one, and I mean NO ONE speaks to Agent Bennett before she's finished her first cup of coffee in the morning. You're lucky she's not armed," Reed admonishes.

Nic pipes in from the range top, "That used to be true, Reed, and although it's still her preference, I've managed to break that horse."

Cara scowls. Nic says she can't shoot him or the children if they speak to her before she's fully caffeinated. He can be so unreasonable.

"You and Jinx skipping breakfast or you want something? I'm only here till 9:00 AM," Nic warns.

She would hurl during the run if she ate anything. Maybe Jinx will take pity on her and get them back here by nine.

"Speaking of which, hurry up with that coffee and let's go," Jinx urges.

It's a rare, beautiful morning for late April in Northeast Ohio. The daffodils and crocuses are blooming. The sun is peeking its way out. The golf course has been cleaned and landscaped after the winter abuse. The 55 degree temperature is perfect for a leisurely jog.

"Jesus, Jinx, my lungs are frigging burning. Slow down, bitch. You know you're like two inches taller than me. That stride of yours is killing me."

Jinx glares back at her over her shoulder. "Stop bitching and start breathing, slut. We're almost back to your house." She hadn't noticed. She can't see through the sweat pouring into her eyes.

Two of the FBI agents are running with Jinx and Cara as protection. Sasha and Nic had insisted. They have flanked the girls for the entire run, but now one agent slips behind Cara as she begins to lag.

About 50 yards from the house, Cara gives up completely and walks the remaining distance while chatting up the FBI agent. They are deep in conversation when she suddenly hears Jinx scream, "Oh NO, NO, NO... HELL NO, NOT HAPPENING!"

Cara breaks into a sprint. As she rounds the corner and heads up the driveway, she sees the cause for alarm. Cara stops dead next to

Jinx, who's standing, hands on hips, staring at the five gorgeous men wearing nothing but shorts or track pants, and sneakers.

Jinx turns to engage Cara. "This is not acceptable. AT ALL. Nic parading around the women in front of Starbucks was obnoxious enough, but this?!" She's waving her arm wildly in the direction of the half-naked band of brothers. "THIS is absolutely intolerable!"

Cara uses her shirt to wipe the sweat from her face, exposing her not so tight abs as she takes her time walking the rest of the way up the driveway. She takes in the view and asks, "Gentlemen, is it really your intention to run the course together dressed like that?"

Nic and Sasha know better than to answer her, but Reed doesn't understand her concern. "Yes, what's the issue?"

Jinx jumps at him. "You can't go out there together and shirtless! The women of this neighborhood will faint! Have you no clue what you all look like? This is Cleveland. Men don't look like you here – let alone five of you together! You look like a Chippendales act!"

Nic complains, "Cara, you know I don't like to wear a shirt when I run. The fabric hurts my nipples when I start to sweat." It comes out like a whine.

"Yeah, honey, you know I have sensitive nipples, too," Jake adds placing his hands over them protectively while flexing his pecs for effect.

Jinx stomps her foot, infuriated now. Cara just sighs knowing they won't win this battle. She places a calming hand on Jinx's arm and says to the group, "Fine, but I hope one of you is carrying."

Carter raises his hand. Cara moves in to inspect his shorts and locate the weapon, then faces the rest of them. "The Women's League is on the course this morning. Please don't give any of the older women a heart attack."

The men head down the driveway but Cara catches Sasha's hairy arm as he passes by. She looks down past his exceedingly hairy chest to his shorts, "I see you're packing a weapon as well."

Sasha gives her a rare ear-to-ear grin. "No, but I've had other women refer to it that way."

"EEEEWWW!" Cara screams as she chases Sasha down the driveway trying to punch him.

THIRTY-ONE

CARA ARRIVES LATE TO THE PARTY at 10:09. She was held up from her shower serving breakfast to the kids, who overslept Nic's cut off time. Apparently, they cannot locate cereal and milk on their own. She's dressed casually in jeans and a light sweater paired with the Olaf boots. She loves how they feel, even after only wearing them once. She blowdried her hair, but skipped the fuss of straightening it. She even managed a little make-up.

She rounds the corner into the living room and sees she's not the only one who was missing. Reed is there. He's wearing a striped, collared shirt and a blue blazer over jeans. Her boyfriend looks like he's going to the club for dinner after the meeting. Jinx, fresh from a shower in Mia's bathroom, has on a fitted long black skirt and a blouse. Cara's thinking she might be underdressed for this meeting. *I should go change.*

Nic arrives a moment later and, giving her a peck on the cheek, he says "You look lovely, baby, and you smell great."

She gives him a little smile and decides to stay dressed as she is.

Sasha comes up from the lower level wearing a T-shirt that says 'BAZINGA' on it. Painted footprints adorn his jeans.

Cara stops him as he passes by. "I know yesterday's jeans paid homage to that *Supernatural* show you watch with the kids, but what's this?" she asks, pointing to his legs.

"These are my *Just Dance* pants."

Reed tilts his head and winces. "Don't you have any *Call of Duty* jeans? I think they would've been more appropriate."

"I play that with the boys but they don't decorate," Sasha says mock seriously. "Where ARE the chosen ones by the way?"

Nic leans into the back stairwell and yells up to the kids.

As the teenagers arrive, everyone finds a seat, except Reed, who remains standing. Cara runs to her favorite chair and sits, but can't get comfortable. She stands back up to inspect the cushion. It seems fine so she sits back down but is still bothered. Rising once again, she pulls the cushion off to look underneath it. She suspects one of the kids hid some contraband below. It's clean. She repositions the cushion but does not sit. Instead, she stands rigidly staring down at the offending armchair. It's not the cause of her discomfort, though. She feels restless and uneasy, as if the air around her is pressurized. She surveys the room. Something is wrong. *There's a threat. I know it. I feel prickles on my neck.* Slowly looking around her, she rests her gaze on the wall of windows facing the backyard. It's not out there. The danger is here in the room with her.

Cara turns to her children who are seated on the couch with their backs to the glass wall. Eli is next to them and they all look bored. She shifts her eyes to where Jinx is reprimanding Jake for setting his coffee down and not using a coaster. Nic and Sasha are seated in the two leather club chairs across from them deep in conversation. No one is paying her any attention; all seemingly unaware of her growing alarm.

Her scrutiny ends with Reed. He's still standing, and he's right next to her. His eyes lock on hers and Cara's sense of peril is heightened. He is the menacing force she feels. She tilts her head in confusion. Reed is wearing an icy expression and it's directed at her. She is dumbfounded. Reed has looked at her with anger, rage, frustration, betrayal, but never like this. He looks ready to kill. Without taking his eyes from her, Reed slowly reaches inside his jacket.

In an instant, Cara lunges towards him, grabbing his wrist with both her hands. "Stop."

"Stop what?" Reed asks quietly.

She backs away slightly, but he moves his hand further into his jacket. She tightens the grip on his wrist. "NO, STOP!"

Her shout gets Nic's attention. He rises to head towards the confrontation but Sasha jumps out in front of him stopping him in his tracks.

Still locked in a battle over his wrist, Reed calmly inquires, "C, what's the matter?" but his face and pale blue eyes are cold and cruel.

Cara stares intently into those glaciers with determination, and demands fiercely, "Take your hand out of your jacket, NOW!"

Reed, still with the forbidding glare, replies, "But I'm just getting my phone, C."

She shakes her head trying to break this spell, but nothing changes the threat level radiating from her best friend. "You're lying. Your phone is not in your jacket."

"C, let go of my wrist, now, before I have to hurt you."

Nic tries to push past Sasha, but Sasha grabs hold of him, and Nic's confusion prevents him from fighting back.

Cara is panicked now. This is all wrong. Reed wants to hurt her. She's sure of it. "No, you ARE trying to hurt me. Why do you want to hurt me? TELL ME!"

Reed grabs Cara so quickly, she doesn't see it coming. He has restrained both of her arms and is shaking her. A bewildered Nic jerks his head back and forth between the confrontation and Sasha, who only clamps tighter to Nic.

Cara is close to hysterics. Reed is in her face now. Those awful eyes on her. *I feel his hatred. This makes no sense. He loves me.*

Reed yells into her face, "TELL ME WHAT'S IN MY JACKET IF IT'S NOT MY PHONE! TELL ME!"

"YOU HAVE A GUN!"

Reed shakes her harder, "OF COURSE I HAVE A GUN. IT'S ALWAYS HOLSTERED IN THERE!"

She feels a sudden jolt go through her brain. It's dizzying, but she now has a clear picture of what's under his coat. "No, no, not that gun!" Cara whispers, her eyes pleading with him to stop this crazy train. She wants to get off.

"WHAT DO I HAVE IN HERE, CARA!?" Reed demands.

"You have Sasha's gun!" Cara blurts out not understanding where the knowledge came from.

CHAPTER

THIRTY-TWO

WITH CARA'S DECLARATION, all eyes are now on them. Reed releases his hold and gently massages her arms where he was gripping her. He opens his jacket and carefully pulls out a vintage Makarov PM pistol. He walks over to Sasha and hands it to him. Nic is staring at the gun, recognizing it as one from Sasha's collection. Frozen in place, he looks up at Cara, questioningly.

Cara puts one shaky hand on her forehead and returns Nic's gaze. When Reed slowly returns to stand in front of her, his heart is bursting with emotion. He loves this woman and is feeling contrite but vindicated. "I am so sorry, my sweetheart, but it had to be done. We had to prove our theory and we couldn't figure out a better way to do it," Reed says as gently as possible. Cara looks up at him with tears in her eyes, unable to speak.

Nic finally tries to move and finds Sasha stepping out in front of him, again. "Nicolae, please, we must see this through. Trust me," Sasha says, soothingly.

Reed is watching Cara closely. "C, sweetheart, I have been remiss. I was your handler and I just didn't see it. The clues were all there but I never put it together. Maybe, I didn't want to see it. Again, I am so sorry," he tells her, his voice echoing the guilt and resignation he feels.

Cara questions him in a trembling shaky voice. "What did I just do?"

Stroking her hair, he contends, "You did what you've been able to do since I met you, sweetheart. We just didn't see it."

Cara always had this amazing ability to predict everyone's next move. She was one of the best in the field, yet she couldn't get through a simulation. Her intuition was sharp, she was a natural, but only in real time with real people. He feels like a fool now as he looks back. He should have realized what she was doing. It wasn't until the plane ride back from Berlin, that each event, each interaction clicked into place. He had a moment of illumination when she started singing the song Nic was humming. That's when the light came on and it was incandescent. She asked if he remembered about Nic's humming, and of course he had, but Nic wasn't humming. He was sitting right next to Nic, and Cara was across the table, at least four more feet away. And he knows for a fact her hearing is not as keen as his.

"You don't hear Nic humming, C, you hear the music in his head." Cara is backing away from him, tears streaming down her face. "You hear a lot of stuff in everyone's head, C. I'll wager you feel what's in their hearts, as well," he continues, his tone pedantic. "You're not a natural, my dangerous, little sweetheart. You're actually a bit of a cheater."

At this accusation, Nic tries again to push Sasha aside but Sasha continues to restrain him. Cara is fully focused on Reed and his revelations.

Reed thinks back to Kabul and Geneva. It all adds up now. Kabul was a failure. But why? Why didn't Cara sense those men coming into the alley after her? There were six of them, for God's sake. Then, there was Geneva; she was a mess. First time Reed had ever seen her like that. "You were so fucked up and out of sorts in Geneva, it spilled over to me," he confesses.

But the answer was revealed yesterday morning when Reed listened to the tapes of Cara's conversation with Vlad. She was doing great. She had him talking, and giving up information, and then suddenly, she shut down. Training gone. Sonar gone. Signal jammed. She went off to seizure land. "Those three were the only times you fell apart on a mission. So what do they all have in common, C?"

Cara's gaze shifts to take in her husband. Nic brings his eyes to hers, but his features give nothing away.

Reed persists with his theorizing. "I berated you over Nic, your fascination, your obsession, your failure to listen to reason. You had NEVER reacted that way to anything before. So what made Nic different? True love at first sight? That's for Hollywood and romance novels. No one gets what you two have from just seeing one another across a dusty Afghani alley."

Now Jinx and Jake are on their feet. Jinx can't stop herself. She interrupts Reed's monologue. "I'm sorry but he's right, you know. It's not normal what you and Nic have. You two are just something else, sometimes. Like too in sync. Unnatural for a couple. And the chemistry still after 17 years together?"

Reed needed to confirm his suspicion. Cara is much more than she appears to be. The clues were everywhere. He just didn't pay attention. "You have the mental capacity to read people's minds, but for some reason your subconscious is keeping that fact hidden from you. And I don't believe you're the only one," he delivers with zeal.

Cara begins to sway as Reed backs away from her. Can this be true? How is it even possible?! She sees movement to her right and notices Jake coming closer to her. She turns her head to glance at him and... *He's so scary. Why does he always have that awful menacing look?*

That's the only look he has. In her mind, it's as clear as if he spoke.

She spins her head so hard in Nic's direction, it causes her to become unbalanced. *Nic?*

Baby?

Cara goes down, knees crumpling beneath her at the sound of her husband's voice in her head. Jake manages to catch her before she hits the ground. Nic's still frozen in his spot, just staring wild-eyed at her. He's as shocked by what's happened as she.

Cara mia!

I'm okay, I'm okay. She sends that thought out to him with a little more force.

WHAT THE HELL IS HAPPENING?

She can not only hear him, but also feel his fear and confusion. Nic breaks free of Sasha this time and scoops her out of Jake's arms. He falls to his knees cradling her close. The children are horrified. Everyone freezes as they gawk at the two of them, recognizing their distress, but failing to comprehend its source.

Nic turns to Sasha and Reed and through gritted teeth growls, "This is what you two talked about last night instead of fighting, isn't it?!"

PART TWO

THIRTY-THREE

CARA'S THROBBING HEAD HAS BECOME more of a dull ache.

Her body is still trembling as she not only hears her husband's thoughts for the first time ever, but also feels his rage. All of it directed at Reed and Sasha. With one arm wrapped around her and his other arm out, finger pointed at both, Nic screams, "This what you two talked about last night instead of fighting, isn't it!?"

Sasha doesn't look apologetic when he answers. "It was all there, Nic. Reed is correct. I am to blame as well. You...you are different. I grew to love you like a brother, so I didn't want to see it. But it was there. You are like Cara, somehow. You are you, but more. It explains so much I've taken for granted over the years."

While Sasha is talking, Reed approaches and leans into her, placing his lips to her ear. She flinches, but he holds her head, firmly. "Tell Jinx it's time to start drinking, and to get some alcohol out here...with your mind." He backs away, but his eyes are fixed on her in silent command.

She places her hand on Nic's face and gazes into his eyes before

Jinx jumps up and announces, "Shit, I don't know about you guys, but I need to start drinking. Do I have any takers?"

Cara inhales so hard, her heart literally skips a beat. She's not even sure how she did that. Reed answers Jinx, calmly requesting she open a bottle of red, but his eyes remain on Cara.

Sasha adds, "Jinx, do you mind going down to the wine cellar and getting the Russian River Pinot, please? You know I love that one." He smiles at his joke.

Oblivious, Jinx heads out to descend the stairs. When she is out of earshot, Reed commands, "C, tell her to grab the Vinho Verde for something lighter, as well." Jake moves towards Reed when he realizes the game they're playing with his wife. Reed puts up his hand to stop him from overreacting. "I'm sorry, it must be done. Please let this play out."

Three minutes go by while no one speaks or appears to breathe. All eyes are darting around the room, looking from one to the other. Jinx starts talking as soon as she's at the top of the stairs. "You know, I grabbed a bottle of the Portuguese Vinho Verde, too. It's nice and light for anyone not looking for the heavy Pinot this early." There's a collective gasp heard around the room.

Jake reaches for his wife and gently pulls her into the living room, taking the two bottles from her. "What happened?" Jinx inquires seeing the shocked look on all their faces.

"When the mission script had to change, how did you know where C needed you to be in the field, Jinx?" Reed demands.

Jinx is confused by his inquisition. "Most times I guessed based on what she would do."

"But you always guessed correctly. By some miracle, pairing you with Cara negated your nickname."

"Well, sure?" Jake takes Jinx's hand and tells her discreetly what just occurred. "WHAT?" Turning and glaring at Cara, she yells, "You've been manipulating me?!"

Reed, again, takes control, "Ellie, calm down. I don't believe C does it consciously. When she NEEDS you, it projects to you," he quells by calling Jinx by her real name.

Cara and Nic are still on the ground speechless, both feeling anxious and perplexed. Cara's head is starting to clear, though. *Nic, it's all true, isn't it?*

It would appear that way, cara mia.

Do I manipulate you?

No.

How can you be so sure? I mean, I manipulate people all the time. It's common knowledge, but I didn't realize I had mad skills at it.

I'm not sure how, but I do know, and you don't have that effect on me. I think Reed has a direction he's going with this. Can you read anyone else's thoughts like you're reading mine right now?

She scans the room. *I'm getting a sense of some thoughts from Sasha, Reed, and Jinx. None are clear like yours and mine, though. Jake is closed off completely. So are all three kids.*

Interesting. He muses.

Are you processing with that brilliant brain of yours?

Yes.

Why can't I hear or see that, the processing? Just your words. I imagine you're speaking in your head like I am.

I am speaking them, but I don't know why you can't see more.

Cara deflates. She takes in a big breath to reorient her body. *Nic, did my cliché B grade romance movie life just become science fiction?*

She can hear him sigh in her mind. *Which answer do you want, cara mia? The one that makes you feel better, or the one my brain is processing right now?*

Before she can mentally respond to Nic, Jake comes to their side on the floor. "You're talking to each right now, telepathically?" Jake inquires, kindly, considerate of their feelings.

"Yes," Nic states.

"So, you can hear her thoughts like Jinx can, but you can also project your thoughts to her?" Jake questions, directing his inquiry only to Nic.

"Yes."

"You have never done this consciously before?"

"No, we have not."

"But you have had a connection to one another that's deeper and more intimate than most couples." This genteel Jake is foreign to Cara. Nic nods his answer and Jake continues, "It never occurred to you to explore that, or think it odd?"

"No." Nic hesitates for a moment. "Maybe?"

Jake very calmly sits back on the floor with his legs spread to each side of Cara and Nic. He leans into the couch behind him, getting comfortable, before turning hard, and casting a menacing glare towards Sasha and Reed.

Pointing his finger between the two of them, he accuses, "You two little co-conspirators have no idea what you've just done." He points to her and Nic, who are obviously in distress, before addressing Sasha and Reed again. "Subtlety is neither one of your talents, is it?"

Reed suddenly looks very guilty as his eyes move to Cara's tear-stained face. He immediately babbles on about how he did some quick research on the plane and read how their gift could be pushed into the conscious level with an emotional breakthrough. He admits he spoke to Sasha about the situation last night, and they couldn't think of a better way to make that happen than to trick Cara.

Sasha jumps in and apologizes but adds they were both tired and knew they didn't have much time to come up with a plan.

"You are both dumbasses," Jake reprimands. "Did it not occur to you this emotional scene could have been avoided by just discussing it with them?" Jake continues to chastise Reed and Sasha. "Break-throughs can occur many different ways. Sending someone over the edge is only one means. You came at this ill-equipped and unprepared. Although you achieved the required result, you could have accomplished it with a kinder, gentler hand."

Placing one hand on Nic's leg and one on Cara's, Jake decides he needs to elaborate for all of them to contain the hysteria he feels building in the room. "What just happened isn't magic or fiction, it's only science. What I'm about to tell you may be hard to take, and may blow your minds a little bit, but hear me out.

"Many great physicists, including Einstein, have envisaged the existence of the particular anomaly you've just seen displayed, and Nic and Cara are, by far, not the first to have this gift. It's all about the ability to convert thoughts into energy. Our thoughts have a molecular structure like everything else in the world. Those molecular particles have energy. Some people can manipulate that energy with their minds the way your brain tells you to lift an arm when you want to reach for something. It's the same concept."

Research and experiments in this field of science have been going on for decades. The physics portion aside, it begins with the notion of intuition. Why do some people have more acute intuition than others? Some minds process information on an intuitive level first, while other minds can only process information given the facts. Many personality tests, like the Myers Briggs, for instance, have been around for decades and are used to determine which type of mind one possesses. These tests are often utilized to gauge someone's career choice, learning challenges, even which type of mate is most suitable.

Other researchers began to look more closely at the concept of intuition. What occurs organically in the brain to cause it to view the world from an intuitive level? That research has led to a more biological understanding of neuropathways in the mind, and how information is moved on the synapses firing on those pathways. It's sometimes referred to as neuroplasticity, the ability to alter and change the neurons and synapses in the brain. Much of this research has led to breakthroughs on ways to approach and treat traumatic brain injuries, how to help Parkinson's victims, and has aided in mental illness solutions and drug therapies. But what is ultimately known of the human brain is still a very fractional understanding.

Still other doctors and researchers have moved toward the concept that our brains are only functioning at ten percent of their capacity. Those scientists have been more inclined to believe intuition is the result of a special talent. A gift. They believe the mind can acquire the ability to utilize and manipulate those neuropathways to produce an evolved outcome. "Tons of research has been funded in this direction, although some of it may be questionable in its ethics. Regardless, there have been some documented results of psychic gifts." Jakes looks around the room to find all eyes directly on him.

"Here's where some of the confusion and perhaps skepticism presents itself." Jake continues with his lecture. "Despite your brain's capacity to possibly produce a 'gifted' moment, between the biology, the psychology, and the physics associated with the event, everyone's mind has some conflict with it."

First off, the concept of the 'breakthrough' is highly debated. Psychologically, every mind is broken into levels of consciousness and sub consciousness. Consciousness is the editor of the mind. It inherently filters inconsistencies for the mind. Any input it's getting from the subconscious, or any input it receives from the reality around it, will be discarded if it makes no cerebral sense. Normal, sane brains function this way.

Jake points to Cara and uses her as an example. "Cara may have been hearing people's thoughts at an early age. Her subconscious released that chatter to her conscious, but it rejected it. It may have rejected it because it was incongruent. It made no sense. Or it may have rejected it because all the chatter was too overwhelming to process. Either way, her subconscious has been protecting her, keeping the chatter to a minimum. So, the information is there, but she is accessing it only on an instinctive level."

Pointing to Nic to make his next example, Jake expands, "Nic's brain may have been receiving the input but, biologically, the neuropathways didn't exist yet to allow the chatter to make the clear jump from subconscious to conscious. So, again, the information is there, but it has no means to move because the synapses to reach its destination don't exist. Neuropathways can be created and repaired in the brain. Doctors have discovered this by monitoring the progress of healing from brain injuries. A breakthrough can be that path suddenly developing."

Jake adds, "The physics portion of this, well, that's complicated and confusing."

Physics theories would argue both Cara and Nic were born with these abilities; their brains were engineered with the ability to manipulate energy on an evolved level. The details on how they are doing it is the complicated and confusing part. And none of those details are factual at this point. It's all theories and equational math. "String theory, quantum mechanics and the God particle are all still only theories to suggest we are one with our universe," Jake says, glancing at the three teenagers on the couch. "Are you still with me?" he asks with a wink.

Nic has been listening to Jake intently. He's looking much more composed as he pulls Cara tighter to him and runs his fingers through her hair. Nic lets his gaze travel around the great room before resting on Jake. "Thank you, Jake, for your assistance. Apparently, our handlers are a bit inept when it comes to 'handling' a situation. A simple game of guess what number I'm thinking in my head may have sufficed, don't you think?" He glares at Sasha and Reed before turning his attention back to Jake. "But, how is it you know so much about this?"

A shot of panic runs up Jake's spine. He has offered too much. He shakes his head sadly at Nic and resignedly asks, "Ever hear of the Stargate Project?"

THIRTY-FOUR

NIC COCKS HIS HEAD AT Jake, but Cara releases the death grip she has on her husband to gawk at Reed in puzzlement.

Reed's mouth has dropped open as he studies Jake. He may know who Jake is, but his knowledge of the Stargate project? This is new intel. The mysterious Jake is starting to make more sense. He finally gets his mouth to work. "Were you a part of that program?"

Nodding solemnly, Jake admits he was placed into the program initially, when he was 13 years old. Nothing came of it, but he learned much about what they were trying to accomplish. He was admitted back in for more tests before he left for college. After that, involvement became voluntary, and he chose not to be a part of it. When he did run into people who were still in the program, he would get updates, but never offered to come back in.

Reed catches on before realizing not everyone else knows what Jake's talking about. Mostly addressing the kids, he explains, "The Stargate Project was the overall code name for a cumulative directive during the Cold War to find and test individuals for psychic, or what they referred to as RV, or Remote Viewing, capabilities. RV was the term used for decades to describe the ability to project one's mind to a particular location. Nowadays it's also referred to as astral projection. During the Cold War, the superpowers decided research into RV had some merit. The research was funded with the hopes of locating, or producing soldiers, who could project their minds over an area to gain intel, the concept being one could 'spy' intel by remotely viewing it."

Sasha adds, "Both the USSR and China had similar programs."

Reed continues, "There have been some stories circulated of small successes during the 70's and 80's, but the understanding was both the Russian and US programs were abandoned in the 1990's. In the US, the talk was the program didn't have adequate success, and with the advent of technology, intel-gathering has been allocated to satellites, high tech listening devices, and most recently drones."

Mia interrupts Reed. "So, you're saying governments were spending considerable time and money trying to find people and test them to see if they could RV, and like read minds, to get information for military purposes? But then just scrapped it when they saw their efforts weren't producing their army of mind readers, and realizing technology could adequately replace the need?"

"That was the word on the street, so to speak. Remember, these programs were originally developed well before computers, let alone stealth planes and bugging devices," Reed confirms, but adds, "While your mom, Jinx and I were at Langley, it was circulated the program just couldn't be justified, and the money better spent on technology.

"The Stargate Project originated within the CIA by taking much of the private research being done at Institutes and Universities and bringing it in house. In the late 70's, the CIA transferred the project to the Defense Intelligence Agency. Offices were established at Fort Meade Army Base, and the research continued there until 1995 when the project, and all its files and data, were transferred back to the CIA for evaluation. A panel at the CIA determined the Stargate Project hadn't produced significant results, and the project, and any funding for it, was shut down," Reed concludes.

"So, that's how I know so much about this," Jake sadly offers when Reed is finished with his explanation. However, before Reed can ask him more questions, Jake changes direction with, "Because of that, I would like to try something with Nic and Cara."

Curious as to what Jake has in mind, Reed moves closer to the three of them on the floor. Sasha is right behind him, also anxious to listen to the conversation.

"Cara, can you see past what Nic is projecting?" Jake inquires, kindly.

"No, we were talking about it. I can hear his voice...but can't hear or see anything else," Cara explains with a shaky voice Reed is feeling guilty about. He wants to wrap her in his arms, but now isn't the time.

Jake continues with patience and surprising calm. "I'm going to hold your hand. I'll explain why later but will you take my hand?" Cara reaches out to him and clasps his hand.

Jake wants Nic to mentally rapid-fire random numbers out to Cara. But before he does that, he wants Cara to close her eyes and search her mind to see if she can pinpoint where they are appearing. "If you can locate them, you're going to...people describe it differently...but...build a bridge, create a path, form a tunnel, follow a thread." Cara jerks at his last choice of word. "Can you follow a thread?" She nods. "Good, let's try this. Nic, start."

CARA SHUTS HER EYES AND CAN SEE WHERE THE NUMBERS ARE, AND THE thick thread-like pull string they are attached to. *I see them, Nic! I'm going to pull the thread.*

Suddenly, Cara's eyes go wide, and her breathing becomes shallow and fast. Nic has grabbed her shoulders at the same time.

"Cara, can you say out loud what you see, please?" Jake requests, again, using a soothing voice.

She raises her head to the ceiling, and her eyes are open, but she only has the visual of what's in her mind. She gets to her knees while Nic is still holding her shoulders. She struggles to verbalize what she sees. All she can do is stare blankly at the sight above her. "Nic, what is this? It's amazing."

"It's my grid," Nic answers matter-of-factly.

She is gazing at the ceiling, eyes darting from section to section, her face displaying complete awe at what she's seeing. It's like looking at a massive computer screen with over twenty separate search windows open for viewing. "You see this all the time in your mind?"

"Yes, it's how I work the different sections of my brain. How I do the math and calculations. Do you see the bottom right quadrant? That's the math area. See, it's running numbers now. It's always calculating."

"What's the upper left doing?"

"It's scanning the area around us, kind of like a GPS. It's plotting each item and where it is, its mass, volume, density, distance, etcetera." Nic seems unfazed by this.

Cara is still looking up. She's squinting without realizing it, trying vainly to focus with her eyes. She just now found the quadrant with all the music. She smiles wide. "It's like a massive iTunes account. Your song lists have associated sheet music attached. It's your running Soundtrack. It's always on in the background, the music, isn't it?"

"It runs at different volumes, but it's always playing," Nic offers.

Cara's head falls to meet her husband's eyes with horror. "You do realize this isn't, um, typical or normal?"

"You don't have a grid?"

"Babe, if I had that in my head 24/7, I would be institutional-ized." She points to the ceiling. "This is intense. How do you stay sane?"

"I can turn it down, watch."

And suddenly the multi-windowed screen loses most of its illumination. "Ohhhh, it's like you dimmed the lights. Does it turn off completely?"

"No, but I can 'dim' it down quite a bit," Nic answers with a chuckle.

"So, you've always had this...grid, and you've learned to live with it?"

"I guess." At this, Nic turns to look at Sasha. "Do you have a grid?" Sasha shakes his head. "How do you do the math thing in your head?" Sasha only shrugs.

Cara surmised early in her relationship with Nic that he possessed a photographic memory. He could also solve complicated math equations in his mind. Since she has known Sasha, he's displayed the same talents. Come to think of it, so has Jake.

This brutally organized mind screen is nothing she could have ever imagined. If she forgets her shopping list, she can barely recall half of it at the grocery store. A grid would be handy, but she could never look at that in her mind all the time.

Cara looks back to Jake to ask if he has a crazy grid, but he's smiling proudly at her with his thumb rubbing the top of her hand. She smiles back at him, unsure why he appears so pleased.

"Little darling, do you realize what you just did?" Jake asks her.

Cara slowly lets out, "I visited Nic's mind?"

Jake laughs before pulling her into a hug. "Visited is one way to put it." Getting a hug from Jake is usually reserved for celebrations. She's not sure why he's so thrilled. He must sense her hesitation because he pulls her from his chest. Looking only into her eyes, he explains, "What you did was take a portion of your consciousness and bring it with you as you traveled over Nic's thread. Essentially, passing a piece of you to Nic." He studies her before adding, "I have only heard of the possibility of doing this but have never known anyone to have success with it."

As he continues to peer only at her, Cara receives an image, like a snapshot of Jake's thoughts. She blurts, "You're wondering if I have successfully made the jump and cleared a path between my sub and waking mind, or established a few new neuropathways." He gives her a big smile in acknowledgment, so she adds, "You have an eidetic mind." He nods to her in affirmation. "Do you have a grid like Nic?"

Jake cants his head. "Not that I am aware of, but can you look in there and see if I do, little darling?"

Smiling at his endearment, Cara shakes her head. Jake has been referring to her as 'little darling' for years. It's odd because at 5' 6" and almost 140 pounds, she is built like a brick shithouse. But compared to every single person in this room, she is the smallest. It's nice to feel petite in a crowd. That's a rarity, when by today's standards, she is considered a beast if she can't fit her ass into size two pants.

The movement is subtle, but her husband's hands tug her bottom, easily drawing her onto his lap. His arm wraps tightly just under her breasts. His lips to her ear, he blows out a breath, but his words are for her mind only. *Don't ever put yourself down. This body could always stop traffic and still does.* All she can do is place a hand over his and promise to watch her self castigation in the future; now that her mind is apparently a public space.

Turning back to Jake and his question, she refocuses. "I tried earlier. I tried to scan everyone in the room, but I only get fleeting glimpses, more feelings than thoughts. You were completely closed off, until just now, when I 'received' a peek."

Wrapping his huge hands around her biceps, Jake positions her off Nic so she is kneeling between his spread legs. It's the most intimate she's ever been with Jake. For the first time since she's been speaking with him, she glances to her right at Sasha and Reed. They are kneeling right behind Nic and watching raptly. "That's because I'm blocking you," Jake says drawing Cara's eyes back to him.

Then she receives another peek at his thoughts. Jake suspects everyone in the room is blocking her without realizing it. He's certain that's why they are all friends. It's not as Reed has inferred. Rather, she and Nic are special because they found each other. Yes, their gifts complement one another, but so too do Reed and the others. To some extent, they all must possess some gifts. If Cara and Nic were around people with no special gift, they would be constantly bombarded with their thoughts. It would have been too overwhelming.

Understanding Jake's explanation, Cara cries out, "My seizures! I was getting too much input from the outside world."

Realizing she once again read his thoughts, Jake smiles at her and asks, "What about growing up with your family? Do you recall if your seizures came as often, or starting early in your childhood?"

She must think about this answer. They are her family, so they irritate her sometimes. It's not the same as feeling overwhelmed or bombarded. From her own experience, she knows dealing with one's family elicits a generally accepted level of distress for everyone. She can't recall having any of her meltdowns or fugue states with them, though. She finally answers simply, "No."

Jake chuckles at her hesitation, almost as if he heard her thoughts. But he becomes serious once again, directing, "I'm going to let you inside my head, but you need to promise to only look where I let you, okay?" She nods, understanding he is a man with secrets, and this is a big step for him. He moves those huge hands down from her biceps until he's threading his fingers into hers. "I'm going to reach out to you, now. Find the thread."

Closing her eyes to block out everyone, she focuses only in her mind. What she visualizes, as a result, can only be described as amazing. She can see that thread to Jake, but she can see many other thicker threads, as well. Only her side of them is visible, but it's extraordinary. She's momentarily lost in the landscape before she remembers what the objective was. She concentrates on Jake's thread and attempts to travel along like she did with Nic. She's struggling, though. It feels like walking through a murky fog, slow and dark. It's nothing like the experience just now with Nic.

Trying to walk the group through her experience, she narrates, "I see images. But they're not clear like with Nic. Wait, I see your grid! It's not like Nic's...it's...less complicated but there's a resemblance. Everything is opaque, though." Cara is trying to see in the fog but isn't getting anything to come into clear focus. "Jake, may I try something?"

Before he can answer, Jake inhales and shudders. "What did you do?"

"I tried to send you a picture of Nic's grid," Cara responds, alarmed that she's hurt him.

"Holy shit! I see it crystal clear. I just didn't know what the hell it was!" Jake jerks his head to Nic. "THIS is in your mind?" Nic nods. "It's fucking fantastic! Okay, we need to try something else now that I've seen this." Cara has never seen Jake so animated.

Jake asks Nic, "Can you see on your grid where Cara is coming through?" Nic confirms he can. Jake wants him to go to Cara the way she came to him. Follow the thread to her, and travel over it. Jake releases Cara's hands and places them into Nic's. "The physical contact is like support. I'll explain later what else it does. Go ahead and try it."

Ready, baby?

Go for it, my love.

Suddenly, Cara's head jerks back violently, and she shudders, spasms, and screams in violation and pain, "STOP!"

Nic releases her mind in a panic and grabs her shoulders. "What did I do?"

Cara tries to get her breath back, slowly. She feels like her eyes are rolling around in her head. It takes a minute for composure. "I can't believe I'm going to say this...but I can SEE you in there." She saw a blurry vision of Nic's outline.

She stops to gather her thoughts. It's like being in a room with those old rolling file systems that were popular in attorney and medical offices. The file cabinets were on tracks, and could be pushed along the tracks, one cabinet at a time, to get to a section and find a file. It was a system created to house a lot of paper files in a small amount of square footage.

Nic nods he understands her analogy. Cara looks to the group to confirm they understand. The kids look confused, so she adds, "They're mostly obsolete now. Many companies have moved to digital conversion of files and reduced their paper consumption in the name of going green."

What Nic just did felt like he ran into her brain and started slamming all those files along the tracks, yanking file folders out of their sections, and throwing them into the air in a crazy mess. Looking apologetically at her concerned husband, she blurts, "You just raped my mind." There is a collective gasp around the room, but Jake places his hand against the small of her back.

Nic needs to go back in slower and treat it like a file room. Open the door. Turn on the light. Look at the catalog showing where the files are, how they're organized, by alphabet, chronologically, or by emotion. Then slide the cabinets gently along the tracks until he finds what section he wants to be in. Once there, he should skim the sides of the files until he locates the exact one he's looking for and slip it out of its resting spot.

Cara looks at Sasha, who at this point is hiding behind Reed acting like he had nothing to do with the revelations that have taken place this morning. Pointedly, and with some indignation, Cara narrows her eyes at him and barks, "Don't think you're getting away Scot-free here. My handler missed my ability to read thoughts and emotions. Where were you all this time that Nic was doing the same and reading memories, as well." Sasha and Reed both inhale sharply, sinking down in an attempt to avoid her barbs.

Turning back towards her husband, satisfied Sasha is suitably chastised, she asks, "Nic, ready to try it again?

"You sure? You scared me before."

She can feel Nic's concern. She tries to allay his fears. "Don't sweat it. It was just a shock. That's all. Hell, they are my private memories and you violated them. That doesn't happen every day, babe. You're in a lot of them, anyway." She winks at her husband trying for levity but not really feeling it.

"Just talk me through it so I know each step of the way I haven't caused any discomfort."

They clasp hands, again, as Nic enters her mind. "I see you in there," she says. Gently this time, he draws open her memory. "Good, door's open." Suddenly her memories appear to illuminate. "Oh, pretty with the lights on. See the catalog?" Cara asks.

"Yes, organized by emotions, that's how you catalog them," he confirms.

"Decide which emotion." It's the strangest phenomenon to watch her husband's physical manifestation appear in her mind. He's standing in what looks like a file room, studying the cabinets, zeroing in on a subdivision. "Good, pick something out from that section." Slowly fanning through, he stops at one memory from the beginning of their courtship. "Nice skimming, my love. Open it and look inside."

Cara suddenly moves her hands to Nic's face. He does the same thing until they're holding each other, gazing directly into each other eyes as the memory plays out in her mind with him.

Sasha jumps down to them. "Tell us what you're doing."

Nic raises his eyebrows. "Not sharing, that's what we're doing." He tilts his head to look at her. "I didn't know that," he delivers with such emotion.

Leaning in, she places a soft kiss to his lips. "Now, you do."

Reed squats down next to them. "Find another memory, one you can share with the group. Get sentimental later, please."

"Reed!" Cara cautions, "These are MY memories. They are all sentimental and PRIVATE!"

Jake steps back in and pushes Reed aside. "Cara's right, back off." He stands up, looming over Reed and Sasha and places his hands on his hips. "I am still very disappointed with the two of you. I suggest neither of you do anything to piss me off," Jake threatens. Both men slink slowly away from her and Nic.

Nic chuckles at Jake's protection of them. He leans out and grabs Sasha by the ankle to prevent him from getting too far. He understands neither man meant any harm. And he comprehends why Reed needed to explore this, and quickly.

He gives Sasha his 'I forgive you' face. "Sash, I guess it's what I've been doing all these years without knowing it."

It's understandable his mind didn't recognize his talent as anything but intuition. It's overwhelming to consider the alternative. He's performing these processes at a rapid pace, most likely always scanning and calculating without even realizing it. "I see now how I've been able to track and trace people so well. I guess I was reading their memories, at least their short-term memories."

Sasha draws closer to him and drapes his arm over Nic's shoulder. "Like in Berlin yesterday morning. You knew to go see Olaf, yet you didn't know the story of Cara and Olaf...but I did."

In Cara's case, when she is in a confrontation, she sees the intent before it happens. She aims her gun before someone's hand reaches for his or her pistol, because she can read their commitment like she did with Reed earlier. The difference being Reed isn't a real threat. He had to build the image of hatred and loathing in his mind for Cara to see it and react. His conflicted emotions caused her confusion, but in the field, it's very clear to her. Targets and adversaries have lethal resolve, and she knows it.

Cara also knows when to extend compassion to an adversary. She can sense their hesitation and unease. She can distinguish possible friend from foe, like she'd done with Olaf, Lucien, and countless others, which earned her the respect of many agents in her field.

"With you, Nic, someone's memories determine their patterns. You know which way someone's going to swing at you, based on the patterns you see. You're processing those patterns at an alarming rate, but essentially, it gives you the advantage that Cara has, knowing intent," Sasha states, confirming Nic's thoughts.

Sasha adds, "Again, I'm sorry Reed and I felt this course of action was the quickest way to confirm our suspicions."

"Are you going to tell me I'm a cheater, too?" Nic glowers at the man he has considered a brother since he was just a boy.

Ignoring his scowl, Sasha turns his own scowl at Reed, instead. "No, and neither of you are cheaters. It's a poor choice of words. You have gifts, and you've used them to your advantage. It doesn't matter if you utilized them with or without knowledge of it."

Sasha stands in an attempt to be closer to eye level with Jake. He focuses his mind on him before stating, "This is no surprise to you. You suspected Nic and me of having gifts. Somewhere along the way, you began to suspect Cara, too." There's some accusation in Sasha's tone.

"You and your new buddy have thrown down the gauntlet. I hope you're both prepared for the full repercussions," Jake replies with ice.

CHAPTER

THIRTY-FIVE

ARA'S FEELING MUCH BETTER. SHE stands and stretches her back out. She walks around some furniture toward where Reed is just rising from the floor. She flicks her boyfriend in the head. He yelps and grabs her hand, pulling her into a hug as he whispers his apologies in her ear. She pulls away and seductively runs her fingertips down his chest before punching him in the stomach. "And you have the gall to accuse me of melodrama."

Reed is hunched forward, wincing, and placing his hands over his crotch, knowing that's her next target. Cara shakes her hand out because Reed's abs are rock hard, and now her knuckles hurt.

Nic, meanwhile, is up and making his way around Sasha and Jake, who are still glaring at each other. He pulls her away from Reed and toward the back window wall where their children are seated.

Nic, the reason Reed started all this is because it made more sense the kids would be targeted because of our gifts, not because of our skills. He was trying to determine if that was the motive. Also, he knows Mia and Max 'heard' your humming.

Cara mia, it's the reason I made my way closer to them. I'm liking this new form of communicating, by the way.

Knowing exactly what her husband wants her to do, she responds, *Max first, on three.* Simultaneously, Nic and Cara reach out and grab their son.

"No way, stop it!" Max yells trying to resist. Cara and Nic hang on long enough to get an answer to their suspicions. But before they can process their reaction to Max, Cara sees Mia jumping off the couch to flee.

Get her!

Nic grabs Mia by the nape of her neck while Cara reaches for her arm. All four of them are now linked together, physically. Mia is struggling to wiggle out of their grasp. Any onlooker might view the scene as child abuse.

Mia screams, "HELL NO!" and suddenly Cara is physically thrown onto Max's lap, except no one has pushed her. Nic is yanked hard, ripping his grip from Mia, causing him to lose his balance. He manages to stay on his feet, struggling to maintain his hold on her. Small trickles of blood run down Cara, Max and Nic's noses.

As if someone hit the pause button, none of them moves, speaks, or even breathes. Then, Nic grabs Mia by the neck again, and yanks her hard out of the room toward the Primary Suite.

Cara is stunned, still on her son's lap. Both are unmoving. The rest of the room finally reacts. Jinx goes running for a box of tissues, while Sasha and Reed lunge for Cara and Max. Sasha plops down next to Max while Reed kneels before them. Taking the tissues from Jinx, Reed removes some for Sasha while he takes a few to wipe Cara's nose. Sasha gently cleans Max.

There's still no communication until Cara breaks the silence. "What was that?"

Max looks up at her and sighs, doing his best impression of Darth Vader. "Obi Wan, the Force is strong in the girl."

This brings a slow smile to her face. She repositions herself slightly off her son, but pulls him in for a tight hug, taking the opportunity to get physical, having abandoned this contact long ago when the kids stopped letting her. She runs her hands over his beautiful face before... *Max, are you okay?*

Yes, Mom, I'm fine, but my head feels weird, and I have a little headache. How about you?

Same thing. Mia did this to us?

Yup.

You knew?

His head slowly shakes. *Not about this little trick of hers, no. Mom, please don't take this the wrong way, but I don't like having you in my head. It's freakish. Like when we catch you and Dad sucking face.*

She snorts out loud. *You mean it's too intimate for your mother to be here? I understand, let's use our words. But Max, everyone is going to hear the rest of our discussion.*

Taking a deep breath, Max responds, *I am prepared for the disappointment, Mom.*

Drawing him closer to her by pulling his head to her neck, she inhales his maturing scent. *Dig in deeper inside my head, Max. You might be surprised.*

Argh, no thanks, I'll take my chances. He pulls away from her, looking for space.

Ignoring his attempt, Cara cups his cheeks and looks him straight in the eyes. *Max, always remember how much I love you. You will always be my beautiful baby boy. Nothing you could ever do would change that. Nothing.*

Cara rises from Max's lap but sits next to him. She inhales deeply before speaking. "Jinx, can..." Jinx is at Cara's side with a glass of water and 4 Advil. "Did I...?"

"Yes, you did, but I can recognize the difference in my head, now. It's fine." Jinx hands them the pills and water.

Cara knows Max is uncomfortable, but everyone is looking for answers so she starts, "Max and Mia have been communicating telepathically for as long as they can remember. But you don't do it as often now?"

"No, a few years ago it got weird being in each other's minds, so we only use it if we need each other or... to talk in front of you or Dad, mostly."

"You have extended each other privacy," Cara says making a statement. Max can read thoughts and feelings like her, but he's also capable of his father's talent. Max can read some memories. "Can you read past the short term and into the stored ones?"

"Sometimes, yes, it depends on the person," Max replies with some anguish in his voice. His eyes are downcast.

Sasha places his hand on Max's leg to comfort him. As if reading the need, Reed places one hand on Max's other leg and wraps his second hand around Cara's calf. Cara pauses and ponders, her head tilting to one side. She sensed a tiny jolt of energy. She shakes her head slightly and looks to Jake.

Jake slowly nods to Cara and says, "Yes." Again, as if he knew what she was thinking. She nods back in understanding, but Sasha and Reed are confused by their exchange.

Cara continues, not addressing the small side interlude, "Max has been utilizing his talents in a not so discreet way these last few years... haven't you?"

Max lowers his head. "Yes."

Cara inhales, "You investigate people's thoughts, and then give them what you think they want to hear or feel. You do it a lot with girls. You scan them and come on as their fantasy boy."

"You use it to be a player!" Sasha exclaims, grabbing Max by the head in more of a congratulations than a reprimand.

"Sasha! No encouragement required here, please," Cara scolds.

She attempts to parent her son by explaining what he's been doing isn't appropriate on so many levels, but she does understand at his age why he would be tempted. He must appreciate, though, having a girl like him based on a façade, isn't how relationships should develop. Girls should like him for who he truly is.

Max looks at her with disdain. "I am not an idiot, Mom. Having a relationship with them isn't what I want at the moment."

He admits he's taking advantage of this added talent. It gives him the competitive edge, especially playing sports. Max scans everyone on the field; knows what their next move is and what their strategy is going to be. "It's why I'm so good at everything. I WANT to win, Mom. Is that unfair?"

Cara is momentarily at a loss and looks to Sasha for help. Sasha seems to understand and takes over. "Ah, my sweet Westley. There is a time to be Westley, and there is a time to become the Dread Pirate Roberts. But you cannot be the pirate all the time. Sometimes you can even be both, but always, you must be sweet Westley."

Reed interrupts, "Is this *The Princess Bride* thing again?" She nods. "Okay, I get it, now."

Sasha continues, "Do you understand the difference, Maximillian?" Max nods solemnly. "Do you have the grid like your father does?"

"No, but Mia does. It's what makes her so smart and...crazy," Max replies while rolling his eyes.

Cara suddenly has her own moment of illumination. She looks to Jake, who is already in motion, walking towards his son. Elijah, who is sitting quietly on the other side of her, has not uttered a sound since this whole reveal began. Jake moves behind him and places a hand on Elijah's shoulder. Eli shudders a bit at the touch.

Knowing Jake wants her to lead the questioning, Cara turns to the boy. "Sweetie, have you seen Mia's grid?" Eli nods. "Do you have a grid, too?" After a hesitation, Elijah nods. "Do you and Mia speak telepathically with one another?" A slow look moves across Eli's face before he finally nods an affirmative. Her eyes bolt up to Jake's.

Jake comes around to kneel in front of his son. "Eli, can you read thoughts and memories?"

Elijah speaks his first words of the day. "No, just Mia's, but sometimes I can get some images from others, like Aunt Cara described yours, opaque... muted," he confesses quickly.

All Jake has to say to that is, "Interesting."

Cara asks Max, "Can you speak to Eli?"

Max and Eli glance at one another, before Eli responds, "I speak to Max through Mia. We need her to facilitate the path. We can't do it alone."

Jake considers the phrase as he repeats, "Facilitate the path."

Cara looks back to Eli. "She just did that for you and Max? She's in your head right now?"

"Yes, she's frightened in the other room with her dad and needs comfort," Eli admits, reluctantly.

Cara immediately sends a short transcript of their conversation to Nic. She isn't even sure how she's done it, but the need for him to know seemed to 'facilitate' the expertise.

Nic responds immediately, *Got it. I'm trying to be delicate, but this IS MIA, you know. I'm not getting shit from her. She's getting a piece of my mind over the charge she threw at us, though.*

Cara smiles and thinks aloud, "Facilitate, I like the terminology, Eli. It's appropriate."

Jinx jumps up and states, "I'm starving. I'm ordering pizzas and salads for lunch. We can do a healthier dinner, agreed? And no Cara, I didn't 'receive' that from you. My stomach growling told me that." She struts out of the room.

After Carter returns from picking up their lunch order, he and Jinx start spreading everything across the kitchen island as a buffet. Having decided the boys had been interrogated enough, the rest of the group is seated at the kitchen table with the two boys standing, waiting impatiently for the food.

Nic and Mia arrive. Appearing worn and haggard, Nic tells the boys and Mia to fix a plate with some salad, take a pizza, and go downstairs to eat at the bar. They are relieved by their dismissal. Carter joins them, following the kids' lead.

The adults fill their plates and eat at the table. Jake has opened the bottles from earlier and Jinx has put out wine glasses. The bottles are passed around, but still, no one wants to communicate.

It's Sasha who finally breaks their occupied silence with, "Nic, we should talk about what we learned while you were gone."

Nic waves him off. "No need. Cara sent me a transcript while I was with Mia."

Reed puts his slice of pizza down quickly. "You. Did. What?"

Cara only shrugs. "It seemed prudent at the time, and I'm not sure how, but the ability to do it just came to me. Like I typed a quick text message and sent it off to Nic."

Jake saves her. "Now that Cara's brain has processed her abilities on a conscious level, the new neuropathways will start forming at an alarming speed. All brains have the capability; Cara's will do it on her level with her gifts, though. Nic will have the same thing happen, but with Nic's brain the new abilities will get a position on his grid. His brain is organized that way, where Cara's is...scattered like most folks."

"Scattered?" Cara accuses.

"Sorry, little darling, but you can't have everything," Jake mumbles to her while chewing.

"Jake, were you and Cara communicating during the Eli discussion?" Jinx asks with a bit of accusation in her tone. "You seemed to be."

Cara answers, "Not really. Like I did with Nic's grid, I sent a picture of my thoughts to Jake. And I get small snippets of Jake's thoughts back."

Jinx appears confused. "But you weren't touching him like before."

Cara doesn't need to anymore. She can identify Jake's thread in her mind and simply tap and send. It's reminiscent of a text message on a phone; if the phone was like the two cans and string game they played as children, as her kids would say, "like a hundred years ago."

Jake is very closed off, more so than the rest of them, but she suspects, like Jake has, they all have some talent. Cara does not have a grid of organization in her mind, but she is processing all this new information at an alarming rate of speed, even for her.

"Like you, Reed." Cara points to him with accusation. Reed cocks that one eyebrow at her in question and concern. She stops to take a sip of wine. "You and I have always done the thing with our foreheads when we're in distress. I've always thought it strangely intimate, and now I understand why."

THIS I want to hear. Her husband murmurs into her mind.

Shut up, you.

Reed considers this for a moment, "Are you asking me what I feel when we do it?" Cara nods while Reed appears to be thinking hard about this.

She truly senses Reed's emotions right at this moment. He loves the intimacy they share. There's a special bonding between them when they connect, but he's uncomfortable discussing it with the group. Squaring his shoulders, he tries, "It is strange. Like we're sharing something...not just you giving, but me providing...there's involvement by both of us... but it feels..."

Watch it, Reed. Nic's threat shoots into her brain.

Shut up you, again. Her husband's constant jealousy is muddling her sonar.

"It feels...enlightening?" Reed finally gives up.

"Yes, that's what I feel. Like we've resolved something and found closure. It's like healing," she confirms.

"But I don't hear your thoughts when we do it," Reed adds.

"Nor do I hear yours, but I'm certain it's more of an emotional exchange between us, empathic versus telepathic. And we have always had it. It was our connection to each other from the start. How I was able to manipulate you. I took advantage of your emotions."

"That's harsh," Jinx chimes in.

Cara's not feeling particularly harsh. Maybe she should have used Eli's word. She facilitated her need for Reed years ago when they first met. And now, she's feeling the beginning of complete acceptance for what has transpired. As traumatized as she felt earlier, the discovery isn't so shocking after all. Like an epiphany. All the jigsaw puzzle pieces are falling into place. All those times, she thought she was weird and a little unhinged for sensing things about people. Her aversion to spending too much time in large groups or keeping most people at bay. It's been enlightening. Reed's right. It's an illumination.

Narrowing her eyes on her boyfriend, Cara confesses, "But, Reed, you have facilitated, as well. You have been on the receiving end just as many times. It's why I don't feel I'm being harsh."

Everyone resorts back to silence at this small admission. But Reed breaks it with, "I'm beginning to see where this is going, and I'm not sure I'm ready to accept it. You think I possess this empathy talent. You think on a subconscious level, I have used it toward my career."

Cara rises from her chair and slowly approaches Reed. She takes his head in her hands and lowers her forehead to his, gently. They remain locked in this position for a minute before she releases his head and brings her face back just inches away from his. "I don't think you used it...I know you did," and she walks back to her chair to start eating again.

Their table companions have stopped eating and are sitting with their eyes darting between her and her boyfriend. Reed is watching her consume food. His expression is blank. When she's had enough, Cara puts down her fork and goes for the wine glass.

After taking a sip, she looks back to Reed and states with conviction, "You and I, sweetheart, we are brilliant together. Me, alone, not so much... at least not in the same way. Why is that? Because you are the master manipulator. You are the Spin Doctor with a premiere PhD in it. You are the big idea man. Maybe, all I did was pull those ideas out of your scattered mind for you as an assist, so to speak."

Getting up and back into his face, Cara adds, "Think about it, my dearest friend, think long and hard, back over these past 25 years. You will see the truth in my words. And when you do, you'll see you are a bigger cheater than I am!"

Sasha interrupts before anyone can react, scolding Cara and Reed. "Stop using words like cheat, advantage, manipulate or use. You need to refrain from any of that kind of talk. None of us has done that. We are all emotional right now and it's dictating our responses. More importantly, there are the children to consider. They don't need to feel guilty for their talents." Sasha, as usual, is the calm, clear voice of reason.

"Wise words, Sasha, I agree," Nic adds before turning his attention to her and Reed. "Can you two conclude your lover's quarrel and kiss and make up, please?"

This makes both Cara and Reed chuckle. They lock eyes on each other and smile. Reed reaches for her hand and squeezes it. All is forgiven. It's always been that easy between them.

Cara turns her attention to Jake. "Can you explain the touch thing now? What happened with Max and Elijah? I know you felt it earlier when Sasha, Reed and I sat down close to Max because I sent you my feelings."

JAKE PUTS DOWN HIS FORK AND PEERS AT ALL OF THEM. HIS EYES LAND AND fix on Reed, though. He's sensing Reed wants to take back what he's unleashed today.

Reed stares back at him on full alert, preparing for another confrontation.

Jake breaks the staring contest and addresses Cara's question. "Some people possess the ability to harness energy. They amass it and expend it into different outlets. They may not show outward signs of this talent. Take me for instance." He can't read minds or thoughts or feelings per se, but he does have the ability to harness the energy, or so he's been told. "People with visible talent like Cara, Nic, and the children may or may not have the ability to stockpile the energy needed to use their talents for long periods."

Until they try to do it, they won't know for sure, but by touching someone who's a collector or enhancer, the gifts will increase. It's a power boost, simply stated. When Sasha and Reed touched Cara and Max, they sent a surge of something extra. This rush can manifest itself in different ways. In this case, they sent calming comfort to Cara, and that's the feeling Cara sent Jake. It was the added boost of warmth she and Max needed at that moment.

"But how did they know to send that particular energy to us?" Cara asks him.

His knowledge in this particular area is limited. "I'm not sure if you facilitate the energy yourselves into what you need it to be at the time, or if we're already sending it in a specific form."

Nic jumps in, his mind always processing on that grid Jake is envious of. "Jake, all that added energy, is that why Cara and I had a breakthrough today? I mean versus never before? All of us together in the great room with all the extra energy boosts?"

Jake sits back in his chair like he was pushed. Nic hit the nail on the head. It's exactly what he was thinking about. Reed. He must be the missing link. This is the first time they've all been together with Reed. The Director's reputation precedes him. Jake's guessing that Reed stores a massive amount of energy. He reflects on the stories he has heard, some he witnessed firsthand, of the exploits of the Reflex and the White Night. They truly were quite the Duo. Not in the same way as the Dark Angel and the Widow Maker. Less lethal but more cunning. Cara is correct; together they are brilliant, maybe more so now than ever before. People still talk about the things the Duo could make you believe.

Jake points at Reed. "It's the Director. He's never been with all of us together." He explains his rationale and a lively discussion ensues regarding the Reed addition to the group, and how the odds favor him being the catalyst to the breakthrough.

EVEN THOUGH EVERYONE IS TALKING ABOUT HIM, REED ISN'T LISTENING. HE can't fathom the notion that he, more so than any of them, can be powerful. He's still contemplating the empathic notion Cara threw at him, and the idea he used it to enhance his career. He hates that she's right. Worse, now Jake is implying the reason he and Cara were such an effective team is because of their combined gifts and his power. He is a fucking big, fat cheater.

Reed feels a foot knock against his. What the hell? He knows just from the touch it's Cara's. He looks up to see her give him two signals. The first is their 'I have your back' signal, followed by their 'love you, always'.

Cara gives him a big, warm smile. She can feel his guilt and self-doubt from across the table. She knows he's questioning their antics over the years. Sasha is right about it not mattering. So, what if all their successes were aided by a few gifts? Doesn't take away the successes. The conversation has now turned to Nic and Sasha and the energy they may have been providing each other during their missions as a team, but Cara's eyes are still wholly focused on him. There's the start of a small tingling up his spine. An awareness of something to come.

The tingling works its way into his brain to settle in one spot. He shuts his eyes for a moment. The prickling sensation has the feel of a mild ocular migraine. He can almost see a sparkly spot on his frontal lobe. The spot suddenly comes alive, and he can feel a torrent of respect and faith pass through his mind, like the hand of God just anointed him.

His eyes fly open, and Cara is staring intently back at him.

CARA HAD TRIED SOMETHING WITH REED'S THREAD. HER THREAD TO HIM IS thicker and more pronounced than her connection to Nic. It's the thickest filament in her mind. The thread has a funky, shiny element woven into it. Continuing to ignore the conversation around her, Cara tapped Reed's thread and sent over all the respect she has for him. She was rewarded when with a jerk of his body, Reed's eyes opened and locked onto hers.

She can only smirk at him and sneak a wink when she suddenly feels an overwhelming sense of being loved. Thinking it's Nic, she turns her head towards him, but he's still engaged in conversation. Then she spies Reed's eyes still on her. He smirks and winks right back.

She snickers. Her boyfriend has found her thread in his mind and figured out the trick.

What the hell is going on over there? Nic interrupts.

She quickly sits upright. *Nothing, just experimenting.* She stops playing with Reed's thread and refocuses on the conversation.

Jake is correcting Nic about the use of the phrase 'shared talent' when describing his relationship with Sasha. "You can't think of it as one taking from the other. Think of the relationship as more symbiotic. With you and Sasha it's still unclear. But there is something there, trust me, I've seen you two together often enough, and it's a thing of great beauty. We just need to explore more with Sasha."

At this suggestion, Cara can see Sasha stiffen and for the first time, she feels his apprehension clearly. Needing to quell it, she shouts over to him, "Hey, Broody, don't be alarmed. No one is going digging in your head. Only when you're ready. But until then, just enjoy the ride." She winks at him but he's still brooding. Cara takes a piece of pizza crust and throws it at his head. He catches it with those quick reflexes of his and puts it in his mouth.

Sasha turns to Jake after he's chewed the crust. "This energy thing is power, and the power can be conveyed when necessary to another source?"

"Yes," Jake responds, "power fuels power."

Cara is reaching for her wine glass, but with those words her hand jerks and she knocks over her glass, sending the remaining contents across the table. Meanwhile, Reed lurches out of his chair so abruptly, it falls to its side, and he stumbles over it. Cara is unmoving and unblinking, while Reed is fumbling in his pocket for his phone like a crazy man. Nic, understanding the situation immediately by reading Cara's thoughts, grabs her by the shoulder and leaps right into her mind.

Her head is rocking back and forth in rapid sequence while Nic's face is inches from it. Within seconds, Nic has released Cara, and is yelling at Reed, who is flipping through his phone to find a number, "It's over 90%, Reed!" Reed finds the number he's looking for and rushes out the back door into the garage, his phone on his ear.

"Now, what the hell is going on?!" Jinx screams.

Cara is just sitting there in shock. The quick violation of her memories, coupled with the memory itself, too much to process. Nic takes her hand and announces, "I believe we may have just identified a prime suspect."

CHAPTER

THIRTY-SIX

CAUTIOUSLY, CARA RISES FROM HER seat. Her face is set, and her brows furrowed. Nic's hand is still in hers. She releases it, and walks deliberately toward the garage door. Nic is following her, but she turns and stops him with her hand up. Purposefully, she places her hand on Nic's chest. His body shudders with the touch that sends intense emotion through his mind.

You are connected to Reed. There is accusation in his mental voice. *These are his emotions. You can do that now?*

I located his thread, earlier.

Seemingly resolved and back in control, he offers, *Baby, based on his emotions, my calculation is 100%.*

I know. Please go ahead and tell the others the story. She and Reed never gave Nic the details on the plane. But he was able to pull her entire memory of the first couple months of her relationship with Reed. *I need some alone time with my boyfriend.*

I understand. It's all coming full circle.

Nic turns back to the gang sitting at the table expectantly waiting for an explanation. He will need to tell them the whole story for them to understand. He shifts his head back to the now closed

284

garage door hoping neither Reed nor Cara will have an issue with their first interaction being discussed. He can assume Jake does not know the story but wonders if Jinx is even aware of the details. Although, she and Reed did tell him no one knew the real story of their first contact.

Inhaling deeply, Nic heads back to his chair at the kitchen table. He pours himself some red wine and begins. "Just before Cara turned 20 years old, one of her sorority's housemates was raped at knife point on campus coming back from a frat party. Cara found her on the ground in shock. Unbeknownst to Cara, this was the third rape with the same MO on campus."

Looking around the table he can see three sets of big eyes watching him. He lowers his voice so he can't be heard by the kids. "Reed was an analyst in the FBI Hartford office at that time. They sent him to UConn to interview witnesses. Cara was his third witness, and she basically grabbed all his files and started reviewing them. Then she blackmailed him to let her assist on the case or she would tell his boss that he let her see the files." This gets a nervous chuckle from the group because despite the horrid subject matter, it's so Cara to do that.

Reed, being young and still a bit inexperienced agreed and worked with her to develop possible profiles for the rapist. "When a fourth rape occurred, the Hartford office sent Reed in undercover as a collegiate. Cara decided he would be her boyfriend from Harvard as his cover. They were both sure the rapist was a frat boy."

Jinx interrupts his story with a scowl on her face. "This is how they met? Why do I not know this story? Those little bitches." She leans back in her chair waiting on him to continue.

Nic explains how they attended frat parties as a couple for a few weeks. On the fifth weekend, Cara decided Reed should do his own mingling at each party so as not to appear connected to Cara. On that weekend, a fifth rape occurred. Except this rape had an additional element. The victim was raped at knife point by a masked man, but the man used the tip of his blade to carve the words, "POWER FUELS POWER" on the victim's abdomen.

He also spoke to his victim for the first time. The rapist kept repeating, "You are not her. I must find her." The team involved in the investigation couldn't come up with any additional leads on the words carved, or his comments.

The latest victim resembled Cara, so much so, they were mistaken for each other on campus. Reed believed Cara may be the actual target, but he did not share his hunch with his team, only with Cara. Of course, Cara pretended to disagree. Still, she decided they should break up and attend subsequent parties as singles. If this guy was after her, she wanted to be the bait.

There's a collective gasp around the room. Sasha whisper shouts, "Bait? An untrained civilian?"

Jake shouts, "Reed let her do that?"

It is Jinx who comes to Cara's rescue. "Really guys? Since when have any of you been able to talk Cara out of anything when she sets her mind to it?" They all lower their heads in submission. "That's what I'm talking about! I get it. She placed Reed in either a win/win or lose/lose situation. She has always done that to him. Mostly, it's win/win, so she gets away with it."

The more he understands his wife's relationship with her boyfriend, the more he feels sorry for Reed. The man has taken the brunt of Cara's abuse all these years. In retrospect, Nic got off easy. Before he can reflect further on his relationship with his wife, he notices she and Reed have come back in through the garage door and are headed to her office.

Figuring it's time to get to the climax of the story he continues, "Cara announced to her sorority sisters she broke up with Connor. The first night they went to a frat party separately, Reed flirted with girls and danced, while Cara drank and danced with groups of other girls."

Apparently, Cara was approached by a young man who asked to dance with her to a slow song. As soon as she placed her arms on his shoulders, she sensed a threat. She spied Reed on the other side of the room and made sure he was watching her. He had many girls around him, but she was pretty sure he saw her dancing.

When the boy, who introduced himself as Ed Grotto, asked if she would go to the backyard with him to get more beer for the house, Cara followed. She had a feeling this innocuous, shorter boy was hiding something. But his explanation for being the "beer boy" made sense.

Meanwhile, Reed lost sight of her and panicked. He knew she would not wander upstairs, so he checked the first floor than asked if anyone saw Cara. He was told she went outside with Ed. As he went through the back door, he unholstered the gun hidden in his boot.

When Cara and Ed approached the large ice cooler, Ed suddenly produced a knife and pointed it at Cara. With a lunatic calm Ed said, "It's you. I've been looking for you all this time. All the other girls were mistakes. You are my power and you, alone, will fuel me."

Reed was close enough to see the knife and hear Ed talking. He wasn't sure how to approach. Should he grab Ed from behind, or try to get a shot at him and risk hitting Cara? Before he could even calculate his advance, Reed watched as Cara stepped directly into Ed, pushed the arm with the knife away from her while throwing a solid punch with her right fist into his throat. Ed fell back a bit and Cara kicked him hard in the nuts. As he bent forward, he was met in the face with her knee.

Jake asks, "How did she know to do that?"

"You have met Tony, Cara's dad, right? The man trained his daughters early on. Taught them self-defense and took them to the shooting range. Tony is straight out of central casting for the Sopranos. I think he's a hoot. Cara has other ideas," Nic advises.

Before they can continue their questions, Nic tells them Ed was on the ground screaming "POWER FUELS POWER" when Reed got to them. Cara was holding the knife and threatening to cut off his balls. Reed managed to extricate the knife from Cara and wire tie Ed's hands behind his back. He called the incident in.

"By the time the shock wears off, Cara starts to worry. She doesn't want her family or anyone to know she took down Ed Grotto."

Again, Jinx interrupts him, "Because of her mother. Nina would have made Cara's life a living hell. She would have demanded Cara come home immediately and never leave the house. She would have made the incident all about her because that's what Cara's mother does. Her children are an extension of her, and they need to have their thoughts, feelings, and actions always approved by her." Jinx snorts, "Talk about central casting Italian mothers."

Funny, hearing Jinx say that about Nina gives Cara's complaints concerning her mother some credence. Nic always thought it a bit bratty of Cara to bitch about her mother, but he does see that Nina is all about herself. When they dine at Cara's family home, it is expected everyone compliments Nina on her cooking, her home, her efforts over the get together, her grandchildren, etc. It's always about Nina. She barely asks her children how they are doing. She only talks about how she is "getting along" with her life.

No wonder Cara let Reed take all the credit for the capture. Cara's relationship with her mom is a huge reinforcement of her keeping secrets mentality. She's never told either of her parents anything about her life then or now, for that matter. Admission of truth would only bring her grief.

Her rambling analogy back in Berlin about Pavlovian response and reaction to threats makes sense to him now. She is so accustomed to secrets. And because of their previous working relationship, of course she would go running to Reed instead of her own husband. The same applies to her family. In her mind the truth hurts, something reinforced throughout her childhood and adult relations with her parents.

And speaking of truth, Nic is not comfortable letting on he knows that particular successful capture was the catalyst for Reed's new position as Team Leader for the CIA. He will keep that secret for Reed to tell if he chooses. Nic only wraps up with, "Cara did testify at Ed's trial, and he was linked to all five rapes and an additional attempted sixth rape. He was indicted and sent to jail for life."

GRATEFUL NIC DIDN'T HAVE ANY ISSUES WITH WHAT HE SAW IN HER memories from her first weeks with Reed, Cara walks out the garage door. Reed is immobilized, staring at his phone. The look of terror, frustration, anger, and guilt is evident on his face. The associated emotions are passing through to her, penetrating her mind.

Reed sees her, tilts his head slightly and says, "He's out. Been three weeks now."

"I know. I felt your reaction when you discovered this information."

"This is entirely my fault." He lets out a big, stuttering breath.

"No, it's the circle. It's time to come 360 degrees." Cara puts her hand out to him.

Reed takes it, reluctantly, and she begins to pull him into the house. They proceed back through the door, and as they pass the kitchen, they can hear Nic reciting the tale that altered their lives. They pay it no attention as Cara continues to lead Reed to her office at the front of the house.

Upon entering, she shuts the French doors and motions him to the sofa. She sits next to him, but there's a penetrating silence before they both hear the distant hum of voices from the kitchen.

"I just realized we never told the details during our recounting of the story to Nic on the plane," Reed thinks aloud.

"Nic could see the memory in my head and went in hard. He yanked it all out. His speed is amazing." Cara responds as if they're chatting about the weather. She looks forward and not at Reed.

"You knew you were always Ed's original target at UConn. All along. You knew that." Reed accuses. "Grotto altered his MO on the rapes right before his attempt with you. He etched those words into the abdomen of his final victim. 'Power Fuels Power'." Again, he accuses, "You knew."

At the time, the words meant nothing to her and Reed's investigation. They couldn't make heads or tails of the added twist in Ed's MO. It wasn't until Ed had her in the backyard, and he was shouting 'power fuels power" at her, she suspected he specifically wanted something from her. "Not originally, no, but I knew it wasn't just the connection to finding one of the victims that prompted my interest in the investigation. It was more. Then, when I met you, I don't know, I felt an opportunity."

Studying her for a moment, Reed's eyes sparkle with understanding. "You think the circle starts there with us, in that moment, in a campus police interview room."

"Yes. You have my thread, and Ed has my thread."

"Are you referring to this connection that allows you to read thoughts and feelings?"

"Can you see mine, now, in your mind?" Wrapping her hand around his wrist, she pulls gently.

Reed looks down at her area rug. For some reason he can't look at her when he confesses, "The sparkly one. It's my connection to you. But what is it?"

"The threads unite everyone, somehow. They bring us together." Cara has heard it referred to in science as a collective consciousness. Everyone is a part of it, but some people can see the actual threads. She could always sense the cohesion of those around her, but now, she can view it.

"So, it was fate driving us to meet all those years ago?" Reed questions, delicately.

Fate means a lot of different things to different people. Destiny, divinity, a calling, Cara doesn't know what it truly is, but some of the threads are much thicker than others, much more vibrant as well. "Best way to describe it is some people appear to be hardwired, while others are just coming in Bluetooth. You are hardwired to me, big time."

"You don't want me to feel guilty. I'm sensing or rather receiving that message from you," Reed whispers.

"Guilt is not a component of this. It's irrelevant. Anger, on the other hand, is acceptable." With this statement, Cara turns to him, her face radiating rage. "How did it happen? How was Ed released without your knowledge? It was the only promise I asked of you. I needed Ed Grotto to stay in prison; if he was released, I was to know immediately or prior to."

"There was always a standing order for me to receive any change in status on Edward Grotto. Last I checked, Ed wasn't up for parole until 2024. I'm being told, between a new warden and some State snafu, he was released. You said Ed has your thread. Do you have his?"

She is certain Ed has her thread because the past makes sense now. He was pulling the thread to try to locate her. He felt her presence on campus. He was getting so close at the parties, but just missing Cara. Ed could not have known how it worked, precisely. He just felt the pull, or the power. His body searching for the source; knowing he wanted it. He knew just enough to etch those awful words on the last victim's abdomen.

"Remember, he kept reciting it over and over when the police were taking him away. Is that when you realized you were always his intended target?" Reed questions.

Thinking back, Cara admits, "No. The words meant nothing to me. It was when we danced, back in the frat house. As soon as he touched me, I felt his connection. He did, too."

Reed is trying to contain his frustration with her. It's obvious, without even needing to say it. She always led him to believe he was crazy for thinking she was Ed's intended target. It's his turn to grab her wrist and tug. "This is one of those perfect examples of me knowing in my gut that I was right, despite what you said. So, you have his thread?"

Cara nods confused. "I can't recall it, though." She leans against him and sighs. She didn't understand any of this until much later, not until she first saw Nic. Somehow, with Nic, her subconscious and her conscious began to coexist in spots. She sensed Nic's thread strongly at first contact but didn't know it was an actual thing. Of course, their cliché fairy tale relationship has a rationale now. Really, all her relationships are making sense.

She did know she and Nic were different, somehow. Cara could always sense Nic's thoughts and feelings. And she suspected he could sense hers. "When I first saw Nic in Kabul, my thread to him pulled at me, obsessively, much in the way Ed's was pulling him to me."

"You're saying the thread claws at you like a madness?" he questions, interrupting her ramblings on the intense intimacy she has with her husband.

"Yes, it can."

Cautiously, Reed asks, "Were you meant to end up with Ed and not Nic?"

"No. I think the thread makes the power connection." To Ed, the connection manifested itself into something obsessive, sick, and disturbed. "Without knowing what gifts Ed has, it's hard to say what the actual connection was meant to be between Ed and me."

Baby, you know I've been in your head listening to this, right? Nic's voice doesn't surprise her.

Yes. I know when you're here, now. I kept you here for this purpose. Besides, I find it...soothing.

Oh, cara mia. When you're ready to return, everyone has questions, and I would like to try something with you.

She already knows what he wants to attempt. *I needed to take a moment to gather my emotions and get control over Reed's reactions flooding my body. Be there shortly.*

"What I don't understand is the timeline," Reed states, cutting into her mental conversation with her husband.

"Everyone in the kitchen is wondering as well. Ready to join them?"

"Before we go back," Reed confesses, while drawing her onto his lap, "you were right about the two-way street between us. Like you, with this newfound gift, I've never considered how or why I made the choices I did. How easy it is to ignore the gifts. Treat it like some sort of intuition."

Cara pulls Reed's forehead down to hers and then wraps her arms around him. "Connor, I'm sorry I lied about the Ed thing. I knew you would worry if I told you the truth and...you were leaving." After Ed's trial, he was moving away to a new job and the life he always wanted with the CIA. "I wanted you to have a fresh start. No worries, no guilt."

He pulls her face to his until they're nose to nose and whispers, "C, did you think I wasn't going to keep in touch?" Cara can only blink at him. She had no idea if Reed would move on with his life and only think of her occasionally, until he didn't think of her at all. "Sweetheart, I may have gone six weeks before I saw you, but how many times did I call after I moved to DC?"

Cara smiles at him and takes a swipe at his lips with her tongue. "Every night when you came home from work."

He grabs her chin, firmly. "And yet, you continued to let me think I was crazy with my Ed theory. You are just filled with secrets, and it's beginning to piss me off. You truly are the biggest pain in my ass."

Giving him a little headbutt, she asks, "Ready to solve a crime, Agent Reed?" This gets a big smile from him because he remembers when she first spoke those words to him 25 years ago.

CHAPTER

THIRTY-SEVEN

SASHA IS UP AND PACING when Reed and Cara arrive back in the kitchen. The chatter stops as everyone notes her entrance but not for long. The discussion immediately continues as Sasha reasserts his feeling the timeline is all wrong.

"Vlad was hired months ago, and Edward has been out for only three weeks on a technicality, which means he had no foresight. Hiring Vlad would've been futile unless he knew he was getting out. And, there's no money trail." Taking command, Sasha barks to Reed, "What do we have on Ed and his assets? Could he have funded the hit?"

Reed shakes his head. "Ed has nothing substantial. Nothing we can find. My team at Langley has already ascertained his financial info. Ed's phone records are being pulled as we speak, as well as all records of visitation. He did have use of the Internet once a week. And, of course, I have agents heading to the address Ed listed with his parole officer."

"They're not going to find him there. He is long gone," Nic states as if he already knows.

"I suspect as much, but it's worth the visit to collect any

evidence. I should hear shortly on the outcome of the premises search," Reed advises.

"He isn't in this alone. You know that, right, Nic?" Cara inquires. She has some precognition of this fact. Plus, Reed received confirmation the pilots were roofied before their near fatal flight home the day before. And it was in Berlin they were drugged. The dinners and everything on the plane were clean. They did venture into the private terminal in Berlin for coffee and lunch. Analysts are looking for footage within the terminal.

"This is a coordinated effort by several people. I just can't make the connections between them. Is that what you're surmising?" Nic counters.

"Very strongly through my experience with Vlad," Cara tells him. It's so weird how much of this back and forth is going on in her mind with Nic, but they are speaking aloud so everyone else can hear.

"I'm accessing as much of his short-term memory as I can from my visit with him," Nic offers.

"You can do that? Go back before you realized your gift and still assemble information?" Sasha asks, shocked.

Based on the memory of their meeting, Nic can pull some info from the confrontation. It's not as clear as if Vlad was standing in front of him, but he did get some insight. Because of it, he wants to try something with her.

Sasha grabs Nic's arm. "I don't think that's a good idea."

"You know what I want to do?" Nic turns to his friend, surprised. "Because you have processed the options, or because you pulled it from my mind?" Nic only spoke to her, mentally, about his plan.

Sasha steps back from Nic, like he was pushed away. He ignores the questions and instead, he cautions Nic, "If you try to connect to Ed's thread, he may be able to re-connect to Cara. There is a high probability of it. She would be bait, once again."

She winces. After six weeks of investigating together, the connection happened the first weekend they attempted their new plan, separately searching for clues instead of as a team. Just like then, Cara knows she must be bait, again.

Noticing the concern on the faces around her, she explains, Nic's bait plan for this go around. Nic thinks he can go into her head to the memory moment when Ed touches her, and she feels his thread. From that instance, Nic believes he can follow Ed's thread back into his 1989 mind, or possibly into his mind now. It's probable a thread is a thread and is timeless.

With this revelation, Reed rises out of his chair. "I agree with Sasha, too dangerous."

Sasha rephrases, "I'm not saying it isn't an option, just not yet. First order is to establish whom Ed is working with. We must know who our adversaries are." It will change the entire equation to their favor if they can identify the targets. "Nic, please first think about what you and Cara can do to get those answers."

"Can you try something else for me?" Jake inquires, interrupting their current train of thought. "Can you scan an area?" He wants them to attempt to extend their talents, collectively, around the house and see if they can pick up anything out of the ordinary, anything malicious. "It is highly probable we are being watched."

Cara and her husband look at each other. With the added power boosts sitting around this table, it would be intriguing to try it. She offers, "I could cast out my sonar, with Nic reading the results on his grid."

"Let's do it," Sasha insists, going back to his seat at the table convinced this should be their next move.

Nic sits down motioning her onto his lap. She straddles him and points the rest of them to place their chairs closely around them. Once they're in a tight circle around her and Nic, she looks to Jake to direct the experiment.

"Let's try this in increments. Nic, you and Cara do your thing by yourselves, first. See what you accomplish. One by one, we'll add our support by placing a hand on each of you. It will direct the power to you, marginally," Jake decides.

Cara leans all in, putting her head on Nic's shoulder and traveling over his thread. *And there's that complicated mind. I've missed it.*

Welcome back. He nuzzles her neck.

I don't know if I can look directly at your grid, Nic. It's sort of disorienting for me. But if you tell me where I should focus during this exercise, I can do that. I just can't take it in all at once like you do.

I'm not sure where the information will place itself because we've never done this together, but if we're successful, I'll show you. I'm going into your head, but not into your memories just yet. Cara stiffens. *I'm in.* She didn't feel any discomfort this time. As a matter of fact, she's feeling quite the opposite. *Um, Nic? What are you feeling right now?*

Very turned on. He's moved on from nuzzling her neck to kissing her jaw.

Me, too! Is it because you are, or I am, and we're projecting it to each other? His hands on her ass draw her tighter to him. *OOHH, I do feel your physical arousal now, too.*

I think it's the intimacy of our minds together. And thank God you're sitting on my lap covering that physical arousal. It might be humiliating, otherwise.

Cara hides her face in Nic's neck to stifle a giggle. *Okay, back to work. You want to lead?*

Nic directs Cara to start by scanning out from the kitchen and let him play with that. *I can see what you mean about the four in the room with us. Jake is sealed tight, and the other three are foggy. But I can see their short term memories fairly well and their feelings, just not their immediate thoughts.*

She notices Nic concentrating on her thread to Reed. It's hard not to. It's the thickest thread in her mind and glittery. She offers, *That one is Reed's.*

Now it's Nic's turn to stiffen. Very calmly he says, *I think I see too much of that connection. Can you tone it down? Reed's emotions are overpowering, and a source of future debate for you and me later, my dear.*

Duly Noted. How's that? She makes a concerted effort to block Reed's thread.

Better, thanks. Now, see if you can scan the kids downstairs. She located all three kids' threads earlier in the great room, but Carter and Far Guard are downstairs with them now. She has nothing on them. Deciding to push, she gathers Nic's strength and extends her reach.

Good, Nic praises, *and yes, the kids are like granite. Even more so than Jake. Carter's worried about what's happening up here, and Far Guard is happy he was fed.* She giggles because Far Guard is disappointed with the Ohio pizza. Which does suck compared to the East coast. *Focus, baby. Push out and see if you can read the FBI agents.*

Again, she draws power from Nic, pushing beyond the boundaries of the house. Now, she is not only getting all the feelings from in the room, and the thoughts from downstairs, but the minds of five agents outside.

Wow, holy input! Nic shouts as all the jumbled mess reaches them.

It's the overwhelming noise thing. Can you help me zero in?

He's working on something on his grid while he muses, *It's so different from within the house. You can hear all their thoughts. No wonder your mind blocked the talent at an early age. How the hell did our children handle this, Cara?*

Her stomach clenches. *I feel a 'bad mommy' moment coming on if we keep talking about it. Can we bench the guilty parent conversation for later, as well?*

Nic can clearly sense her distress, and it's not helping. *Cara mia, the kids are fine. Please don't stress.*

Jumping back and forth between his mind and Cara's, Nic is attempting to combine their gifts. He had the ability to organize his mental grid and add quadrants before, but with Cara's talent and boost, the ease and speed is remarkable. A new section is complete, but Nic is studying Cara's threads in her mind.

Besides the connection they have to each other, the other threads share a resemblance except for the one to Reed and her thread to Sasha. Nic jumps back into his own mind to identify his threads to the group. He can locate the one to Reed, but the thread doesn't share any resemblance to what Cara has to him. His thread to Reed looks like the ones to the others. Nic locates his thread to Sasha. That thread is the thickest of any of his.

Sasha's thread to him has some of the same coloring in it he observed in Cara's mind, but it's not identical. He zeros in on Sasha's thread. It appears to have a subtle vibration to it.

Refocusing on his new quadrant, he moves all the chatter she's receiving straight to his mind.

It's quiet! Did you do that? He instructs her to look at what he's done. *Are you using your GPS with some of the other talents to do this?* Poor thing. She's lost.

Something like that, he answers because he doesn't want to complicate this for her.

He moves back to Cara to ask her if she can take all their threads and hold them, mentally, at once. Treat it like pulling the strings and keeping them in her hand. Cara practices it while Nic assists her. She can do it, but it's like touching them all, versus holding them. More like keeping her mental fingertips on each thread. When he feels they have achieved the required result, Nic travels back to his mind to work on his new quadrant.

He has left Cara, alone, with mental fingers on all their threads, but he can hear her thoughts. She's comparing the marginal difference in each thread's energy. Oddly, despite her connection to him, it is Reed's thread emanating the clear energy boost. She's contemplating whether Jake's hypothesis about Reed is the rationale for that, or their years of history together. Wondering if the synergy she and Reed have mastered through their training could cause a thread to develop, or if the threads exist as is from inception. Cara can recall always having more energy when she was with Reed, from the very beginning. She even sleeps better when he's around.

Nic's trying to focus on the task at hand, but this new gift reveal is only making him more jealous. Getting back on topic, he asks Cara to keep her grasp on those threads as she makes her way to his mind. He's not sure she's going to be able to do it when he suddenly feels her presence behind him.

Good girl! You never cease to impress, baby. Now, watch the section just to the left of the GPS on my grid. I'm going to cue into each Agent outside, separately, so we can hear.

Cara busts out laughing while Nic chuckles.

Jake is getting impatient with the lack of conversation. "What the hell are you two doing?"

"Chill, Reacher," Cara scolds. "Nic and I had to get the mojo correct. We just got outside with the two agents in front of the house. And...let's say their conversation is enlightening."

"You can actually hear them talking?" Jake asks, excited.

"Yeah, they're discussing which of the two MILF's in the house is more fuckable," Cara offers as explanation for the laughing. "Is fuckable a real word?"

"What!" Jinx jumps up. "Wait...which of us is, you know, more fuckable?"

Nic responds they've decided Jinx has the nicer ass, but Cara's tits win and actually in the end, they want to do both. "Sorry ladies, it's a tie." At this admission, Jinx turns and starts shaking her ass in Cara's face. Cara slaps it. "Ladies, please, it's clear you both can get laid, can we move on?"

"Back to work, fine," Cara announces right before she and Jinx high five each other. As if there was any question either one of them could get laid. Men have been, and are still, very drawn to his wife. She has male clients hanging on her every word and making excuses to meet with her so they can spend time in her company. Heads turn all the time, but that never bothered him. He has always been proud she chose him, and is secure in their relationship. Well, except for Reed.

I heard all that.

Fuuuck. This mind reading may take some getting used to. He empties his thoughts and refocuses. There will be time, later, to address his concerns.

Once he's prepared, he instructs Cara to scan away from the house as far as she can. From there, they can start adding the others for energy one by one. She relays the info coming off Nic's grid. Neighbors are arguing on the right, on the left are not home. Across the street is very concerned about the black cars and scary looking men.

"Nic, you need to go see them and assure them. I've forgotten about our neighbors noticing the FBI boys outside," Cara admonishes him.

Wait. What? "Why can't you go, Cara?"

"Check the wife's memories, Nic!"

Nic zeroes in on Mrs. Landers particular thoughts. "Oh, eeewww, ummm, wow..." He's speechless.

Cara announces, "For our studio audience this afternoon, my friendly neighbor across the street has some interesting erotic fantasies of which my husband is the star." Guess there's no question he can get laid, as well. "That's why you get to go talk to them, Nic. Moving on down the street. How fast can you go?"

Feeling the strain on them, Nic makes a request. "I think we need Jake now, and see if we can scan with some more speed and accuracy." Then he adds, "Jake, can you empty your mind as much as possible and try to bring down your blocks? We promise not to pry." Jakes composes himself for a moment before placing a hand on Nic's shoulder and Cara's arm. "Cara, did you feel that?"

As soon as Jake touched them, they could feel the additional energy coming from his thread. He instructs Cara to take his thread and pull lightly to bring Jake into the collective. She does as he requested, and he can feel a very small part of Jake's consciousness enter.

Jake's body jerks, and his eyes grow wide. "Is this what you're seeing?"

Nic is ecstatic it worked. He coaches Jake to focus on the top left corner of his grid, and then follow the grid to the right to the next quadrant. Nic has the play by play on the street, and the dialog, coming through as images and texts. He is converting the thoughts Cara hears into texts so they can read them, as opposed to hearing the jumbled garb. It seemed more streamline.

"Nic, you are incredible! I can totally follow it," Jake states with true admiration.

Nic begins to slowly expand the scan area. He can tell by his wife's thoughts he's losing her on the play by play. "Cara, just focus on the threads in your mind and the scan only. Let me process from now on."

Cara is relieved she doesn't need to look at Nic's disorienting mind anymore. Attempting to mentally multitask, she heads her scan in the direction of the South half of the neighborhood with a portion of consciousness, while maintaining her fingers on the threads. The extra energy from Jake's thread does appear to add a boost to her own mental efforts. Cara is trying to get outside their neighborhood, figuring anyone watching them is likely to be outside the gates, closer to the shopping plaza.

She can sense the further they go, the harder it becomes.

"Cara, more power, who do you want next?" Nic asks knowing they are slowing down.

"Reed, can you do the same thing as Jake? Empty your mind AND your emotions for me?" Cara inquires a little too harshly.

"Let it rip, C," Reed teases her as he places a hand on Nic's arm and Cara's shoulder.

Cara gives Reed's mental thread a gentle tug. As soon as she does, Nic and Jake gasp while her mind lights up like a Christmas tree, all circuits firing.

Reed grips her shoulder and she realizes he has become dizzy.

Her hand comes down over his firmly, and her other hand grabs his leg. When she is certain Reed isn't going to fall, she pats his hand. "You okay, sweetheart?"

Before Reed can answer, Jake injects, "That's some serious energy you got there, Director. I think our hypothesis about you is spot on."

Cara warns Reed she's going to try and connect him like she did for Jake so he can see. Jake has a grid but Reed doesn't. Just a fair warning to him, it may be more disorienting. If it is, Reed's to let her know. She will keep him on her side of the scanning.

Reed squeezes Cara's shoulder and she pulls his thread a little more. "OH MY GOD! Holy shit! Where am I supposed to look?" His eyes are wide in panic.

Cara giggles out directions. The images and texts are scrolling fast. Nic and Jake are processing them. She feels vindicated she isn't the only one who can't look at that grid for long. "Look quick at the Supermind, then stay with me on my side."

"I see the images, but you're right, it's like watching the credits of a movie on fast forward," Reed admits, trying not to sound too drone. "Sorry."

"I can use the company, watch this instead." Cara brings him back to her and sends him the scan, which is strange in itself.

It feels like they are flying above the houses and plopping into each one. The thoughts of everyone they pass are over on the mind screen in Nic's head, but Reed can sense the emotions as they travel. It's remarkable he can pull that from the scan. Trying to release his initial anxiety, he focuses on those emotions he's feeling.

"See the shopping plaza? That's my grocery store. I like it there. Everything is organized in the aisles, as it should be. There's always plenty of checkout lanes open and..."

Cara's yapping is disrupting Reed's concentration. "Shut up, C, and just drive," he teases her. "Wait. Can you pull to the left more toward... what's the big boxy building?"

"Movie theater."

"Head that way while you scan. I'm feeling something there," he instructs, sounding like the Director he is.

Aware they made the longest leap with Reed's energy, Nic requests Jinx join them next. Wordlessly, Jinx saddles up in front of her husband and takes a spot on Nic's arm and Cara's leg. The group inhales collectively at her touch.

Reed must comment, "That's some fine hot ass energy you got there, Jinx."

Jinx thanks Reed for his sarcastic compliment, but she hesitates when Cara asks if she's ready. "Based on what you all are saying, I'm really intimidated by Nic's mind and what Cara's about to do."

Sensing her anxiety, Cara assures her it will be fine. She softly pulls Jinx's thread, hoping the transition will be easier. "I'm going to give you a quick peek at Supermind, and then bring you back...now," Cara warns.

"Jesus Nic, you're a hot mess! Jake, you can follow that?" Jinx shouts.

"Yes, my scatterbrained love, I can," Jake responds to his wife flatly.

"Almost through the plaza. Reed, how much further to the area you're getting something from?" Nic inquires.

"About 100 yards."

"Sasha, it's time. Ready, my friend?" Nic asks with some concern.

Nic wants Sasha to do the same thing, empty his mind, and then latch on. Cara will take it from there and throw him the moving picture. Sasha should try and stay with Jake and Nic for a moment. Cara can take him, afterwards.

Sasha stands behind Nic and places one hand on Nic's head and one on Cara's head. As soon as his hand lands on Cara's head there is a collective buzz. Her hair stands straight up. Jinx's hair does the same thing. Reed feels goosebumps spread across his skin and a charge shudder through him causing the scan to static out for a moment. Everyone is speechless for a full minute feeling the effect.

"My brother, you have always had an electric personality. Do you feel this?" Nic jokes.

Sasha says nothing but, "Cara, picture."

"Don't ignite big guy, it's coming. I'm sending you straight to Nic, though, tell me when you need to come back," Cara counters defensively. Reed can sense her struggle for Sasha's thread. It's distinctive and much more vibrant and colorful than the others. Whereas his thread has a metallic filament to it, Sasha's is iridescent. When she tugs it, the thread latches on, like a mental hand has grasped her mental finger. He can feel Sasha pass through her with such speed and force; Reed swears her hair swings with the momentum.

"Welcome to the show, Sasha. Let me explain..."

"I got it Nic, no explanation required," Sasha snaps.

Reed, Cara, and Jinx watch as Sasha migrates quickly and effortlessly through Nic's mind. He's moving from quadrant-to-quadrant sorting through it all, absorbing like a sponge. Cara has stopped scanning because she's enthralled by Sasha's ability to navigate and process Nic's grid so easily. Next thing they know, Sasha is back in Cara's mind returning to them of his own accord.

"Reed, show me the target you see," Sasha barks out. "Cara, I feel it too, skip everything, go right there. Better yet, let me."

"What the...did you just take the helm? How the hell did you... STOP!" Cara shrieks.

Sasha keeps the controls but ceases all forward movement.

REED IS CORRECT ABOUT THE LOCATION, BUT CARA'S HEAD IS SPINNING FROM Sasha commandeering control from her. She needs Sasha to stop and proceed with caution. Cara can feel the man in the blue four door Camry parked North of the theater. He appears to be a blocker though, maybe, with his own gifts. She's getting a similar vibe to what she feels with her group. There is no strong connection between them to tap into. But she does see a faint thread extending from him to her. It's too weak and indistinct to pull, but she wonders if she can travel on it. She brings a part of her consciousness close to his faint thread to feel his emotions. "I'm getting malice and rage and..."

"Revenge," Reed offers.

Cara warns, "Nic, you need to be very cautious. Just you and I are going to get closer."

Nic refocuses in Cara's mind to mystery man's thread. She is going to try to travel it while pulling Nic along. She wants to attempt to invade and violate.

"Pull on my mark. Get everything you can from his mind, Nic. We can process it later. Reed, Sasha, see the thread he has connected to me? It's faint, but it's there. If you see it quiver, scream."

Nic and Cara covertly move along the thread. She isn't registering much in the way of thoughts, but the emotions are evident. She creeps forward pulling Nic along with her. Nic is beginning to access his memories.

"There's movement!" Sasha says abruptly.

Before Cara pulls out, Nic runs the thread and does a smash and grab. He snatches everything he can and takes it with him as Cara quickly travels off the thread.

"Everyone off," Cara yells.

The group removes their hands and Cara releases their threads. Her head falls back as if she was punched. Nic's head falls forward. Everyone appears a little disoriented, eyes dazed and hands trembling.

They start to back away, but she reaches out roughly for Sasha's shirt and pulls him back to her and Nic. Holding him by the collar, she yanks Sasha's head in between them. "Guess we figured out your gift... Captain." She salutes him before pushing him away.

"I'm on it, Cara, pot of coffee coming right up," Jinx says with a mocking smile toward Cara before shaking her ass across the kitchen. Obviously, Cara only needs to crave coffee and poor Jinx is in action.

Nic gently tries to calm Cara's hair down with his hands. He gives up and leans in for a kiss, advising, "We should take a break, and then mind palace the smash and grab loot from the Camry man." Pausing for another deeper kiss, he pulls back to add, "That was impressive, my love."

It really did look like a smash and grab from inside Cara's mind. The fact Nic's calling it loot is even funnier. She rises to use the bathroom and get a hairbrush as she chuckles to herself, picturing a thief's black sack filled with memories.

Before she walks out of the kitchen, she spies Reed pulling Sasha aside, and stops to listen. "Argh, Reed, I know what you're about to say to me. What the hell? We're all getting way too intimate," Sasha says, disgustedly.

"What was I going to say?" Reed wants to know, but he whispers his request to Sasha.

"You were about to comment the six of us could take down a small country. And you're correct, we can. How fascinating would that be?" Sasha winks at poor Reed.

"Cara's right, you are the Captain." He salutes Sasha and runs up the stairs.

Of course those two particular men would already be contemplating political and borderline nefarious uses of their gifts.

CHAPTER

THIRTY-EIGHT

WHEN CARA RETURNS TO THE kitchen, Nic hands her a full mug of coffee as she passes by him heading to Jinx. She gives the other woman a hairbrush and pats her head, thanking her for making the coffee.

Jinx still appears dazed as she rhythmically starts brushing her hair. She finally looks to Cara. "I'm feeling like the duh in our little evil franchise. Can someone explain to me what just happened, and how we were all in your brains?"

His wife's gaze rests on him and Nic gathers his thoughts before speaking. "Nobody was in my or her brains, per se. Cara combined some of her consciousness with all of yours. In doing so, she created a 'pocket', for lack of a better word, to store shared pieces of consciousness from each of you."

That's how they could see what the others were doing. Cara couldn't reach the people outside their bubble on her own. She needed the thicker thread connection, and collaborative effort of this close group of friends inside the house, to create a path to the outside.

That very faint connection they were able to make with everyone they passed after leaving the house, was obtained through what might be referred to as a weave of mankind's thoughts, a universal mindfulness. Scientists are calling it collective consciousness.

It's a term originally coined in 1893 by a noted Sorbonne sociologist, Émile Durkheim. Durkheim observed that people's beliefs, standards, and principles make up a shared way of understanding in the world, a collective consciousness. It's what binds individuals together to generate social assimilation.

Later, in the 1970's, scientists continued to develop the hypothesis of a human collective consciousness. And in 1998 a coalition of scientists developed the Global Consciousness Project. They set up and monitor a hardware network of random number generators that have been placed around the globe. They examine output before, during, and after significant worldwide events to measure for common emotional responses of large groups of unrelated people, thereby proving the theory of a global consciousness. Although many scientists have written opinions debunking the claims, the project received a significant boost when these generators registered a spike in activity during the 9/11 attacks.

This collective consciousness is mind-centric parapsychology, the concept of our brainwaves interacting with the physical world. The concept is not groundbreaking. Similar to meditation and prayer, it's the theory of mind over matter, of using the infinite power of the brain to overcome limitations. Lately, people refer to the spilling of positive energy as manifesting. It's not an original idea. It's been around since the dawn of man. Every human being is doing it without realizing his or her thoughts are reaching a common denominator. They are all using willpower to influence reality.

As to how everyone is connected, he's not sure. While eavesdropping earlier on Cara's conversation with Reed in her office, Nic overheard her suggesting it could be divinity or fate. Whether the connections are placed there by a supreme being, they're a metaphysical result, or just plain physics can be debated, but the threads do exist.

As Jake previously mentioned, if the general consensus is we only use 10% of our brain, and if we do evolve, our brain should be able to harness more and more of its potential with each subsequent generation. On the physical plane, think of the powerful effect of social media and the way it has exploded exponentially across the globe. We are all linked, and only now with technology, we are starting to see that link.

Imagine with evolution, the powerful capability of the brain to move beyond the physical world. "Well, in our case we appear to have gone beyond the physical, and even the metaphysical, into telepathic, sharing our thoughts and spilling them into a cosmic consciousness."

Nic shakes his head slightly after his explanation to the group. It's humorous or eerily intentional that he knows so much on the topic. He acquired the knowledge well before he understood his own 'superpowers'.

His daughter's favorite programs to watch with him are *Ancient Aliens* and any show investigating unsolved phenomena. He's heard plenty of theorizing and debating about psychic abilities, shared consciousness, hive minds and the powerful capabilities of the human brain.

Furthermore, Cara's sister is a psychologist and a "New Age Guru" as Sasha refers to Danni. Danni has Cara's head filled with all the latest therapy techniques, meditation hints, and the power of sage. During the celebration of Beltane, or May Day as some may know it, Cara and Mia light a fire in the outdoor pit. They sing, dance and chant while they smudge the property with burnt sage. Mia really enjoys this bonding moment, so Nic has never bothered to investigate the why.

Besides, the why can be harmful to his mental health. Once, after an hour-long conversation on the phone with her sister, Cara hung up and stared at him for several uncomfortable minutes. When she finally spoke, she said, "I am trying to figure out what Love Language you are." This led to a debate on whether he was Touch and she was

Words or vice versa. It ended in a stalemate, but they did both agree Sasha was Acts of Service. Nic has now learned not to pursue details on any of these topics unless he has the time and the interest. All in all, Danni's fascination with all of it is also eerily ironic.

Between aliens populating the earth thousands of years ago, all the psychobabble, and the Pagan rituals, he knows surprisingly more about the topic of collective consciousness than he would have guessed. Although, what he and his wife just achieved is beyond anything he can explain. It borders on the fantastical. Yet maybe it can be rationalized. Maybe they 'will' the talent into existence. Whatever the explanation, he senses they are only beginning to grasp the enormity of the gifts they may possess.

"But how was Sasha able to commandeer the steering of Cara's scan?" Jinx asks, still looking puzzled after his lengthy explanation and interrupting his thoughts.

Nic peers at his friend. "Ah, Sasha was different."

When Cara pulled his thread, not only did Sasha come into the pocket, but he was able to go beyond it, starting to travel on his own on the thread between Cara and himself. Sasha's mind can see the process and adapt.

"Like a computer worm or virus, Sasha can get in and decipher code, and reroute or reprogram. He's a mind hacker," Jinx says by way of an explanation that makes sense to her computer engineering background.

"Nice description, Jinx. Makes me sound despicable," Sasha huffs.

"I think she's onto something, Sash. It could be the thing of beauty Jake describes when we're together. You are directing your gift and capitalizing my talent," Nic agrees.

Cara comes to Sasha's defense. "You are selling poor Broody short on this. There's more, but he's holding back. His mind and thread are different from yours, more dazzling and stouter. Remember the electrical charge we received when he attached himself to the group? He doesn't have a grid, but the grid may only be indicative of the photographic memory, not raw intelligence, or talent. When we tried to attach to Mia earlier, the charge she threw at us was very similar to the energy I felt from Sasha." Cara rests her eyes on Sasha with some scrutiny. "But yours was more subtle and controlled."

"Who was the guy we spotted?" Jinx asks.

Cara responds, "He's part of this, for sure. I received enough from him to know."

"Was it Ed?"

"No," Reed answers as he's coming down the stairs with a laptop in one hand and an IPad in the other. He hands the tablet to Sasha and the laptop to Nic informing them he has the results from the search of Ed's apartment and his records from prison. He has the Wi-Fi password but to plug in the printer password in case they want a paper copy for everyone to review.

Cara goes off topic while they are reviewing the search results, "I feel the overwhelming need to cook." She lifts a chin to her boyfriend. "Reed, how about you and I head to that fine grocery store I was telling you about?"

From the look on Reed's face, Nic isn't the only one reading Cara's thoughts. Reed tips his chin back at Cara. "On the way to the store, I want to hit the spot mystery man was parked. He is long gone, but there might be some residual haze left behind that we can work with."

Cara points to him, Sasha, and Jake, barking her own orders, "You guys can play with Reed's new intel," before adding in a sweeter tone, "and please check on the kids. Make sure they're not driving poor Carter crazy."

"Vizzini, I don't think it's wise for you to go out right now," Sasha comments with concern.

No one has noticed, but when Cara returned from the bedroom, she was wearing a light jacket. She swings the jacket open on the left to reveal she's holstered with the Glock, having lifted her favorite weapon back from Reed, earlier.

"Besides, have you already forgotten I can read minds? I can identify mystery man's thread now. And we can take Far Guard and post him outside." She looks to Jinx. "Wanna come?"

Jinx gives Cara her 'are you joking' face. "No way I'm missing all the fun when the ladies of this community see us with a fourth hot guy at the store." Jinx jumps up, grabbing Cara's arm. "Promise you'll throw me their thoughts when they see us with Reed, please?"

Cara giggles while pulling out an Indians baseball cap from her jacket pocket and handing it to Reed. "Take off that ridiculous blue blazer and put this hat on."

She gives him one of Sasha's leather jackets on the way out. "On the rare chance someone actually watches CNN in this town, you should be unrecognizable."

CHAPTER

THIRTY-NINE

"WE'RE BACK!" CARA ANNOUNCES, BUT no one is in the kitchen.

She heaves her grocery bags onto the counter with Jinx and Reed following suit. Cara immediately starts pulling out pots and pans and ingredients to make her mother's Sicilian meat sauce, sugo.

Reed is watching his girlfriend, carefully. Their little trip to buy groceries was quite the experience. Successful, yet heartbreaking. While Cara was able to throw thoughts to Jinx in the store, she sent all the emotions to him. It was truly horrid. Jinx finally had to stop Cara. She was in tears over the mental insults being hurled at them. Vicious soccer moms judging Jinx and Cara's appearance and wondering how they so undeservedly got their claws into such astonishingly handsome husbands. Even their children were commented on. No vile stone was left unturned. And the emotional lashing...it was a crash course on the seven deadly sins. It was unbearable. No wonder Cara has always been so humble when it comes to her looks. As strong as she appears on the outside, she's obviously vulnerable to the chatter that has been attacking her subconscious.

Reed can't get the nastiness out of his head. Looking at Cara now, she seems composed, but those words and emotions likely caused some damage. Or maybe, they didn't. Maybe she's lived with the criticism so long, she has adapted. Judging from her focus on making the sauce though, he can tell she is affected. She has always told him women are their own worst enemies. He never understood until now.

Men don't evaluate each other with the same kind of venom. They can't be bothered with any of that. But women...are vipers. He understands the "boys club" and "glass ceiling" issues that have existed. That's enough for women to have to deal with. But he believes women are the far stronger sex and has often wondered why more haven't progressed further in industry and politics. In the last 70 years, women have just begun to make a dent in the overall one percent. But who can achieve success with that kind of scrutiny and self-flagellation?

Cara always said she could never work for a woman because women don't have each other's backs. Women cannot see each other as anything but competition in the business world. They will use sex as a tool and pit men against each other, but they will not allow another woman onto their playing field. She used to joke about it being some dormant genetic code from the past to be the last woman standing in the field. Let all the cavemen fight over her. After hearing the backbiting and cruel contempt from those fake-tanned, Botoxed, dimwitted housewives at the grocery store, he must agree.

Wait, did he just judge those women? Holy shit, he's becoming a woman himself from all this oversharing with his girlfriend. Doing the only thing he can think of, he pulls Cara to his chest for a long, solid hug. Without thinking about it, he pulls Jinx into the hug as well.

Bringing their heads to his mouth, he whispers, "I know I didn't tell you both enough how proud I am of you. Not only are both of you gorgeous on the outside, but brilliant and kind and caring on the inside. Even more, you both have a set of brass balls most men would envy. I love you guys."

Jinx punches him in the abs. "Stop that, Reed! You are going to make me cry again today."

His girl kisses the spot Jinx hit, and then wraps her arms more tightly around him.

MOST OF THE PREP WORK IS DONE WHEN THE OTHER THREE MEN MAKE THEIR way into the kitchen. Reed is rolling out meatballs as Jinx washes the dishes and cleans up the cooking mess. Cara stirs, adding some final spices. Short of Reed's emotional moment, they have kept conversation to a minimum during the preparation. Both Jinx and Reed know she requires mental solitude on occasion and this looked to be one of those moments.

Cooking for her is an outlet. She will take on tasks like cooking or cleaning, hyperfocusing on the exercise, essentially emptying her mind of any other thoughts. Reed keeps watching her from the corner of his eyes. This realization does reconcile all the, sometimes, odd behavior she's exhibited in the past. Although, when her need to cook and clean happened at Reed's place, he couldn't be happier or more encouraging of her oddness.

With his eyes still on her, she finally turns to give Reed her full attention. It's apparent he is highly disturbed by what happened at the grocery store. He need not worry. Cara has already disassociated, or compartmentalized, or whatever psych term is correct.

"I thought I was the Meatball Making King of this house," Sasha declares, offended, and interrupting everyone's deep thoughts when he suddenly appears in the kitchen.

"No, I'm the Meatball Making Queen, and Reed is a fine Roller. He has held that position far longer than you, Sasha," Cara quips back.

Nic questions this as he's waltzing in. "You make sugo with Reed?"

Cara glares at her husband. "Nic, I've been making sugo for Reed since the 80's. I still make it for him when I visit. It's tomato sauce, not children. Where were you guys?"

Her husband is watching Reed roll out the final meatballs while he responds, "We were down in my office using the work boards to create a flow chart of facts on all this new intel. Did you guys get anything from the theater parking lot?"

"Not really. A few little things I've stored. You ready to mind palace, or do I need to see your flow chart first?" The little mental game they have always played together as a couple to sort out their issues received a name a few days ago.

"Skip the chart, it may hamper rather than help."

"K," Cara says without looking at him. She needs twenty minutes to finish, wash up and core dump the intrusive thoughts from earlier. Forget disassociating, she wants them erased.

They relocate to the living room and everyone sits down comfortably, except Cara, who remains standing. Jinx has a pen and paper. Reed has his tablet poised, and Sasha is sitting between them. Jake is seated next to Nic, ready to assist if necessary.

"You ready?" Nic asks her.

Cara starts to pace. She has a bad feeling this exercise is going to prove difficult. "Nic, let's start with the actual man in the Camry. Middle aged, foreign, been here in the States for a while."

"Incarcerated," Nic adds.

Cara nods her affirmation. "That's the connection to Ed, same prison. But who is he?"

"Connection to a third interested party," Nic blurts out.

"Yes, but let's focus on one person at a time."

She asks Nic to scan through and find Camry guy's memories of Ed and feed them to her. Cara can see Reed tapping away at his tablet, probably requesting inmate and release records.

"He didn't know Ed previously, and didn't like him when they first met, but somehow, they find a connection and become friends... or is it partners with a common enemy?" Nic asks.

Cara is still pacing, but she likes the direction they're going in. "Partners. I like partners. Commonality?"

Nic's eyes are moving back and forth quickly. "Pictures. I see pictures, moving pictures. Recent but also, maybe a year or 18 months ago."

"Yes, that's when they make the connection. It's a video. Leave it for now, Nic. Zero in on his memories of Ed. Besides the obvious motive, what else are you getting? Why the kids? Why are we feeling the kids with him?"

"He hates the kids. No, not hates, fears. He fears the kids. It starts with you, though. You, and the kids by extension. Why fear?"

"Ed has his own talents and he is using them now. We need an inventory of his gifts. What can he do? Can you see his talent in the memory?" She needs to get to the bottom of why her children feel like the real target.

Nic places his fingers to his temples. "I can't see past..."

Cara comes around, closer, and stops behind her husband. "It must be done, Nic," she says very calmly, and places her hand on the back of his neck.

"Baby, he may know."

"What does it matter? He already knows more about us than we know about him. We must, Nic, it's the only way." Without some solid clues, they will never figure this out.

"What are you going to do?" Sasha asks, interrupting them.

They are going to follow the threads after all. The thread mystery, middle-aged, foreign man has to Ed. The second thread, a memory from what Nic seized during the smash and grab, and the third thread, the connection from Cara to mystery man.

"Won't mystery man know you've come knocking?" Sasha questions, concerned.

The best defense is a good offense. It's time to take down the door and storm the castle. Camry man knows where they are, and he knows of Cara's abilities. They are at a disadvantage by not going in. If they can determine his motive and true capabilities, it will move the advantage back to their team.

Nic places his hand over Cara's on his neck. They both shut their eyes and their heads tilt in unison. Motionless, even their breathing seems to slow. Suddenly, Nic's eyes pop back open, again in unison with Cara's. Nic removes his hand from Cara's and places it back on his lap. They are in a trancelike state for a few minutes. No one in the room dares utter a sound. Slowly, Cara comes out of the trance and moves her hand away from Nic's neck. She thoughtfully shifts around him so she's standing in front of him, all while looking at his face.

When Nic finally looks up at her, he states with no inflection, "You are his Voldemort."

"Who?!" Reed yells out.

Cara turns to him. "He Who Must Not Be Named," she says, still in deep thought.

"What the hell are you talking about?" Reed asks, losing his patience. This causes Cara to snap out of her thoughts.

"Jesus, Reed, you really need to start reading fiction more, or reading People magazine or something. Now, that we don't hang out on a regular basis, your knowledge of contemporary pop culture is severely lacking," Cara quips.

Sasha tries to quell the tension. "Reed, I think Ed thinks he's the 'Boy Who Lived'. He thinks he's Harry Potter. He believes Cara is his Voldemort. One must die for the other to live."

Cara manages a small smile for Sasha. "Mia would be very proud of you, Sasha."

"How many frigging times have I had to watch those movies with her? I can quote them for God's sake. So, what are you saying, Ed's become delusional?"

Nic jumps in explaining that Ed's talents mimic Cara's. He is a telepath and an empath. "He thinks he was spared for a reason in the confrontation with her years ago. Ed became obsessed with the

Harry Potter books in prison and related everything about Harry to his own life and his gifts. Ed believes he's the 'Boy Who Lived.' In his mind, Cara became the evil Voldemort. He thought she was dead until he met the Camry man in prison. The information the man provided lets Ed know for certain that his Voldemort truly lives. And just like in the books, only one of them can survive."

"He's insane, we knew THAT from the beginning," Cara exclaims. She suddenly turns to Reed, seething, "You should have let me cut off his nuts like I wanted to. He would have bled to death, and Voldemort would live. The maniacal villain wins this tale."

Nic stands and grabs her wrist, firmly. "That's it, Cara! That's the thread between you. You WERE supposed to kill him 25 years ago!"

Reed whispers quietly, "Or he was supposed to kill her. The thread had to be cut, but it wasn't."

The room is silent once again. Jinx is still writing on the pad, but Cara can't imagine what the words are.

It's Sasha who breaks the silence. "What's with the kids? Why hunt them?"

Nic mumbles, "He sees them as an extension of Cara. Evil minions, Death Eater spawn, so to speak."

"Okay, this is bad, but it's good we know. We can factor in 'fucking crazy' on your flow chart and move on. At least my life is starting to elevate from B movie status," Cara adds to lighten the mood.

"So, back to the middleman," Nic says dismissively, walking back to his chair.

"Nic! That's what he is, a middleman." Inspiration hits her hard.

Camry man has no connection to Cara. He's an intermediary between Ed and another interested party. The connection was random. Serendipitous. The middleman doesn't have any motive of his own. He's tied to someone else, aside from Ed. They must follow middleman's thread out to that second party, the interested party, to discern their motive. It must be the person or group that funded the hit from Vlad and wants the kids.

"Wait, Ed is after Cara Bianco, but is this second interested party after Chase Bennett?" Reed asks trying to follow this mind palace routine they are doing with each other. It's obvious he's very disturbed she has yet another adversary he's failed to protect her from.

Nic and Cara give each other the look, again, the one nobody in the room seems to understand. Nic reaches his hand out to her. While Cara places her hand in his, Nic says a little too calmly in response to the question, "No. This second party has no prior connection to Cara, at all. The other person or group...is connected to me."

Sasha jumps out of his chair, gesturing at Nic. "You mean to tell me that Ed is looking to kill Cara and her kids, and then he runs into someone in prison who knows of a second party also looking to kill Cara and her kids but because of something you've done, Nic?"

"Yes...sort of," Nic admits, reluctantly.

Jake who has remained quiet and alert during the whole mind palace act finally decides to comment. "Don't get me wrong; I am thoroughly impressed today with what you two have done with this breakthrough. It's fucking remarkable. But why is it so hard to get intel on the second party when you had so much on Ed?"

When Nic did the grab, he went looking for memories of Ed because he knew Ed was involved. Only having seconds to find relevant memories, he focused where it made sense. The other memories had some heavy blocks on them. Nic didn't bother to dig. The time would have been wasted. Those blocked memories were peripheral at that point. There, but slightly out of his reach.

Middleman was mostly blocked like everyone else in the house is. Cara did receive some emotions from him but no thoughts. She recommends they make another mind palace attempt combining Nic's fringe memories and the emotions she came away with.

It was a set up, you know, Cara transmits to her husband.

Yes, the middleman wanted us to see Ed memories. He covered the 2nd party. He's connected more intimately with that other party. I believe they were going to let Ed take the fall for the murders. This was planned.

I agree, but let's think about this. I get the feeling we need to proceed with caution. Why do I feel that way? Like I'm about to walk out onto a minefield.

I'm sensing that, too.

"Wait." Jake states. "Isn't it too coincidental that you're given free passage to the Ed memories, but the other party and their motive is blocked from you? It sounds like a set up. This middleman has talent. He came here specifically to lead us to Ed, thus concealing the greater threat, the second party."

Damn that Jack Reacher.

"You already figured this out, didn't you?" Jake accuses.

"You read minds now?" Nic inquires with some attitude.

"No. It's written all over you. Nice poker faces, guys. Were you not going to share that?"

"Yes, we were, but we're still processing. Don't get your panties in a bunch, JACK," Cara retorts. This produces a menacing growl from Jake, but Cara catches an emotion from Reed at her comment... What is it?

Satisfaction, is Nic's telepathic response.

Shit, I forgot you were in here! Sorry, babe. Welcome to my world of talking to myself!

This does take some getting used to, yeah?

They both begin laughing, appearing insane. Noticing the others staring, they shake their heads trying to regain composure. Neither feels an explanation is necessary. Releasing Cara's hand, Nic sits back in his chair. "Round Two in the mind palace."

Cara, again, begins to pace around the room. She is visibly squinting her eyes this time as she walks. There is tremendous emotion around the second party. Whereas Ed is delusional, this person or group is all regret, rage, and revenge. It's different though; somehow inconsistent. "I feel it through the middleman but it's not..."

"It's not the same level of emotion," Nic adds. He can feel the difference, too. He doesn't recognize what it is, but it feels like one person, not a group.

Cara has moved to pacing a smaller portion of the living room, directly in front of everyone seated there. Her fingertips rub her temples while she paces. The afternoon's mental activities are taking a toll. After two full rounds of pacing with no one speaking, Cara stops in front of Nic and looks at him. She turns abruptly to gawk at Jinx, and it hits her. A straight punch to her gut from the memory of the grocery store gossip.

Jinx looks up defensively. "What?"

"OH MY GOD, NIC!" Cara exclaims. "We don't recognize the emotion because we're looking at it all wrong. It's FEMININE!"

Nic reexamines the processes in his mind and his face registers the result. "The second party is a woman!"

Cara begins to scowl and leans in to place her hands on Nic's chair. She gets right in his face. Her eyes become hard, and she speaks clearly, positive she recognizes the emotion now. "Not just any woman, Nic. The Hell hath no fury like a woman scorned kind of woman! Care to elaborate?!" Nic's face falls flat while Cara's turns to seething, jealous fury. "What haven't you shared with me, my love?!"

CHAPTER

FORTY

T HE VISIBLE FURY EMANATING FROM Cara is making the group uncomfortable. Nic is lost, not being able to reconcile what his brain is receiving from Cara with what's being processed in there.

No, you're jumping to conclusions here. You're correct, she is a woman scorned, but it can't be me, Cara. I told you I've never been in a relationship. I didn't lie to you. Yes, there were women, but none I saw more than a couple of times.

How about during ops? Seductions? Cara drills.

No, that wasn't my area of expertise. I told you already.

Nic, with your looks, you're telling me you didn't seduce women as part of your work?

Sure, I flirted and 'preened' as you refer to it, but no, bedding them was not my specialty. I...would've had some issues with that.

What are you talking about, issues? You're like a sex machine! You're amazing in bed. I thought you were a total player after our first night.

Player?! You need to calm down, Cara, and trust me. It was all about you on our first night. I've never had anything like that happen to me. I'll send you my memory of it...later. Although, I sort of like this crazy,

324

jealous bitch thing you have going on. I must admit, it's very reaffirming.

You trying to defuse the situation?

YES, you're going postal on me and I'm losing focus. SO. ARE. YOU.

Fine, you're right, I'm calming down. I do want that memory later, though. I shared mine with you, earlier.

Which, by the way, was very emotive. I had no idea you felt that way the morning after our first night together. AND YET, you still question me?

I trust you. I do. But are you sure there isn't some crazy bunny boiler you slept with once who's out there trying to kill me and our kids? Because that IS what we're feeling on this. Clearly.

But it doesn't make sense.

They need to reexamine the connection to him. It isn't clear. Her motive is, her targets are, but the connection is hazy. There is some deep emotion there. This isn't a one-night stand gone stalker. This is a woman who has some time invested, who is avenging a deep, dark betrayal.

Cara leans away from Nic and composes her face. She turns and sees everyone watching in curious horror. She doesn't think she can continue to mind palace this out loud to the group anymore. Reed, feeling her distress, is on the edge of his seat, the Captain, ready to pounce. She's not getting rid of either of them easily. She sends a message to Jinx.

"Jake, let's get dinner started. The sauce should be ready. You set the table and I'll make the penne...and Cara, thank you for asking instead of just throwing the suggestion at me." Jinx gives her a smirk and a wink as she drags her husband out of the living room.

Cara reciprocates with an appreciative smile. She looks to Reed wanting to try something. She can see her own concern on his face and feels his alarm coming back at her.

Connor? It's fine...I'm okay...I just had an overreaction. Nic and I would be more comfortable without so many people in attendance for the rest of this. Do you hear me?

Cara is only watching Reed from the corner of her eye. She sees him tilt his head and wipe his face with his hands. Then, a slow, subtle nod comes from him.

We would like you and Sasha to stay, but if this gets too emotional, I'm going to ask you to grab Sasha and get out, as well. Capice?

Reed moves his head towards the kitchen and touches his ear, their signal for 'all set'.

Nic interrupts, *You and I are soooo having a little 'talk' tonight, cara mia.*

Duly noted, once again. Let's proceed. As painful as this woman's betrayal is, you know we need to get inside of it to find the answer. Her emotion is the only thing we have at this point to go on.

Standing, Nic stretches his back, knowing this isn't going to be easy.

Reed and Sasha watch as Cara and Nic get up and move towards the center of the room, closer to where they're seated. They clasp hands, more from the need to touch than the need for connection.

Ready? Cara nods toward Nic.

OH GOD Nic, it's awful...the pain...it's everywhere. Cara leans forward to clasp her abdomen from the physical pain. Even Nic is hunching towards her, his face flinching.

She was hurt, wounded physically and emotionally by this man. She's never recovered. He has ruined her life. His death isn't enough. She needs him suffering...emotionally devastated as her revenge. Nic gets this out. She can hear the pain in his mental voice.

She doesn't want to hurt him, physically. She doesn't want to KILL him. Just annihilate him emotionally...she still loves him. She knows the way to do that is through me and the kids.

Yes, she keeps something of him...Cara, what is it she keeps...a memory?

No...something more tangible.

Yes...she always keeps it on her. Like a talisman. However painful, Cara, the talisman is the key. Please, try and see it.

Cara takes a deep breath. The pain is so intense. Pain like she has never experienced before, deep, wrenching, and anguished. It makes her shudder, tears bursting from her eyes. The emotions twist with desperation and rage. Nic releases her hands to pull her closer. His face etched with torment.

Even in her mind Cara can barely give Nic the words...*Erghh, it's... a picture of them. She keeps...keeps...a photo.*

Baby, focus. Please focus on the photo. Can you make out faces?

OOOHHH Nic, it hurts so much!

Cara's practically convulsing, shaking so hard. Nic tightens his grip around her. The photo begins to materialize in their minds. First the woman, she is young, vibrant, and very beautiful. She has a cascading flow of copper hair. She is smiling like she has everything in the world to live for, a woman madly in love.

Nic jerks back slightly at the sight of the woman. *Baby? I've never in my life seen this woman before, and please remember I have a photographic memory. I'm sorry, but you need to expand the picture and see the rest of it.*

Cara moans as she continues her assault on the pain-stricken emotions. The only thing holding her upright at this point is Nic. And suddenly the photo expands. It's an old school selfie. Shot with an instamatic type of camera. The man is clearer. He's young, and he's smiling that same wide grin as the woman. He has dark, slightly disheveled wavy hair. He could be standing in the wind, or just had it tousled. He is strikingly handsome.

Nic immediately drops his arms and steps away from Cara, causing her to go crashing to the carpet. She is outright sobbing. Reed lurches for her and scoops her up onto his lap in one fluid movement. He begins rocking her and wiping her tears. Sasha moves with the same grace to Nic's side full of concern. The handlers appear as if they are taking sides in a marital battle.

Nic is immobile. His face has transformed. Evil Nic. Deadly steel eyes.

REED'S ENTIRE FOCUS IS ON CARA. SHE IS A MESS, INCONSOLABLE AND emotionally anguished. He's clutching her to his chest, hoping he can send her this comfort energy they say he can emit. He finally lifts his eyes to Nic.

Her husband is just standing there, his arms at his sides. His fists are clenched, and he is emanating pure furious wrath. Reed's mouth drops open because he can feel it. He looks quickly to Sasha and notices the man registering Nic's anger, leaning away from him.

"Cara, you know what must be done," is all Nic says.

She can't even verbalize, mentally, but nods to her husband while she roughly removes Reed's arms from around her.

Nic is a blur. He steps behind Sasha while Cara jumps up into Nic arms, essentially wedging Sasha between them. The reaction is instantaneous. Sasha groans while thrashing, not in an effort to hurt them, but from the violent assault they have perpetrated on his mind. Sasha continues to moan from the intrusion, and then from the memory as Nic and Cara wrench it from him with no thought of sparing him the rape.

When Nic releases his arms, Cara stumbles back away from Sasha. Reed catches her before she falls. He's completely clueless and growing more alarmed while he clutches her back to his chest. Why did they do that to Sasha?

Dropping down to his knees, Sasha's head falls forward and it hits the carpet. He looks like he's praying except his body is trembling. Still standing, with his head inclined and staring at the only person he called family until he met Cara, is Nic. His face is a mask showing no emotion. He really is one scary son of a bitch.

FORTY-ONE

REED, TAKE ME TO THE family room and grab Jinx and Jake along the way, please.

Reed pulls Cara up into his arms and carries her out. Cara is crying harder than before. As they pass the kitchen, Reed motions for Jinx and Jake while they continue through the kitchen to the smaller, more intimate and casual family room on the other side.

On their way in, Jinx flips the switch to turn on the gas fireplace in the room. Reed sits on the stone hearth with a sobbing Cara still held tightly in his arms. He doesn't know what to do to calm her down. He's wiping tears and rocking her, rubbing her back and stroking her hair. But she knows none of Reed's efforts are going to shake what she and Nic pulled from Sasha.

Then Cara starts to hear it...in her head. The music...she knows it... it's the strums of a bass guitar from one of the songs she hears late at night coming from the music room...maybe October Project? Then comes the voice, shaky, anguished, and tormented, singing about haunted dreams and being caged, the past never leaving his mind, and a funeral in his heart. It's not Nic's voice, though. It's

Sasha singing. *Please Nic, disconnect. I can't take it right now,* Cara pleads mentally.

After Nic vacates abruptly, Cara realizes she's not alone. Reed. She kept his thread pulled in her mind. She looks up at him and his eyes are red rimmed and glassy. He's just experienced all of that with her. She places her hand up to his face and leans in for their foreheads to touch. *I'm sorry, I didn't mean to have you feel that awful anguish, first hers, then his. I'll be ok. I just need to let the emotions pass. It's crazy, isn't it? I've cried more in the last 72 hours than I have my whole life.* Cara releases Reed's connection and attempts to process all this chaos and try for some semblance of composure.

When she can finally have a clear thought, she reaches her hand out to Jake. He doesn't hesitate and clasps it with both of his, engulfing her small one inside his very large paws. He nods to her in understanding. His face suddenly changes; he inhales a hard, shaky breath, and drops to one knee, involuntarily.

Cara gives him a moment to process what she sent him. When he looks back up at her, showing the most emotion she has ever seen on his face, Jake utters the only words he can form, "Holy. Shit."

"Yes," Cara confirms.

With her voice still shaky, she makes some requests. It's a music video the ginger made the connection with. It's something the kids posted online, probably YouTube. Cara wants Jake to grab the kids downstairs and use Nic's office to have them pull up all the videos of their open mic night performances, and the ones they film in the music room. Find any that have Sasha in them. Nic and Sasha have a rule. They don't let the kids post the ones they appear in, but somehow one or two have made their way to the Internet. They must find them.

"Delete all the videos, regardless of my children's protests, but download a copy of any you find with Nic or Sasha in them, first." They need to watch those. While Jake is doing that, she is going to endeavor to explain to Jinx and Reed what has just transpired. Her final request is he leave Sasha and Nic alone on his way by.

Cara turns her face back to Reed. "Do you know who Katherine St. John is?"

"I know of a Katherine St. John who's the daughter of the former MI6 serving Chief, Thomas St. John," Reed acknowledges.

As Jake quickly passes by the living room, Nic catches a glimpse of him in his peripheral vision. Nic is staring down at Sasha who is still on the floor. All he can think is, *this is a fucking mess.* Nic's rage has subsided and he's left with nothing but emptiness and the sound of Sasha's tormented singing in his head. The lyrics tell of a person who has lost himself and is alone in his life. It's seriously depressing. As he listens to Broody, Nic can't prevent the tiny smile on his lips when he thinks of his wife's accurate description of him and Sasha with their dark, moody, and broody personalities. He hates when she's right.

Not knowing what he should do, Nic gets down on the floor next to Sasha, sitting tailor style. He listens to Sasha hit the chorus with haunting echoes, but otherwise he just sits.

Um, Cara? I know I'm not supposed to bother you but, um, I'm at a bit of a loss here. Comforting middle-aged anguished men is not my area of expertise. This is sort of your domain, no? I mean you are Italian, and melodrama and tragedy are in your DNA.

What. The. Fuck? You are the man with the ANGST! Suck on that for some inspiration! For God's sake, put on your big boy underpants, place your hand on his shoulder and ask him to start telling you the story, from the beginning. I'm finishing the wrap up in here. I want to start Reed and Jinx on some research and data collection. Oh, and I've sent Jake to look at videos to find the point of origin. And Nic?

Yes?

You're starting to appear as the weak link in our partnership.

I'm starting to believe I am, cara mia.

I'll be in there as soon as I'm done here. Get him to talk, please.

Nic follows his orders and reaches out to Sasha, placing his hand tentatively on his shoulder. He gently asks Sasha to tell him what happened. He even throws in a couple of 'pleases'. Sasha doesn't acknowledge him, though. Nic tries to do that energy thing Jake was talking about where he can send comfort and warmth through his touch. He isn't sure if he's done it correctly until Sasha finally looks up at him.

"Are you trying to comfort me?" Nic nods. "DO NOT EXTEND ME ANY COMFORT," Sasha says articulating each word. "I don't deserve that."

"Sash, story, from the beginning, NOW!" Nic barks, deciding more force is required.

Instead of talking, Sasha sings another verse of the song aloud, but softly, as he pulls his head from the floor and leans back, slouched against the front of a plush chair with his legs spread.

Then, abruptly, he just stops singing and peers to Nic, looking resigned. "Just after you got settled at your new job, I was sent away for nine months on assignment." Nic nods at the recollection. "I was only 20 years old...I was sent under deep cover to infiltrate England's Military Intelligence, Section 6."

He was supposed to use his high marks in Whore School, as well as his exemplary training, to seduce, bed, and eventually get engaged to Katherine St. John, the daughter of the then Assistant Chief at MI6, Thomas St. John.

Sasha was a young man. He didn't really understand what was involved. Even if he had, Sasha would not have been able to deny the order.

He was given a new cover as a student at Cambridge, where Katherine was attending. He was supposed to be the son of West German, wealthy parents, but most of his academic life was spent in Great Britain at various schools.

Someone, already inside, on a lower level, had paved the way for Sasha by forging documents at all the proper primary schools in England. He was to sound like a Brit, but with a slight German accent. That was the only easy part of the assignment.

Sasha arrived at Cambridge looking and dressing the part. He was matched into three of her classes. Katherine was only 18 years old. She was far more beautiful than he thought she would be. He took his time trying to get to know her, and then courting her. He utilized the sum of his education. That's all he had, what he had studied. Sasha hadn't really dated or spent any time with women. They didn't have those kinds of opportunities in training.

He looks to Nic waiting for some acknowledgement, and when Nic nods, Sasha continues.

He found he enjoyed her company. She was very bright. She loved life and appreciated all its nuances. She relished life's simple pleasures. Katherine wasn't what Sasha expected from a girl raised in a privileged environment. It took him by surprise if he's being honest.

Sasha pauses for a moment to reflect. His brain feels melted from both the rape and the memory.

He tried to match all his interests with Katherine's. Nineteenth century Romanticism was her specialty, so it became his. They would read Byron and Shelly under a tree together and go for long walks to discuss the literature. Sasha was enjoying it.

Katherine wasn't the type of girl who savored crowds or attention. Their occasional trips to pubs and parties in the academic environment were something he had never experienced, and he found them entertaining. But she was more content with her solitary time spent with him.

The weeks turned to three months and Katherine finally asked him to meet her parents. They went into London and met with her folks at their flat for dinner. Her father seemed tentative, but cordial. Sasha was pleased, as he still saw the meeting as progress.

During this time, he tried to keep their physical relationship to stolen kisses and light contact. Sasha attempted to follow the books Katherine was so fond of, becoming the courteous, romantic hero. He never pushed for more than that.

The University was going into break for the holidays and he was invited to spend New Year's with her in London. Again, he saw Katherine's father who was beginning to show more kindness, even complimenting Sasha on his care of Katherine. The man commented he had never seen her happier. Sasha was getting more excited by his progress.

When they got back to the routine at school, Katherine began to press the physical part of their relationship. She wanted more. He had to give in at some point, so Sasha let her set the pace. He thought it prudent.

Sasha lets out a big sigh. "We progressed on that front quickly to an all out sexual relationship. She was very prolific, and, I was afraid, beginning to fall in love with me."

"Did you love her?" Cara asks very softly as she comes in behind Sasha and sits next to him on the floor.

Sasha winces slightly before answering, "I don't know. I wasn't an experienced man. I was never loved and I don't think I knew what love was at that point. I knew training and duty. My only bond of affection was what I had for Nic. But I knew enough to realize what she was feeling for me. Still, I had my mission." Sasha inhales deeply before continuing.

Their relationship progressed hot and heavy until spring when he was sent orders to propose. Sasha discerned the timing was quick. They were both still so young, but his superiors were thrilled with his progress and wanted him poised to infiltrate the family.

Sasha took the opportunity on their next visit with her family to speak to her father, alone. He explained his feelings for Katherine and that he wanted to ask for her hand, promising not to marry until they were older and out of school, but explaining he wanted to commit to her and only her. Her father didn't object.

Subsequently, he planned a very romantic evening and asked her to marry him.

"Of course, she was thrilled." Sasha has his head in his hands, barely capable of talking.

They were engaged for eight weeks when it happened. They went for a walk in the woods to discuss books and admire nature. When they returned to her flat, she opened the door to find her father and two of his agents pointing pistols.

Sasha is beginning to lose it again. Tears are running down his face. He is not sure he can continue. "I don't know what happened to me, but in that instant, nothing was in my head but my training... nothing." He takes some quick, shaky breaths just to resume.

He placed Katherine in front of him. He knew he was the target. He knew that somehow his cover was blown, so he used her as a shield. Her father was screaming at him to let her go, but he couldn't. He wouldn't. He backed them up to the doorway. He was going to drag her through then run, but that's not what happened.

Very gently Nic coaxes Sasha on, "What happened, Sash?"

The two agents panicked. They aimed their weapons at any exposed part of Sasha's body, hoping to get a shot off before he got past the doorway, but he kept Katherine perfectly in front of him until the door. At the door, he was going to push her back into the room, but the exact moment he propelled her forward, one of the agents fired at his leg. Katherine was already in motion. The bullet hit her in the abdomen.

"I didn't stay to see her fall to the ground. I was around the corner, out the door, in the cover of shadows, and on my way to a safe house before I even heard the ambulance." Sasha gets the last part out quickly. He can't tolerate speaking the words that changed his life.

Nic looks to his wife before refocusing on Sasha who is wiped out. His head is down, his body slouched. He just can't continue, but he knows they need more.

CHAPTER

FORTY-TWO

CARA KNOWS HER HUSBAND IS useless right now. It's up to her. She cajoles Sasha into continuing. "Katherine survived the shooting. She lived, but the damage to her reproductive organs...they couldn't be salvaged. Katherine became unstable when she was told who you really were, Sash. Between the shooting, the loss of her fertility, and the betrayal, she had a breakdown. Her father institutionalized her. She spent the next 15 years in an asylum. You tortured yourself and kept track of her, didn't you? DIDN'T YOU?" Cara shouts.

"YES, YES, I did! How could I..." Sasha just dissolves.

Nic is up and out of the room, heading to find Reed to see what he's gathered on intel. He can't bear the sight of his 'brother' falling apart. *Sorry, baby, but you really are better with the Angst.*

Cara tries to gather Sasha in her arms as best she can and holds him. She strains desperately to tone down the tremendous guilt flooding her from his emotions. *Max? Can you and your sister come upstairs and show your Uncle Sasha how much you love him, please.*

We're feeling his distress, Mom. Mia gathered the story, as well.

Then you understand what I need you to do.

Cara is still holding Sasha when she can hear the kids on the stairs. She quickly wipes away his tears and tucks his hair behind his ears. She stands, leaving a spot on each side of Sasha open for them. They plop down and do what children all over the world can do with a just a smile. They mend his tortured heart.

Mia hugs him hard, whispering her love and praises, giving him encouragement. Max only cuddles with Sasha, something they've always done together. Max was the more physically affectionate of the two kids and Sasha the recipient of most of his attention. He also whispers kind words of love and his reassurance, reminding Sasha how much he has meant to them, even conceding Sasha has done more for them than either parent.

Cara stands back and watches her children interact with Sasha, struck by their love for him and his for them. She is so proud of her children right at that moment. But the moment passes and her lips frown. The frown is slowly replaced with a look of calm. The calm, still transforming her face, and hardening her features. Her eyes turn cold and dark. Her jaw becomes set and her lips thin. A look of steely determination takes over.

THE TWINS ARE STILL GATHERED IN SASHA ARMS WHEN NIC AND REED approach the living room. Taking note of Cara's expression, Reed stops Nic in the archway. "Look at your wife's face." Nic stares at Cara and turns back to Reed with questioning eyes. "You don't see that look often, I imagine. I haven't seen it in quite some time. That's her mission set face. Best we hang back and watch from a safe distance."

Cara looks down at her children and informs them it's time to get ready for dinner. "Head upstairs to your rooms and wash up. Be back in 20 minutes, please."

The twins register her steely mood and rise quickly to exit, passing Nic and Reed on their way out of the room.

When Cara knows they are far enough away, she says, "Sasha, please stand up."

Sasha is hesitant, but he stands facing Cara. She winds up and slaps him across the face with as much brute force as she can manage. While he's still registering the shock from her assault, Cara shoves him hard, sending him backwards to land seated in the plush chair.

She gets right into his face and starts screaming, "You need to snap out of it, now! You need to get over this guilt for hurting her NOW! And do you know why, Sasha, DO YOU? BECAUSE I WILL FIND KATHERINE AND KILL HER!!!"

Sicilian Personality Disorder has set in, firmly. Cara has had some success learning to control the overwhelming fury that can ignite her into an insane rage. Over the years, Reed has helped her figure out when to use it to her advantage and when to hold back. It's an interesting phenomenon, and her family jokes about it so often, it has received its own name and acronym, SPD. They all have it. She has an entire extended family of crazy hotheads. Unleashing her inner SPD in certain situations can provoke a positive result. Cara has obviously concluded this is one of those moments.

Sasha's eyes grow wide as Cara continues her full-on offensive. "NO ONE THREATENS ME OR MY CHILDREN AND LIVES, SASHA. I DON'T GIVE A RAT'S ASS ABOUT YOUR GUILT OR YOUR ANGST! YOU WERE DOING YOUR JOB, SOLDIER! ANY ONE OF US WOULD HAVE DONE THE SAME THING!"

Nic looks to Reed, and they both say simultaneously, "The Italian Love Treatment."

Reed starts to chuckle, but Nic adds, "The guy's a fucking mess. I hope it works."

Cara grabs Sasha by his shirt pulling him even closer to her face. She looks like the quintessential drill Sargent at Army basic. Her face, her body language and emotional onslaught, are nothing short of terrifying.

"You must get a handle on this, Sasha. You've carried it too far.

She was not the love of your life, and I understand she was collateral damage, but SHIT HAPPENS! It sucks, but you compartmentalize and move on. WHAT THE FUCK?! Did they not teach that in your training?!"

Sasha finally gets the nerve to respond to her, "What do you know of this? YOU, who were raised in a loving home."

Cara turns away from him to try for some composure, but she fails, turning back and hitting him hard in the chest. "That's exactly where you learn it, dumb ass!"

Reed can't prevent the smile forming on his lips. Of course, Cara is correct. Compartmentalizing is a learned behavior everyone acquires in a loving home. If you have a brother or sister, you learn to tuck away your anger and disappointment. Some siblings thrive on ratting each other out to their parents or accusing them by telling wicked lies. Some steal favorite clothes and ruin them. They destroy perfect Friday nights out with friends by getting a parent to insist they tag along. They compete for attention and sabotage each other. But these mutinous heathens have to live together.

"And when you're at your lowest, beaten, battered, and hopeless, you must march to the family dinner table and sit right next them and make nice – every night! That's where you learn to compartmentalize!" Cara screams, on the same wavelength as Reed's thoughts.

She finally stands back, stepping away from Sasha, and takes a deep breath, "Don't you see, Sasha, you missed that class growing up. You never got the invite to that one. I am truly sorry about that. But you got the chance and attended the class, later. Pity, you didn't get a very good grade in it."

Sasha's face grows confused. Cara enlightens him. "Here, dipshit, for the last 15 years. WE are a family; you're like my brother. We tease, we beat on, we rip, and then we come to the table, and we LOVE! We love because that's what you learn in a family. You learn that despite what you've done, or what you intend to do, we LOVE YOU!"

Cara steps forward once again, and stares down at Sasha. "Get up, give me a hug, and tell me you love me, NOW!"

Sasha jumps up, but Cara doesn't give him a chance. She grabs him firmly and holds him for a few seconds before pushing off and getting back into his face. "YOU have 15 minutes to get your act together and I expect you at the dinner table, capisci stronzo?"

She must be really pissed when instead of saying the phonetic "capeesh," Americano style, she tells him, do you understand, asshole, in real Italian.

Sasha is at a loss for a moment. He hesitates before turning on his heel and heading to the stairs for the lower level.

Cara whips her head towards the two members of her audience. "Who's next?!"

Nic quickly scampers away, but as Reed watches Nic run out the garage door, he decides to make his way into the living room. Cara has her head down, shoulders slumped, looking utterly wiped.

He wraps her up in his arms and whispers in her ear. "Ya done good, sweetheart. Broody needed a good kick in the pants. He was spiraling out of control."

Cara wraps her arms around his waist and leans into him as she exhales, letting all the rage drain from her system. At the same time, he lets go of all his warmth and love for her. Slowly, she melts into their embrace.

He takes her face with both hands, forcing her eyes to his. "You are still standing on your own two feet, even after everything that's happened today, and you have accomplished so much." Leaning in, he brushes his lips to the side of her mouth and whispers, "As usual, you couldn't make me prouder, my sweetheart."

He sweeps her off those two feet and carries her back to the family room to get comfortable on his lap in front of the fire. He needs to take care of her. Just like he has always done from the beginning.

FORTY-THREE

EVERYONE ASSEMBLES FOR DINNER, INCLUDING Sasha. Cara decides to stay by his side in case she needs to comfort him during the meal. The dinner conversation is kept away from the impending threats and focuses more on the children. The kids share what Carter has taught them about different video games he plays. They talk about schoolwork and upcoming games, recitals and concerts. Weirdly, they do most of the talking, an unusual role reversal, as if they recognize the discussion must remain light. Even Elijah offers some discourse.

After dinner, Jinx promises the teenagers dessert but in an hour. They clean up quickly, while Jake delivers pasta and bread to the agents outside. When he returns, they sit to watch the uploaded video. Jake has only found one with Sasha and none with Nic. The kids had only flubbed up once. Although, she and Nic are shocked to find out that both Max and Elijah had posted over 24 videos. Jake confirms they were all removed.

Jake sets the video to play on the flat screen in the family room. The six of them get comfortable and watch as Max appears doing his best Michael Buble, singing Sinatra's *Fly Me to the Moon.* Mia is on piano while Eli is playing the bass. In the background, Sasha is playing an acoustic guitar.

Cara keeps her eyes on the Sasha in the video, while her mind cues into the Sasha sitting next her. Video Sasha is playing but watching the kids; a smile and absolute pride showing on his face. The look of cherished love is so evident.

Sasha, I'm feeling your distress level. Please share.

You need to get out of my head, Vizzini.

Impressed he was able to clearly respond to her, mentally, Cara pushes, *Make me.*

Sasha leans in close to emit a low growl in her ear. *I'm not ready for more intrusion today, please.*

Deciding to extend him the mental privacy, Cara whispers, "Fine, then share with me or share with the group, because I know this is affecting you.n How did she find this and why?"

When the video is complete, Sasha clears his throat and explains, "I used to play this song for Katherine on an acoustic guitar. It's the first song Nic taught me to sing and play. She loved it when I sang it to her." He looks wiped out just from that statement.

"That makes sense then," Jake states. "The video is over a year old. It's categorized on YouTube as an acoustic version. Katherine probably stumbled upon it in search of the song. From there she could have investigated the names listed for the kids. They didn't place Sasha's on the video, but they did use their own when they set up their YouTube channel."

Reed takes over the conversation offering up what he has learned from his analysts at Langley. "Apparently, an inmate matching the description of the Camry man was charged with a B&E eight months ago in Connecticut. His name is Simon Joseff, and he was incarcerated at the same prison as Ed Grotto. According to prison guards, Simon Joseff befriended Ed and remained in prison with him for almost 4 months. After that time, Joseff's attorney pulled his British citizenship card and got him released back to England. That happened a little over three months ago."

Reed also briefs them on his analysts' review of Customs and Immigration records since that time. Simon Joseff isn't listed as returning to the States according to their search, however, they're also looking for any possible cover names he may be using when he did come back. Reed's final piece of intel gets their undivided attention. "Simon Joseff spent seven years at the same institution as Katherine St. John in England. So, that's the connection."

"And Katherine?" Nic inquires.

Reed explains, "I am hitting some roadblocks on her. Because of whom her father is, I must tread lightly with my requests for information. Customs and Immigration don't report her in the States either, but it's likely she is here with a cover name similar to our suspicions about Simon. My analysts are searching through all phone records and possible addresses for Katherine in England, but it's a common name, and the process is slow," Reed declares. "I have reached out to the current MI6 Chief with a polite request but haven't heard anything yet. Her father Thomas' listed address and known records produced nothing of substance leading to Katherine."

Jinx admits she personally did a comprehensive search utilizing her login with the NSA. "I also came up empty," she states.

"Does that mean he doesn't keep in contact with his daughter?" Cara questions.

"It would appear that way, based on his records," Jinx confirms.

Reed leans into Jinx and places a soft kiss on the top of her head. Jinx has been his finest analyst. His cyber genius. She could hack her way through any network. Such a critical component to his success, he thanked her by getting her the very high paying job she has now. Jinx has since repaid him by performing special favors over the years.

The NSA is not always quick or courteous in response to the CIA's request for access and, in fact, is sometimes a hindrance. A phone call to Jinx tended to remedy those situations. Just like now, without her, Reed couldn't even guess how long it would take to get approval for a search of those records. Because the NSA falls under the Department of Defense, the Director is a military General. The Pentagon is known for its secrecy, and its personnel play their cards close to their chest. They don't play nice in the sandbox with the other agencies.

Reed shrugs involuntarily, thinking about how much time he spends finessing the US military; more than he does running his own Agency. The Patriot Act gave the NSA carte blanche and they, in turn, left the CIA and the FBI in the dust. Concerned at any given time their funding might wane, the NSA maintains a stranglehold on its information and resources, purposefully choosing when to share these assets in a continuous effort to prove its worth. Reed often contemplates what this country could achieve if all the agencies remained apolitical, ended their turf wars, and actually worked together.

His internal bitch fest is interrupted when Nic asks a question. Which, ironically, is the same type of bitching Reed does on a day-to-day basis with Nic's wife. Cara has been his most valuable sounding board for ideas and resolutions. She even acts as his therapist.

Nic blurts out, "Setting aside the lack of any intel on Katherine's current whereabouts, we can establish her and Simon's activities fit into our timeline to have hired Vlad. But how do they connect Cara Andre, the married woman, to the intelligence agent known as the Reflex?"

Ed knew Cara as Cara Bianco. Katherine found Cara Andre through the kids' social media accounts. From there, making the connection between the two names was elementary. Things like marriage records, Facebook friends and phone records could be used for that. Once they connected the names, a search of 'Bianco' would have produced court records of her involvement in, and connection to the Ed Grotto case. That information is public. But the Reflex? There's still no correlation whatsoever for that.

Also, if Katherine makes the Bianco/Andre connection, doesn't she already know where Cara lives? Maybe not an actual address, but she would know the general area to search. Why hire Vlad?

Reed looks to Cara for assistance but she appears exhausted. She doesn't make eye contact with him. Instead, she turns to push with her legs against the side of the slippery leather sofa, causing Sasha's body to give way enough for Cara to place her head down on his leg.

Sasha gives her a disgusted head shake before adding, "Katherine would definitely know where we live. As Cara Andre, she is listed as the owner of your design and construction business. The business is on enough websites and State and Federal lists to produce this address. I, too, utilize this address versus my apartment. By all appearances, we live together and share a last name. The underlying link we need to resolve is why Katherine would pursue The Reflex. Why hire Vlad to find the ex-agent? We need the reasoning behind that jump," Sasha adds with less emotion. He looks down with a reassuring smile at Cara's head on his lap. It's obvious to everyone in the room she is staying close to him to feed him comfort.

"I really must be the weak link here. None of this makes sense. If Katherine can manage to trace your history all the way back to your involvement with Ed, doesn't she realize, Cara, you are married to Nic and not Sasha? Why hate you? You haven't betrayed her by taking Sasha from her," Jinx questions.

Nic proposes, "I don't think that's what's in her head. I think her hatred for Cara may come from producing the children Sasha loves so much. She's the vessel."

They all sit quietly for a spell processing all the information they've gathered and trying to come up with any new potential links.

Sasha has something to offer first. "Is Cara just a vessel, or is Katherine's hatred tied to the Reflex in some other way, or is it both?" He places his hand on Cara's forehead as he speaks. "Cara, did you ever work with any of the agents at MI6 during your tenure with the Agency?"

Cara looks to him to answer for her. The day has finally taken its toll on her. Reed responds, "Cara did work with many of the agents at MI6, and she spent considerable time there. Our agencies have always had very cooperative relations, more so then, than now, honestly. Why do you ask?"

With this acknowledgement, Sasha gently lifts Cara's head from his legs as he rises from the sofa. He places her head back down on the leather and stands to look at Reed and Nic. "Can we speak in private, Reed? You, me and Nic?" Interesting, Sasha did not invite Jake.

They follow Sasha out of the room without questioning. They pass Carter on his way into the kitchen.

Carter continues to the family room and sits in the spot Sasha vacated. He stares down at Cara sprawled on the couch. "Agent Bennett, your children have sent me to request their dessert."

Cara slowly lifts herself to a sitting position and studies him. "My children have sent you to do their evil bidding for them?"

Carter is about to come back with a derogatory retort of his own but stops himself. "You have wonderful kids, Agent Bennett. I'm very impressed with them. How you and Mean Man managed that is beyond me, but I compliment you."

Struck by his sincerity, she places her hand on his arm and thanks him. "And you know my name is not Chase Bennett, right?" Carter nods an affirmative. "Please, call me 'Cara' from now on."

Carter gives her one of his wry smiles. "Director Reed expects me to call you Agent Bennett."

"Carter, this is my house, my rules. While you're here, you will refer to me as Cara. After that, you may decide what you're more comfortable with. Besides, you know I don't always adhere to Director Reed's rules." She gives him a wink. "You may still refer to my husband as Mean Man, though."

"Deal." Carter smiles, "Now, when are you serving dessert?"

Cara rises and heads to the kitchen to put out pie and ice cream for everyone.

FORTY-FOUR

NIC ISN'T SURE WHERE TO lead them for some privacy. The kids are on the lower level, but he can hear Cara's thoughts so he knows they're looking to eat. He takes the chance and leads the other two men down to his office. As expected, Nic passes his two and Elijah on their way toward the stairwell after he descends.

"I hear there's pie and ice cream. Save us some." He reaches for Mia's hand, just brushing it, needing the contact after everything that's transpired.

Mia senses his need and doesn't pull away from him. Instead, she leans in and gives Nic a tiny peck on the cheek. God, he loves his kids.

Once in the office, Nic takes a seat at his desk while Reed sits in the plush chair. Sasha is pacing the length of the office before abruptly turning to Reed to ask, "How much do you know about the executed plan to keep Nic and me here in the States?"

Reed looks to Nic to acknowledge that some of those details were only just given to him on the plane ride the day before. "I heard of the initial plan where you killed Nic, and then you were killed by an agent from MI6sss." Reed lets the six-sound slur from his lips realizing why they are going to talk.

"Yes, precisely. Were you ever given the name of the agent who allegedly killed me?"

"At my level 15 years ago, I wasn't privy to that intel." Reed had heard the story and knew it wasn't true. Obviously, Nic was alive and well. Reed also knew how close Nic and Sasha had been. "Cara always made that clear. Looking back on it now, I realize she was preparing me for the truth of your presence here should it ever come out."

Reed shrugs his shoulders as he continues, "I always assumed you found a way out for yourself and rode off into the sunset." After some thought he adds, "I was curious as to who you found to cover for you at MI6, but to have investigated would not have been prudent. Don't forget, I was already harboring the crime of concealing Nic. I didn't need to call any attention to myself."

"I'm in a precarious position, Reed, and I need you to respect that," Sasha goes on, waiting for Reed to acknowledge.

When Reed nods subtly, Sasha confesses, "There was an agent in service for MI6, 15 years ago, who owed me a favor. This agent was… not always faithful to the Queen. He wasn't a double agent, per se, but he was reasonable. He and I developed a relationship over the years where we would sometimes share intel if one of our teams could be protected, or if the intel was dangerously inaccurate. We would squelch rumors. It was a mutual, working relationship, fully reciprocated. I had many of these types of associations."

Reed nods again in understanding as, obviously, he maintains his own similar relationships, currently.

Sasha takes a deep breath before adding, "After what happened with Katherine, I came back a changed man. Rules, orders, and loyalties became more nebulous to me. I began to understand the need to separate the truth from the rhetoric. I developed my own rubric."

For some reason, Reed feels the need to interrupt Sasha. "You and I are very much alike. No one will understand the concept of judge, jury, and executioner more than me." He apologizes if he hasn't made it clear. "Sasha, I never believed you were the monster characterized by your reputation. Especially after I got to know Nic, who considers you a brother. I mean the man lets his wife be best friends with another man, and he hasn't killed me." Reed shudders slightly, "Early on I did think Nic might exterminate me." He shrugs and admits, "Instead, I respected and admired your expertise, skills and knowledge."

Nic did consider killing Reed. If he thought it wouldn't devastate Cara, the man would have perished. Over the years, he's realized how happy he is that he did not. Cara abuses Reed more than him. Connor Reed divides his wife's sass. He suspects Reed gets the brunt of it.

Reed laughs to himself for a moment, "And as for the creation of your own rubric? Well, in this country, it's called, 'Politics.' Welcome to my world. You don't need to explain or defend yourself, ever, with me."

Sasha studies Reed for a few moments. "Thank you...Now I should probably get to the point."

Reed assumes this is the reason they are sequestered in Nic's office without Jake. Sasha is going to reveal more counterintelligence secrets. It blows his mind to think of what has been shared in the last three days. Nothing short of treason.

With a deep breath, Sasha continues, "It's possible this contact who assisted me 15 years ago knew about the Reflex. Not because I came out and said it, but because the MI6 agent wouldn't strike a deal with me without some additional information. He wanted to know where I was going, why and with whom. He wanted the truth. When I told him I was working with Nic, and what we were going to do, the Agent insisted on being the hero, protecting some poor civilian woman from the Dark Angel of Death. Apparently, he was concerned Nic's eternal love was going to damn this woman to Hell." Sasha makes a disgusted face at Nic. "I had to tell him the woman was a CIA operative. She could handle herself. He may have connected the dots."

Nic scowls at Sasha, "You never told me this."

Sasha glares back at Nic, "You did not need to know."

Reed smiles at the exchange. It's the first time he's seen Sasha act like the handler he was. "Sasha, if I'm connecting the dots correctly, you believe there's a possibility this man may have directly or inadvertently betrayed you by conveying this information to Katherine?"

"This agent is an old man, now. He's friends with Katherine's father, Thomas. He is also the man who was providing me with updates on her. Could Katherine have extrapolated this from information or stories he shared...yes. It's not much of a stretch. But why she needed to discover if Cara Andre was the Reflex is where I become confused. What's the motive? There is something more we're missing," Sasha admits.

Reed summarizes, "Katherine hears neither you, nor Nic are dead. You are in the US with Nic and the woman he married who happens to be former CIA. Best guess? She may have been told the agent is the Reflex. She may even have been given Chase Bennett as a name. Katherine then hires Vlad to confirm Cara and the Reflex are one and the same. At some point she received verification and released Vlad to kill her. Best case, Cara's dead. Worst case, her identity is confirmed one way or the other."

"Win/win, but why?" Nic looks to Reed. "Possible political ramifications?"

That's where Reed's leaning. It's one thing to go after one or two former KGB rogue agents. It's entirely another level of reprisal to hunt down and kill a former CIA agent and her children, potentially on her own soil. It must be the rationale behind the acquisition of Ed. Place him as the fall guy to placate any political backlash.

Nic shakes his head. "I like the reasoning, until Ed." He points to the flowchart and information up on one of his war boards.

"Katherine could only have confirmed Cara as the Reflex on Friday, Thursday at the earliest. Ed was planned for and brought into the mix months ago."

"Back up plan for her if she received confirmation? I'm calculating a good probability for that," Sasha says.

Nic confides he's feeling strange. "Since the discovery of our gifts, the computations in my head have gone a bit off. The math is trying to fold in feelings. The equations that are trying to solve for variables are collecting sentiments through the threads, or through Cara's empathy. It's messing with my head. The probability of this scenario being entirely accurate right now, I'm calculating at less than 20%. Not because of finite math, but because of infinite variables added for the emotion."

Reed comes to Nic's aid, advising him not to fight it. His mind is weaving the emotion into the calculation as it should. It's the next progression for his grid. As they recently learned, all of Reed's intuition over the years has been based on his empathic ability. Nic shouldn't discount his advice. He just needs to give his mind time to adjust. "If you're calculating less than 20%, we are missing something."

"I have to concur," Sasha agrees. "Is it time for pie?"

Reed stands but turns to Sasha. "You weren't comfortable asking Jake to this meeting?"

They trust Jake for his loyalty to them and his skills. They don't trust Jake with information concerning their past, or their networks. "Without knowing whom Jake works for, or who he is associated with, we will not take that risk. Jake understands this. Without full disclosure on his part, there will always be some secrets between us," Sasha states.

"But you trust me with this?" Reed inquires raising one eyebrow at Sasha.

"We trust Cara. Cara trusts you. You get extension rights." Sasha cocks one eyebrow back at him.

Reed just stares at him for a moment longer before asking,

"You're not going to tell me who your former MI6 contact is, are you?"

"No."

Reed adds, "You don't trust me enough with that intel, correct?"

"Yes."

At this admittance, Reed clasps Sasha by the shoulder and laughs, "Sasha, you would've disappointed me if you had trusted me!"

Before it all disappeared, Cara saved a slice of apple pie for Sasha and blueberry slices for Reed and Nic, their favorites. The guys added their ice cream and ate on the island stools. Cara waits until they're halfway done to let them know Jake and Jinx have gone home, explaining she assumes they wanted some alone time together. They left Eli to sleep over. The couple will be back bright and early at 8:30 AM.

"You haven't seen 8:30 AM on a Sunday since the kids were young, Cara. I can't believe you agreed to that," Nic teases.

Cara retorts, "I didn't. I said I would be sleeping. Jinx responded by telling me the world does not revolve around me. So, to spite her, I do intend to sleep."

"You look tired now, sweetheart," Reed comments concerned for her.

"I feel fried. Mentally. I asked Jake if that was, you know, normal for us."

Nic looks up at Cara. "What did he say? I feel the same way. Mentally spent."

"He said he's heard the gift can be overtaxed." Just then their landline starts ringing in the kitchen. "Nic, don't answer it, I can't talk to anyone right now." The phone rings four times, then goes to voicemail. The machine is on speaker; therefore, they can hear the message.

"Um, Cara, are you there? It's Danni. I've tried your cell, both call and text, and no answer from you. I had to resort to analog. Is everything okay there? Um, I'm somehow worried..."

Reed reaches for the phone and hits talk. "Danni, hey, it's Reed. How the hell are you?"

Because it's still in speaker mode, the group can hear the conversation. "REED! OMG, it's been forever! Are you visiting Cara?"

"Yes, sorry, we've all been hanging out and having fun. Keeping your sister busy cooking and cleaning so she didn't see your calls or texts."

"Is everything okay there? I was suddenly...worried today and wanted to check in."

Reed looks to the group at the island who all register the same AHA moment on their faces. "Everything is fine. When do I get to see you again? Planning a trip to DC soon, I hope?"

"Nah, but maybe the next time I visit Cara, you can join us. I know Mr. Super Powerful is busy, but I always hope you remember us little peons who enjoy you for you."

This makes Reed smile. "Mr. Super Powerful? I like it, Danni. And 'peon' is not the word I would use to describe you."

"How would you describe me?" Danni asks playfully. Cara's sister is an in-demand marriage counselor in Connecticut. She is also an incessant flirt. She assumes Danni does not show her clients that side of her.

"Um, HOT. You still married to that unworthy of your great beauty and wit man?"

"Yes...but you are my first exception, Reed," Danni purrs.

"Exception?"

Cara is already shaking her head in disgust, making her way to the phone. Her sister, Danni, has even fewer filters than she does. Reed pushes away from her.

"Yeah, you know, exception. I get to pick two guys I can have sex with, and my husband gets to pick two women. We made our list when we got married. You're my first exception and let me tell you, I saw you while I was channel flipping on CSPAN the other day, and I'm still pleased with listing you as number one 10 years ago when I married."

"I'm flattered, Danni, and I believe I'll be taking you up on the offer. But out of curiosity, who is your second exception?"

"That would be Sasha. My sister knows how to pick'em. Lucky bitch."

At this revelation, Sasha is completely humiliated dropping his head down to hide his reddening face. Cara is practically climbing Reed to get to the phone. Danni has always flirted with both men over the years.

Nic decides to intervene, grabbing Cara and pulling her away from Reed, because the conversation is too entertaining to stop.

"So, who are your husband's exceptions?"

"He's a dimwit. He chose Jessica Alba and for some strange reason, Diane Sawyer. Like that's going to happen. I went with viable and available. So, you let me know when. I figure someone in this family should take you out for a real ride, if you're up for it?"

Reed delivers his words slowly, and dripping with sexuality. "I promise you, Danni, it will be one hell of a drive."

"I'm counting on it. Has my sister heard enough yet? Is she completely mortified? I'm on speaker, am I not?"

Reed rolls his eyes and hands the phone to Cara, who grabs it, changes the setting to take her sister off speaker, and puts the receiver to her ear.

"You're an ass, Danni." Now they can only hear Cara's side of the conversation. "Yes, Sasha turned red, and yes, he still looks hot in that shade." She winks at Sasha. "And you are warned, Danni, you can't tell Reed shit like that. He won't hesitate to take you for that 'drive.' Although, I'm guessing it would be more fast and furious than long and pleasurable." Reed flips her off and Nic laughs.

Cara tells her sister she's busy with a full house all weekend and she'll call on Monday. She hangs up and turns back to the group in the kitchen. "So, it seems it's very possible everyone in my family has some gift. They're too far away to make any connections from here, but Danni somehow knew. Reed, you'll eventually need to do some prying with your own sister. I wonder if there's something there, too?"

"You know Olivia and I have regressed to only a cordial relationship at best," Reed spills with some regret.

"I think your sister is very nice, despite her uber position in Manhattan high society."

Reed and his sister are very much alike but Olivia has managed to lose her sense of humor along the way. Cara blames Olivia's husband for that. Eugene is so uptight and boring. He's rubbed off on Olivia.

"My sister never had a sense of humor. That's the problem." Reed exhales as he states this. She knows that is not true. It's Reed's regret talking. He and his sister were close when Cara first met Olivia. She and Olivia are closer in age, and until Olivia met Eugene, they often went out together as a threesome. Olivia was fun, gorgeous and enjoyed making trouble. Then she met Eugene, who is not attractive but very wealthy and connected. Not that the Reed family require more wealth or affluence. Cara never understood the attraction. Olivia changed slowly after she met him. She became distant and superficial. Speaking of Olivia, Cara remembers the last text she sent begging her to plead with Connor about a blind date she wanted him to go on. "Is she still trying, desperately, to get you to date that Isabelle woman?"

Nodding his head, a defeated Reed offers, "Yup, she still is."

Isabelle Harrison was seventeen years old the last time Reed saw her. Cara went with him to his cousin Peter's wedding, like 22 years ago. Isabelle sat on the other side of Reed at the dinner reception.

"Do you remember her?" Reed asks.

For some reason Cara has never forgotten her. She was a super skinny, no boobs, tall, redhead with hair in her face. "Poor girl, so shy and withdrawn. I don't recall if she even spoke during dinner. What ever happened to her?"

"Some sort of academic now, PhD in something boring. I don't want to ask and show any interest in her. If I opened that door, and Olivia had her way, she'd have me dating every pretentious, dull, rich woman in New York."

"Jeez, Connor, speaking of pretentious...some of those women may offer more than you give them credit for, sweetheart. I am standing up for all of them when I say give them a chance," Cara announces with pride.

"How utterly feminist and considerate of you. So out of character for Cara Callous," Reed ribs.

Cara juts her chin out at him. "Maybe I'm turning over a new leaf with today's epiphanies. I'm going to be kinder and more welcoming...ah, who am I kidding, that ain't happening."

"Truer words have never been spoken," Nic declares with great flair, reaching for her.

Cara jumps onto her husband's back. "Sasha, you and Reed have cleanup duty. Nic and I need to go have a much overdue conversation with our progeny."

CHAPTER

FORTY-FIVE

NIC AND HIS WIFE FIND the three kids with Carter in the Music room. Nic gives Carter a quick nod before asking if they can borrow Max and Mia for a few minutes. Carter, responding with a knowing glance, offers to keep Eli company and work some chords on the bass together. Eli only offers a faint smile. A smile is an affirmative from Elijah.

Nic motions his two out of the room, leading them around the corner into his office. When they enter, Nic places himself on the floor in the center of the room sitting with his legs out in front of him. Cara shuts the office door and joins him, sitting with her legs crossed. They wait for a moment before Max and Mia conclude they are supposed to get comfortable on the floor across from them.

Nic begins, but he no longer feels patient, he feels like a parent. "Why didn't you ever tell us, and did you know we had the same gifts?" Max and Mia start to look to each other, but Nic leans in as they do. "DO NOT SPEAK to each other! You will not discuss this between yourselves. If I even sense you're communicating, I will invade your minds, privacy be damned. I want the truth, not some agreed upon riposte from you both."

It's Max who speaks up first. He apologizes, but states he and Mia were always able to speak to each other. "Then, we found out Mia could speak to Eli. We didn't think it odd at first. It wasn't until we started school that it became more a freaky thing. Because we could never read you, Uncle Sasha, or Eli's parents, we thought all little kids could do it, but the adults had somehow outgrown it. We could sense some emotions from all of you, but we thought it might just be physical cues.

"You know, like when Mom is about to lose it, it shows on her face," Max uses as an example. "When we started school, that's when it hit us, we weren't like the other kids. And you weren't like the other adults. We began to hear everything and everyone."

Cara inhales sharply at this admission and Nic can sense her stress level increase, but she doesn't interrupt.

Mia starts in, "Mom, you're doing the face right now. STOP! On top of seeing it, now, since this morning, I can FEEL your distress."

Mia shudders at her mother before adding, "When we realized we could hear the chatter in everyone's mind, we all didn't handle it the same way. Max learned quickly to filter it. For some reason, his brain could, and still can, turn it off completely. I had more problems with it though, and that's when I decided to try and tell you about it." She points to her mother.

Cara's face falls at this news. Mia can see her mother searching her memories for the years ago moment she can't recall. "Mom, let me help."

Cara jolts as the memory is deposited into her mind. Nic lowers his head to watch it play through his wife.

It's their kitchen in their old house. Cara has just returned from taking the kids to see The Incredibles *at the movie theater. Mia is coloring and Max is on the floor with his Legos. Cara is busying herself making dinner. Mia calls out to her mother, "Mom, did you like the movie?"*

"Yes, honey, it was one of my favorites, so far. It was funny and I really liked the storyline. Did you?"

"Ahhh, I LOVED it. I wanna see it again." Little Mia pauses watching

her mother cook. You can see her beautiful face preparing itself. "Mom? Is that real? You know, how people can have secret lives and superpowers?"

Much younger Cara stiffens immediately at the question, standing with her hands in the sink. The reaction is evident in her body language. She seems to compose herself before responding. When she turns to her daughter, her face is reflective and somewhat sad.

"My sweet girl, everyone has secrets, sometimes secret lives, and secret talents. Secrets are easy to hide...but superpowers? No."

The memory fades to a new scene. Cara is shaking her head comprehending the confusion Mia must have experienced at her long-ago reaction and response.

The scene starts with Nic pushing Mia on the swings at the park. He is laughing as Mia screams, "Higher, higher!"

Sasha is swinging Max in the air like an airplane while Max squeals, "I'm flying!"

Suddenly Mia yells to her father, totally out of context, as young children are prone to do. "Daddy, I loved the movie yesterday, can we see it again with you?"

Nic smiles warmly at his daughter, his hair longer and all golden blonde with some loose strands hanging in his eyes, blown there from the wind. "Yes, darling, we can see it whenever you like."

Mia yells to her uncle, "Sasha, will you come with us next time?"

While swinging Max, Sasha calls out to her, "As you wish, Buttercup."

Mia screams, "Yeeeaahhh! You're going to LOVE it, Sasha. It's about parents with secret lives!"

Younger Sasha almost drops Max, grabbing him just before he hits the ground. You can see him clutch Max to his chest, walking quickly towards Nic. Sasha's face has panic written all over it.

Mia registers her uncle's shock and says, "Daddy, I wanna stop now."

Nic grabs her on the pass back and brings her to a stop. She jumps off and looks at her father and uncle with her little serious face. "You will like it, Uncle Sasha, I promise. The mommy and daddy keep a big secret from their kids. They were superheroes before they got married and had them."

Nic's body stiffens as he pulls Mia tight to his leg while looking at Sasha, his eyes wide and frozen.

Mia squirms out of his grasp and gazes up at her father. "I know it's okay to have secrets. We can hide our secrets really good. But I know there are no superpowers. That part is just make-believe." Nic and Sasha continue to stare at one another but say nothing in response.

When the memory is over, Cara looks to her husband, whose face is guilt ridden. She isn't sure whether he's feeling her emotions or experiencing his own.

She takes a slow, deep breath and faces her children. "So, you thought based on our reactions, we knew, and preferred you not talk about it? Keep it a secret?"

Mia glares at her. "Yeah, like it was some special thing we had that we were never supposed to talk about. A secret just for us. Mom, I was 5 years old."

That's what they interpreted back then. Of course, after last night and the big secret agent reveal, the twins finally figured out why their parents and Sasha had reacted the way they did. It had nothing to do with hiding their talents. Their parents didn't know about them. Mia continues, "We thought long and hard about it all night after your meltdown. We considered everything we could derive from the conversations around the house. Finally, we decided it was time to say something about our talents, but we never had to. Uncle Reed took care of that for us this morning," Mia concludes.

Nic responds, "But Mia, as you guys got older, didn't you question the 'secret' idea?"

Mia puts her head down at this inquiry. Suddenly, Cara feels it, the emotion, and the thoughts coming from her daughter. Just a small drip like Mia has formed a tiny crack in a dam.

Mia did think about it, often, but like Max, she enjoyed the consequence of her parents' cluelessness. School was easy for her. She didn't have to do any work. Mia learned to dim down the voices at school. She kept to herself. She adapted. She could hear the teachers talk about her. They wanted to recommend a better school for her, one offering even more challenging classes. Mia didn't want to leave Max and Eli.

"You thought we would send you away from us, split you up from your brother and Eli," Cara recites as these revelations enter her mind.

Cara takes a deep breath and tells her children they have nothing to feel ashamed of. She and their father, on the other hand, do. She admits when she was their age, she would have handled it exactly as they had done. And on some level, it's what she did. "But this is out now, in the open between us, and no more secrets, got it? We're going to proceed as if this is ground zero. Full disclosure from here on out."

Cara stops and looks to Nic before she adds, "Well, full disclosure with the nine of us, only." It still must be treated as a secret to the outside world. No one in the general public is prepared to accept their gifts. They may never be ready for that." It's their communal secret, now.

"As a rule, we will respect your privacy and not intrude on your thoughts, but in the event of need, all bets are off. We WILL intervene. I expect the same from you two. You give us our privacy but reach out to us at any time if you need us. Are we in agreement?" Nic urges.

As the children nod and start to stand, Cara stops them. The way they rectified this revelation about themselves is still bothering her. "I need to understand. What did you guys think was the reason you had these gifts?"

Max starts howling with laughter as Mia pushes him over. She's trying to cover her brother's mouth. All Max can get out is, "The Great Debate!"

Their father gently pulls Mia's hands from her brother's face.

"Tell us." There is a compulsion to his request.

Sitting upright, while Mia crosses her arms, Max admits, "When we were really young, Mia decided we were witches." Cara's son looks to her. "Because you always called Nonna a witch."

Okay, that's true, but not necessarily meant literally about her mother.

Before Cara can contemplate more, Max continues, "Later, Mia began to read all kinds of paranormal books. She then decided we were mages."

"Like sorcerers or wizards?" Nic asks.

Mia cuts her brother off. "Yes. And no, not like Harry Potter crap. More based on the Wicca faith. I started there with their pagan based beliefs and looked more deeply at the Druids, their history and practices. The elemental aspect of their rituals intrigued me." She shrugs, "Max was convinced we had the Force." Mia shudders at her brother. "The Force is elemental as well. It's essentially all the same. We are tied to our Earth and the forces around it."

Finally letting her brother speak, Max continues, "We always see or read something new and alter our conclusions. I do like to watch fantastical movies and science fiction because I think I can gain some clues. Mia does the reading."

Rolling her eyes, Mia adds, "I've been studying physics more now. Like Jake explained, it's all theoretical, but possible."

Knowing her husband has a dozen scientific questions, Cara jumps in before he can speak. What she needs to know is more important than the why. "Have the three of you played with, tested, or experimented with your gifts?"

Both of their heads drop before Mia cants hers offering, "We have been...reluctant...to do that." She picks her head up to face them both. "What I did this morning to you three was a test. I...am sorry. But the result is why we do not experiment."

With relief and understanding, Nic interjects, "You three needed a monitor or a control for any experiments."

Mia confirms, "Yes."

"I am pleased you are astute enough to understand the dangers of experimentation. Let us neutralize this current threat. If you feel you can assist, please let us know, otherwise, when we are done, let's plan on working as a family to investigate our gifts," Nic proposes.

Apparently, the discussion is over as both her children and Nic stand. Cara motions Mia to stay while Nic and Max walk out of his office together.

"Mia, one last thing. I can see your thread to Eli, and I see it isn't like the others between us. It is not a thread." Cara looks long and hard at her daughter before continuing, "The connection you have with Eli resembles the one I have with...your father."

Mia snaps at her, "I'm not ready to have this conversation with you, Mom."

"I know, and this conversation will only be between you and me. When you're ready to go there, please know you can talk to me. That's all I'm going to say on it."

Mia nods her acknowledgment and leaves her sitting on the floor in Nic's office.

Cara pulls her knees to her chest and places her head down on them. She is so drained. So much is flying around in her mind. The three days of threats, confessions, reveals and discoveries are playing with every nerve in her body.

Looking at her wristwatch, she realizes the last 16 hours were the longest and the shortest of her life. From a jog on the course, to finding out gifts exist, to using said gifts, to finally finding out why Sasha is emotionally stunted, to discovering who is after them and why, and concluding with bad mommy guilt. Existential, surreal, amazing, and disappointing. She sighs and rubs her temples.

Her consciousness literally looks like it's spinning. Now that she can draw herself into it, the visual in her mind is startling. There's a section of her consciousness moving in a funnel cloud. Cara snorts to herself. She has always said her mind is swirling, never realizing her brain quite literally does.

She's so inside her mind watching the vortex, she doesn't notice the legs standing before her. Cara looks up to see the painted footprints of Sasha's Just Dance pants, evidence of Mia's handiwork in decorating his clothes. The images grow closer before his hands pull her gently towards the chair behind her.

Sasha gets down on the ground and pulls her under his arm and leans them back against the chair together. He just leaves her to her thoughts.

When he feels she's ready, he says, "You did well with the kids. Despite what you may think sometimes, you're a great mom, Cara. You and Nic are doing a tremendous job so far. I know the next phase appears more daunting, but we, as a family, will get through it."

Finally looking up into his eyes, she apologizes, "I am sorry for the tough love earlier. It felt like the natural direction to take."

"It was. And you have no need to apologize. I need some time to sort it all out. I've lived with this anguish and guilt for a very long while." Sasha glances up to see they're facing the war board with the flowchart. He stares at it in silence before asking, "Do Katherine and I have a thread?"

"Everyone is threaded but, no, you two are not connected by a thread like all of us are with you." Cara pauses, not sure how she should proceed. "Katherine wasn't supposed to be in your life. I feel her presence again, and it isn't scripted, if such a thing exists."

"You think the six of us were always meant to find each other?"

"Yes. What drew you to Nic? Do you recall?"

Concentrating, Sasha finally says, "I heard about the new boy. Some of the instructors said he was extremely intelligent. But the gossip amongst the boys was Nicolae was a useless, weak, pretty face. I don't understand why I went looking for Nic, but I felt compelled to find him and meet him. When I did find him, I knew I had to help him." He looks down at her. "Is that what it's like, compulsion?"

"In various degrees, yes. I see it that way."

"Did you feel that with Reed?"

"The moment I met Connor, I knew he was meant to be a part of my life."

"You know I still don't fully comprehend your relationship with Reed."

A second involuntary snort comes from Cara. Her relationship with Reed isn't what she feels like talking about. It's never what she wants to discuss because it's not simply a conversation. For 25 years, Reed has been a demanded explanation. There was Nic constantly badgering her, her family incessantly teasing that Reed must be gay, or their superiors at work insisting they come clean about their couple status. Cara has spent the better part of her life mounting a defense when it comes to Connor.

Their relationship is odd. Neither would ever deny that. How it got that way, and why, can be debated. In the end, though, Connor was Cara's whole world before she met Nic. And after, he was no longer her world, but she could never live without him in it. Reed fills a void and a need even Nic and the kids can't. Maybe it's because they have so much history together? Cara has never been sure why, but his importance to her life she will not question.

She focuses back in her mind at all of the threads. Reed's thread to her is so interesting. After examining it, Cara turns her attention back to Sasha. "Can I be honest with you?" Sasha nods slowly. "Unlike our thread to the others, the diameter of the thread between you and Nic resembles the thread between Reed and me. There are other differences, but the thickness is the same. I'm not going to ask you to talk about your feelings, but it makes me wonder...if Nic had been a woman, what would you have expected of your relationship?"

Sasha contemplates this interesting concept for a moment before turning seriously to Cara. "Nic would be my bitch. I would've kept him tied to a bed for my sexual pleasure most of the day." She plugs him in the chest. "Okay, maybe that's extreme."

Laughing, Sasha admits, "I had beautiful agents reporting to me. I was their handler, and I was very protective of them. I never slept with them, but I don't believe I was threaded to any of them. Although there was one once, right before I came here to see Nic when I heard about your pregnancy..." He doesn't finish his sentence and goes back into thought. When he opens his mouth next, nothing comes out.

His mouth closes and reopens with, "If Nic had been a woman, maybe it would be like you and Reed. That's what you're trying to make me understand?"

"Yes, but I wanted your honest answer, you know, for posterity." Cara smiles, referring to yet another quote for him from *The Princess Bride*. "I think the fact Reed and I aren't the same sex makes it more complicated. His emotional connection, coupled with the testosterone, causes his feelings for me to become indistinct. And...," poking Sasha as she completes her thought, "at least my handler doesn't live with us."

SASHA CONSIDERS HIS WORDS BEFORE SPEAKING. IT'S BEEN BOTHERING HIM since last night. After today's epiphanies, it's disturbing him more. He's already spoken to Nic about it, not because he was trying to cause trouble, but because he was very concerned that Nic also believes what Sasha suspects about Reed. The man adores her. Reed reveres her. Sasha can see beyond their biting repartee with each other. There is a deep devotion there. "You are aware Reed's in love with you."

Cara doesn't jump at him as he expected. She simply sits with her head on his shoulder for a pause before her head drops in defeat. "He THINKS he's in love with me."

"Is there a difference?"

"Very much." She inhales, as if for patience. "If Reed were truly in love with me, we would have been a couple."

Deciding that's a loaded statement, Sasha goes quiet. But Cara changes direction. "Like you with Katherine in a way."

"I don't understand."

"She was your first girlfriend, really. The first time your emotions and body experienced the thrill of passion. It doesn't mean it is love; it really is more physical desire. It can be confusing to someone with little experience."

"Are you saying Reed is inexperienced?" Sasha asks with a little mocking in his voice.

Cara looks at him disapprovingly, before attempting to elaborate for him. "I am quite sure Reed has a lot of sexual experience, but that's all he's had. His relationship with me is opposite of what you had with Katherine. I have been Reed's single source of emotional connection. He's never had another emotional relationship with a woman. That can be confusing. There's all this love pouring between us, yet the physical portion isn't there.

"Honestly, had I not found Nic, it may still be confusing for me to understand. With Nic, the emotional connection was definitely there, but the physical connection...that was intense. No questions, no conjecture, no hesitation. I can see and feel the difference, now. Reed just hasn't found both yet to be able to understand the distinction."

Thinking about this confession, Sasha recognizes the truth in it. He sees the similarity to his relationship with Katherine. He found the physical with Katherine, but the emotional connection never existed. It was only the hormonal lust of the young and inexperienced. Quite typical and appropriate, according to Cara. The real issue for him now is guilt over the tragic outcome. It's prevented him from forming any emotional ties to another woman. He doesn't need Cara to say that aloud. He can sense all her thoughts in his mind, loud and clear.

"You don't believe I have an emotional connection to you?" Sasha asks her, concerned.

"Yes, of course we have that connection, but our relationship is different. You and I, Sasha, we are family."

He does feel like a brother to her, but even better than that. He comes with all the benefits of having a brother but without the sibling torment she experiences in her constant squabbles with her real brother, Robert. He wonders...if they had met before she encountered Nic, would their relationship be as confusing as hers and Reed's?

Cara smirks at his musings because she is listening inside his mind, uninvited. "For some reason I think we would've been close but not sexual, either."

"I would have tied you to a bed as well, and made you my sex slave," Sasha quips but pauses for a moment to admit, "I feel more protective and loving with you, the way I assume a brother would of a younger sister." He gives Cara one of his rare ear-to-ear grins. "I have a confession to make. When I came to meet you for the first time, I was convinced I wouldn't like you. I had heard the stories of the famed Duo, and you didn't seem like the kind of girl I would've wished for Nicolae. It didn't take long to see I was so wrong, however. Not because of the love you have for each other, but for who you really are. You are not what you like to project. You are capable of great compassion and loyalty. You altered the course of my life and made it worth living. You're still doing that."

Cara tries not to react to Sasha's confession. She doesn't want him to feel uncomfortable about sharing his emotions. She knows she needs to stay silent as positive reinforcement for what she understands is a difficult task for him. She sits still with her head against his chest and his arm around her shoulders.

"Sasha, thank you for sharing and...well, you're giving me energy while we sit here. I'm feeling much better. Did you know you were doing that?"

"Yes...I'm beginning to recognize the ability." Sasha states with earnest. "Cara, can I ask one more question?"

"Shoot."

"Funny pun. I'm sensing the guilt you're feeling about your connection to Reed. Are you thinking you need to assuage that guilt somehow?"

Cara doesn't hesitate. Reed means so much to her, but up until today, it was easy to be in the Land of Denial about his emotions, and her monopoly of them. Reed deserves so much more. And like Sasha, she's concerned he has missed an opportunity to connect to the correct thread. She believes IF they meet the one, they will know. But she considers she can't trust that to happen. Cara is still not sure that's even possible for them. Her only experience to draw on is Nic.

"In my head, the empathy and telepathy still fight with the plain old thinking portion of my brain. That part of my brain is racked with guilt. And I'm carrying enough guilt because of all of this." Cara waves her arms to encompass the war board and the whole house.

"I'm beginning to think I can feel enough to understand. You know if you need me for anything, just ask." He draws her closer with this statement.

She suddenly feels compelled to share a thought. "What your organization did to you all those years ago with Katherine was a horrible thing. Had your cover never been blown, you could be married, a father, and potentially working at MI6 as a double agent. Your whole life was mapped out for you without your consent. You could have been stuck in a loveless marriage where you resented your wife and potentially your kids."

Placing her hands on each side of his face, she continues, "Sasha, the best thing that could have happened was what occurred. Yes, Katherine was injured but you were saved. It may not feel like that but it is the truth."

Sasha sighs out slowly, "I do understand that, Cara, but you of all people know the demands that are placed on us working in counter-intelligence. In Russia, it's a lifelong commitment one way or another, and one does not deny a direct order."

Before she can retort, he adds, "And don't try to tell me the CIA hasn't been as ruthless in its methods over the years."

She is left only blinking at him. He is correct, of course. Cara is ashamed she was part of the organization at times. The CIA was so politically motivated during the last decades. The decisions they made, and the things they did, were nothing short of criminal. Look how many Central and South American countries have been manipulated by the CIA, and what happened in the Middle East that eventually brought down the Twin Towers. She could go on and on, and all of it makes her sick.

She and Reed were never a part of that, however. Their team was allowed to fly solo as long as they achieved results. And those results... they determined... only them. If massaging the truth was what was required, that's what they did. Even after she left, Reed kept up the ruse. He manipulated the organization so their efforts were viewed as worthwhile and successful - because they actually were. That effort, and the hard work that came along with it, just may not have been exactly in line with the agenda outlined for the mission or the organization.

Sasha whispers into her ear, "I hear those thoughts. You understand I did what I could within my group, too."

Snapping at him, she says sharply, "Because you were there! You didn't die in London undercover. You did the right thing and saved yourself. Then you went back to Moscow and made a difference!" Grabbing a fistful of his shirt, she expounds, "You rewrote the script. You probably saved countless altercations from occurring. You might have saved the world for all we know. Can you not appreciate what you did achieve?"

Huffing out, Sasha states, "You make me sound like a hero."

Shaking him, Cara tries again, "You are a hero. I see both you and Reed that way." She gives him a big hug. "Just think about that as well, when you reconcile all of this, okay?"

Now he is left only blinking and speechless. Deciding he needs to mull over this new nugget for a minute, she moves back into her original position under his arm. She can hear and feel his muddled thoughts and emotions. When his brain seems to quiet, she releases her final concern.

"Sasha, one more thing," Cara sits up and turns her body towards him, so they're face to face. "I will kill Katherine. Are you emotionally prepared for that?"

Sasha takes a large breath before speaking, "Cara, I'm prepared to destroy her."

FORTY-SIX

CARA WANDERS THE LOWER LEVEL. Sasha has gone to his room wanting some private time. Carter is out of the music room and watching a movie with Far Guard and Max. There's a lot of exploding noises and guns but that's all Cara can get from it because they need the special 3-D glasses they're wearing to view the screen. She takes the steps up and wanders the first floor. No one is around.

She goes up to the next floor and finds Mia and Eli in her room. They're at her computer watching Internet videos and laughing. Cara wants to walk in on them but changes her mind and walks towards the closed guest room door. She raises her hand to knock but decides against that as well. She moves back to Mia's door and knocks gently while calling out, "Don't stay up too late, promise?"

Her own bedroom is calling. She stops by the kitchen to grab bottled water and heads to bed. The door to the suite is closed. Cara quietly opens it to find Nic sitting on the floor in front of the lit fireplace in only his boxers. He appears zoned out. No lights are on in the bedroom, only the shadows of the flames flickering on the walls and his face.

She walks past him to the bathroom. She brushes her teeth, washes her face, and takes her clothes off. She makes her way back into the bedroom and sits directly behind Nic, spreading her legs until she has full contact with his back. She wraps her arms around his waist and leans her head on him.

They sit unmoving and quiet until Cara feels the memory she shared with Nic that morning come into her mind.

She must have fallen asleep after their first night together. She slowly awakens to the memories of the most amazing night of her life. The previous evening was the object of dreams, more passionate and sensual than she could have ever imagined. But suddenly, she feels confined. She is bound. No, no, it can't be true. He would want to hurt me after all? Her heart is utterly breaking.

As her eyes open, she realizes she is not bound, but wrapped in Nic's arms and legs so tightly, any movement is restricted. His head is in the crook of her neck and he's sound asleep. He is the most beautiful creature she has ever seen. Ethereal. His face and body are perfect, but her feelings at his nearness are intensely passionate. He has truly fallen from the heavens.

After a few minutes of admiring him, she cautiously tries to wiggle out from his grasp to go to the bathroom without waking him.

Just as she's free, he mumbles in his sleep. "Cara mia, don't leave me, please. Ever."

At that moment, looking at his face, she knows she never will.

Nic has wrapped Cara with his arms behind him as the memory played. He lets his hands run up the sides of her torso until he can't reach any further, drawing her tight to his back. Releasing his grip on her, he runs his fingertips down her arms slowly until they meet her hands at his waist. He wraps his hands around hers, tightly, and lets his memory flow to her.

It's the same morning and Nic has just completed a dozen rounds of lovemaking with her. He lifts his body from her to see she's sound asleep, completely exhausted. It's then he notices he has left some bruises and marks on her. He frowns and becomes upset. He gently kisses each bruise and red welt. He doesn't seem to notice the scratches and marks on his own body.

When he's done kissing each injury, he runs his hands over her face, softly, and moves her hair away. He places tiny tender kisses all over her face leaving her lips for last, lightly brushing his across hers. He slowly pulls her to his side, wrapping his legs and arms around her, needing her close. His last thought before falling asleep, Cara mia, don't leave me, please. Ever.

Still holding her hands, Nic brings them slowly up his chest and neck until they reach his face. He kisses each fingertip. Rising, Cara moves in front of him to straddle his lap. She sits comfortably and just stares into his eyes which are reflecting the flames behind her and burning crimson.

She gradually sees his grid as she enters his mind. He has dimmed the lights on it, so it appears like thousands of twinkling stars in the night sky. Instead of the dizzying sensation of his grid before, this version is peaceful. There is the serenity and veneration of gazing at the heavens. It's spectacular.

Caught up in the sight above her, Cara starts to sense his emotion, the intense love he has for her. She releases her own emotion to soar into his mind. The result is so overwhelming; they both inhale sharply. It's all there. All the love, trapped under the blinking, sparkling night sky of his mind.

Nic leans in with their special lip caress, but instead of deepening the kiss, he slowly lifts her and rises to bring them to the bed. He lays her down gently, caringly, bringing his body over hers. They take that long and pleasurable drive; but this drive is filled with the sights and sensations of seventeen years of wonder, respect, desire, and adoration.

With his arms and legs wrapped around her once again, just like on their first night together, Nic closes his eyes. The lovemaking was

altogether divine, and his body is completely sated. Peace and sleep are awaiting him.

Suddenly, Cara jerks out of his grasp. His eyes do not need to be open to know she is sitting next to him with her knees up to her chest in contemplation. He is not going to be able to sleep. Finally, he acquiesces, "Baby, what's the matter?"

He pops one eye open to see her facing him. She is naked, but her position prevents him from seeing anything. Doesn't matter, she is still beautiful, maybe more so, with the freshly fucked glow to her. Despite the contented luminosity, her face is serious.

"Nic, I may not have been entirely forthright in my story of how I came to work for Reed."

Deciding he needs to be more upright for this, he props the pillows behind him. "You two said Reed invited you to lunch when you visited him, Jinx picked you up from Security, and then you were hired. New job, new roommate and a new name is what you said."

Canting her head at him, she states, "That part is all true, but… Reed never had any intention of hiring me."

"Okay. Did you omit something?"

Cara winces, "Kinda a big something." He just wanted to sleep. But now, the adrenalin has entered his system.

Placing his hand on her knee, he questions, "And you are going to tell me this big something, now?"

She nods, unapologetically. "I said on the plane ride back from Berlin, I was coming to DC to interview for a job at World Bank. That is true. It's what happened at that interview I didn't disclose."

Eyeing her carefully, Nic summarizes, "You hadn't seen Reed in a few weeks, you get this interview, and you go down and stay with him to attend. It's this interview that changes his mind?"

Sighing, she admits, "I am going to pull the memory of the interview and the evening after it. Will you watch it, please?"

There is tension coming off her in waves. He thinks back to when she and Reed were sharing their tale on the plane. She did prevent Reed from telling this story. Nic recalls her placing two fingers in her mouth. A signal? A sign between the two of them to skip the tale. Why? And it was his wife making the decision. Resigned, he requests, "Send me the memory."

Cara is in an office. She's being interviewed by a woman who is sitting across from her behind a desk. The woman is from Human Resources, and she is explaining some general attributes of the World Bank job Cara is applying for. She is excited and elated over the possibilities of the position. Nothing she has interviewed for since she graduated college has been nearly this interesting. The pay is decent, and Cara believes she may really enjoy this job. The woman explains there will be extensive travel, much of it international, and asks Cara how many languages she can speak.

The woman appears impressed with Cara and tells her she would like the hiring manager to meet with her. They continue to talk before a man in his late twenties strolls into the office without knocking, casts a cursory glance at Cara and interrupts the interview.

He then turns to introduce himself to Cara, and while they are still shaking hands, he pulls her from the chair. He insists they have lunch and starts negotiating Cara away from the office, down the hall and out of the building to a café across the street. His hand on her arm, he never gives her a chance to protest.

They order their lunch, and he continues the interview, asking her questions about her background, experience, favorite subjects, favorite things to do when she isn't working. Once the food arrives, he begins to describe the position, but he keeps his explanation rather obscure.

Pretty soon, he's asking more personal questions. He explains the job would require a tremendous amount of travel, so he wants to know if she has a boyfriend or any serious relationships preventing her from keeping an open schedule. Cara tells the man she isn't in any kind of relationship, and nothing would inhibit her time. He nods approvingly and then explains how important it is that his assistant and he get along very well because they would be spending a significant amount of time together.

Nic knows where this is going. He stares dead on at his wife. She simply nods for him to continue.

Cara asks the hiring manager how he intends to determine their compatibility. The man gets up, comes around to Cara's side of the table, pulls her from the chair, bringing her body against his. He leans into her, and with a whisper, proposes they meet at his place for dinner that evening to find out. Cara sets a time for dinner with the letch, and leaves the restaurant, smiling.

"Please tell me you didn't." Nic breathes out.

"Just keeping watching."

The memory jumps to Cara walking into Reed's apartment. She immediately picks up the phone in his kitchen and calls him at work. With eerie composure, she relays everything that happened at the interview. She calms Reed down by the end of the conversation before asking him, "Reed, feel like helping me teach a bad boy a lesson?"

The memory jumps again... Cara is dressed to kill in fuck-me shoes, a skintight dress that leaves nothing to the imagination, and sultry hair and makeup. She looks incredible. She's walking down an apartment building hallway, heading to a door. She knocks and the hiring manager opens the door. The look on his face when he sees her is priceless. He is practically panting with desire.

He is speechless as he lets her into the apartment, so she starts talking first. "Do we plan to have dinner, or do you want to start with dessert?" She drops her eyes to take in the raging hard on, albeit the size of a stack of dimes, pushing out his trousers. She leans in and brushes her fingertips over his little bulge, just very lightly, and tells him, "I think dessert, first."

He still can't speak, so she adds, "You need to let me get my dessert ready." She starts to undress him, slowly unbuttoning his shirt and taking it off. She unbuckles his belt and pants, letting them drop to the floor. He steps out of them and remains where he is, wearing only his underwear. He leans in to touch her for the first time, but she backs away and tells him, "Please remove your underwear, because I need to admire the full view before you can touch me." He complies and is standing there completely naked when there's a knock on the door.

Cara heads to the door, before he can stop her, and opens it. Reed is there in just jeans with flip-flops on, no shirt and muscles everywhere. A young Reed with messy hair, body cut, and carved, and menacing. He walks in and shuts and locks the door behind him.

Poor little naked man is horrified. Cara offers, "This is my fuck buddy, Troy." He doesn't appear to understand her. She endeavors to clarify for naked hiring manager. "I can only fuck two guys at the same time because one guy is too boring for me. I can't get hot anymore with just one." Hiring manager looks panicked, so she says reassuringly, "It's going to be the best experience of your life."

Naked man is only slightly mollified until Reed whines, "I don't know, Cara. This one isn't of your usual caliber. He's so small. I don't know if he's going to do it for me."

"I know, but I'm making an exception in this case. I really want this job, and he may be fun. We won't know until we try."

"Fine, but he needs to suck my dick real hard, and then I can put it in his ass while you have your fun with him. Does that work for you?"

"I love to watch you get your cock stroked and sucked. You know it always makes me so hot and wet," she purrs seductively.

The hiring manager finally speaks. He begins to stutter, "I don't think I can do this," over and over. Meanwhile, Reed has unbuttoned his jeans and is pulling down the zipper.

Cara moves in real close to naked hiring manager and whispers in his ear, "Yes, you can, you're going to love it. I promise." Then she kicks his legs from behind, dropping him onto to his knees with his face inches from Reed's crotch. Reed grabs hold of the guy's head, holding his face directly in front of his pants. The moment the guy begins to struggle, Reed reaches out with lightning speed and cuffs his hands behind his back in a wire tie. He's so fast, you can't even see where he pulled the tie from.

Reed tells him, calmly, "Dude, don't fight it, you know you want to suck it. It's beautiful." Then he pulls down his jeans just enough to give him the full view. Hiring manager is close to tears. Reed studies him for a moment before he turns to Cara and states, "I think he's too upset for the blowjob. I should just put this in his ass and let's get this party started."

Grabbing the man's head and pushing him down, Reed has him on his knees with his ass in the air and his head on the floor. He spins around and gets into position to sodomize the asshole. By this time, the man is crying hysterically.

Cara discreetly places her purse next to Reed before she walks in front of the guy and gets down on her knees so she can be at eye level with him. She picks his head up and tells him, "I need to see your beautiful face when Troy pleasures you, darling. How am I going to get wet if I don't?" And then on cue, Reed takes the biggest cucumber Cara could find at the small local grocery store from her purse, and places it against the guy's ass.

Naked hiring manager starts screaming. Cara frowns at him like it's just occurred to her he isn't having any fun. She asks, "You're not enjoying this? I'm so sorry but it's the only way I can get off." She pauses for effect before saying, "I guess this means I don't get the job?" He's frantic by this point.

Cara gets up. Reed puts the cucumber away, zips up his pants, grabs her handbag and they walk out of the apartment leaving hiring manager cuffed, crying and convulsing.

Nic is shaking, with rage, with indignation, with horror and with exasperation. The only words coming from his mouth or mind are, "You planned the whole charade."

His wife shrugs before trying to defend herself. Nic stops her with his hand in her face. Her defense is not what he needs. He requires a moment to solve the enigma that is his wife.

Making her employment with the bank contingent on sex is nothing short of despicable. It's harassment at the highest degree and inexcusable. Having only just survived a rape attempt months before, he could understand Cara's rage. She was only 20 years old when all of this occurred.

He is starting to comprehend the perplexity of the human jigsaw puzzle he married… a young woman, a civilian, able to channel her rage into such a diabolical plot to 'teach a bad boy a lesson', to humiliate the man, debase him so thoroughly, he most likely never harassed another woman again. It's no wonder Reed would want to hire her after that farce.

Part of the mystery of Cara is solved. It all started with her. The

Duo was born that night. They could have extrapolated anything they wanted from that poor shlep. Anything. It's sick and brilliant all at the same time. Not sex as a weapon, but sex as a tool in an arsenal of manipulation and subterfuge. Forget Whore School. Sex as a seduction tactic has nothing on sex used to defile. And her plan, it prevented any blow back on them. Hiring manager was not going to admit he asked her over for sex. She and Reed held all the cards.

Nic looks at his wife with new eyes. By 20 years old, she must have become so accustomed to harassment, the emotional response became rote to her. She was and is a gorgeous woman. How many times was she placed in a position to defend herself?

And Reed, he capitalized on her abilities. Cara was a weapon 25 years ago he wasn't going to lose. He asked her to Langley for lunch the very next day and laid out his proposal. Cara had conditions, though. Now, knowing the full story, the outcome of those conditions makes sense.

Before he can continue solving his puzzle for more unknowns, Cara interrupts, "I can hear all your thoughts, Nic. And yes, Agent Connor Reed, not fuck buddy, Troy, visited naked hiring manager after my lunch at Langley. He blackmailed him into hiring me and giving me a paycheck, a desk, and a phone at World Bank. Naked Hiring Manager, whose name is Steve, received a new assistant who was never there."

"And a convenient cover is born," is all Nic can say.

Lowering her head, she admits, "Yes." Again, before he can say more, she adds, "I am sorry. I was not ready to divulge this information to you on the plane. Not only is it a breach of security, a breach of trust, and a breach of honor, I realize it's a hard pill for a husband to swallow."

Hard Pill? The idea his wife spent a decade with her boyfriend utilizing practices in their repertoire that included lots of physical contact? It's more than a hard pill. It's a revelation. No wonder these two have no physical boundaries with each other.

"We do have boundaries. No mouths below the waist and no

penetration," Cara responds matter-of-factly to his thoughts. Then she adds, "And no one was ever allowed to touch me during a mission. Connor forbade it. I am for his hands only."

Of course, 'not even a scratch on you' Agent Connor Reed would never allow Cara to feel uncomfortable. He protected her. He had the skills, the power and the resources to do it.

As Cara finally drops her knees and lays next to him, she wraps her arms around his waist. Speaking into his chest, she states, "Reed always protected me. He still does. And you needed to understand that part of our relationship. More importantly, you needed to understand me."

She takes a deep breath before adding, "I will never allow sexual abuse or harassment perpetrated on myself or anyone I love. I lost my patience and tolerance for it a long time ago. I WILL get even. No hesitation. I wish more women in similar situations had my fortitude in confronting it head on, but I acknowledge not all have the means."

Scooching down so they are face to face, Nic wraps her up in his arms. Cara was almost gang raped in Kabul. He saved her. Or was it true that he had to come to her rescue because his grid jammed her sonar as Reed accused? But, then again, she was never supposed to be in Kabul. Reed did not know of, or approve of her mission. Strange. Or maybe just a weird irony they should meet then, there and under those circumstances.

Grabbing his chin, she scolds, "Don't. Don't think about Kabul. Maybe if you weren't there, I would have sensed them coming for me and killed them based on intuition alone. Maybe not. Doesn't matter. I found you. That's all that matters." She snuggles into him. Eventually, her breathing evens out...

His wife awakens to the sound of dogs barking, incessantly. Nic has her cradled against his chest. His legs and arms still wrapped tightly around her. *Nic? Can I have your gun to shoot the dogs?*

Forget the dogs; I'm going over to shoot the neighbors. It's not the dogs' fault.

"How can they always do that? They leave them out there barking to wake the entire neighborhood. We should definitely at least kick their asses," Cara whines.

He presses his arousal against her bottom and between her thighs. He's been awake for a while watching her sleep and admiring, his thoughts a conflicting clutter of emotions. The journey with her in his mind last night was enlightening. He has always loved her with every molecule of his being, but to literally see and feel her complete and committed love for him was affirming. On the other hand, there are components in their love for each other that do not measure up to what his wife shares with her boyfriend. Obviously.

After she fell asleep, he let his mind wander through so many scenarios involving the two of them. The memories and revelations weighed heavily on him all night.

Cara and Reed share a love filled with respect, pride, and absolute faith in one another. Although Nic wants her to feel that same intense devotion for him, he is realizing this morning, he does not feel it for her, either. He respects Cara, and she makes him proud, but he doesn't have the kind of blind faith in her as he does in Sasha. That kind of reverence can only be earned. As successful mission partners, it's understandable that absolute trust would be a byproduct.

Cara asks, snapping him out of his deep, blocked thoughts, "What time is it?"

"7:30"

She sighs in disgust before leaning against him until he's on his back. She crawls onto his chest to sensuously rub her body across his. "Argh, so early...but you do feel good. How about I make you a deal? Let's finish this in the shower where I can't hear the dogs?"

"Sex before coffee? I'm making good progress with you. These new gifts are going to be very advantageous. You have yourself a deal."

By the time Cara is dressed for the day, Nic has already made coffee and is working on pancakes for the crew. He knows she's headed to the kitchen and has a large mug waiting for her. Nic hands it to her as she passes him, leaving a small kiss on his cheek. Although Nic's thoughts were blocked this morning, his emotions were not. She was afraid he would think her a deviant, but instead, she feels only resignation from him. The truth of her employment needed to come out of the closet of her mind.

With Ed Grotto running around out there, Nic needed to understand her compulsion for revenge against sexual abusers. She will find Ed and kill him, once and for all.

Seated at the table this morning are Jinx, Jake and Reed, all of them eating their pancakes.

Cara sits and watches as they wait for her to take some sips of her coffee before they give her any direct eye contact.

Once it appears safe, Jinx inquires, "The dogs again?"

"Yes, or I would still be asleep."

"When this is over, we need a plan of attack on those neighbors of yours," Jinx adds.

"Agreed. Are Carter and Far Guard sleeping in?" Cara inquires.

"It appears that way," Reed says admonishingly.

"I'm certain they were up late watching action movies downstairs with my son. Max can be a bad influence. Don't be too hard on them," Cara tries to soothe.

"Like mother, like son?" Reed looks right at her for the first time this morning.

Cara meets his eyes and smiles. She observes Reed has more casual clothes on, but soon notices they are beyond casual.

"Wait a minute, are you wearing an A & F T-shirt?" Cara implores with concern.

Reed rises slowly to reveal his fitted shirt and the jeans he's wearing. The jeans have colorful painted medieval shields, swords, and Templar symbols on them. Cara inhales when she recognizes them.

Reed smiles wide at her reaction. "I asked Sasha if I could borrow some clothes. I ran out. Apparently, he has a very keen sense of irony."

"Apparently. Another favorite show, the BBC's *Merlin*." Cara adds after some thought, "At least he gave you a plain T-shirt."

"Max gave me the shirt." Reed runs his hands over his torso. "I guess teenagers like the snugger fit."

Cara apologizes profusely. It didn't occur to her that Reed, Carter, and Far Guard would run out of clean clothes. She promises to dig some up for them and run a load of their laundry after breakfast.

"C, we're big boys, we can fend for ourselves. No need to apologize."

Cara smiles knowing he's right, but she is struck by the camaraderie developing within the walls of her home from this divergent group of people. She's jolted out of her thoughts when she receives a flick to the back of her head.

"You like my choice," Sasha says from behind her, making it a statement rather than a question.

Cara should reach back and smack him for the flick, but his choice of jeans for Reed is still resonating in her mind with inspiration and concern. Feelings she's going to have to resolve later when she has more time to process them. Sasha takes the seat at the end of the table with a cup of coffee and gives Cara a little smirk. Then she notices his outfit.

Deciding not to address the jeans choice for Reed, Cara inquires, "And what the hell are you wearing? You look...um...normal."

Sasha has on a long sleeved fitted black shirt with army green cargo pants. No decals, paints, or jewels. His hair is pulled back into a small bun on the back of his head. He looks like a hipster. He's adorable, and younger looking with his hair pulled entirely off his face. He hasn't shaved, adding to the cuteness factor because he's sporting a fuller, trimmed beard. Cara turns to cop a glance at her husband. Nic hasn't shaved, either.

"Nic, Jake and I are going on a weapons mission," Sasha advises, raising one eyebrow.

Cara looks to Jake for some sort of explanation. "We are going to put together everything we have between the three of us, locally, to see if we have enough firepower. Then we'll stockpile it in the garage and start outfitting the vehicles and the house," Jake declares impassively around a mouthful of pancakes.

"We need to make sure we're ready in case something should go down. Reed has offered up some additional weapons if we determine we require more," Jake adds.

Nic serves Cara and Sasha each a plate of pancakes. He leans into his wife. "We need to decide if we're going to send the kids to school tomorrow. Jake and I have discussed it, and we think they should go."

Schools have already become a dangerous place, lately. The high school has excellent lockdown procedures and utilizes the ALICE plan, an acronym for alert, lockdown, inform, counter, and evacuate, but the thought of the kids being away from them all day is frightening. Both Cara and Jinx feel the kids should stay home. Missing some school won't kill them, but going, may. She discussed the topic in depth with Jinx last night.

"Reed's working on something he thinks may make us feel better about letting them go," Jinx sighs out.

Reed explains he's working on getting Carter and two of the FBI Agents inserted as substitute teachers at the high school in the classes the kids have. He hopes to speak directly with the School Superintendent today. Reed just needs to figure out what spin he wants to place on this to protect all of them from speculation.

Nic adds, "Cara, we can't keep them hidden here at the house, indefinitely. We can pull Max from all sports, because I don't like the odds of him exposed in an open field, but at school, with protection, I think we do it."

"I see the logic, I do, but..." Cara can't finish her thought out loud. *As their mother, I can't get the wretched fear for their safety out of my heart.* For the first time since their enlightenment, Cara sends this statement out to all their threads.

Shifting their heads around to one another, they attempt to determine if they did all hear that.

"Nice trick," Reed says when he realizes they have all received the same message.

It's a trick I intend to use often if it keeps us all safe. Cara's response is delivered with a stern reprimand to the group.

Jake asks, "Can anyone communicate back to you, besides Nic?"

Cara looks subtly to Sasha, wondering if he's comfortable with her letting them know. He nods slowly. "Sasha and I can communicate. He can with Nic, too."

Jake's eyebrows shoot up in surprise, but then he thinks for a moment. "I'm not surprised, really. I think we all may be able to perform that at some point." Questioning Sasha, "How did you do it?"

Sasha gives Jake a boyish shrug. "I'm not sure, but I believe it has more to do with trusting than anything else. I figured out where I need to be in my mind to push my thoughts to them. You called it blocking. The natural block must come down on that section of your mind. Because Nic and Cara don't have many blocks to each other, they found the connection easily. I also figured out the energy push. We do convey it preformatted, Jake. I can send whatever emotional energy boost I want. Again, not entirely sure how I'm doing it, but I only think of the emotion I want to convey and push it out."

Sasha looks to her with a nod to confirm his statement. Cara adds, "Last night I sent him loving energy at dinner and again during the video. Later, he sent me something that felt like courage after our discussion with the kids. We can both do it."

Again, Jake's eyebrows rise. "Interesting."

Jake ponders for some time and no one speaks, sensing he is deep in thought. Finally, he advises, "It would be prudent to practice some of that today. As Cara indicated, if we can communicate to each other nonverbally and quickly, the odds in any confrontation are going to rise substantially in our favor."

Nic sits at the table with a plate of pancakes for himself. Cara rises to get more coffee and brings the carafe to everyone for refills. They decide Jinx and Cara will work with Reed and the school administration this morning. Cara has a neighbor who's a teacher at the school. She will be able to provide cell phone numbers for the superintendent and principal.

The boys can work on creating their armory, and then everyone will spend time practicing their gifts on each other.

Nic announces as he eats, "I'm done cooking. Kitchen is closed."

"Carter will be disappointed he missed Mean Man's Mean Breakfast," Cara giggles out as she places the carafe back on the warmer.

CHAPTER

FORTY-SEVEN

T HE MORNING GOES WELL. REED spins a yarn to explain why the kids will require additional protection. Carter and the two other agents, or new substitute teachers, will be armed and at the school before drop-off for this week. Nic, Sasha and Jake have assembled what looks like a military arsenal in their garage. Reed and the girls wander out to inspect their activity. Cara and Jinx are stunned to learn the boys have this much firepower hanging around.

Jinx, don't tell them, but I'm impressed this has all been local and we never found it. I'm not sure if that's kudos to them, or a hand slap to us.

Sitting on a set up folding table is a stripped down M4 Assault rifle. Jinx approaches it. Jake sees her and warns, "Honey, be careful not to touch that."

Scowling back at her husband, Jinx reaching for the pieces, quickly and effortlessly assembling the rifle. Before he can react, she has it pointed right at him. "What part of be careful are you referring to? The part about shooting your ignorant ass?"

Cara and Reed burst out laughing, almost uncontrollably. Nic and Sasha join them. Jake is still staring at his wife with disbelief.

Jinx lowers the rifle and field strips it once again, all while keeping her narrowed eyes primed on her husband.

Jake draws closer to her and says rather loudly, "You don't know how turned on I am right now." Of course, this elicits a further round of laughter from the group. Bowing his head to Cara and Jinx, he adds, "My apologies, ladies. I haven't wrapped my head around any of your skills, yet. But it must be years since you've handled a weapon."

Cara and Jinx cast a quick glance at each other before Jinx offers, "Not really. Cara and I go to the gun range once a month to practice. We find it... therapeutic."

Nic snaps his head to Cara with this admission. "You do? Wait... but you don't train?" Her eyes shift to Reed quickly, and that's all it takes for Nic to sputter, "Oh my God! Your weekends away with Reed!" Shaking his head with derision, he admits, "Here I was picturing you both arm in arm at some Gala, or seeing a show, but it's more than that, isn't it? You've been running ops!"

Moving closer to her husband, she admits, "No, not ops in that sense. Not. At. All. It's more training. And sometimes I do Reed a favor and attend functions as his date but...with an ulterior motive... to gather intel. It's perfectly safe, and no threat of injury to me." Nic is scowling at both Cara and Reed. "I've enjoyed it, like you have. It keeps me sharp without feeling threatened," she adds.

Nic processes this new information for a moment. "So, what do you two do when you aren't on an intel gathering mission?"

Reed responds, "We train in the ways we've always trained together. C is my best field partner, and I think we both derive the maximum benefit when we do it together."

"And what exactly is this training?" Nic narrows his eyes at the man.

Reed glances subtly to Jake. "I don't think it's warranted we discuss it. All you need to know is C's still training."

Baby, I'm not sure how I feel about this. On the one hand, I'm very relieved to find out you and your boyfriend aren't spending romantic weekends away together as I envisioned. But on the other hand, now being privy to your team MO, I am not happy about Reed having his hands all over my wife.

Nic, there's none of that. Honestly, we evolved beyond those sex scams, early on. This other training is...unorthodox, and not something I'm prepared to share with the group. I'm not prepared to share it with you either, at least not yet. It's complicated, NOT romantic, but a very different approach to training that Reed and I mastered early on in our professional relationship.

I feel your emotions, cara mia. You think I will judge you. More so than last night?

Yes, and to be honest, I would rather show you the training someday versus explain it.

Fair enough. I guess I owe you that after the Jake mission omission thing.

Cara smiles at her husband. The trust between them is so evident, even with those few mental comments. Cara wanders over to the weapons cache to see if there's anything she isn't familiar with. "No Tasers? I think I need a Taser since I've recently been on the receiving end of one."

Jake looks at her disapprovingly. "I will see what I can do. Reed, you want to help outfit the vehicles?"

Reed reviews the collection with a critical eye. "No, I'm going to help Cara and Jinx with lunch, practice the mind thing, and see if I can get you guys some Stinger portable surface to air missiles this afternoon."

Sasha is impressed and gazes at Reed with new appreciation. "Dude, that would be awesome!" Reed smirks at him as they head back into the house.

After they are out of earshot, Jake turns scornfully to Sasha. "You're liking him now?"

"Maybe." Sasha looks around the garage before continuing, "I do like Reed, much more than I thought I would. I'm beginning to respect him, too, which is unusual for me. You know I have a very short list of people I respect."

Jake looks at both Sasha and Nic with piercing eyes. "You know this person isn't Director Connor Reed of Washington, DC, right?"

Nic and Sasha are stunned by this admission, as if Jake is insinuating this Reed is some sort of doppelgänger.

Realizing his misuse of words, Jake adds, "Of course, it's Reed. But DC Reed is a ruthless bureaucrat, a master manipulator, and aggressively aloof. He's a scary man. No one likes to go up against him." At the Pentagon, people begin to sweat when they know he's coming to a meeting. Most of the military know Reed's reputation. Not only do they fear him now, but they know all his background stories. Unlike most of his predecessors, Reed was in the field. He came up through the ranks at the CIA. There were no special bureaucratic confirmations. Reed earned that job, and he does it better than anyone before him.

Jake looks at the door he just left through. "I don't know THIS Reed."

Nic nods in understanding. "You believe this Reed is not to be trusted?"

Jake's not comfortable sharing any detailed knowledge he has about Reed. If Nic and Sasha knew the stories firsthand as he does, they would understand his trepidation. Honestly, he is having serious trouble still reconciling Cara is Agent Chase Bennett. He was blown away when he found out. He never saw that coming, let alone that his own wife was her analyst. Jake has respected his wife and Cara over the years for their wit and intelligence but now he's slightly intimidated by all three of them.

He's going to withhold that concern from Nic and Sasha as well. "No, I'm not saying he's not to be trusted but...I'm just...I'm having difficulty reconciling the two Reeds," Jake merely admits.

NIC CONTINUES TO NOD IN SUPPORT AND HE CAN'T BELIEVE WHAT HE'S ABOUT to verbalize, but he knows this is genuine Reed. He doesn't know how to be anything else when he's with Cara. There is no pretense between them. Nic's been around the two of them together, often and long enough, to know the real Connor Reed.

Shaking his head at the memories, Nic lets a secret smile form on his lips while thinking about his wife and her ridiculous boyfriend. They were always so funny and entertaining, albeit, disturbing to watch. "DC Reed is the persona he has worked hard to create. Sound familiar?"

"I'm not an idiot, Supermind. I get the correlation you're making to us, but it's different with us. We are ruthless killers on some level, always. That being the case, then on some level Reed is also innately ruthless," Jake retorts.

Nic disagrees. He learned something from his experience with Cara in Berlin. After his rage over his wife running to her boyfriend instead of her own husband, he understood how she could have done that. He is not the Dark Angel when he's with her. He is just Nic. He has never shown her the slightest inclination otherwise, and not because he was trying to conceal it. "I am Nic Andre, businessman, father, and husband. The Zen Master of this household. Not ruthless. Pacifist. No cover. It's who I am."

Jake stares at Nic trying to digest his words. "Are you losing your edge?"

"There are 546 different ways I could kill you in this garage, including 15 ways with my bare hands. And I wouldn't hesitate to do it, if provoked. But that's the difference. Provocation." When he needs to, Nic can be the Dark Angel. That training exists, but it doesn't define him. "If you don't feel that way, I guess I'm sorry for you. I'm certain Sasha shares my sentiment on this."

Jake is mildly distressed by Nic's words. He is rendered speechless.

Nic, trying to infuse some humor, adds, "I believe the girls would say you need to put on your Freud hat and examine your feelings. Maybe you are not what you imagine yourself to be. Then again, maybe you are. Only you can resolve that."

Pausing for a moment, Nic winces, "And I believe my wife and I are now sharing too much with each other, because I'm beginning to sound like a girl."

While the other three are in the kitchen making sandwiches for everyone, they practice trying to connect to Cara. Jinx and Reed can hear her clearly but can't seem to project their thoughts. Cara admits what they are trying to convey is coming across, but it's jumbled and unclear. Like a bad cell phone connection, their words staccato and intermittent sounding.

Lunch is served on paper plates to everyone spread throughout the house and yard. The kids are in the family room with Carter watching something on Netflix. Far Guard is outside with the FBI boys all trying to help Nic, Sasha, and Jake load the vehicles with concealed weapons. Reed utilizes Cara's office for some privacy. He's making phone calls and is on her computer when she enters with a cold drink for him.

"Knock, knock, can I come in my own office?" She calls out before walking right in, affording him no privacy, as is her norm. Cara has her sandwich balanced on top of her drink in her other hand. She gets comfortable in the guest chair facing her desk.

Starting to eat lunch, she watches Reed bang out email after email. She doesn't try to communicate. He's in the zone. She just wanted to be near him for some reason. She wants to talk to herself, but she needs to check that Nic is not in her head. Cara does some looking around in there and doesn't sense him.

Weird. Does this mean Nic will always know how much I really spend on shoes? I need to learn how to put memories away where he can't find them. I don't mind sharing, but not the shoes. The shoes must stay hidden.

Cara watches Reed some more. She's almost ready to start talking when Reed, with his back turned to her says, "You want to see something cool? Bring your chair over here."

Dragging her chair around the desk, Cara seats herself in front of her monitors right next to him. He begins to click at the keys and the next thing she sees is an aerial view of her neighborhood scanning across both monitors.

"Watch this." Reed slowly zooms in, and the top of their house comes into view. She can see Sasha's G wagon and Jake's Suburban on the street with the two black sedans. Nic's BMW and Cara's Audi are both parked in the driveway. Nic's Ford Truck must be in the garage getting worked on.

"COOL, Spy drone?" Cara asks, her eyes are wide.

"No, can't seem to shake down the military to get one of those here." They have a lucky satellite position for the next couple of days, though. By the end of the week, Reed will lose this ability with the rotation of the earth. It's always potluck on the surveillance with satellites. "Tell Nic to walk out to the driveway."

Cara and Reed watch the screens as they see Nic appear from the garage and look up.

Now wave, we can see you.

They watch Nic tentatively wave. They see him go back into the garage and he emerges again, dragging Sasha out with him. Sasha is left gazing up at the heavens as Nic disappears.

Cara articulates a countdown. "8,7,6,5,4,3,2, and 1." On one, Nic appears in her office.

"Let me see. Let me see!" He calls out, dragging Cara from her chair. "That's so cool. Satellite?"

Realizing Cara is standing, it occurs to Nic he was rude. He pulls her onto one leg to sit. They're all watching the view of Sasha when they see him turn and look up, like he knows where the camera is. Sasha flips them off from the driveway.

"How did he know?" Reed asks laughing.

"I told him where to look," Nic admits. "Can you zoom back out, but slowly?" They begin to see the street. Sasha appears in the office and stands behind Reed and Nic, wedged between them and the desk. "This is so cool!" Sasha exclaims.

REED CHUCKLES AS HE GRASPS HOW LONG THESE THREE HAVE BEEN AWAY from all of this. They haven't had the opportunity to have fun with the new technology. It's a different game out there now. Most espionage is done this way, or with Internet and phone tapping. Seems barbaric in hindsight to think they would send agents to 'spy' and gather intel. Nowadays, field missions are reserved for the final action after countless months of technological analysis. And even then, it takes an act of Congress to commence.

Reed patiently explains to Nic how to control the satellite. Nic catches on quickly and takes command, moving the view towards the neighborhood entrance, but slowly, so the lens can stay focused.

While they watch the screen, Reed details some new protocols they utilize with this technology. He has far fewer field operatives than analysts, currently, under his direction at the Agency. Those analysts spend most of their time just watching video feeds of doorways, for instance, noting who comes in and out, and how often. Personally, he would have hated that kind of work. Reed's thankful his role for the last decade has been merely managing these activities, and not actually performing them.

Nic whines, "Baby, I want my own satellite, and I want it now."

Cara pats his head, "There, there, Veruca. I'm sure Reed will let you play with his."

"But I neeeeed one. How can I be Ernst Stavro Blofeld without it?" Nic continues to pretend whine.

Reed leans back in his chair while Nic plays with the controls. He doesn't know who Veruca is, but Blofeld is his personal favorite villain, Leader of SPECTRE, arch nemesis of James Bond. He lets his mind wander through the possibilities.

Cara must sense the emotion from the diabolical fantasy he's constructing and slaps Reed's chest. "I know what you're feeling, Connor Reed, so get that despicable idea out of your head right now," she scolds.

"Come on C, the villains have all the fun," Reed faux whines, trying to mimic Nic.

Sasha must catch a glimpse of his thoughts and adds, "SPECTRE. I like it," and places his hand on Reed's shoulder. Nic gives him his killer smile.

"OH MY GOD, the three of you! Stop!" Standing from Nic's lap, she narrows her eyes at them. "I will make you a deal. WHEN we get over this threat, you three can do whatever you like, but until then, please curb your rule the world enthusiasm. Now, don't you two have something to do?"

Reed interrupts her. "Actually, I need to go pick up the missiles. You can stay and play if you like." Nic offers to help Reed, but he hesitates for a moment before responding, "Thanks, but I was going to ask Jake to come and maybe drive me."

Cara goes back to narrowing her eyes at him. "Somehow, I think this is clue number one for who Jake is."

It's Nic who looks long and hard at him before offering, "It's clue number two." Ah, the Dark Angel may be figuring it out.

Cara salutes Reed. She turns back to her husband. He is sure she is going to drill him on what was clue number one she may have missed. Too funny these guys haven't put it all together yet concerning Jake's identity. Reed is especially disappointed in Cara. She should have figured it out by now. Really, when she first met Jake. Jinx, as well. Knowing these two women, they only saw big, gruff, hot, bad boy, and didn't bother looking beyond that.

Reed moves past them with a sly smile as he leaves her office. He asks Cara to log him off when they're done playing. "And do something worthwhile while you're farting around and check for threats." Cara salutes him again.

CHAPTER

FORTY-EIGHT

DINNER IS IN THE OVEN. Four loads of laundry have been done, including Reed's and Carter's. The kids have been pulled from their weekend party mode and are forced to do homework. Jinx is still hacking ex-British Intelligence officials on her laptop in the kitchen. Nic and Sasha have finished tricking out the last vehicle and are in the process of placing weapons throughout the house. Cara is relaxing while doing work emails in her office.

Nic comes in with a Beretta like the one he used in Berlin, but without the scope and silencer. "Where do you want this, baby?"

Cara stops typing and looks at the 9mm semi-automatic. She places her hand out for it. She releases the magazine, inspects it, and checks the springs on the cartridge. "When's the last time this was fired?"

"Recently."

She snaps the magazine back in, makes sure the safety is on, and reaches for a mailing tape dispenser. She pulls out about 18 inches and tapes the gun under her desk above the kneehole space. "Happy?"

Nic leans in close to her and places his lips on her neck. "I think Jake is right. Watching you handle a gun is a big turn on."

"That's because they're phallic. Now get out and let me finish working. Dinner will be served when Jake and Reed return. Go." She manages to grab his butt while he walks away.

Everyone, including the kids, Carter, and Far Guard, is at the table tonight. It's like a traditional Sunday dinner. The mixed company, a mashup of ages and roles, opens the conversation to a myriad of subjects. The topics are interesting and entertaining.

They learn Agent William Carter, or Willy at home, is from New Orleans. He regales everyone with stories of gators, creole traditions and jazz music. New Orleans is one of Cara and Nic's favorite cities in the States, so they add their beloved places to Carter's list. They realize quickly, as the discussion continues, Carter hasn't experienced his hometown on the same kind of budget they have.

When did WE get to be snobs? Cara asks her husband.

We're not snobs…just because we stay at and eat in four- and five-star establishments when we travel?

Um, yeah. That was sort of embarrassing just now. I feel like Carter was one of those little bayou boys fishing for catfish to make a living. Or whatever it is they fish for in the bayou.

THAT sounded snobbish. And there are catfish in the Bayou and bass… and crappie.

Cara smiles at her husband. She's enjoying this telepathy thing, even if it means she needs to come clean about the shoes. She looks around the table, struck again by the fun and camaraderie. Even Jake and Reed seem closer since their little ride together, the details of which they shared with no one.

No, cara mia, they all can't come live with us.

Cara frowns, but she notices Nic looking at Sasha. *They must be talking. Those two. Too cute.*

Heard that. Still connected.

Damn, do you know about the shoes?

What about the shoes?

Nothing. What are you and Sasha talking about?

We're trying to figure out a gameplan for dropping off the kids tomorrow morning.

Can you patch me into your conversation?

Sash? Cara?

Cara giggles, *Ha, you sound like a conference call. Did you have to hit the flash button on your grid?*

You are a wiseass even in my mind, Vizzini.

Captain, what course of action do you intend tomorrow morning?

Appreciating her deference, Sasha states, *That's better. I was thinking you and Reed take the kids to school in the Audi. Jake will drive in with Eli at the same time. Nic and I, with my wagon, will be in the area.*

You guys want back up position?

I think we're more comfortable watching and scanning, yes. Does that work for you?

Sure, but you know I HATE drop-off. Although, it'll be fun to put Reed through it.

It's a plan then. Cara, convey that to Reed. After dinner, I'm going to my room to try the UK again. I still want to reach my associate there. I assume Nic told you about that?

Um, I was in attendance during your conversation. Sorry.

Nicolae, I am disappointed. Are there no secrets anymore?

Chill Broody, we've had enough secrets for the last 17 years. Welcome to the Brave New World.

Welcome, indeed.

Nic finally gets a thought in. *You two are cracking me up. I'm hanging up now.*

Dinner is long, but entertaining. By the time it's done and the kitchen is cleaned, it's 9:00 PM. Jinx, Eli and Jake leave, and the kids head to their rooms. The plan is set for the morning.

Cara heads to her bedroom to get comfy in her yoga pants and a T-shirt. She finds Nic in the bathroom stepping out of the shower. Taking a long look at his body as he towels off, she reaffirms she will never tire of admiring him.

Catching her seductive stare, Nic goads her with, "Reed is leaving tomorrow afternoon." He must attend some meetings but is going to leave Carter there and be back by Thursday. For some reason, though, Nic doesn't think these three co-conspirators will wait until Thursday to strike. "I feel it's imminent."

"I do, too. Reed feels badly about leaving, but I know he must get back at some point. In an extremely surreal way, this has been sort of fun, you know?"

"Fun?"

Of course, it's not fun because of the looming threat hanging over their heads, but Cara has enjoyed their time together. This group is calming, but energizing and inspirational. Even Carter. His thoughts don't come exploding at her. She needs to dig a bit with him. Not having to deal with all that outside chatter has made her feel more focused, despite the recent chaos. All the energy these others provide, and emit, probably has something to do with that. "Mostly, I've enjoyed the camaraderie we've established."

"You sure it wasn't just fun because you got to be with Reed?"

Cara folds her arms over her chest and glowers at her husband. Nic drops the towel and turns to her, naked, and folds his arms over his chest.

"He's in love with you, cara mia."

"Argh, he THINKS he's in love with me," Cara states firmly, stomping her foot on the tile floor.

"Yeah, yeah, yeah, I heard you hashing it out all day...but what is it you feel? Have you at least figured that out?"

Uncrossing her arms, she plops down on her vanity chair in deep thought. Nic pulls on a pair of gym shorts. They are having a mental confrontation. They have been all day, ever since she saw Reed in those painted jeans and Nic read her thoughts. There is a tension filled silence in the bathroom for several minutes while Nic reprimands her, mentally. Cara adds a few barbs back at him, but he commandeers the mental discussion until finally, she acquiesces.

Resigned and worn out, Cara sighs softly, "You are right, Nic, I do need to deal with this once and for all."

She gets up to leave the bathroom, but as she passes her husband, he grabs her arm. He concentrates on her face for a long while before commanding, "Yes, you do. The way I want, and the way we agreed earlier, but know one thing...I won't wait for you." Cara nods in understanding and walks out of the bathroom, through the bedroom, and out the door.

She heads up the front stairs towards Reed's room. His door is shut, and she knocks gently. She doesn't wait for a reply, but walks in wordlessly. Reed is sitting in bed wearing only drawstring pajama pants. His legs are out in front of him, and his tablet is on his lap. He has his reading glasses on, and Cara is struck by how attractive he is. Sometimes she forgets.

She closes the door and stands in front of it, steeling her emotions, trying to draw some courage from anywhere. Reed places the tablet on the nightstand and takes his glasses off. He motions to Cara by patting the bed beside him.

She approaches the bed and crawls onto it to sit side by side with him. He reaches out to place a hand on her leg. "Tell me what's wrong, my sweetheart." The request comes off his tongue with hesitation, apprehension and fear.

It's a relief he's already figured out why she's here. "Geneva. We need to discuss what happened in Geneva."

Motioning Cara onto his lap, she complies and sits facing him. Reed takes his time processing his thoughts and emotions as he searches her face. Fucking Geneva. The bane of his existence. Geneva changed his life. He's not surprised she finally needs to discuss what happened. He releases his breath and speaks thoughtfully and succinctly.

"You were my girl. From the moment I met you, you were MY

GIRL. I always wanted you in my life. Sometimes, I thought you were my life. So many times, and I mean so many times, I just wanted to take things to the next level, but something always prevented me from doing it. At first, it was the cover guilt, but then, later, it was the work thing. I just thought...I just thought, eventually, it would work out. I always thought you were my girl. Then, Geneva."

He never thought it could happen. She wasn't into dating, and didn't seem to want a relationship with another guy. Just him. Always, just him.

Until Geneva.

Of course now, in hindsight, he can say he felt her emotional pull towards Nic and it's what caused his additional distress but, "You broke my heart that night."

When Cara softly places her hands on his face, he wraps his arms around her waist and continues. "You were a mess in Geneva. Really, you were a mess after Kabul. I knew it. I FELT it. I didn't want to acknowledge it, but on some level, I knew it was all coming to an end. You stopped being my girl the moment you came back from Kabul. A place you never should've been in."

Reed took Cara to Geneva thinking he could teach her a lesson. He believed he could convince her of the foolishness of her fixation on the Dark Angel. But she only got worse. She became obsessed. And then she spotted Nic at the Summit, smiling, in the arms of another woman. Reed saw it on Cara's face, and he felt it in his heart.

"It was devastating for me." Reed lowers his head, unable to look Cara in the face. She begins to run her fingers through his hair as he continues. "I panicked. I had to get you out of there. I couldn't bear the look on your face."

He was beyond emotional when he physically dragged her back to their hotel room. Then she fell apart on him and did the one thing he had waited 10 years for her to do. He was screaming at her about being immature and naïve to think she could manufacture a relationship with the Dark Angel of Death, like some spy versus spy love affair from a movie plot. Then, in the middle of his tirade, with her in tears, her devastation apparent, she blurts out she wants to move their relationship to a physical one. She begs him to become her lover.

"Why did you make that offer? And why then, C? Why, after you break my heart, did you think I would accept?" Reed looks back up to Cara, beseeching. Her hands are still in his hair and their faces are mere inches from each other.

Cara finally responds, "I have seen you angry enough to scream at me, mad enough to want to hit me, and frustrated with the need to strangle me. I spent a good portion of my career testing your patience. But I had never seen you like you were that night. You scared me."

He drops his head in grief. He was awful to her that night. He called her a huge disappointment. Told her she was acting like a teenage girl with her first crush. Blamed her for blowing their mission, and accused her of not caring. It would have been one thing if Nic had shown her any interest, but he never even looked her way.

Before he can respond to her, she adds, "I started to think everything you said to me was true. I had become unbalanced over some crazy crush on a lethal killer. And then the insanity of the night came into clear focus. You weren't just angry or mad or frustrated with me. You felt betrayed."

The pain. It's like it was yesterday and not 17 years ago. He struggles for air as his head falls to her shoulder. He's having trouble verbalizing as she cradles his head into her neck. She continues to run her hands through his hair. All he can do is whisper, "But why would you choose to ask me for a sexual relationship on that night?"

He can hear her inhale. "I felt I had never been fair to you. I felt I owed you the chance, first. I felt...guilty."

There it is. Confirmation of what he suspected all this time. Lifting his head, he finally has the strength to draw closer until his lips are faintly against Cara's. He tells her quietly and softly, "I felt your guilt, and I was damned if my first time with you was because you were harboring that emotion."

So much happened to him in the 24 hours after he left Geneva. He didn't shun her as she suspected he had. Instead, he laid out plans to seduce her properly without the guilt, shame and betrayal of the hotel room. But, best laid plans and all…he never got the chance to implement. Nicolae Interruptus came along and swept her off her feet. Telling her the truth now, all these years later, will not make any difference. It will only hurt her. He would never willingly hurt her. His feelings and emotional well-being will be secondary to hers. Always.

Before he can continue to dwell on that long ago time, Cara does the unexpected. She pulls slightly away to look him in the eyes. She tugs his head towards hers and places her lips hard against his. Her kiss turns passionate as she explores his mouth. His hands unconsciously pull her tight to him. His arousal is nestled between her legs. She runs her hands from his hair down to his face while his hands move under her shirt.

He finally breaks the kiss, his hands on her rib cage, his fingertips brushing the bottoms of her breasts. Placing soft kisses to the side of her mouth, he whispers, "I was your White Knight. I guess, I thought it meant I was also your Prince Charming."

CARA CAN'T TAKE IT ANYMORE. SHE PULLS HIM INTO A TIGHT HUG, CRADLING his head against her neck again. "You ARE my dashing White Knight on his noble steed. You always will be, Connor." No matter which direction her life takes, no matter what man she lays in bed with every night, this man will always be the one who gets the credit. He made her, as much as she made him. "Did I ever tell you about the reasoning behind the name I gave you, the White Knight?" Reed shakes his head while still huddled on her shoulder. Picking his head up by the chin, Cara forces him to look into her eyes, tear-filled and remorseful.

"Do you know the Legend of King Arthur? As the story goes, one of the Knights of the Round Table is named Sir Galahad. He is called the White Knight. Not just because he carries a white shield, but because he was the Knight known for his tremendous gallantry and purity. That's how I have always seen you. My White Knight...my PURE love." Cara waits for him to process this before continuing.

"I somehow knew our relationship was to be kept pure. Perfect and innocent as if tampering with it could possibly destroy it."

It didn't really come together until she saw the jeans he wore today. The white shields Mia painted on them were symbolic of Galahad. She knew why Sasha gave them to Reed, but it was the other symbols on the jeans that struck her instantly and more profoundly. It was the full circle again. It all began to make sense in her head, the thinking portion and the feeling portion coming together.

She moves her hand from his face to place it over his heart. She leans in to cradle her head against his throat and chest. "I have always thought it sardonic the Deputy Director Knighted me Sir Reflex." She remembers the awful day of her simulator debacle at Langley. "I wasn't aware at that point the Assistant Director knew the code name YOU were going to use. My nickname for you."

Ironic, how they both ended up as Knights.

Then, the jeans. It was when she saw the jeans and noticed the various shields that she identified another connection. "You've heard of Sir Lancelot, right? He is known as the Black Knight. He was highly skilled, very brave, and very noble. But Lancelot had a flaw. He fell in love with the King's wife, Guinevere. Lancelot gave up God, country, King and duty to consummate his love." She glances up to him searching his face for understanding.

"Your Dark Angel is the Black Knight," Reed gets out with some pain in his voice.

"Yes."

"It was going to take an act of eternal sacrifice to win you."

"Maybe...but it's the light and dark metaphor I couldn't escape from this morning. And the metaphor was caught on the Templar symbols on your jeans. The Templars, or the Knights of the Round Table, were on a great quest. The quest for the Holy Grail. Do you know who finds the Grail? Only the purest of hearts can. Sir Galahad finds the Grail in the legend. He's the only one worthy of its treasure and knowledge."

He understands the direction she's headed and tries to compose himself. "So, if this analogy of yours is to be followed, you're saying our relationship was always supposed to be kept pure because you think I am on a quest to find some treasure?"

"Metaphorically speaking, yes."

Cara pauses to get more comfortable on his lap. Reed needs to really dig down deep for her and put away the emotions and the hormones. Raising her arm to wrap her hand around his nape, she calmly inquires, "Why didn't you ever just take me?"

She knows he's a very sexual guy, yet he never touched her beyond innocent caresses and kisses. Almost as if he knew he couldn't. They have slept together and cuddled. They have been naked together, often, but it's never sexual. It's always pure.

"Connor, you have talked the talk on occasion, but with thousands of opportunities, you have never tried to go down that road. You must realize how odd that is. Particularly for you, Reed, the man who has always taken what he wants."

Reed is driven. He sets his mind on something and he achieves it. Nothing stands in his way. Yet he did not pursue her sexually. If he wanted her that badly, if he had the passion for her, and if being a couple meant that much to him, he would have taken her. She never gave him any indication he couldn't for the first ten years of their relationship. She even offered it to him in Geneva, and he turned her down flat. He grabbed his bag and walked out of their room, leaving her in Switzerland, alone and reeling.

Taking it a step further, what if he had taken them to the next level? What if she never went to Kabul, and never encountered Nic? What if she always stayed his girl? "What if we did finally make love? Then what?"

Reed is confused by this line of questioning. "You mean would we have gotten married?"

"Yes, what would you have done, Connor?"

He knew what she wanted all along. He knew she wanted out of the government work someday. He knew the agent thing was wearing thin on her. If they got married, what was she supposed to do? Get a career? That works for a while. Would they have had children? She wanted kids. Would her career have been over at that point? And what of Reed's career? Would she have been the supportive wife? Home alone while he traveled, caring for their children like a single mom?

And now, with him in his current capacity, what would her life be like? She would have no career whatsoever. She would have a multitude of expectations placed on her as the wife of the Director. Hosting and attending functions would become her full-time position. Cara Callous, with her chatter filled head, among the glitterati. She would no longer be her own person.

Connor Reed was meant for the life he has now. He is destined to make a difference. He is Galahad on the great quest. This fulfills him. Cara would not have fulfilled him in the capacity of lover and wife, partly because she herself would not have been content in that role.

She believes he would've given up everything to make her happy, but would he have been happy? As compatible as they are to each other, ultimately they never did want the same things from their lives.

Yet, he has spent decades thinking he's in love with her.

"But you're not in love with me. You love me and I love you, but we are not intended for physical love. My thread has always been as your Knight, your comrade in arms. It was in the cards that way. And there's the irony. I am the Knight tasked to provide emotion, love, loyalty and support. I'm to assist you on your own Knight's quest. I am not, and will never be, your actual quest. You're looking for the Grail, Connor, and I believe you'll find it. It is scripted. I see it now."

Cara sends Reed everything she can, the emotion, the thoughts, the logic, everything, including her love. She knows it's too much for him, though. She can tell immediately. But she continues transmitting, sitting still with her head on his chest, hugging him hard while he processes all of it.

When Reed can finally articulate, all he says is, "I think I get it."

She gazes back into his eyes again. "I will always feel guilty for not having this conversation with you years ago, but honestly, it never made much sense to me until this morning. Initially, I felt guilty that I somehow held you back from meeting the right girl and falling in love, but it wasn't your fate yet. I can't tell you how I know that, but for some reason I feel this quest thing comes first. It's the rationale explaining our bond. I'm embedded in your world providing the pure love you need on your journey."

Cara leans in to place her forehead against his. "I love you, Connor Reed. I always have and I always will. It's a coveted position I take the great honor on being bestowed. I've always said I have your back, but I can stand by your side when you need me, too." She places a gentle kiss on his lips and makes her way out of the bedroom.

CHAPTER

FORTY-NINE

WHEN CARA GETS BACK INTO her bedroom, the lights are all off but her small nightstand light is on. It takes a few seconds for her eyes to adjust to the semi darkness. She looks to Nic's side of the bed, and sees it's empty.

Cara lowers her head and leans against the closed bedroom door behind her. She tries to control her breathing while emptying her mind. The session with Reed had been emotionally draining and she's relieved it's over with. She can't manage to release the metaphor from her mind, though. The sight of those jeans struck her so hard this morning. Its symbolic nature materialized out of nowhere and clues began to populate. It was reminiscent of watching bacteria multiply in her mind. Clues were randomly being pulled from sections and attaching themselves to the image of those painted jeans.

It was enlightening, but frightening. She really does see a script for Reed. He is on a quest, a journey involving these gifts. The last couple of days have brought about a breakthrough on so many levels. Cara can't yet determine why the timing coincides with this threat,

411

but it's all tied together, somehow. The last 72 hours were meant to happen. She is positioned at a pivotal moment for all of them. A moment she's beginning to sense was scripted. All these years, everyone kept their secrets, and not one slip up, by any of them. Then, all the secrets and the gifts get revealed with this threat. There is no such thing as a coincidence.

They have all accomplished a great deal in this short period. But Reed? There is so much more to Connor than the others. She isn't sure how she understands this, but she does. Despite the breakthrough that revealed Cara's gifts, she continues to feel a strong intuition she's unable to tie directly to them. Like with the metaphor, her mind is arbitrarily pulling clues based on nothing but symbols. Neither thoughts nor emotions have anything to do with it.

She isn't even sure how she knows the King Arthur story. Cara can't recall ever reading it. Maybe a couple of Monty Python movies from long ago but that's all she can remember. Yet the clues found their way into her mind. Whatever it is Reed is meant to achieve, she will be by his side when he does. This was in the cards for her from the moment she looked into those fierce baby blue eyes of his from the other side of that campus police interview table.

Suddenly, Cara is shaken from her thoughts. She hears music streaming into her brain. Realizing she's been leaning against the closed door; she pushes off and stalks toward her bathroom. Opening the door, she spies Nic leaning over his sink spitting out toothpaste.

While she rests on the door jamb with her arms crossed over her chest, she watches Nic rinse his mouth and stand upright to face her. He is naked and very, very aroused. She flashes him a quick grin. "I thought you weren't going to wait up for me? And I can't believe you're playing New Order's *Bizarre Love Triangle* in your head right now."

This causes Nic to start gesticulating wildly with his arms. "Are you kidding?! After that bizarre love triangle I was just involved in?!

How could the song be any more appropriate?" He grabs her hand and places it on his engorged cock. "I just had some sort of strange, homoerotic experience, and I'm very turned on, and VERY freaked out by it!"

Cara begins to giggle as she releases his manhood and steps to her own sink to brush her teeth. Nic is following behind, just inches from her body. As she starts to brush, he begins to paw at her clothes.

"Cara mia, you have too many clothes on. I need them off."

Cara tries to push him away, but he's successful in getting her yoga pants removed. He struggles to get her T-shirt over her head while she has the toothbrush in her mouth.

He stops and moves his lips to her ear to whisper, "Did you really need to have a full make out session with Reed?"

Cara spits her toothpaste out while giggling, "You felt that? I couldn't get a clear path into his mind. It was all over the place. I needed him to hyperfocus, and the making out worked."

"Yeah, it worked, but you shot me into Reed's brain right at that moment, and I was immediately assaulted by the man's desire for you. I was sort of 'overcome'. Full pun intended."

Cara snorts at the image he's just conjured, then glares at him in the mirror. "You are the man with a plan. You are the man that asked me to implicitly trust you. You are the man I was supposed to covertly sneak into my best friend's mind, despite my protests."

Nic can't deny Reed doesn't have some serious sexual desire for her, but that's all it is. She was correct, there is no passion between them. It's only a hormonal, therapeutic appeal. It's like having a piece of chocolate cake placed in front of you. You eat it because it looks good, even if you're not hungry.

He watches his wife wash her face. She and her boyfriend never ate that slice of cake. They sniffed it, they may have even taken a lick, but they did not consume it. They didn't, because on some level they understood they weren't hungry and the cake was just empty calories. It's the only explanation that makes sense to Nic. As much as he hates to do it, he must give Reed credit. He never took advantage. He watched the cake, he protected it and saved it, but Reed never took a bite.

Cara rinses and moves to use the toilet. Nic is still following on her heels. She peers at him from her position and pointedly reminds him, "You swore to never tell me what you did in Reed's mind. I don't want to know. I need to have plausible deniability. Just promise me you didn't leave any damage."

They had struck a deal earlier, before she entered Reed's bedroom. Nic's plan had been to enter Reed's mind stealthily, facilitated by Cara as she distracted him. After that, Nic was on his own with the promise that he would not hurt Reed, but only assist in getting him past his misunderstood emotions for Cara.

"Store that memory somewhere I can never see it, Nic," she demands.

"It's already gone. Have no fears. I didn't do any damage," Nic swears with his right hand up. He is sure he didn't do any harm, but what he did do was risky.

Cara grins at him while he blocks his thoughts from her. "You look too precious, naked, aroused and pledging your allegiance." She washes her hands and turns to him. Taking her bra off, she offers, "Now, you may have me."

Nic wastes no time. He grabs her hand and leads her to their bed. He sits with his back against the headboard and motions for her to get on his lap. Complying, she lowers herself to take him in as she does.

His head falls gently back to hit the headboard as he sighs, "Much better, thank you. You don't need to do anything, just sit. I needed the connection."

Cara leans in so her body is against his. "I guess we'll never know if your plan was required. I thought my discussion with Reed went well."

"Really? The metaphor that's been running in your head since this morning?" Nic teases while he begins to kiss her jaw.

"You don't like my analogy?"

"I like the Gallant Galahad and the pure love part. That does seem to fit you two. It's accurate for what you feel, emotionally. The Grail concept is intriguing, as well. But me, the Black Knight?"

"Are you not more a Black Knight than a Dark Angel?"

"Yes, I see what you were going for, but you are not Guinevere in your scenario. You're another Knight. And furthermore, in the legend, Galahad is Lancelot's illegitimate son, which is way too weird to insert into the equation."

"You are such a smart ass, Nicolae Maximillian Herrmann Andrychenko Andre, whatever your name is." Cara states this as she wiggles her bottom trying to get him riled up. She adds, "By the way, I never had the heart to tell you, but Nic, N.I.C, is the way women in this country spell the nickname. Men use N.I.C.K."

He pushes her away, but only to place his hands over her breasts. "I was teasing you before, and yes, I did figure out the lack of a K was emasculating." Even the Dark Angel gets some things wrong. "You did a great job trying to get Reed to wrap his head around his emotions. I was struck by a thought though, while I was listening to you after I left Reed's mind."

Cara turns serious. "You have a question?"

"I was wondering... if you and Reed had ended up sleeping together in Geneva, where would that have left me?"

Dropping her head, she mumbles, "I don't think you want to ask that question."

"Why?"

"I think you need to ask a different question," Cara says as she rubs her face lightly against his growing facial hair with interest.

"You need to ask yourself first, what would you have done if Reed were in my room in Geneva making love to me? Would you still have followed me and tried to make contact?"

He gets thoughtful for a moment before he answers, "I did think you were in a relationship with him. It wouldn't have made a difference. I needed to be with you. I still would've pursued you."

"Okay," Cara says calmly, "then the question you want to ask me is, if Reed and I were in a physical relationship, whether it started in Geneva or earlier, what would I have done when I did meet you?"

She must recognize the pleading look on his face because Cara smiles and lets her lips rest against his as she whispers, "The exact same thing would've happened. Just like all those years ago. No one and nothing will ever change the outcome, my love."

Nic bites her lower lip gently before releasing it to place his lips on hers, showing her what a passionate kiss should feel like. He breaks from the kiss leaving her panting for breath. "Cara, we spent last evening in my mind. Can I try something in your mind tonight?" He delivers this with a wicked gleam in his eyes.

"I'm all yours," she breathes while arching her neck to expose her throat.

While leaving small kisses and bites on her neck, Nic gathers all his raw passion for her. Not his love, or any other emotions, he only brings his need. That fire he has always felt for the gorgeous, intelligent and complex woman he holds in his arms. It's a desire so intense, the overwhelming need to claim her takes him every time they make love. He takes his burning desire and travels into her mind.

When she realizes what he's done, her mouth drops open. His hunger and craving bounce around in her head, like they are trapped inside an isolation tank with no other thoughts or emotions allowed in. *I thought you needed a reminder of what true passion feels like, baby.*

Slowly running her fingertips up his torso, she somehow surrounds his emotions with her own inside her mind. The effect isn't just fast and furious. It's frantic and frenzied and completely erotic as they practically attack one another. Hands and mouths are everywhere. It's out of control pure passion and lust reminiscent of their first time together.

They are lost for what feels like hours, with only their longing to lead them. They're grasping for breath and each other as the hunger slowly fades, and exhaustion takes them.

CHAPTER

FIFTY

THE ALARM GOES OFF RIGHT at 6:00 AM. Cara doesn't usually hear Nic's alarm, but today it startles her awake. She finds herself sideways on the bed. Most of the blankets and pillows are on the floor in total disarray. She leans over Nic to shut off the alarm. He's still asleep, lying perpendicular to her. Pulling closer to kiss him, she spots the crusted blood on his lip and on the sheet under his face. Her quick inhale wakes him. He opens his eyes and sees her, his killer smile coming first before his face changes and his brows furrow.

He pushes himself upright quickly to look her over with concern. "Baby, I think we got a little out of control last night. You're covered in beard burn and some bruises."

"Yeah? Here's the funny part. I look better than you. Your lip is cut and bleeding." Then she motions to his torso which has scratches over his chest and neck.

Nic touches his lip and winces. "Holy Shit, but that was awesome and so worth it. You look like the morning after, 17 years ago." He is smiling broadly and proudly. The lip cut oozing more blood.

"Yes, but next time we try that trick, let's give ourselves some heal time after," she admonishes him.

He starts getting out of bed, but not before giving her another inspection. Just as he rises, he grabs between his legs. "Even my dick is sore."

This sends Cara into fits of laughter. "Get cleaned up and go make me coffee. I'm jumping in the shower, ALONE. We can't be trusted naked together."

"Agreed," Nic says as he gingerly makes his way to the bathroom.

Cara forgoes the usual morning drop off attire. She pulls her wet hair into a ponytail and heads out for some coffee. She barely makes it into the kitchen before she hears the whistles and catcalls. She stops dead when she sees the three men seated at the table, all wearing big, stupid grins of delight. She keeps her eyes on them while moving slowly toward the coffee maker to pour hot coffee into a mug Nic has left for her.

"What?" She questions as she draws closer to the table.

Reed rises and struts over to her. Taking her in from head to toe, he walks behind her for the same examination. He's still clutching his coffee mug when he releases that long, slow whistle again. "Agent Bennett, I haven't seen you look like this in decades. And no one ever filled out cargos as nicely as you. Are these your lucky ones?"

Cara waits to respond so she can admire Reed's outfit. He has opted out of his usual suit and is also wearing black cargos and a fitted off-white shirt. He's like a photo negative of Cara, who has on her lucky sand-colored cargos with black combat boots and a fitted, high neck, long sleeved black shirt. Her cargos are a smidge too tight. She isn't entirely the same size she was 20 years ago.

Sasha lets out his own high-pitched whistle. "Cara, you look, I hate to say it, HOT. The beard burn adds a nice touch. We've already harassed your husband over the shot you gave him to the face."

Cara flips him off before asking, "What is it with you guys and girls with guns and combat attire? They're just my mission clothes and yes, Director, sir, these are the one and only lucky cargos."

Reed doesn't respond but gives her a quick pat down. "I see you're armed as usual for this outfit, Agent."

"Yes, sir, standard protocol."

"Good, Agent Bennett, now sit down and have some coffee and breakfast," Reed commands.

Nic is still smiling, the cut on his lip slightly bleeding from the pull. Cara makes the motion for him to dab the blood before adding to Reed, "Sir, I see you've brought your mission clothes."

"Why Agent Bennett, would you have expected less of me?"

Nic starts giggling and her heart warms. Maybe her husband has finally let go of the consuming jealousy over her antics with her boyfriend. After last night, he's much more relaxed about it. It certainly helps that Reed isn't emitting anything but pride and respect this morning.

Nic points to them. "So formal?"

Cara laughs a little before explaining they really try to be professional in public, especially if anyone of rank is present. Otherwise, she never addressed Reed with any formality.

Sasha is still smiling as if he can't get over the rapport between her and Reed. Then his smile fades a bit. "You ready, Vizzini?"

"Yes, as much as I'll ever be. Are Carter and the FBI in position?"

Carter has checked in. They're registered at the school and in their classrooms. Reed will text him when they leave. Carter will wait for the kids just inside the drop off doorway. Jake has checked in. He'll time his drop off with Eli right behind them.

"Good. We are a go then. Um, I see all three of you are sporting the no shave, concealing your facial features look," Cara points out.

"It's a proven fact the disguise works, and anyway, it can't hurt." Sasha comments.

"Well, maybe my beard burn will contribute to my concealment." Cara jokes.

They all finish their breakfast while Nic prepares the requisite lunch sacks and pushes the kids along. They arrive in the kitchen at 7:10 AM. Max is his usual calm, but Mia appears distressed.

"Mom, what the hell are you wearing? Your regular drop off uniform is bad enough, and now this?" Mia hisses, pointing towards her.

Before Cara can answer, Reed rises and places a gentle hand on Mia's shoulder. "Your Mom is mission ready. Get used to it."

This causes Mia's eyebrows to rise. She has no retort.

Without thinking much about it, Cara gets up, grabs the two lunch sacks and prepares to walk out to the car.

Nic stops her before she hits the garage door. He pulls her in for a tight hug as he whispers, "Please, be careful."

It's then she realizes this isn't a normal morning but a potentially dangerous mission. She stops and turns to her children who are behind her. She pulls them both in for a group hug with Nic. They resist, but she doesn't care. As she grips them tightly, the strangest sensation comes over her. She takes each child's hand and states firmly, "Promise me you will do exactly as I ask if it should ever come to that. PROMISE ME." Max and Mia nod solemnly. "Good. Let's rock and roll."

Cara drives while Reed takes the shotgun position. Max is behind his mother in the back seat; Mia is right behind Reed. They pull out of the driveway only 30 seconds after Nic and Sasha leave in Sasha's G wagon with Sasha driving.

As they leave the neighborhood, Max requests the music from channel two on Cara's satellite radio. She knows he likes to listen to music on the ride, so she complies, leaving the volume low. Only the music can be heard while no one communicates. Cara glances at the cup holders. She realizes she forgot her coffee but notices Reed's. She takes his and drinks.

With a frown on his face, he watches her consume most of his coffee while she navigates the car. Except for his dick, nothing of Reed's is off limits to her.

They approach the school turn off and spot Jake in his Suburban on a side street ready to pull behind them. Problem is Cara has two other parents stuck to her ass. Jake must wait for the two cars before he can pull out. They take the final left turn into the school before taking the first right into the oval.

Drop off is more congested than usual. The slight misty rain is most likely contributing to the volume of traffic. As they proceed into the oval at the 6:00 position, Cara looks in her rearview mirror to see Jake is still two cars behind. She looks forward again and slams her brakes. A teenager has darted out right in front of her.

"Jesus Christ, don't they look?" Reed yells.

Mia giggles in the back seat. "Uncle Reed, welcome to my parents' worst nightmare. The Oval."

Cara smiles. "It's true. On most mornings, I could kill everyone in here."

From the back seat both children yell, "NO!"

"What?" Cara asks, alarmed.

Max states calmly, "Mom, you can't say stuff like that anymore. Now we know you can kill them. Please don't."

"Your father and I promise not to shoot to kill, just maim, deal?" Cara smiles once more.

They advance with the usual rubber-necking stop and go until they get to the 12:00 position. Cara is scanning all around her and she can see Reed's head in motion, as well. The one-way in moves in a counterclockwise direction. The school building doesn't begin until the 11:00 position and the front doors are at 9:00. Almost there.

Cara glances in her mirror again, looking to spot Jake. For some reason, she feels the need to call him via Bluetooth in the car. She quickly uses the controls on her steering column and Jake comes through on the car's speaker.

"What's up? You good?" Jake inquires.

Before Cara can respond, their thoughts hit her like a landslide. She doesn't wait to process, she doesn't bother to speak, she lets her years of training take over. Cara throws the car into reverse, backing up so fast and accurately, she misses the car behind her by a hair. She throws the car back into drive, yanks the wheel hard to the right, hopping the curb and flooring it across the adjacent soccer field.

"JAKE! Incoming from the parking spaces!" Cara yells in her car.

She looks in her mirror to see two cars emerge from the end interior parking spaces of the oval, gunning towards the spot she just vacated.

Nic. Grid. Now! Location of the weapons in the car.

A grid emerges in Cara's mind like a map of the interior of her vehicle. She quickly sends it to Reed, who immediately pulls open the glove box and reaches under his seat. She's still flooring it across the soccer field and can see the two other vehicles following. Simultaneously out loud and in her mind, she yells, "Black Tahoe and black Crown Vic in pursuit. Can't see plates."

Jake responds, "Am bypassing queue to drop off Eli and will be right behind you. Get Carter outside to meet up with me!"

Reed has his phone in hand and is texting. They can hear Jake opening doors in his car and screaming at Carter who's now standing in front of the school with his gun drawn.

"Carter, take him inside and lock down the school, NOW!"

Cara veers right off the soccer field onto the adjacent street and puts the pedal to the metal. She begins to weave around every car on both sides. She reaches quickly behind to her daughter. "Mia, I need paths! I know you can do this. Your father, your brother, Sasha, Reed and me, all together. Make it like a conference call in our minds."

Mia struggles a bit, but within seconds, Cara can feel them all on the same path.

We're heading East on Elm; I want to get away from the school and collateral. Trying for Route 89. It's open and more accessible. Head that way. Again, she says it out loud so Jake can hear her.

Reed is on his knees in the front seat. He is locked and loaded when he begins to pull at Mia. "Mia, switch with me, now." Mia looks terrified but complies getting into the front seat. He tells her to stay down, try to get most of her body into the footwell as low as possible, but put her seatbelt on. He turns to Max. "You too, down as low as the belt can take you. C, they're 100 yards and closing."

60 seconds to the intersection of 89 and Elm, Cara. Sasha's voice is lacking its usual calm.

We are approaching...now. Cara swerves onto State Route 89, avoiding all the cars, and begins weaving through traffic at a much higher rate of speed. She's clocking 85 in a 45, the Audi darting around the stunned vehicles. She glances quickly behind her to see the two vehicles still in pursuit, keeping up but not making as much progress.

"Jake! Where are you in proximity to them?" Cara calls.

"I have them in my sights, but they're 120 yards ahead."

That's when Cara hears it. She turns to see Reed's hands reach out for Max and Mia on instinct. He hears it, too.

"Jake! Incoming rotors!" She sends that out the path as well.

"WHAT THE FUCK!? How did they get air power?!" Jake yells back.

"I need a visual!" Cara commands.

Reed checks the grid map and pulls binoculars out from under the backseat. He starts scanning. "Incoming at 3:00, three armed Apaches, no markings."

"No identification visible?" Cara calls out.

"No. Jake, you need to see this. These guys look familiar to you?" Reed demands.

They can hear Jake over the speakers, "SHIT, SHIT, SHIT, I need to look! Hang on. I'm trying to get to the binoculars without slowing down."

Don't bother. I have them on mine; sending visual to Jake.

"Jake, Nic's sending you the picture."

There's quiet from the speaker as Cara continues her assault on the road, not stopping or slowing. She looks like a Grand Prix racecar driver.

"What the... Reed?" Jake asks.

"YES!"

"This is the blue team," Jake says very calmly with some confusion mixed in. "I'm digging out my other phone."

Reed yells, "If you have a contact for them, I suggest you use it, NOW!"

Cara begins to open the full sunroof on her vehicle knowing Reed is already prepping the Stinger.

Poor Max is gawking at the weapon laid across the backseat of the car. It's a personal portable infrared homing surface to air missile, and his Uncle Reed is rapidly throwing a battery-cooling pack into the handguard. Cara barks out, "They're on approach. Sasha! ETA?"

We have Jake in our sights. I need to plot a course to intercept. Where are you headed? Nic is prepping the Stinger in this vehicle for the second Apache, so have Reed aim for the lead.

I want open spaces. I'm headed for I-480 South. The highway should be less congested this time of the morning.

Reed has the Stinger armed and is hoisting it up on his shoulder as he aims through the roof for the closest Apache. "We only have one missile in this car, C. Let's hope it scares them off."

Nic is requesting direction from Reed on the open mental path. He has never fired an American Stinger, and is having some issues arming it. Sasha is driving like a madman, cutting through yards, across low bed streams and a nature preserve. The Mercedes wagon, with the price tag of a small house is performing as advertised as Sasha expertly switches the lockable differentials on the wheels. Cara continues to hear all the mental conversations as she drives like her mother's crush Kimi Raikkonen, the Formula One Ice Man.

The first Apache closes in just as they hear Jake through their speaker talking on his other phone to someone other than one of them. They can only hear Jake's side of the conversation.

"Trickster, it's Bishop! What the hell are you doing up in that Apache? What?...Being paid to hunt down rogue KGB agents and a CIA double agent? Do you realize who you're about to shoot at, you asshole? See the man aiming the Stinger at you? Yeah, that would be the sitting Director of the CIA. You're about to shoot Director Connor Reed if he doesn't blow your stupid ass up first, you fucking moron! STAND DOWN NOW! There are civilian children in the vehicle!

"Who paid you and gave the intel? British Intelligence?! Did you verify the contact? You've been duped, you asshat! See me? I'm in the gray Suburban about 100 yards back. I'm going to find your ass when you land that copter and kick the shit out of you! ABORT NOW!"

Sasha, Nic, you getting this?

So that was the angle. The one they couldn't figure out. Katherine set the three of them up for collusion. She needed the final confirmation of who the Reflex was to put her plan in motion, a full-on assault. It's diabolically brilliant. Connect a former CIA Agent to two rogue KGB agents and you have the makings of a full-blown international conspiracy. She built a case with British Intelligence, somehow getting them to exclude Reed from the intel. The Brits hired the mercenaries to take them out, not wanting their people on US soil.

Cara is furious. *How can they do this without checking in with the Americans? Tricky bitch is a dead woman walking!*

Katherine has been building a case against them for some time, only needing that final confirmation from Vlad to release her assault. She had been working the angle long enough to get Ed sprung from prison as the fall guy when all was said and done.

She knew about Reed. Katherine was aware of his connection to Ed as the arresting officer. Whatever tall tale she spun for MI6, she managed to throw Reed under the bus so far, they would deem it necessary to exclude him from the intel. Reed is either anticipated collateral damage, or included in the conspiracy scandal with them.

Nic's the one to finally verbalize where all their thoughts have gone. *Katherine factored Reed into her plan. That's what we were missing the other night. Reed is the connection. She needed the final confirmation of Cara as the Reflex. In order to set the plan in motion and have Ed play the fall guy, she promised to take out The Reflex AND The White Knight as revenge for his capture and arrest so many years earlier. MI6's only possible exposure would then be for the elimination of rogue KGB agents she's proven are alive and kicking, and not long dead. It's perfect.*

As the pieces fall into place, Cara suddenly feels a hand on her shoulder. She knows Reed has heard the conversation on the open path. She can feel both his acknowledgement of the hypothesis and his rage.

"Reed! Do not stand down with the Stinger until they do!" she warns. Cara watches the Apache formation about to retreat. Just then, they hear the gunfire. "Shit!" She knows the Tahoe has taken position to take the Audi out in a firefight.

Cara uses one arm to steer and maneuver, while with the other, she reaches behind for Max's shirt. She pulls him forward through the opening between the two front seats. "Max, I need you to drive. Can you do it? Sasha says you're great." Max looks nervous but he nods his affirmation.

He begins to crawl through the opening and positions himself on the armrest between the front seats. Cara instructs him to hold the wheel and put his left foot over the gas pedal. She pushes the seat back and gets him on her lap moving his right foot over the gas pedal. She motions for him to raise his butt as she slips around him and onto the armrest.

"Perfect, honey. Great slip in! Two hands on the wheel and hunch down as low as you can without impeding your visual, seatbelt on. Awesome, job!" Cara says as she sneaks a quick kiss to Max's cheek before reaching over to Mia and squeezing her arm. "I am so proud of you both. Max, keep the pace I had and head to the highway entrance for 480 South. Lay on the horn as you hit any intersections, but don't stop. And follow my command, okay, my man?"

Cara slips off the center console and gets into the back seat. She views the grid map and pulls the automatic rifle from the open trunk and the Glock from her cargos. They're being fired upon, but from a distance too far away to make any accurate hits. The Apache helicopters have retreated, and Reed has placed the missile back down across the backseat. Once the gunfire started, all the traffic in between them quickly pulled off the road. Nothing between targets now.

She takes a moment to try and scan the occupants in the vehicles. She relays on all frequencies. "Tahoe is in the lead position. Simon Joseff is front passenger. There's a driver and two others in the back seat. Crown Vic has Ed for sure, getting one other, but no clear read. Probably Katherine. She's blocking, and there's no heavy thread to tap. She has talents." Cara can see that much.

"They're gaining on us." Cara stops to think for a moment. She looks down at the missile and sees the battery pack still engaged. "Jake, I have an idea. Slow down to 30 MPH, on my mark."

Cara tries to lift the Stinger off the seat, but it must weigh over 50 pounds when prepped. Reed is in position by the open window on the passenger side of the car. She motions to him to take the missile. "These are heavier than I remember." She forces a smile while she sends Reed her idea.

"I LIKE IT. You call it, on your mark," Reed confirms as he places the missile back on his shoulder, scooting back down to keep it concealed. He's adjusting the range and placing the targeting on manual.

Cara slides her window down and pulls the seatbelt all the way out. She wraps it around her torso for stability in the event she needs to hang out the window and fire back. "Max, slow down to 30 MPH, 10 MPH AT A TIME! Reed, in position!"

Reed nods. He has the Stinger ready and armed. He places one foot on the backseat floor and one foot on the seat but stays crouched. Cara accesses Nic's grid and calculates the math.

"Jake, adjust your speed now! Steady, Max. Perfect. Reed, ready." Cara watches as the Tahoe gets closer, now within 30 yards. "Reed! Now!" Reed pops his head out the roof, aims and manually fires the Stinger as Cara yells, "MAX, GUN IT NOW! FULL THROTTLE, MY MAN!"

The Stinger missile makes a direct hit on the Tahoe, and as if in slow motion, the Tahoe catapults into the air with full forward motion. It is in flames, somersaulting back over front heading directly towards the Audi. Max gives it all the car has, and it looks like they will barely miss getting hit by the flaming SUV, when it slams onto the road right behind them.

"Four down!" Cara yells for everyone to hear.

She watches as the Crown Vic maneuvers around the flaming wreck and guns it for them. Cara leans out her window with the assault rifle and starts firing on them, hoping to slow them down. Reed takes a duplicate position at the other window. The distance is still too great to have any accuracy. She pulls back in.

"We are half a mile from the start of the shopping district just before the highway entrance ramp. ETA to intersect Route 91 is 60 seconds at current speed," Cara calls out.

Cara, we are on 91 and will intersect with you in 45 seconds. Will take out target if possible, Sasha calls out. He really should stop talking. His emotions are resonating through his mental voice. It's making her angry. Her children can detect fear. This is a no fear zone.

They can hear Jake, "Carter has alerts into the state police. I-480's being closed before our ramp access. Police taking position at the exits and entrances. FBI copter enroute to highway Southbound between exits 191 and 192."

"MOM!"

Cara and Reed spin to see the line of traffic in front of them stopped dead.

"Max, slow down and try to use the sidewalks to get around them. You can do it, my boy," Reed calls to him.

FUCKING GREAT, everyone needs to shop this morning. Nic, we're coming to a standstill!

I see the congestion. Close enough, proceeding on foot to you with sniper rifle.

Just as Max is about to jump the curb, a group of daycare children emerge onto the sidewalk. He slams the brakes so hard; they all jolt forward. Mia is snapped up from the footwell. Reed hits the back of her seat as Cara is twisted by the seatbelt still wrapped around her.

"Seat belts off! Out of the car, now!" Reed yells as he opens his door. He waves the daycare kids off the sidewalk with authority. "Get them back inside!" he barks to the two women with them.

Max and Cara materialize from their side, simultaneously. Cara still has the assault rifle over her shoulder, her right hand at the ready and her Glock in her left. She immediately takes position between the Crown Vic and Max, waiting to send cover fire. There are too many cars, though; all pulling out from plaza entrances between her and the Crown Vic.

Cara is about to tell Max to run to Sasha when she sees it. On the other side of the car, Reed is desperately trying to get Mia out. Her seatbelt having jammed, all it takes is that split second of exposure and...it's slow motion, again.

Reed is bending over to pull Mia out. Just as he frees her from the belt, Cara hears the wiz of the bullet hitting him. It was a lucky shot from the woman hanging slightly out of the window on the passenger side of the Crown Vic.

There is just a moment of hesitation as panic sets in, but she regains her composure in time to catch Ed aiming and preparing to fire right at Max. Her right-handed weapon is down from the panic. The assault rifle isn't ideal to try for Ed without causing collateral damage, anyway. Her left hand isn't accurate enough with the Glock. She does the only thing she can think of and hurls herself at Max to knock him over. She makes contact with him just as she feels the bullet rip into her hip. She hits the ground with Max underneath her.

"Are you hit, baby?" she whispers in Max's ear.

"I don't think so," he whispers back, petrified.

Send your father this intel and our position. I am hit. Reed is down. Max, take the gun from my left hand. Safety is off. All you need to do is pull the trigger and keep firing until the magazine is empty. Hold it as steady as you can, but keep it hidden underneath me until I tell you. On my mark, only.

Cara peers beneath the Audi to see a woman's feet step over Reed's body and start dragging Mia away. Cara can't catch her breath. *Max, tell your father Katherine has Mia. She's walking North on 91.*

Nic's soothing words squeeze into her brain. *I can hear you, baby, hang in there. I'm on Mia. Sasha and Jake enroute to you.*

Cara looks up to see Ed approaching them from about ten feet away. She's surprised by his still boyish appearance. He's wearing black-rimmed round glasses and giving her a sideways smirk.

"I was afraid I had killed you first, Cara. What fun would that be if you died before you had a chance to see me kill your son? Now you can watch as the Death Eater spawn dies."

She is lying on the ground almost directly over her son. Max's head is still exposed. He has her Glock hidden in his right hand under Cara's body.

She's just waiting for Ed to get closer to increase Max's chances of taking him out.

Ed kicks the assault rifle away from Cara's grasp; the contact sending ripples of pain through her body. He raises his gun and aims right at Max's head. Cara is trying to use what's left of her mental energy to access Nic's grid and calculate the moment she must take the chance and have Max expose the Glock and attempt a shot at Ed. Then Cara hears it, his voice coming through her mind crystal clear.

It takes all her energy, but she scoots up over Max's body to cover his head and his eyes as she watches Ed's head explode. She can feel Ed's thread connection to her snap. And she knows...the 360-degree rotation is complete. She has come full circle. What was her true destiny, 25 years ago to the month, has finally been fulfilled.

Standing with one arm stretched over the top of the Audi is Reed. His 9mm still smoking hot from the shot.

Sasha, Ed down, I have Jake in my visual. Go to Mia, please!

Max is trembling under Cara. Reed reaches them and Cara can see the blood coming from his left shoulder. He gets down on his knees and gently lifts her using only his right arm. He wraps it around her waist and applies pressure to her wound. With what little use he has of his left arm, he pulls Max around and under him to cover his face. He doesn't want him to see what's left of Ed, and he knows what's coming next...the media blitz.

Cara is searching over Reed's shoulder for any visual of Nic and Sasha. Her head is falling backwards from the blood loss. She sees nothing but the people running from their cars. She hears nothing but her daughter screaming in her mind.

"Sweetheart, you need to stay with me, please. Promise you'll stay with me." Reed looks at her with pleading eyes before leaning into her son. "Max, it's going to be fine. Are you hurt anywhere?"

Max shakes his head. His eyes are watering and all he can get out with a shaky breath is, "Mia."

"Your Dad will get Mia. He's the best," Reed tells him trying to be reassuring.

Jake hits them from a full out run. Phone in hand, he's on it before he even reaches them. They can hear him yelling, "Two Medevac's, NOW!" He ends the call and kneels next to Cara.

"Five minutes. They're landing in the green. Cara, can I lift you up?" Jake requests, but it comes out a shout.

She lets her eyes wander over to Jake as an answer because she can't even muster a nod. Jake collects the weapons quickly and hides them in the Audi. Then he reaches for Cara.

CHAPTER

FIFTY-ONE

NIC IS SPRINTING AT MAXIMUM speed. His lungs are burning. His long leather coat is concealing the rifle and a multitude of other weapons. In this moment, he's not the steely-eyed cold-faced assassin. He's a husband and father. He's operating on emotion, his mind reeling. As he runs across the congested main intersection, he can see the top of the Audi on his right. He can also see the G Wagon cutting off pedestrians and cars as it hits the Town Center Green, tearing up the grass as it flies across it. Mia's screams of terror echo in his mind.

Mia, my beautiful girl, it will be all right. I need you to stop struggling with Katherine. Just go with her and try to stay calm. Daddy is coming for you, I promise.

Sasha, I see them heading past the pharmacy. Katherine has a gun in Mia's back. She will most likely turn right past the store and take cover between the buildings.

Nic can't seem to run fast enough. He has lost connection to Cara, unsure whether she shut him down out of pain, anguish, or her lack of consciousness. Katherine does indeed take Mia around the corner past the pharmacy, and they're now out of his sight.

MIA IS PUSHED INTO THE ALLEY BETWEEN THE TWO BUILDINGS. KATHERINE has one arm wrapped tightly around her waist and her other hand holds a gun pressed into her back. Mia has stopped struggling, but her whole body is trembling with fear. Her only open connection is to her father at this point. She has lost her mother and Max. Eli is too distant to connect. Katherine continues to push her down the alley, but she seems to be getting tired and they're moving slower.

Dad, she's slowing down.

Mia, whatever happens I need you to stay as perfectly still as possible and ignore what you hear, okay? Do not react. Everything will be all right. Just listen for me to instruct you.

Just as Katherine and Mia are more than halfway down the alley, Sasha appears at the other end, facing them on their present course. His face is blank and hard. He's wearing his leather biker jacket. He looks ominous, arms held calmly out to his sides, his hands empty and open, palms back. Katherine sees him and comes to an abrupt halt. Mia can hear her loud, sharp intake of breath.

"YOU!" Katherine screams as she tightens her grip on Mia.

Sasha remains motionless, his eyes locked on Katherine. He watches her every move and reaction. Speaking to her very softly, he keeps his voice flat. "Katherine, my love, what have you done?"

"DON'T SAY MY NAME, STEFAN, or is it Alexander, or Sasha!? It should be SATAN! You're an abomination on this earth!" Katherine screams at him.

She is wild eyed. Her face contorted with pain and hysteria. Her hair is gray and disheveled. She resembles a witch from a fairy tale.

Again, Sasha answers her, but very calmly with no inflection. "You were so beautiful, Katherine. So young and innocent...you were... so easy." He pauses and tilts his head, "What happened to you? You look wretched now."

Katherine pulls the gun from Mia's side and aims it at Sasha for just a split second before bringing it back to Mia, but pointing it at her head. "I want to kill you so badly for everything you've done to me, but that's not enough punishment for you. I will kill the girl first, and you will watch and enjoy."

Sasha lets out a snort and laughs, "You mean to torture me by killing the child? Really Katherine, you expect me to care? The girl means nothing to me."

"No, you LOVE her. I SAW it. You LIE!" she screams at him defiantly.

Sasha composes his face again. "I lie? You saw my love for the girl? Katherine, you saw my love for you on my face years ago. Did I not lie about that?" He's completely poised when he delivers each blow.

"YES! You're incapable of love. You're the Devil, pure evil!"

"You are correct. I am evil. I did not love you, and I do not love the girl. I do not love anyone," Sasha delivers with total serenity.

Katherine is trembling with rage. Her eyes are frantic as she looks to Mia, and then back at Sasha. "DO NOT TRY TO CONFUSE ME! The girl dies, then I will kill you..."

Katherine loosens her hold on Mia to get a proper angle for a shot at her head.

MIA, DOWN TO YOUR KNEES, NOW!

Obeying her father, Mia just lets her legs give out. She catches a glimpse of him behind her. In a split second, her dad has Katherine's gun arm in one of his hands while the other hand rips at Katherine's jaw, snapping her neck. Not a speck of blood, and the wicked witch is dead.

Nic watches as Katherine's body crumples to the ground. He doesn't hesitate or let his eyes linger. He reaches out and grabs Mia into his arms, fiercely. He pulls her tight against him and cradles her head into his chest letting every emotion he was feeling loose.

Sasha runs to them and tightly wraps his arms around them both. No one speaks. They just hang on to each other.

Sasha finally releases them in an effort to regain his composure. "Nic, I will take care of this. GO."

Nic turns to him and understands, still clinging to Mia. He begins to move them back down the alley towards the Town Green. He can't seem to release his grasp on his daughter. She hasn't spoken since the episode began. Her breathing is shallow and rapid and Nic can feel her trembling beneath his arms, although he's not sure if the trembling is all coming from Mia.

He whispers softly to her, "It's all over, beautiful. You were awesome. Try to breathe slowly. Let's go find Mom and Max."

Nic brings them out to the public sidewalk, loosening his two-arm grip on her, keeping just one arm tightly over her shoulders so they don't appear conspicuous.

Jake is carrying Cara across the street towards the Green. Reed is up and walking on his own behind them, but he has Max concealed beneath his right arm. Forget the pain and start spinning, he thinks to himself.

"Max, listen to me. I'm not sure your mom is conscious enough, but you need to understand how I must spin this." He doesn't want Mia, Nic, Sasha or Jake involved if he can help it. He needs to protect them. He needs to shield them. Cara and Max may be too exposed already, but he's still trying to cover Max's face.

Max acknowledges he understands what his uncle is trying to do and reaches out to his father.

Dad, are you and Mia, okay?

Yes, my man, we are fine and on our way to the Green.

Max relays the good news to Reed. He trusts Sasha will know what to do with Katherine. He needs Nic to keep himself and Mia as concealed as he can on approach. They're the grieving, concerned husband and daughter, but they must try not to be photographed. Cameras are already out. Local news vans are approaching.

"Tell your dad to stay in your head. Listen to my story and follow my lead," Reed barks out to Max, but then holds him closer and runs his right hand through Max's hair, affectionately. "I told you your dad would get Mia. And your mom is going to be fine." Reed isn't convinced about the second part of that, but he's forcing his emotions away to focus on damage control.

When they get to one end of the Green, they notice the local police have cordoned off an area for the first of the two helicopters to land.

Jake slows his approach to coincide with Reed's. "Reed, I am no one."

"I'm already on it, Jake. I sent the info through Max to Nic, as well. Deliver Cara and disappear. Check in with Sasha, he may require assistance," Reed commands.

People are beginning to snap photos with their phones and Reed can hear sirens everywhere. He draws Max's head further into his chest for coverage. He looks over to Jake who places his head down, but over Cara's, as they walk. The local police have created a barricade around Reed and Jake. They are escorting them toward the one landed medical helicopter.

The EMT's are rushing to them, pulling a stretcher in their hands. Jake gently places Cara on it and she moans. She's growing pale; her breathing is labored.

Reed barks at the medical personnel. "Get her in the chopper now, out of view!" He continues to walk Max to the helicopter door and pushes him into it. "Max, keep your head down until your father gets here."

Turning to scan the area, he spots Nic approaching. He tells the police to let them through. He is aware and in control despite the blood pouring down his chest from his shoulder injury. Good. He's got this. Glancing around him, and despite his size, Reed has already lost Jake in his visual.

One of the EMTs attempts to look at Reed's gunshot wound but he pushes him away. Reed tries to send Nic his thoughts and emotions, hoping he gets a glimpse. Nic seems to understand and walks directly toward the helicopter with his head down, partially covering Mia. Reed meets him there.

Nic can't help himself; he grabs Reed by his good shoulder and brings him in close for a hug. He winces from the motion, but Nic places his mouth to his ear. "I can never thank you enough for what you've done for me and my family."

Grabbing Nic's head so it appears as if they're embracing, Reed keeps it inclined away from any cameras. "I would gladly do it again, my friend. Please take care of her. I need to work this out; come up with an angle to keep the rest of you out of it. I can't risk any of you being exposed."

Katherine will be a very complicated political spin, but ultimately easy to keep Cara out of. Ed, on the other hand, is going to be connected to Cara. Reed will work it as best he can, he promises Nic. "Now go, and I'll speak to you at the hospital later. Tell Sasha to expect a call from me. I may need his...expertise." Reed releases Nic's head and turns his back on him while Nic and Mia get into the helicopter.

THEY TAKE OFF IMMEDIATELY SO THE OTHER HELICOPTER CAN LAND. NIC finds Cara being worked on when they enter. She looks bad. They have placed an oxygen mask over her face, but her eyes are partially open, and she's holding Max's hand. Her lucky cargos have been cut off and they're field dressing the wound. One of the EMT's is adjusting an IV drip to her arm when they announce the take-off.

Cara sees her daughter under Nic's arm. The anguish leaves her body and undeniable relief overtakes her face. *You got her.*

It's then Nic can hear his wife and feel her suffering. He tries to conceal it from his face, but the pain and the emotions get the better of him and he begins to cry. He's trying to keep it together for her, but the tears are collecting in his eyes. *Cara mia, failure was not an option. I wouldn't let you down, EVER.*

You were scared?

I was...concerned.

This makes her crack a small grin. *You can let the death grip you have on Mia go now, Angel. I think you're scaring her more. Can you ask her to hold my other hand and sit by me?*

Nic smiles back when he realizes he is still clutching Mia. He motions for her to go to her mother, sit in the jumpseat, and put her seatbelt on.

Cara looks at her daughter and forces another smile while squeezing her hand. Appearing slightly traumatized, but otherwise fine, Mia squeezes her mother's hand in return. Nic scoots in closer to his wife so he can brush the hair from her face. Affectionately, he takes a few moments to run his fingers through it as they fly through the air.

The look on his wife's face is so serious as she addresses their children. *Agent Max, Agent Mia...you guys were totally awesome in the face of danger. Your handlers are very impressed by the results of your first mission. How are you feeling about your efforts?*

This gets both his kids to smirk.

I really liked the driving fast part. Max gives a devilish grin.

Mia leans over her mother to flick her brother in the head. *You are such an ass, Max.*

EPILOGUE

"CARA, YOU WERE PRETTY LUCKY, although the irony didn't escape me. The bullet traveled at an angle into your hip toward your uterus. Lucky for you, it was removed five years ago."

Nic continues his update after Cara arrives from the recovery room. The doctors were able to extract the bullet with minimal damage to any other organs or bones. She will be on bed rest for a couple days, and then standard post-surgical recuperation and rehab.

The surgeon believes her existing scar tissue from both the C Section and the hysterectomy assisted in slowing the bullet down. Nic suspects the angle and distance were more the contributing factors. And, it was a .22 caliber.

"They must have given Ed the little gun thinking he was useless with anything larger," Nic adds, sitting next to Cara and holding her hand.

Cara nods, slightly disinterested in her injury, or prognosis, and looks around the room. Her children are seated with bags of fast food in front of them. She cringes when she sees it. Eli is sitting with them eating. Sasha is standing with Jinx on the other side of her bed. Alert, and looking like a mean bodyguard over by the closed hospital room door, is Jake.

Cara tries to find her voice. It comes out hoarse and painful. "First time I've been shot."

"Really?!" Sasha exclaims and starts tugging off his shirt to show her his various scars and explain them in detail. Nic takes his shirt off and shows Cara the scar he received when he was knifed and a bullet he took to the arm. Not to be outdone, Jake has approached the bed with his shirt off, and is beginning to unbutton his pants. Thankfully, Jinx stops him before he can reveal too much.

Cara can only smile at the three shirtless men. She sends a little message to Jinx to get her worked up.

"I know! What the hell is it with you guys and being mostly naked? Cover up already!" Jinx yells at them.

Cara reaches out for Jake's hand. He takes it gently. "We would've been Apache meat if it wasn't for you," she croaks out slowly.

"Little darling, is that your way of thanking me?" Jake teases. Cara nods solemnly. Jake waves her off but leans in closer to her, "Cara, YOU were amazing. I still can't believe it, to be honest. Brilliant."

Sasha adds, "Now I see what all the hoopla was over this Reflex." He smiles wide for her.

Cara tries to wave him off, but she can't bring her arm up high enough, so she gives up.

"Vizzini, you really were impressive. Honestly, you handled it better than anyone. You kept your composure, despite having the kids in the car with you. I felt your steely resolve. You, my dear, have captivated me. You may work for me anytime."

"Speaking of who I work for...or maybe I should rephrase that to who WE work for after today, how's Reed doing?" Cara whispers out.

"The man is a piece of work! He was yapping on the phone and barking out orders while they were wheeling him into surgery. I think Reed might have opted for a local just so he could keep command during it," Sasha says with flair.

Cara narrows her eyes at him and turns to Nic hoping someone will answer her. Nic informs her, "Reed is going to be fine. The bullet went through his shoulder. It caused some tissue, muscle and nerve damage, but all of it they were able to repair. He should make a full recovery but will require some rehab. He had a concussion, though. When Reed was shot, the force of the bullet caused him to whack his head on the side of the car door." Nic teases, "He must have a soft skull."

Narrowing her eyes at him, too, she scolds, "You guys aren't fooling me with the disparaging comments. Tell me what he's spinning. Cuz, I know my various Reeds, and he is in spin doctor mode right now."

Sasha turns serious and leans in closer to Cara so he can keep his voice low. "The man has talent, I tell you. Reed spun the Ed angle to make it appear as if Ed was seeking vengeance against him as the original arresting officer in his rape case. He spun Simon as the link between Ed and a former rival from his days as an agent. Collectively, they paid to have the Director of the CIA assassinated. Reed then called MI6 and worked out a deal with them, so they now owe him big time after he thoroughly ripped them a new asshole. He kept them out of the press entirely, though."

Still with a strange admiration in his voice, Sasha announces with some pride, "As for the former rival...well, let's just say Reed owes ME for that one."

"Sasha, you didn't offer yourself..." Cara argues.

"No! But I did offer up one of my adversaries," Sasha adds with a wicked smile. Cara knows she won't find out the name of this adversary. That will forever stay between Reed and Sasha.

"But what of the Katherine angle? How was she able to manipulate MI6 for the assistance? What fable did she weave to get them to believe in a conspiracy that may have included the three of us along with the sitting Director of the CIA?" Cara inquires.

"Reed isn't speaking of it, Reflex. He may tell you at some point, but for now, he's playing those cards close to his chest. I don't blame him. At this moment, the less we know, the better, as the political fallout unfolds." Sasha cocks that one brow at her.

Nic interrupts to add, "Reed was able to keep all of us but you and Max out of the equation. Kids and parents at school saw Max in the backseat of the car with Reed at drop off. Because of Mia's position in the car and the angle, she was hidden from view. No one has come forward to report they saw her being dragged away from the Audi by Katherine, so Reed is taking the chance that no one will. Mia was kept home from school today for illness as far as the story goes."

Cara nods in understanding but asks, "And Max and me?"

"Reed is keeping close to the truth there, too many witnesses. And the press will eventually link Ed to you. Reed made a statement admitting you and he have been very close friends since he saved you from Ed's rape attempt 25 years ago. It just happened that he was here visiting you when it all went down. Reed has also manipulated his public calendar so it appears the trip had been planned for months in the event someone checks his story."

There are enough photos of Cara with Reed at various events and galas over the years for the press to verify the tight friendship. Nic adds, "As for Max, there are already pictures making the rounds that show you throwing yourself in front of our son. Fortunately, none of the angles show your weapons yet. There are also pictures of Reed shooting Ed while he was all bloodied up from his own gunshot wound. The press is having a field day with it. The man who was the target of an assassination plot saves his good friend and her son." Nic shakes his head slightly amused.

"I told you, master manipulator. He always knows how to spin it to his advantage. In this day and age of optics, you have to respect that." Cara says it as a statement, denoting nothing but reverence.

"There's even a great grieving shot of the pathetic husband embracing Reed in thanks," Sasha laughs out.

Cara looks to Nic, expecting him to jump over the bed at Sasha, but instead Nic appears thoughtful. He says nothing, but Jake chimes in. "The man had every angle worked out by the time he boarded the medevac. DC Reed is an animal."

"No, Jake, DC Reed is about loyalty and honor. You prove to him you trust him, and he WILL trust you, always. But you must trust him first. You must take the leap of faith first," Cara says thoughtfully.

Is this the Holy Grail thing again? Nic inquires with some mirth.

"Only he with the purest of hearts," Cara utters softly, in deep thought, and then adds, "Maybe with a little help from some Merlin magic."

He saved yours and Max's lives, cara mia. There is no spin we can put on that.

I'm glad you finally understand why he's my best friend. He is and always will be my White Knight. He's always protected me, Nic. And he knew you trusted him to protect the rest of our group from exposure. So, he did it. He isn't a complicated man. He always had a deep respect for you and Sasha, but now that he has your trust, he will be your greatest ally. I can promise you that.

Nic seems to think this over for a while as he and Cara ignore the rest of the conversations.

I was going to take the kids home and come back and spend the night with you here.

You know, as lovely as that sounds, I'm exhausted and crave some serious morphine and some sleep. Besides, I'm worried about the kids and what this ordeal has done to them. I think they need a parent tonight.

I get it. I'll be back in the morning after DROP OFF HELL, which subsequently, following this morning, has a whole new meaning... Cara tries for a wide grin and squeezes his hand.

Slowly bringing her hand up to brush kisses to her fingertips, he adds, *I'll give the kids the low down on what to say and what not to reveal at school. They have comprehended some of it already. Reed is supposed to call Sasha later to give him the details of the story he wants the kids to have. He and Sasha believe the kids should go to school tomorrow. The longer they wait to confront this ordeal, the harder it will be. I agree with them.*

Mentally sighing out Nic adds, *Funny about Sasha and Reed…they seem to be really bonding.*

Nic starts to gather up the crew to prepare for their departure. He makes sure to have a nurse administer more pain relief for her. Before he goes, he sits alone with her, placing kisses on her face and running his hands through her hair.

"I love you, baby. See you in the morning. I left your cell phone on the nightstand. I called your family and told them you'll be fine. Your mother had the nerve to say how proud she was of Reed for saving you guys." He gives her a wink.

Cara can barely keep her eyes open, but she pulls him to her. "I love you, Lancelot. Are you sure Guinevere doesn't do any fighting in the legend?"

"Now you're just talking rubbish, my fair lady."

"Kiss me one more time, please, brave Sir."

Cara falls into a deep sleep. She dreams of Knights and fair maidens, goblets filled with wine, and shiny ornate chalices. She dreams of great battles on the fields of England, and boundless lovemaking in the castles. She is woken up twice for a vitals check, and on the second visit, she's given more morphine and her catheter is removed.

Each time, she falls back to sleep immediately. She dreams of Nic, his hands through her hair, gently fingering the loose curls and waves; his lips on her neck, softly trailing kisses leading up to her ear with a nibble. The excitement begins coursing through her blood. Nic can always do that to her. His touch is chemical for her. The feeling has never really subsided, even after all these years.

The lips begin to make their way to her jaw, soft kisses trailing his teeth like little, indulgent bites. Such a turn on. Her pulse is accelerating and she's getting warm. The lips come so close to hers, just brushing across, teasing for more. When Cara tries to capture them, they're gone and onto her jaw line, trailing again to the other side of her face and onto her neck.

Slowly, the kisses and teeth are making their way to her shoulder, ever so sensually. Her breathing quickens and she's getting even warmer. The lips begin to assault her collarbone, then advance lower until they're just over her breast.

Cara's filled with anticipation; she arches her back as invitation. Those amazing lips move and that tongue licks until he reaches her nipple, the teeth lightly grazing it. She can feel the hand now; the brush of fingertips climbing up her leg, over her hip, across her rib cage, until they meet her other nipple with the slightest touch. Cara is losing herself and lets out a soft moan. Those expert hands and mouth causing havoc. Best dream, ever.

His mouth moves leisurely down her rib cage but stops to leave a light kiss across the bandage from her injury. The lips are making their way to her one bare hip, licking, kissing, and scraping. Cara groans her appreciation. The lips are now poised just above her hot spot. She is trembling with need. But the lips pause.

You are so wet for me, my sweetheart.

Cara's eyes open with an audible snap just in time to see Reed take a long, hard lick. She is dazed from the shock of hearing him in her mind, and of relishing the contact, but mostly from the jolt upon realizing he is literally present in her room.

You know how long I've waited to see what you taste like? You taste wonderful.

He takes another lick leaving his lips on longer. Cara shudders slightly from the stimulation of it. She can see him smile up at her with a wicked grin. His mouth moves slowly back to her bare hip with those little kissing lips and scraping teeth. Cara is immobilized. She can't process what's happening. She hears what she thinks is her heart monitor beeping wildly. Maybe that isn't the monitor at all. Maybe it's just her own heart beating out of her chest. His mouth returns to her bandage.

If you weren't injured, I promise you this would be a very long, very pleasurable drive that's VERY MUCH overdue.

Those lips are back, placing soft kisses over her breast before making their way to her neck and onto her chin. His teeth scrape until they're at her mouth. He takes a small bite, pulling her lower lip.

I hate it when you bite your lip because it's always turned me on. All the better when I bite it for you, don't you think?

Reed stops to brush his lips across hers and then pulls away to look her in the eyes. He grabs her chin with a little force. "I know what you and your Dark Angel did to me last night. Tell your husband he made a slight error. He accidentally left a tracer behind in my mind after his intrusion."

If it is even possible, Cara's eyes grow bigger staring back into Reed's.

He lifts one brow and cautions her, "I don't know if I should kill you or thank you. On the one hand, you two had no business being in my mind. How dare you fuck inside my head. On the other hand..." *Look and see what new tricks I can do.*

He rises and backs away slowly, continuing to stare into her eyes. Reed grabs her hand and places it firmly over the arousal stretching out his pants.

Closing his eyes, he tilts his head back. *I am certain I've never been this hard, my sweetheart. PURE LOVE, MY ASS.*

After rubbing it back and forth a couple of times, he gently moves her hand back onto the side of the bed. He places her gown over her and pulls the covers up. Keeping his eyes on hers, he begins to step away from the bed. Cara is still too horrified to move or speak, but she notices he's in a full suit, his left arm in a sling.

"I'm leaving for Washington, shortly. I've checked in with your doctors and you're in good hands." Reed turns to head for the door, but before he reaches it, he flips his head back to her. "You, Nic and Sasha owe me, and I mean to collect, my sweetheart. I'll keep in touch." And with that, he leaves.

ANOTHER EPILOGUE

HAVING JUST BEEN RELEASED FROM the hospital yesterday, Cara is resting in bed. It's been five days since the altercation with Ed and Katherine, and five days since the incident with Reed. She hasn't heard from him, at all. No calls or texts.

Oddly, her husband hasn't said a word to her about it. Nic either has no knowledge of what transpired, or he doesn't want to share. Conversely, Cara has not asked Nic what he did when he was in Reed's mind. The three of them are at a stalemate.

The only person who is speaking, incessantly, with Reed is Sasha. Cara has been getting her updates from him. Apparently, Reed is still healing from his surgery and will undergo physical therapy starting in a few days.

Reed has spun his web, though. No one came forward to say they saw Mia in the car. There are only pictures of her with her father boarding the helicopter. No one saw Jake or Sasha, so they are still ghosts. Reed did admit he and she were close friends and he was in town visiting her family. But nothing has come out about her former position. She is only Cara Bianco Andre, Reed's dear friend for years since he saved her from Ed Grotto when she was a young college student. Heartwarming, really. The Press is eating it up. Reed is once again the White Knight, so dashing and everyone's hero. The optics are incredible. His popularity is skyrocketing.

Max is being coached for the media. Unfortunately, there are many pictures of Cara throwing herself in front of her son. And many pictures of Reed killing Ed and saving the both of them. It is being circulated around Cara will not be able to give interviews because of her gunshot wound. It was serious, and although not life threatening, she is still traumatized by the altercation. Cara Andre is suffering emotionally, and will not be expected to face the Press.

Reed is still protecting her. She will give him that much, for now. What comes down the line later, is still very concerning.

She is broken out of her reverie when both of her children barge into her room in tears. In an automatic response, she bolts up from her lain position.

Pain shoots through her lower abdominal area. She flinches and Max knows enough to throw some pillows behind her back.

"What happened? Why are you both crying?"

Sitting next to her, Max gets comfortable with one arm around her. "I don't think I can talk to the Press, Mom." He wipes some tears on her Tshirt. "I mean, I froze. I didn't know what to do and I got you shot. I could have gotten you killed."

Wondering when this revelation was eventually going to hit her children, Cara is not shocked by the admission. Up until Berlin, Cara was in her own deluded Land of Denial. How could she possibly think the progeny of The Reflex and the Dark Angel of Death would never be targets? And now, she is an idiot if she lets herself believe her children will have "normal" lives. Between their gifts and who their parents are, that is not happening for them. And it breaks her heart.

"Max, my beautiful boy, first off, none of us expected you or Mia to handle that situation even half as well as you did. We are very impressed with how you both did manage." Cara pulls him closer to her. "You are experiencing post-traumatic stress. The shock has finally worn off. But we were expecting this. THIS is why Sasha wants to train you both. We want to replace the shock and PTSD with empowerment."

Mia throws herself on the bed, weeping dramatically. "Mom, the Audi seatbelt wasn't stuck." Her tears are coming down harder. "My hands were shaking so badly I couldn't unfasten the belt. Uncle Reed bent inside the car to unhitch me, and he was shot because of it." Her head now on Cara's leg, Mia wails, "I almost got Uncle Reed killed!"

Stroking her daughter's hair and Max's arm, Cara responds, "Guys, I reiterate, neither of you got anyone almost killed. Ed and Katherine almost killed us, not you. Reed and I were hurt protecting both of you." Cara takes in a big breath. "I am your mom, and as such, I will throw myself in front of anyone trying to harm you. What you do or don't do will not make a difference. Both your Uncles Reed and Sasha put themselves in harm's way to protect you, as well. And they will do it again and again."

Her assurances don't appear to placate her children. Cara tries a different tactic. "Besides, from here on in, you will be trained. Maybe... hopefully... you will never need the training. But also maybe, one day you will return the favor and save your old, decrepit mother from near death."

Both her children look into her eyes. "Is that so difficult to believe? Yes, we saved your annoying little butts. One day, you can return the favor. You aren't going to be almost 16 forever. You will mature and grow stronger." So much debate has been happening about training her children. Sasha and Nic believe the kids need to become mini field agents. "You will be better prepared for these situations, assuming that's what you want."

They both nod passionately before Max adds, "But what if I break down during the interviews? I will look like a pussy."

Trying to hide her smile, Cara addresses him. "Max, women love men who can exhibit their vulnerabilities. It's a serious turn on."

He backs away from her to ask, "Really?'

"Of course. You saw your dad cry in the helicopter on the way to the hospital. Did you think he was a pussy?"

Max vehemently shakes his head. "No way! You, Dad, Reed, and Sasha are bad asses!"

"My point, exactly. Be yourself for the interviews. Keep to the script you are given but allow your emotions through. Don't hold them back. The media wants to see authenticity. It will make the story more believable and relatable. That's what your Uncle Reed wants from you."

Finally getting it, Max utters, "Huh."

Mia pipes in with the obvious, "Uncle Reed is counting on Max to appear traumatized and shaken from the whole incident. That's his hook, what he is going to capitalize on."

Hugging both, Cara wipes their eyes before saying, "You have already learned lesson number one. The Press can be your ally. Mainstream and social media are powerful tools you can work to your advantage. Never underestimate what you can achieve with a good spin on any story."

Mia stares pointedly at her. "But if that's the case, why are you not in front of the cameras?"

That is a bit too complicated for her children. She adopts a more obvious scenario. "We don't need for more people to recognize The Reflex. Agent Chase Bennett is long gone. And that's where she needs to stay." For now.

They both cuddle into her, and if the world wasn't completely changing around her, holding them close and safe is where she would keep them. But her reality has cracked. The illusion is gone. Nothing is the same. Safety for her children means preparation, training, and vigilance. Even then, there are no guarantees. It's best she adapts to the new normal...and quickly.

AUTHOR'S NOTE

I HOPE YOU ENJOYED THE REFLEX. Coming next is **The Reaction**. The second book in The Reflex Series.

Find out how Katherine managed to get assistance from the British Government. Just how big and far reaching was this plot to kill Cara, Reed, Max, and Mia? And are they the only targets?

Will training the twins prove beneficial? How will they adapt?

And what of Cara and Reed's relationship? Has she finally gone too far with him? Has she snapped his last nerve? She isn't even sure what Nic did in Reed's mind. How does she attempt to repair this? After being violated, why does she even feel the need to try and repair it?

What about Sasha? Will he finally be able to place what he did to Katherine behind him? Is he ready to move on from all the guilt and anguish? If so, how will he move on?

All these questions and more will be answered in *The Reaction*, coming soon.

Order The Reaction Now My Reaction

Check out my page at www.mariadenison.com for updates and

info. There are even some bonus scenes from the edit floor. Leave your email address for my newsletter.

The Reflex Series Spotify playlist is on my website and on Spotify. Like my character Nic, music is important to my life. Unlike my character, I have no musical talent whatsoever. For me, it only makes me appreciate how much talent goes into writing and making music. So, a bow and thanks to all of you devoting your life to the arts.

Thank you so much for all your support.

ACKNOWLEDGMENTS

I WANTED TO MENTION SOME of the folks who I could not have written these books without. As always, thanks to my family for pizza night when I did not have time to cook. And thank you Uber Eats, Doordash, and Postmates.

Thanks to Traci, Jan, Beth, Vera, Heidi, Lisa, Kaileigh, and Marion for all your test readings and emotional support. Your input was invaluable. Your love, even more so.

Thank you so much to my cover designer (and best sister ever) Claudia Kemmerer!

Thank you to my new copy editor, Kathy Denison, who graciously offered up her services to my much-needed manuscript. Your edits are the bomb!

Finally, thanks to you readers. Please leave positive reviews if you enjoyed the books. Check out my website for links to all my social media accounts to follow. Personally, I believe I am hysterical, so follow me to laugh with me or at me. Makes no difference. Laughter is a balm to life.

About the Author

Here's what you will not find on my website or the jacket of the book. I'm a voracious reader but craved writing an epic book series in a style I would enjoy reading. No obvious tropes, no whodunnits guessed in Chapter 3, no constant, violent endangerments to keep the reader engaged for lack of content. I wanted a twisting, turning, you won't see it coming at all unless you pay very close attention to the carrots, series of books. But, I needed the books to be based in realism. Fantastical, yet truly believable. Preternatural versus paranormal. Genre bending and mixing all at once.

There are 5 books in The Reflex series, which are all written at this point.

What I lack in publishing experience, I make up for with life experiences. A career that has brought me to all 50 states and to over 40 countries. A life being engaged with countless people and their personalities. I am a wife, a mother, a sister, an aunt, a pet owner, a business owner and entrepreneur. The sum total is poured into my books.

I am a native of New England, spent decades in the Midwest and now hang around the West Coast.